MICHELLE DALTON

INCLUDES
PULLED UNDER AND *SWEPT AWAY*

SIMON PULSE

NEW YORK LONDON TORONTO SYDNEY NEW DELHI

SIMON PULSE

An imprint of Simon & Schuster Children's Publishing Division
1230 Avenue of the Americas, New York, New York 10020
This Simon Pulse paperback edition May 2019
Pulled Under copyright © 2014 by Simon & Schuster, Inc.
Swept Away copyright © 2015 by Simon & Schuster, Inc.
Cover photograph copyright © 2019
by Guitarist Magazine/Contributor/Getty Images
All rights reserved, including the right of reproduction
in whole or in part in any form.
SIMON PULSE and colophon are registered trademarks of
Simon & Schuster, Inc.
For information about special discounts for bulk purchases,
please contact Simon & Schuster Special Sales at
1-866-506-1949 or business@simonandschuster.com.
The Simon & Schuster Speakers Bureau can bring authors to your live
event. For more information or to book an event contact the
Simon & Schuster Speakers Bureau at 1-866-248-3049 or visit
our website at www.simonspeakers.com.
Book designed by Tiara Iandiorio
The text of this book was set in Berling LT Std.
Manufactured in the United States of America
2 4 6 8 10 9 7 5 3 1
Library of Congress Control Number 2018966073
ISBN 978-1-5344-4301-3 (pbk)
ISBN 978-1-4814-0702-1 (*Pulled Under* eBook)
ISBN 978-1-4814-3610-6 (*Swept Away* eBook)
These titles were previously published individually.

PULLED UNDER

For Carey and Terry,

who took me to the boardwalk

and taught me about the beach

June

*D*ifficult questions come in all shapes and sizes. They can be big and philosophical, like "What's the meaning of life?" Or small and personal, like "How do you know if you're really in love?" They can even be evil (Yes, I'm talking about you, Mrs. Perkins), like "For the quadratic equation where the equation has only one solution, what's the value of C?" But of all the world's questions there is one that stands alone as the single most difficult to answer.

"Does this bathing suit make me look fat?"

If you've ever been asked, then you know what I'm talking about. It's not like you can just say, "No, but your butt kinda does." And it's not like you can say, "Oh no, it looks great. You should definitely wear that on the beach, where every guy you know will see you." Instead you have to find that delicate place between honesty and kindness.

I know this because I hear the question all the time. I work weekends and summers at Surf Sisters, a surf shop in Pearl Beach, Florida, where women asking you how they look in all varieties of swimwear kind of comes with the turf. (Or as my father would say, it "comes with the *surf*," because, you know, dads.)

It's been my experience that a great many of those who ask the question already know the answer. This group includes the girls with the hot bodies who only ask because they want to hear someone say how great they look. My response to them is usually just to shrug and answer, "It doesn't make you look fat, but it is kind of strange for your torso." The proximity of the words "strange" and "torso" in the same sentence usually keeps them from asking again.

Most girls, however, ask because while they know a swimsuit doesn't look right, they're not exactly sure why. That's the case with the girl who's asking me right now. All she wants is to look her best and to feel good about herself. Unfortunately, the bikini she's trying on is preventing that from happening. My first step is to help her get rid of *it* for reasons that have nothing to do with *her*.

"I think it looks good on you," I answer. "But I don't love what happens with that particular swimsuit when it gets wet. It loses its shape and it starts to look dingy."

"Really?" she says. "That's not good."

I sense that she's relieved to have an excuse to get rid of it, so I decide to wade deeper into the waters of truthfulness. "And, to be honest, it doesn't seem like you feel very comfortable in it."

She looks at me and then she looks at herself in the mirror and shakes her head. "No, I don't, do I? I'm no good at finding the right suit."

"Luckily, I can help you with that," I say. "But I need to know what you're looking for, and I need to know how you see yourself. Are you a shark or a dolphin?"

She cocks her head to the side. "What do you mean?"

"Sharks are sleek and deadly. They're man-eaters."

"And dolphins?"

"They're more . . . playful and intelligent."

She thinks it over for a moment and smiles. "Well, I probably wish I was more of a shark, but . . . I'm a total dolphin."

"So am I. You know, in the ocean, if a shark and a dolphin fight, the dolphin always wins."

"Maybe, but on land it usually goes the other way."

We both laugh, and I can tell that I like her.

"Let's see what we can do about that," I say. "I think we've got a couple styles that just might help a dolphin out."

Fifteen minutes later, when I'm ringing her up at the register, she is happy and confident. I know it sounds hokey, but this is what I love about Surf Sisters. Unlike most shops, where girls have to be bikini babes or they're out of luck, this one has always been owned and operated by women. And while we have plenty of male customers, we've always lived by the slogan, "Where the waves meet the curves."

At the moment it also happens to be where the waves meet the pouring rain. That's why, when my girl leaves with not one but two new and empowering swimsuits, the in-store population of employees outnumbers customers three to two. And, since both customers seem more interested in waiting out the storm than in buying anything, I'm free to turn my attention to the always entertaining *Nicole and Sophie Show*.

"You have no idea what you're talking about," Nicole says as they expertly fold and stack a new display of T-shirts. "Absolutely. No. Idea."

In addition to being my coworkers, Nicole and Sophie have been my best friends for as long as I can remember. At first glance they seem like polar opposites. Nicole is a blue-eyed blonde who stands six feet tall, most of which is arms and legs. This comes in handy as heck on the volleyball court but makes her self-conscious when it comes to boys. Sophie, meanwhile, is petite and fiery. She's half Italian, half Cuban, all confidence.

Judging by Nic's signature blend of outrage and indignation, Sophie must be offering unsolicited opinions in regard to her terminal crush on the oh-so-cute but always-out-of-reach Cody Bell.

"There was a time when it was an embarrassing but still technically acceptable infatuation," Sophie explains. "But that was back around ninth-grade band camp. It has since gone through various stages of awkward, and I'm afraid can now only be described as intervention-worthy stalking."

Although I've witnessed many versions of this exact conversation over the years, this is the first time I've seen it in a while. That's because Sophie just got back from her freshman year at college. Watching them now is like seeing the season premiere of a favorite television show. Except without the microwave popcorn.

"Stalking?" Nicole replies. "Do you know how absurd that sounds?"

"No, but I do know how absurd it *looks*," Sophie retorts. "You go wherever he goes, but you never talk to him. Or if you do talk to him, it's never about anything real, like the fact that you're into him."

"Where are you even getting your information?" Nicole demands. "You've been two hundred miles away. For all you know, Cody and I had a mad, passionate relationship while you were away at Florida State."

Sophie turns to me and rolls her eyes. "Izzy, were there any mad, passionate developments in the Nicole and Cody saga while I was in Tallahassee? Did they become a supercouple? Did the celebrity press start referring to them as 'Nicody'?"

I'm not about to lie and say that there were new developments, but I also won't throw Nicole under the bus and admit that the situation has actually gotten a little worse. Instead, I take the coward's way out.

"I'm Switzerland," I say. "Totally neutral and all about the chocolate."

"Your courage is inspiring," mocks Sophie before directing the question back at Nicole. "Then you tell me. Did you have a mad, passionate relationship with Cody this year?"

"No," Nicole admits after some hesitation. "I was just pointing out that you weren't here, so you have no way of knowing what did or did not happen."

"So you're saying you did not follow him around?"

"Cody and I have some similar interests and are therefore occasionally in the same general vicinity. But that doesn't mean that I follow him around or that it's developed into . . . whatever it was that you called it."

"Intervention-worthy stalking," I interject.

Nicole looks my way and asks, "How exactly do you define 'neutral'?"

I mimic locking my mouth shut with a key and flash a cheesy apology grin.

"So it's not because of Cody that you suddenly decided that you wanted to switch to the drum line?" Sophie asks.

"Even though you've been first-chair clarinet for your entire life?"

"You told her about drum line?" Nicole says, giving me another look.

"You're gonna be marching at football games in front of the entire town," I say incredulously. "It's not exactly top secret information."

"I changed instruments because I wanted to push myself musically," Nicole explains. "The fact that Cody is also on the drum line is pure coincidence."

"Just like it's coincidence that Cody is the president of Latin Club and you're the newly elected vice president?"

Another look at me. "Seriously?"

"I was proud of you," I say, trying to put a positive spin on it. "I was bragging."

"Yes, it's a coincidence," she says, turning back to Sophie. "By the way, there are plenty of girls in Latin Club and I don't see you accusing any of them of stalking."

"First of all, there aren't *plenty* of girls in Latin Club. I bet there are like *three* of them," Sophie counters. "And unlike you, I'm sure they actually take Latin. You take Spanish, which means that you should be in—what's it called again?—oh yeah, Spanish Club."

It's worth pointing out that despite her time away, Sophie is not the least bit rusty. She's bringing her A game, and while it might sound harsh to outsiders, trust me when I say this is all being done out of love.

"I had a scheduling conflict with Spanish Club," Nicole offers.

"Besides, I thought Latin Club would look good on my college applications."

It's obvious that no matter how many examples Sophie provides, Nicole is going to keep dodging the issue with lame excuse after lame excuse. So Sophie decides to go straight to the finish line. Unfortunately, I'm the finish line.

"Sorry, Switzerland," she says. "This one's on you. Who's right? Me or the Latin drummer girl?"

Before you jump to any conclusions, let me assure you that she's not asking because I'm some sort of expert when it comes to boys. In fact, both of them know that I have virtually zero firsthand experience. It's just that I'm working the register, and whenever there's a disagreement at the shop, whoever's working the register breaks the tie. This is a time-honored tradition, and at Surf Sisters we don't take traditions lightly.

"You're really taking it to the register?" I ask, wanting no part of this decision. "On your first day back?"

"I really am," Sophie answers, giving me no wiggle room.

"Okay," I say to her. "But in order for me to reach a verdict, you'll have to explain why it is that you've brought this up now. Except for Latin Club, all the stuff you're talking about is old news."

"First of all, I've been away and thought you were keeping an eye on her," she says. "And it's not old. While you were helping that girl find a swimsuit—awesome job, by the way . . ."

"Thank you."

". . . Nicole was telling me about last week when she spent two hours following Cody from just a few feet away. She followed him in and out of multiple buildings, walked when he walked, stopped when he stopped, and never said a single word to him. That's textbook stalking."

"Okay. Wow," I reply, a little surprised. "That does sound . . . really bad. Nicole?"

"It only sounds bad because she's leaving out the part about us being on a campus tour at the University of Florida," Nicole says with a spark of attitude. "And the part about there being fifteen people in the group, all of whom were stopping and walking together in and out of buildings. And the fact that we *couldn't* talk because we were listening to the tour guide, and nothing looks worse to an admissions counselor than hitting on someone when you're supposed to be paying attention."

I do my best judge impression as I point an angry finger at Sophie. "Counselor, I am tempted to declare a mistrial as I believe you have withheld key evidence."

"Those are minor details," she scoffs. "It's still stalking."

"Besides, you have your facts wrong," I continue. "It wasn't last week. Nicole visited UF over a month ago, which puts it outside the statute of limitations."

It's at this moment that I notice the slightest hint of a guilty expression on Nicole's face. It's only there for a second, but it's long enough for me to pause.

"I thought you said it was last week," Sophie says to her.

Nicole clears her throat for a moment and replies, "I don't see how it matters when it occurred."

"It matters," Sophie says.

"Besides," I add, also confused, "you told me all about that

PULLED UNDER

visit and you never once mentioned that Cody was there."

"Maybe because, despite these ridiculous allegations, I am not obsessed with him. I was checking out a college, not checking out a guy."

"Oh! My! God!" says Sophie, figuring it out. "You went back for a second visit, didn't you? You took the tour last month. Then you went back and took it again last week because you knew that Cody was going to be there and it would give you a reason to follow him around."

Nicole looks at both of us and, rather than deny the charge, she goes back to folding shirts. "I believe a mistrial was declared in my favor."

"Izzy only said she was *tempted* to declare one," Sophie says. "Besides, she never rang the register."

"I distinctly heard the register," Nicole claims.

"No, you didn't," I say. "Is she right? Did you drive two and a half hours to Gainesville, take a two-hour tour you'd already taken a month ago, and drive back home for two and a half hours, just so you could follow Cody around the campus?"

She is silent for a moment and then nods slowly. "Pretty much."

"I'm sorry, but you are guilty as charged," I say as I ring the bell of the register.

"I really was planning on talking to him this time," she says, deflated. "I worked out a whole speech on the drive over, and then when the time came . . . I just froze."

Sophie thinks this over for a moment. "That should be your sentence."

"What do you mean?" asks Nicole.

"You have been found guilty and your sentence should be that you *have* to talk to him. No backing out. No freezing. And it has to be a real conversation. It can't be about band or Latin Club."

"What if he wants to talk about band or Latin Club? What if he brings it up? Am I just supposed to ignore him?"

"It's summer vacation and we live at the beach," Sophie says. "If he wants to talk about band or Latin, then I think it's time you found a new crush."

Nicole nods her acceptance, and I make it official. "Nicole Walker, you are hereby sentenced to have an actual conversation with Cody Bell sometime within the next . . . two weeks."

"Two weeks?" she protests. "I need at least a month so I can plan what I'm going to say and organize my—"

"Two weeks," I say, cutting her off.

She's about to make one more plea for leniency when the door flies open and a boy rushes in from the rain. He's tall, over six feet, has short-cropped hair, and judging by the embarrassed look on his face, made a much louder entrance than he intended.

"Sorry," he says to the three of us. There's an awkward pause for a moment before he asks, "Can I speak to whoever's in charge?"

Without missing a beat, Nicole and Sophie both point at me. I'm not really in charge, but they love putting me on the spot, and since it would be pointless to explain that they're insane, I just go with it.

"How can I help you?"

As he walks to the register I do a quick glance-over. The

fact that he's our age and I've never seen him before makes me think he's from out of town. So does the way he's dressed. His tucked-in shirt, coach's shorts, and white socks pulled all the way up complete a look that is totally lacking in beach vibe. (It will also generate a truly brutal farmer's tan once the rain stops.) But he's wearing a polo with a Pearl Beach Parks and Recreation logo on it, which suggests he's local.

I'm trying to reconcile this, and maybe I'm also trying to figure out exactly how tall he is, when I notice that he's looking at me with an expectant expression. It takes me a moment to realize that my glance-over might have slightly crossed the border into a stare-at, during which I was so distracted that I apparently missed the part when he asked me a question. This would be an appropriate time to add that despite the dorkiness factor in the above description, there's more than a little bit of dreamy about him.

"Well . . . ?" he asks expectantly.

I smile at him. He smiles at me. The air is ripe with awkwardness. This is when a girl hopes her BFFs might jump to her rescue and keep her from completely embarrassing herself. Unfortunately, one of mine just came back from college looking to tease her little high school friends, and the other thinks I was too tough on her during the sentencing phase of our just completed mock trial. I quickly realize that I am on my own.

"I'm sorry, could you repeat that?"

"Which part?" he asks, with a crooked smile that is also alarmingly distracting.

When it becomes apparent that I don't have an answer,

Sophie finally chimes in. "I think you should just call it a do-over and repeat the whole thing."

She stifles a laugh at my expense, but I ignore her so that I can focus on actually hearing him this go-round. I'm counting on the second time being the charm.

"Sure," he says. "I'm Ben with Parks and Recreation, and I'm going to businesses all over town to see if they'll put up this poster highlighting some of the events we have planned for summer."

He unzips his backpack and pulls out a poster that has a picture of the boardwalk above a calendar of events. "We've got a parade, fireworks for the Fourth of July, all kinds of cool stuff, and we want to get the word out."

This is the part when a noncrazy person would just take the poster, smile, and be done with it. But, apparently, I'm not a noncrazy person. So I look at him (again), wonder exactly how tall he is (again), and try to figure out who he is (again).

"I'm sorry, *who* are you?"

"Ben," he says slowly, and more than a little confused. "I've said that like three times now."

"No, I don't mean 'What's your name?' I mean 'Who are you?' Pearl Beach is not that big and I've lived here my whole life. How is it possible that you work at Parks and Rec and we've never met before?"

"Oh, that's easy," he says. "Today's my first day on the job. I'm visiting for the summer and staying with my uncle. I live in Madison, Wisconsin."

"Well," I hear Sophie whisper to Nicole, "that explains the socks."

Finally, I snap back to normalcy and smile. "It's nice to meet you, Ben from Wisconsin. My name's Izzy. Welcome to Pearl Beach."

Over the next few minutes, Ben and I make small talk while we hang the poster in the front window. I know hanging a poster might not seem like a two-person job, but this way one of us (Ben) can tape the poster up while the other (me) makes sure it's straight.

Unfortunately when I go outside to look in the window to check the poster, I see my own reflection and I'm mortified. The rain has caused my hair to frizz in directions I did not think were possible, and I have what appears to be a heart-shaped guacamole stain on my shirt. (Beware the dangers of eating takeout from Mama Tacos in a cramped storeroom.) I try to nonchalantly cover the stain, but when I do it just seems like I'm saying the Pledge of Allegiance.

"How's that look?" he asks when I go back in.

I'm still thinking about my shirt, so I start to say "awful," but then realize he's talking about the poster he just hung, so I try to turn it into "awesome." It comes out somewhere in the middle, as "Awfslome."

"What?"

"Awesome," I say. "The poster looks awesome."

"Perfect. By the way, I'm about to get some lunch and I was wondering . . ."

Some psychotic part of me actually thinks he's just going to ask me out to lunch. Like that's something that happens. To me. It isn't.

". . . where'd you get the Mexican food?"

"The what?"

That's when he points at the stain on my shirt. "The guacamole got me thinking that Mexican would be *muy bueno* for lunch."

For a moment I consider balling up in the fetal position, but I manage to respond. "Mama Tacos, two blocks down the beach."

"*Gracias!*" he says with a wink. He slings the backpack over his shoulder, waves good-bye to the girls, and disappears back into the rain. Meanwhile, I take the long, sad walk back toward the register wondering how much Nicole and Sophie overheard.

"I noticed that stain earlier and meant to point it out," Nicole says.

"Thanks," I respond. "That might have been helpful."

"Well, I don't know about you guys," Sophie says. "But I think Ben is 'awfslome'!"

So apparently they heard every word.

"And I think it's awfslome that our little Izzy is head over heels for him," she continues.

"I'm sorry," I respond. "What are you talking about?"

"What we're talking about," says Nicole, "is you full-on crushing for Ben from Wisconsin."

"Is Wisconsin the dairy one?" Sophie asks.

"Yes," says Nicole.

"Then I think we should call him Milky Ben," Sophie suggests.

"We are not calling him Milky Ben!" I exclaim.

"Cheesy Ben?" she asks.

"We're not calling him *anything* Ben."

"See what I mean?" Nicole says. "She's already so protective."

"You're certifiable. All I did was hang a poster with him. That qualifies as head over heels crushing?"

"Well, that's not all you did," she corrects. "In addition to the guacamole and the '*awfslome*,' there was the part when you were so dazzled by his appearance that you couldn't hear him talking to you. That was kind of horrifying, actually."

"I know, right?" says Sophie. "Like a slasher movie. Except instead of a chain saw, the slasher has really bright socks that blind you into submission."

"You guys are hilarious," I say, hoping to switch the topic of conversation.

"Are you denying it?" Nicole asks, incredulous.

"It's not even worthy of denial," I reply. "It's make-believe."

"Um . . . I'm going to have to challenge that," she says. "I think I'm going to have to go to the register."

"You can't go to the register," I say. "Besides, *I'm* on register."

"Really?" says Sophie. "'Cause it looks like I am."

It's only then that I notice that Sophie slipped behind the counter while I was helping Ben.

"Wait a minute," I protest. "This is a total conspiracy. I'm being set up."

Sophie doesn't even give me a chance to defend myself. She just goes straight to the verdict. "Izzy Lucas, you have been found guilty of crush at first sight."

"You should make her talk to him like she's making me talk to Cody," Nicole suggests, looking for some instant payback. "Karma's a bitch, isn't it?"

"No," I reply. "But I know two girls who might qualify."

"Really?" says Sophie. "You're going to call me names right before sentencing?"

"Oh," I say, realizing my mistake. "I didn't mean *you two girls*."

"Too late," Sophie laughs. "Isabel Lucas, sometime in the next two weeks you must . . . have a meal with whatever-embarrassing-nickname-we-ultimately-decide-to-call-him Ben."

"A meal? Are you drunk with power? Nicole stalked a guy across six counties and all she has to do is talk to him. Why is my sentence worse than hers?"

"Because she has a whole school year coming up with Cody," Sophie explains. "But Ben said he's only here for the summer. That doesn't leave you much time."

Before I can beg for mercy, she rings the register, making it official.

*P*earl Beach is a barrier island, eight and a half miles long and connected to the mainland by a causeway bridge. I've spent all sixteen years of my life as an islander, and when I think of home, I don't think of my house or my neighborhood. I think of the ocean.

That's why, despite the fact that it's summer vacation and I should be fast asleep, I'm awake at six thirty in the morning putting on my favorite spring suit—a wet suit with long sleeves and a shorty cut around the thighs. The combination of last night's storm, the rising tide, and a slight but steady wind should make for ideal surf conditions.

It's a two-block walk from my house to the beach, and when

I reach the stairs that lead down from the seawall, the view is spectacular. Purple and orange streak through the sky and the sun is barely peeking up from the water.

The only remnants of the storm are the tufts of foam that dance across the sand like tumbleweeds and the thin layer of crushed shells that were dredged up from the ocean floor and now crackle beneath my feet. The early morning water temperature shocks the last bit of sleep from my system, and as I paddle out on my board, there's not another living soul in sight. It is as if God has created all of this just for me.

I inherited my love of surfing from my dad. When I was little, he'd take me out on his longboard, and we'd ride in on gentle waves as he held me up by my hands so that I could stand. We still surf together a lot of the time, but this morning I slipped out of the house by myself so that I could be on my own and think.

It bothers me that I got so flustered the other day when I met Ben. I don't want to make a big deal out of it, but the truth is when it comes to guys, I'm not a shark or a dolphin. I'm a flounder. I just don't have the practice. I've never had a boyfriend or been on a date. I've never even been kissed. Part of this is because I'm introverted by nature, and part of it is because I've grown up on an island with all the same boys my whole life. Even if one's kind of cute now that we're in high school, it's hard to forget the middle school version of him that used to call me Izzy Mucus and tell fart jokes.

Ben is different. My only history with him was less than five minutes in the surf shop. And, while I wasn't about to admit it to Nicole and Sophie, during those five minutes I was definitely guilty of "crush at first sight." I don't know why exactly. It's not just that he's cute. I'm not even sure if most girls would classify him as cute. It's just that there was some sort of . . . I don't know what to call it . . . a connection, chemistry, temporary insanity. Whatever it was, it was a totally new sensation.

And now, because Sophie snuck onto the register when I wasn't looking, I have to try to convince him to share a meal with me. It's a total abuse of power on her part, but I meant what I said about us taking traditions seriously at Surf Sisters. The girls won't hold it against me if I'm not successful. But if I don't give it a real try, I'll never hear the end of it.

I sit up on my board with the nose pointed to the ocean and straddle it so that I can watch for waves. I see a set of three coming toward me and suddenly all thoughts of boys and crushes wash out of my mind. I lie out on my stomach and slowly start to paddle back in. I let the first two swells pass beneath me, and the moment I feel the third one begin to lift me, I paddle as fast as I can, trying to keep up.

Just before the wave starts to break, I feel it grab hold of the board and I pop up on my feet. This is the moment that takes my breath away. Every time. This is when it's magic. In one instant you're exerting every ounce of energy you have, and in the next it feels like you're floating through air as you glide along the face of the wave. You stop thinking. You stop worrying. You're just one with the wave, and everything else melts away.

The ride doesn't last long. No matter how well you catch it, the wave always crashes against the shore and snaps you back to reality. But those few moments, especially at times like this when I'm alone, those few moments are perfect.

If only boys were as predictable as waves; then I'd know just what to do.

*T*he Bermuda Triangle is a section of the Atlantic Ocean where ships and planes mysteriously vanish into thin air. It's totally bogus and based on some ridiculous alien conspiracy theory. But it inspired my dad to come up with The Izzy Triangle. He likes to say, "It's where daughters disappear for the summer."

Unlike the Bermuda Triangle, however, this one has some truth to it. If you're looking for me anytime from June through August, the odds are you're going to find me in one of three places: the beach (surfing), my room (reading), or Surf Sisters (hanging out or working). In fact, I'm not exactly sure when I officially started *working* at the shop. I was just there all the time, and I slowly started to chip in whenever they needed help.

That's where I'm heading now, even though it's my day off. I surfed this morning and finished my latest mystery novel, so I figure I should do something that involves other humans. (Introvert, push yourself!) Besides, both Sophie and Nicole are working, and once their shift's over, we're catching a movie.

The problem is that I know they'll be ready to pounce on me the second I walk through the door. It's been a few days since the Ben Incident (Sophie wants to call it the Bencident, but I refuse to let her), and they'll want to know if I've made any progress with him. If I say that I haven't, they'll give me a hard time and start talking about how I'm going to run out of time. That's why I decide to take a calculated risk and stop by the bandshell on my way to the shop.

The bandshell is our town's outdoor stage. It's at the north end of the boardwalk and where we have little concerts and annual events like Tuba Christmas and the Sand Castle Dance, which we all make fun of but secretly love. It's also where the Parks and Recreation office is located. I figure Ben probably spends most of his time *parking* and *recreating,* so the odds are pretty good that he won't be in the office. If I drop by, I can at least tell the girls that I tried to see him. Even if he happens to be there, I don't have to actually talk to him. I can act like I'm there for some other reason and tell the girls that I saw him, which would technically be true.

The office is in a plain cinder block building right behind the bandshell. Its only architectural flourish is a mural painted on one side that's meant to look like *The Birth of Venus,* except instead of Venus it has a pearl. Written above it is the slogan PEARL BEACH, GEM OF THE OCEAN. It's so tacky that I actually think it's kind of perfect.

When I open the door, I'm greeted by an arctic blast of air-conditioning. And when I look around the office and see that Ben's not there, I have a sinking feeling. I realize I was maybe secretly hoping he would be. This fact surprises me and is just another indication that all of this really is new for me.

Just as I'm about to turn and leave, I hear a voice call my name. "Izzy?"

I look over and see Ms. McCarthy behind a desk. She lives

down the street from us and is good friends with my mom. I totally forgot that she works here.

"Hi, Ms. Mac. How are you?"

"Good," she says. "What's brings you by?"

"I'm looking for . . ." I'm halfway through the sentence before I realize that I don't really have a good finish for it. I stammer for a second and say, "Well . . . there's a new boy who just started working here and . . ."

"Ben?" she asks, with that knowing smile that grown-ups give when they think they know what's up. "Are you looking for Ben?"

Mental warning bells sound as I realize that this information will get back to my mom within seconds of me leaving.

"Actually, I'm not looking for *him*. I'm looking for a *poster*. He dropped one off yesterday at the shop, and Mo, one of the two sisters who own the surf shop, wants me to pick up another one for us to hang up. You know . . . to help support the town . . . and all of its wonderful activities."

Ms. McCarthy gives me a slightly skeptical look. "Okay. If it's just a poster you want, there are some extras over there."

She points to a table, and I go over and see a stack of posters.

"Yep, this is it," I say, picking one up. "*This* is the reason that I came by. It's a nice poster. Attractive and informative. Thanks so much. Mo will be really happy about this."

I realize I'm overdoing it and decide my best course of action is to stop talking and nod good-bye.

As I head out the door, Ms. McCarthy says one more thing. "I know it's not why you came here, but if you had come to see

Ben, I would have told you that you just missed him and that he was headed down the boardwalk to get some lunch."

I find this information very interesting, but I don't want her—and therefore my mom—to know this, so I just make a confused expression and say, "Whatever." I maintain this "whatever" attitude up to the instant that I'm beyond her field of vision, at which point I sprint toward the boardwalk.

The boardwalk is the main tourist strip for Pearl Beach, and it stretches eight blocks from the bandshell at one end to the pier at the other. Normally I avoid it because of the whole "it has crowds and I'm an introvert" thing, but since it's technically on the way to where I'm going and we're early enough in the season that the crowds aren't too bad, I decide to walk along it.

After a couple blocks I see Ben in all of his white sock and coach's shorts glory standing in line at Beach-a Pizza. It's an outdoor pizza stand that has picnic table seating facing out over the ocean. It dawns on me that I can get in line, buy a slice, and if I sit at the same picnic table, we'll be eating together. That will fulfill my sentencing requirement. Clever me.

I slip into the line and see there are a few people between us. It's not until I'm standing there that I realize I'm still holding the stupid poster. I'd kept it so that I could prove to the girls that I really had stopped by the office, but now it just seems awkward. I'm strategizing what I should do about it when he turns and sees me.

"Hey . . . it's you. Izzy, right?"

"Right," I answer. "And you're Ben."

He smiles. "You remembered."

"Tell me something three times and it sticks."

He lets the people in between us cut in front of him and moves back so that he's next to me. I know it seems small, but this instantly makes me like him more. So many people try to get you to move up to them and cut in front of other people, and I'm never comfortable with that. Of course, I'm not particularly comfortable at the moment standing in line clutching my poster. But you know what I mean.

"Something wrong with the poster?" he asks, pointing at it.

"Nope," I say. "I just picked up another one to hang in the other window."

Apparently he's just as clueless about things as I am, because he buys this as an acceptable excuse.

"Good to see that the word is spreading."

"So what are you up to?" I ask, as if there are a wide variety of reasons why someone would be standing in line at Beach-a Pizza.

"Just getting pizza and a pop."

"A pop?" I ask, confused. "You mean a popsicle?"

"No, a soft drink. Don't you call it 'pop'?"

I laugh. "We say soda."

"Okay, this is good. Now I've learned something," he says. "I'm getting pizza and . . . a soda."

"Very nice," I respond, playing along.

"Pretty soon I'll be just like the locals."

"Well . . . not as long as you eat here."

He looks at me for a second. "What's wrong with Beach-a Pizza?"

"You mean besides the name?" I lean closer and whisper. "It tastes like cardboard with ketchup on it."

"It seems pretty popular," he says. "Look at all the people in line."

"Yes, look at them," I reply, still keeping my voice low. "They have pale skin, wear shoes with their bathing suits, and fanny packs. They're wearing fanny packs, Ben! What does that tell you?"

He thinks it over for a moment and shakes his head. "I don't know, what does it tell me?"

"That they're tourists," I say. "Only tourists are waiting here. The people who live in Pearl Beach are not in line. You're living here for the summer. Don't you think you should get pizza where we get it?"

"But you live here," he says. "Why are you in line?"

This one catches me off guard. It's not like I can say, "Because Sophie was on the register and I have to eat with you or be subjected to extended hazing." I pause for a second before blurting, "Because I wanted to rescue you and show you where we go."

"Rescue me?" He likes this. "You're like my knight in shining armor?"

"More like light wash denim . . . but it's something like that."

"Well, you were right about Mama Tacos," he says, reminding me of the horror that was the guacamole-stain recommendation. "That was delicious. I'll trust you again. Where do you think we should go?"

"Luigi's Car Wash," I say.

"I meant for pizza," he says.

"So did I."

"Sounds awful!" He hesitates for a moment. "Let's go!"

It suddenly dawns on me that I may have just asked a guy out on a date.

As we're driving down Ocean Ave. in an old blue Parks and Rec pickup truck, I get my first true up-close look at him since the Bencident. (Sophie can't call it that, but I can.) I'm trying not to stare, but as I give him directions I at least have an excuse to be looking his way.

I will amend my earlier statement in which I said I wasn't sure that all girls would classify him as cute. I think your boy vision would have to be seriously impaired not to rate him at least that high. He has strong features and permanent scruff that gives him a ruggedness I find irresistible. But the clinching feature is still the smile. It's easy and natural, with teeth so bright they might as well be a commercial for the virtues of Wisconsin milk.

"Explain to me why we're getting pizza at a car wash," he says, flashing those same pearly whites.

"It's complicated," I reply. "Back when my parents were growing up, it really was a car wash. But at some point Luigi realized that he could make more money selling pizzas than washing cars, so he decided to convert into a pizza joint."

"But it's still called Luigi's Car Wash?"

"That's the complicated part. Technically it still is a car wash," I try to explain. "It's right on the beach and oceanfront property is really valuable. Developers would love to get rid of Luigi, tear down the building, and put up a condominium or a hotel or something awful like that. But as long as he keeps the name the same and as long they wash a few cars every week, it's protected by an old law that was in effect when he first opened."

Ben laughs and gives me a skeptical look. "I was perfectly happy eating boardwalk pizza, which I have to say sounds way more legit than car wash pizza. Why do I feel like I'm being set up for some kind of practical joke?"

"You're not. I promise."

"Now, before I embarrass myself, you do call it pizza, right?" he asks. "It's not going to be another 'pop' situation, where it turns out I'm using the wrong word again?"

He's funny. I like funny.

"No," I tell him as we pull into the parking lot. "But if you really want to sound like you know what you're doing, just say that you want a couple slices of Big Lu."

"What's Big Lu?"

"It's short for Big Luigi, a pizza with everything on it. It's the house specialty, and trust me when I say that you're going to want to order it."

"You're telling me it's good?"

"No, I'm telling you it's life changing."

"Life-changing car wash pizza?" he says as we get out of the car. "This should be interesting."

Luigi's still has the shape and design of a car wash, which is part of its charm. (It's also part of the legal requirements that protect it.) As we walk up to the counter to order, I'm suddenly extremely self-conscious. I've never been on a date before—and

I'm not sure this would even qualify as one—but I am walking into Luigi's with a guy and I don't know all the protocols. In fact, I don't know any of the protocols. There's no line, so we go straight to the counter.

"I'll have a couple of slices of Big Lu and a—" He almost says "pop," but he catches himself and says "soda."

Then he says something that surprises me.

"And whatever she wants."

I wasn't expecting him to pay for my lunch, but I think it's a check in the "it's kinda, sorta like a date" column.

"I'll have the same," I say.

The cashier rings it up, gives us two cups and a number to take to our table. Ben makes another "is it soda or pop?" joke as we get our drinks, and then we sit down in a booth. I have been in Luigi's a thousand times before, but I have never felt more like a fish out of water in my entire life.

"How long have you lived in Pearl Beach?" he asks.

"Born and raised," I answer. "Third generation. By the way, we usually call it PB."

"More lingo," he says with a nod as he sips his drink. "So far I've learned 'soda,' 'Big Lu,' and 'PB.' Pretty soon I'll be fluent, which is important considering that I'm a native."

I give him a look. "I think you're getting ahead of yourself. You ordered two slices of pizza. That hardly makes you a native."

"No, no, no," he tells me. "It's legit. I was born here."

"You were born in Pearl Beach?" I ask skeptically.

"Nope," he says. "I was born in PB. See, I'm using the lingo."

I laugh. "Now you're messing with me."

"Actually, I'm not. I was born the summer after my father finished law school. This is where Mom grew up, and since his job didn't start until the following January, they came here and stayed with my grandma. That way they could save money and my dad could study for the bar exam. I lived here for the first six months of my life."

"Well then, I guess that means there's an islander in there somewhere," I joke. "We've just got to shake off some of the Wisconsin that's covering it."

"Watch what you say about Wisconsin," he says with mock indignation. "That's America's Dairy Land."

"I didn't mean to imply anything negative."

"You better not. There are a lot of important things that come out of Wisconsin."

"Is that so?" I say playfully. "Like what?"

"Okay," he replies, perhaps a little caught off guard. "I'll list some of them for you."

He pauses for a second, and I impatiently cross my arms.

"Harley-Davidson motorcycles . . . and custard."

"Custard?"

He makes the happy delicious face. "You haven't lived until you've had the custard at Babcock Hall."

"I'll take your word for it."

"And the Green Bay Packers. Everybody loves the Packers."

I shrug.

"And don't forget milk. Without which we would not have our wonderful smiles."

He flashes a smile, and I have to admit that I am sold.

"You've got me there," I say.

I don't know if it's because of the back and forth nature of the conversation or all the endorphins released by the incredible aroma of pizza that fills the air, but I'm actually feeling more relaxed.

"So we'll accept that Wisconsin is amazing and wonderful. But since you're stuck with us for the summer, what exactly does your job with the Parks and Recreation Department entail?" I ask.

"I think I'm responsible for anything that no one else wants to do," he says with a laugh. "There's a lot of scrubbing and cleaning. More than a little mowing. And, starting Monday, I'm one of the counselors for the summer day camp. That should be great—four days a week with a bunch of screaming kids trying to torment me."

"I did that," I tell him.

"You were a counselor?"

"No. I was one of the screaming kids who tormented the counselors. It was a lot of fun."

"The schedule's insane," he says. "Every day it's something different. We've got kick ball, soccer, swimming, and we're even going to the golf course once a week."

"Don't forget Surf Sisters," I say.

"We're going to Surf Sisters?" he asks.

"On Tuesdays campers will learn respect for the ocean, beach safety, and the fundamentals of surfing," I say, quoting the brochure.

"I thought that was at a place called Eddie's Surf . . . something or other."

"Steady Eddie's Surf School," I say.

"That's it."

"Surf Sisters is actually run by two sisters, and Steady Eddie was their dad," I explain. "They are one and the same."

"That's great news," he says with a smile. "Does that mean you're going to be our surfing instructor?"

I try to hide my disappointment as I tell him no.

I leave out the part about how I was supposed to be the instructor but pawned it off on Sophie because I didn't want to deal with all of those screaming kids. Of course, it had never dawned on me that I would want to deal with their dreamy counselor.

"That's too bad," he says. "We could have chased them together."

This development puts me in a funk for a little while, but it's nothing that two slices of Big Lu can't cure. During the rest of the conversation we talk about his hometown and high school. I figure if I let him do most of the talking, I will not put my foot in my mouth, as I've been prone to do in the past. This strategy seems to work, because we keep talking even after we've finished eating, which is pretty cool.

I try to resist my natural instinct to overanalyze every little detail, but I can't help but look for any hint that he might be interested in me. He's good about eye contact; it's not piercing and creepy but he stays engaged. Never once does he make more than a casual glance at the game playing on the big screen TV behind me. Better yet, there are a couple of sharky girls at the next table. They're cute and giggly, and I think more than a little loud on purpose trying to get his attention, but he seems oblivious to them.

"Don't you think?" he says, and I realize that I have no idea what he's talking about. (How's that for irony? My analyzing how engaged he is made me zone out.)

"Totally," I say, hoping that it makes sense based on the question. Fearful of continuing to talk about a subject of which I am unaware, I decide to change the topic. "So how'd you end up here for the summer?"

It didn't seem like a trick question when I asked it, but his expression makes me rethink this. "I'm sorry. I don't mean to pry."

"No, it's nothing secret, just a little sad," he says. "My parents are getting divorced and it's really ugly. There are lawyers and screaming arguments, and my mom was worried that it might scar me for life, so she arranged with Uncle Bob for me to come down here and work with him."

"I'm really sorry to hear that. A few of my friends have had their parents get divorced, and it was hard on them. I'm so lucky that mine are happy together."

"The worst part," he says, "is that my dad is being a total jerk. I don't get it. He's being so mean to her, and I wish I were up there because I want to be there for her. But she thought this would be best for me."

The discussion about his parents brings down the mood of the conversation, and before I can come up with a new topic, he gets a phone call. The conversation is short, and when it's over, he says, "Duty calls."

He takes one last sip of his soda and stands up.

"What's the problem?"

"There's a pavilion at the playground where they like to have birthday parties," he says.

"I know it well," I say. "I believe I celebrated birthday number seven there."

"Apparently some of the kids learned an important lesson about what happens to your digestive system if you eat massive amounts of cake and ice cream immediately before going full speed on the merry-go-round."

"And you've got to clean it up?" I ask with a grimace.

"Like I said, my job is pretty much to do whatever nobody else wants to do." He shrugs. "Let me take you wherever you were headed?"

"It's not far, I can walk," I say. "I don't want to make you late."

"I'm pretty sure it will still be there," he says.

"Okay, I'll take a lift to Surf Sisters."

As we walk out to his truck, I manage to send a clandestine text to Nicole and Sophie. Make sure you can see the parking lot in three minutes. Trust me!

I slide my phone back into my pocket and ignore the vibrating of reply texts no doubt asking for an explanation.

"Thanks for rescuing me from boardwalk pizza," he says as we drive down Ocean. "Luigi's is without a doubt the best pizza I've ever had."

"It was the least I could do," I say. "And thanks for buying me lunch. You didn't have to do that."

"You can buy next time." As he says it he flashes that oh-so-distracting smile, and I'm feeling good.

"Next time." I like the sound of that. Of course, I'm not sure how to read the smile. Is he smiling because he's polite? Is he smiling because he likes being with me? Or is he smiling because he just ate the best pizza in the world?

When he pulls up to Surf Sisters, I look through the windshield and can see that Nicole and Sophie are both looking out the window. They're dumbfounded when they realize that it's me in the truck with Ben, and it takes everything I've got not to react. It also makes me even more self-conscious as I try to come up with the perfect farewell line that will keep him thinking of me.

"Well," I say with a goofy grin, "have fun cleaning up the vomit."

Apparently that's the best I could come up with. My first ever may or may not be a date ends with me turning to a guy and talking about vomit. I am so smooth.

"I'll do my best," he says. "Thanks again."

I get out of the truck, wave good-bye, and watch him drive away.

I'm still not sure what to make of it all, but that does nothing to dampen the feeling of total triumph that I have as I walk into the store. For a moment the two of them stare in disbelief.

"Is there a problem, girls?"

"No," Sophie says, trying to suppress a grin but failing miserably. "Where were you?"

"You know, just eating pizza at Luigi's with Ben. No big."

"Are you serious?" asks Nicole.

I smile and nod. "Absolutely."

"Okay," Sophie says, getting excited. "There are questions that need to be answered. Many questions."

"No, there aren't," I say, trying to project cool for once in my life. "There's just one question that needs to be answered."

"What's that?" she says.

I turn to Nicole, who's working the register. "I'd like an official judgment on this. Which beach girl totally kicks ass."

Nicole grins as she says it. "That would be Izzy Lucas."

And she rings the bell on the register to make it official.

*S*ince the shop is busy, the girls don't get to grill me for information until after their shift ends and we're all riding to the movie theater. Sophie's driving and Nicole's in the passenger seat. (One perk of being a six-foot-tall girl is that you always get the front seat.) She wedges herself sideways to look at me in the back.

"Explain again how this happened?" she asks.

"First I stopped by the Parks and Rec office to see if I could 'bump into' him there," I say. "And I found out that he was taking his lunch break on the boardwalk."

"I'm surrounded by stalkers," Sophie interjects as she gives me a wink in the rearview mirror.

"So I went walking along the boardwalk and saw him in line at Beach-a Pizza."

"BP?" says Nicole. "That's disgusting."

"Which is exactly what I told him," I continue. "So I suggested that he should try Luigi's and that was that. We were on our way."

"Very nice," says Nicole.

"See what happens when you actually talk to the guy," Sophie says, giving Nicole a raised eyebrow.

"Can we get back to Izzy?" she protests, not wanting another lecture on how she should talk to Cody. "What's Ben like?"

"I don't know," I answer. "I mean, he seems great. He's funny. Kind of goofy but in the totally good way."

"I love that," Nicole says. "Give me cute and goofy over slick and sexy any day."

Sophie gives Nicole another look but decides not to press her on Cody. Instead, she looks at me in the mirror for a second and asks, "Does that mean you're into him?"

I think about it for a moment. "I don't know. Maybe."

Nicole grins. "Her lips say 'maybe,' but the redness in her cheeks says 'hell yeah.'"

We're all laughing as Sophie parks and we get out of the car.

"Tell me that you picked this movie because it's supposed to be good," she says to Nicole. "And not because you think 'you know who' will be here."

"He's not going to be here," Nicole says. "He already saw it last Saturday with some of the guys from Interact."

Sophie stops. "And you know this how?"

"I've already been convicted of stalking and as such am protected by double jeopardy," she says. "So lay off."

Sophie and I share a look and shake our heads. Nicole really does need to do something about this.

"All I'm saying is that I pushed Izzy and it paid off," Sophie replies. "I'd like the same good fortune to happen to you."

"Slow down," I say. "We're not sure that it 'paid off' for me. Ben and I had pizza, but I have no idea if he likes me or not. He may just like the pizza."

"Didn't you see any signs?" asks Sophie.

"Yeah," says Nicole. "I've heard there are supposed to be signs."

"The signs were mixed," I reply. "At some points it seemed like he was into me and at others not so much. It doesn't help that his parents are going through an epic divorce. I think it may have soured him a bit on the whole idea of relationships."

We reach the ticket window and Sophie turns to me.

"By the way, you're buying my ticket."

"And why is that?"

"Because you owe me . . . big time."

I think about this for a second. "Because?"

"Because, despite it being a major hassle, I went through the computer and swapped shifts with you every Tuesday for the rest of the summer."

It takes me a moment to realize what she's saying.

"You mean . . ."

"You'll be teaching all the summer campers how to surf, which should give you plenty of opportunities to read signs from Ben."

I wrap her up in a giant hug, and because she's so small it lifts her off the ground.

"You're pretty awesome sometimes, you know that?"

"No," she says. "I'm *incredibly* awesome *all* of the time. And as soon as you two realize that, your lives will improve dramatically."

Needless to say, I am more than happy to buy her ticket.

*O*n Tuesday morning I spend a ridiculous amount of time trying to select my surfing attire. Normally, this is automatic: wet suit in the cold months, spring suit on chilly mornings, bikini and a rash guard when it's hot. My rash guard has two purposes. It's a swim shirt that protects my skin from all the wax and sand on my surfboard. And, bonus, it keeps me from falling out of my bikini top whenever I wipe out.

Of course, *normally* I'm only interested in what's most comfortable and functional for surfing. Today, however, is not normal.

Instead of hitting the waves to find the perfect ride, I'll be teaching a bunch of grade school kids how to surf. That means they'll be staring at me while I do a lot of leaning and bending over. The last thing I want to do is give them a little show-and-tell. But I'll also be in front of Ben, and it wouldn't be the worst thing in the world if I actually looked, you know, cute.

After countless combinations, I finally settle on a pair of rainbow-striped board shorts that have a stylish cut but still cover everything I need covered and a baby blue Surf Sisters rash guard that I put on over a black bikini top. As I take one final look in my bedroom mirror I empathize with all of the women who ask me to help them find a swimsuit. Still, to my surprise, the combination actually looks cute, and in a rare moment of self-confidence I'm willing to say I've gone from flounder to dolphin.

At the beach, Sophie helps me set up before the campers arrive. She's doing a good job of keeping it light and funny so I don't stress out. She can ride you relentlessly, but when you need it, she's nothing but your biggest cheerleader. We're laughing about something when we hear the faint sound of mass whistling approaching us.

I look up just in time to see Ben leading a makeshift platoon of campers over a sand dune and right at us. They are whistling a silly tune as they pretend to march, and it is irresistibly cute.

My guess is that Ben didn't spend nearly as much time worrying about his wardrobe as I did. He's traded in his coach's shorts for a flowery Hawaiian print bathing suit but has maintained the rest of his signature look with a tucked-in polo, white socks, and running shoes. You'd think it was a uniform or a job requirement, except both of the other counselors are wearing swimsuits and T-shirts.

"He's wearing shoes and socks," Sophie says to me. "He's wearing them *on the beach*."

"Yeah," I respond. "I'm going to have to work on that."

I recognize the other counselors from school. The guy's name is Jacob. Even though he's a star soccer player, he runs with the brainy crowd and stays pretty low key. I wouldn't say we're friends, but I've always liked him and we get along well. The girl is a different story.

Kayla is a total alpha, a shark to my dolphin. She lives to make sure that girls like me know that we're not nearly as sparkly as girls like her. For example, just so everyone realizes how unbelievably awesome she is, she's wearing a way too tight Surf City top that shows off her curves—and I imagine also restricts her breathing. Surf City is a megaretail store on Ocean Ave. where girls like Kayla, wearing short-shorts and tank tops, sell overpriced T-shirts and surfboards to tourists who don't know any better. They are our sworn enemies.

"Watch out for that one," Sophie says with a nod toward Kayla. "If she so much as gets a hint you're into Ben, she will totally drop in on you." "Dropping in" is what surfers call it when someone tries to catch a wave that you're already riding.

Although the Kayla development puts a slight damper on my mood, things take a turn for the better when Ben sees me and flashes that smile of his.

Even Sophie can't help but notice. "Well, what he lacks in fashion sense, he makes up for with dimples," she says, accompanied by a friendly nudge of her elbow. "That's my cue to let you two be all alone . . . you know, except for the screaming kids and the conniving camp counselor."

She smiles and gives a friendly wave to Ben and the campers as she walks back up toward the surf shop.

Just as they're about to reach me, Ben holds his hand out like a stop sign. "Campers, halt!"

The kids make exaggerated stops, some even going so far as running into each other in slow motion before crashing onto the sand. Apparently, his goofiness has already infected them.

"I thought you said you weren't going to be teaching this class," he says.

"There was a change in plans," I answer, trying to sound mysterious but probably coming across as clueless.

He thinks about this for a second and nods. "Very nice."

He turns to address the kids, and from the way they hang on his every word I can tell that they love him.

"I want all of you to say hi to Izzy."

"Hi, Izzy!" the kids shout in unison.

"Hi, everyone!" I say back. "Are you ready to learn how to become slammin' surfers?"

There are cheers, and I realize that even if it wasn't for Ben, I should never have tried to avoid this. Kids are great and I love teaching them about the ocean. I can't help but flash back to my own summer camp when I came here for the same lessons. My dad had already taught me the basics, but this was when I really got the bug. It's also when I first started to hang out at Surf Sisters.

"Before we do anything," I continue, "I want you all to repeat these three words. Slip! Slop! Slap!"

"Slip! Slop! Slap!" they shout in unison.

"Who can tell me what these words mean?"

When no one else raises a hand, Ben jumps right in.

"Slip, slop, slap," he says. "That's what happened to me when I tried to stand up in a bathtub this morning."

The kids laugh.

"Good guess," I say. "But not what I was going for. This is why they're important. If you're going to be in the sun for a while, you should always 'slip on a shirt,' 'slop on some sunscreen,' and 'slap on a hat.'"

I open up the two big boxes that Sophie helped me set up and start handing out rash guards, Steady Eddie surf caps, and plenty of sunscreen.

"We love the sun, but we have to respect it," I say. "Too much of it is bad for your skin. Isn't that right, Kayla?"

All eyes turn to Kayla, whose richly tanned skin is a pretty good indication that she does not follow this advice.

"That's right," she says unenthusiastically as she stares daggers at me.

Once everyone is fortified against the sun, I get them all in a big circle so that we can stretch. I don't know if it's coincidence or conniving, but Kayla winds up directly across from Ben so that he has an unobstructed view of her doing her stretches. And, as much as I hate her, even I have to admit she looks pretty spectacular while she's doing them.

Once we're all stretched out, I hold up a thick foam board about three feet long and ask, "Who can tell me what this is?"

Without missing a beat, Ben answers, "A surfboard!"

The kids all laugh because they think he's joking, but I can tell by his expression that he thought he had the right answer. I quickly come to his rescue.

"Ben's trying to trick you guys, isn't he?"

"Yes," they shout, and Ben smiles and plays along.

"This is way too short to be a surfboard, *isn't it*, Ben?"

"Absolutely," he says with a grateful smile. "Way too short. Even for short people like these guys."

"So, who, other than Ben, can tell me what it really is?"

A few of the kids call out, "A boogie board."

"That's right," I answer. "A boogie board. It's also called a body board, and although you use it to ride waves, you don't stand up on it like a surfboard. Do you?"

"No," they reply.

I notice one girl in back is too shy to shout out with the

others. She reminds me of me at her age, so I point to her and ask, "How do you ride a boogie board?" As I ask the question, I rub my hand over my stomach.

"On your belly?" she says with a little uncertainty.

"That's right, you ride it on your belly. Before camp is over we're going to have all of you standing up on surfboards. But for today we're going to just stay on our bellies and ride these. Okay?"

"Okay!" they shout, and this time she shouts with them.

We break the campers into smaller groups and take them out into shallow water a few at a time. This lets them get used to the dynamics of waves and builds their confidence for riding on a board. It's also unbelievably fun.

Most of them pick it up instantly, and I quickly become a fan of the shy girl, whose name is Rebecca. I notice the change in her attitude with every bit of success, and it reminds me even more of the nine-year-old version of me.

The only one who struggles getting the hang of it is Ben. First he has trouble catching a wave, and when he finally does get one, he lies too far up on the board and winds up going face-first into the sand. The kids all get a kick out of this, and the thing that's great about Ben is that he does too. A lot of guys would get embarrassed and try to act cool, but he just goes with the goofy, and the kids love it.

By the middle of the session I am certain that it's more than a crush for me. I really like him and I would love for him to like me. But the problem is that I just can't tell if he's even remotely interested.

He's relaxed when we talk, which makes it seem like he is,

but then he's all goofy with the kids, too, so maybe that's just him. Furthermore, he seems to have no idea that Kayla is a shark in surf clothing and seems mighty comfortable talking to her, too. I don't have the body or confidence to do what she's doing and begin to think that I may be in beyond my depth.

In fact, I don't get a good read on the situation until the lesson is done and we're all carrying our boards back up to the shop. Ben walks next to me.

"This was great," he says. "The kids loved it. I loved it. Obviously, I need a lot of practice and coaching, but it was great."

I can't tell if he's opening the door for me to offer to help him get that practice and coaching or if he's just making conversation. I walk quietly for a moment before I start to stammer, "Well, you know . . . if you really want to get better . . . I could always—"

And that's when Kayla drops in, just like Sophie warned me she would. She sidles right up next to him and grabs him by the elbow with an effortlessness that is as impressive as it is evil.

"Ben, you are so great with these kids," she says, all dimples and boobs. "Don't you think so, Iz?"

I cannot believe that she is calling me "Iz," like we're old friends or something. Of course there's nothing I can do about it but agree.

"Terrific," I say. For a moment she and I lock stares, and I know that war is at hand. Before I can say anything else, one of the campers comes running up to Ben.

"Ben, Ben, Ben," he says excitedly. "You won't believe it. There's this dead fish and its guts are exploded all over the place. It's totally disgusting."

"Well, if it's TOTALLY disgusting," he says with an exaggerated expression, "then I have to see it."

They hurry off and leave me alone with Kayla. Neither of us says another word for the rest of the walk. We're just a shark and a dolphin swimming side by side across the sand.

*Y*ou're my daughter and I love you," my dad says with total tenderness before he flashes an evil grin and adds, "But first I'm going to demolish you, and then I'm going to destroy you."

Welcome to game night with the Lucas family. Always fun, always competitive, always full of trash talk. At the moment we're in the middle of a particularly intense game of Risk, and Dad is about to attack my armies in Greenland. He's feeling good about it until my mom interrupts.

"You know that 'demolish' and 'destroy' mean the same thing," she says, tweaking him.

He stops just as he's about to roll the dice. "What?"

"You can't destroy her if you've already demolished her. Your threat doesn't make sense."

"Donna?" he whines. "I'm going for an intimidation thing, and you are literally raining on my parade."

"You mean 'figuratively,'" she says. "Or is there actual rain falling on a parade I don't know about?"

"You're doing it again," he says, getting flustered. "You're doing it again."

"I'm sorry, but I think if you want to be a global dictator, the least you can do is use proper grammar."

My parents totally crack me up. They're both teachers at Pearl Beach High School. Mom is the chair of the English Department, hence the grammar, and Dad teaches history and coaches cross-country, which explains the competitiveness. At school I might have a slight tendency to avoid them, but they're actually very cool and fun to hang out with. During the summer we usually play board games around the kitchen table a couple nights a week.

"What if I say this?" he offers, having fun with it. "First I'm going to invade your country, and then I'm going to destroy it?"

He looks at her hopefully, but she just shrugs and replies, "It's not great."

"Why? What's wrong with it?"

"Why invade the country if you're going to destroy it? I think you may mean that you're going to invade the country and destroy her army, but that's not what you said. Your command of pronouns is about as strong as your armies in northern Africa."

He's trying to think up a comeback when the doorbell rings. "Saved by the bell," he says. "Literally."

"Thank you," she replies. "In that instance 'literally' is correct."

She stands up and adds, "I'll go answer the door so you can keep up your attacks on Greenland and the English language."

"English teachers," he says under his breath as he shoots me a wink.

Just as he's about to roll the dice, I hear a familiar voice talking to Mom at the door and signal Dad to stop.

"Wait a second. Is that Ben?"

"Ben?" my father asks. "Who's Ben?"

Suddenly visions of embarrassment dance through my head.

I turn to him and give my most desperate face. "Don't be you. Don't tell bad jokes. Don't tell embarrassing stories. Just once, try to be normal."

"I am offended," he says indignantly. "I have no idea what you're talking about."

I give him a look and he returns it in kind.

"Really?" I ask.

"Really."

I hear them walking toward the kitchen and I know I'm running out of time. "If you're good, I'll promise not to attack you in northern Africa and we can gang up on Mom in Asia."

"Deal," he says with a grin.

We shake on it just before Mom walks into the room with Ben.

"Hi, Izzy," he says sheepishly.

"Hey, Ben," I say, trying to figure out why he might be here. "Mom, Dad, this is Ben. He's down for the summer from Wisconsin. Ben, these are my parents."

"Nice to meet you," he says. "I'm sorry to interrupt your game."

"That's okay," says Mom. "We were just about to take a break."

"We were?" asks my father, no doubt disappointed that his plans for global domination keep getting interrupted.

"We were," she says, "so that you and I could head over to the Islander and get some ice cream."

"That's right," he replies, suddenly pleased. "We absolutely were going to get some ice cream."

Without missing a beat Mom picks up her purse and beelines for the door with Dad right behind her. Just before he leaves, though, he turns around and pulls out his phone to take a picture.

"Dad?" I say, suddenly worried. "What are you doing?"

He takes a picture of the game board and gives me a look. "Just in case someone accidentally 'bumps' into the table while I'm gone, I want to make sure we can put all the pieces back where they're supposed to be."

Rather than reply, I just shake my head and let them leave.

"I really am sorry to just drop in like this," Ben says once they're gone. "But I don't know your phone number and I need to ask a favor."

"Sure," I say, trying to sound confident and cool, neither of which remotely describes my current state of being. "But if you didn't know my phone number, how'd you figure out where I live?"

"I stopped by the shop to see if you were working, and one of your friends was there. She told me how to find you."

"Would that be the really tall one?"

"No, it was the one who says I wear the wrong clothes on the beach."

I cringe. "You heard that."

"She has the kind of voice that carries," he says. "But it's okay. It didn't hurt my feelings or anything. I really don't know what to wear on the beach. And I did think that the boogie board was a surfboard."

"I know."

"And I call things by the wrong name."

"Yeah."

"If I'm going to spend the summer here, I don't want to feel like I'm an alien from some far off planet."

"Okay, but what's the favor?"

MICHELLE DALTON

"Can you teach me all that stuff? Can you teach me what to wear? Where to go? How to tell the difference between a surf- board and a boogie board?"

"Sure," I say. "I'd be happy to."

"Really?"

"Absolutely. When's your next day off?"

"Saturday," he says.

"Perfect," I tell him. "I'm off this Saturday too. Why don't we meet here at eleven?"

There's that smile, and then he says the most remarkable thing of all.

"It's a date."

On Saturday morning I wake up early to surf the stretch of beach closest to my house. The waves are better down by the pier, but I'm not really looking for a workout. I just want to clear my mind and have a chill start to the day.

As I paddle out I keep thinking about something that Nicole said to me last night. She came over to the house to hang out and, big shocker, talk turned to Ben. Considering our mutual clue- lessness about boys, it was pretty much a blind-leading-the-blind conversation. That is, until she said, "The girl you are on a surf- board is the girl you have to be with him."

At first I laughed at the whole profound quality of it. But the more I thought about it, the more I realized she was on to some- thing. My problem is that the girl I am on a surfboard has liter- ally been surfing longer than she's been walking, while the girl I am with boys has barely taken baby steps. I have no idea how to convert one into the other.

I try to figure it out as I sit on the board, dangling my legs in the water. Unfortunately, my brainstorming session is as flat as the surf. This morning the ocean looks like a lake, and after fifteen minutes with little more than a ripple, I decide to call it a day. But just as I start to bail, the surf gods surprise me with a sudden gift. I turn to take one last look and see a swell forming in the distance. It's going to be big and it's all for me.

My board is already lined up perfectly, so all I have to do is lie flat on my belly and start paddling. I go slowly at first and then pick up the pace when it gets close. As I feel the wave come up beneath me, I try to study my technique. Maybe it's as simple as Nicole said, and all I have to do is look for hints of how I am on the surfboard to figure out how I should be with Ben.

I feel a rush as the wave catches the board, and I get up on my feet. I analyze every detail—the face of the wave, the placement of my feet, and the way my hand reaches back toward the white water breaking off the crest. I adjust my weight to test my center of gravity and bend my knees to lower my butt closer to the deck. I study everything . . . for about three seconds.

Then I pearl.

Pearling is what you call it when the nose of your board digs under the water and throws you flying over the front. This particular one is a textbook example, and before I even realize what's happening, I slam face-first into the water. It's more disorienting than scary. One moment I'm riding a wave and the next I'm getting slapped around by Mother Nature. When I'm underwater it feels like a weird combination of slow motion and superspeed as the force of the wave pushes me down from the surface.

I get kicked around for a few seconds until it passes over me. Then I wade up to the tide line and plop down on the sand to catch my breath. The back of my shoulder stings where it scraped against some shells, and there's a dull throb around my ankle because it got yanked by the tether line attached to the surfboard. But overall my body isn't hurt nearly as much as my pride.

I'm not embarrassed because I wiped out. Everybody does that. It's just that I did it like some newbie trying to catch her first wave. I'm not even sure what went wrong. Since I was so carefully analyzing each step, you'd think I'd be able to figure it out. But as I run through my mental checklist, it seems like I was doing everything right.

That's when it hits me.

The reason I pearled is *because* I was analyzing each step. I was thinking too much. Normally I don't think at all. I just do it. I mean, you can't fight a wave; you can only go where it takes you. Maybe boys are the same way. Instead of analyzing every little detail and looking for signals with Ben, I should just see where it takes me. I should just be myself.

Okay, so this might not be the most original realization, but it sure is new for me. Normally when I'm around guys, I'm trying to be anyone but me. But I remind myself that Ben's the one who suggested hanging out today and that he's the one who used the phrase "It's a date." He might actually be into me.

That thought gives me a rare burst of confidence as I walk home with my board under my arm. Earlier I was worried about how the day would unfold, but now I'm thinking it might work out fine. Of course, that could just be because I bumped my head pretty bad when I was underwater, but I'm going to go with it.

It also helps that I've eliminated wardrobe drama this time. Unlike the day when I taught the campers, I don't need to spend time obsessing about what I should wear. Nicole and I took care of that last night. I picked out a loose pink halter to wear over the top of my bathing suit and a pair of old denim shorts that seem cool but not in a trying too hard sort of way.

As I look at myself in the mirror I feel . . . cautiously optimistic. I also feel a throbbing in my shoulder. I twist to see if there's any noticeable swelling but stop when I hear footsteps on the porch. My room's in the front of the house, which means I'm always the first to know when someone's coming to the door. It sucks when you're trying to sleep in on a Saturday morning, but it's great at times like this, when you want to make sure you're the one answering it instead of your parents.

I move out into the hall and wait for Ben to knock.

And I wait.

And I wait.

Through the door I can hear the sounds of deep breathing and loud footsteps walking from one side of the porch to the other. It sounds like he's panting and pacing, which doesn't really make sense. It's not like he can be nervous about hanging out with me. Or can he be?

I peek through the window and can't believe my eyes.

"Dad!" I exclaim as I fling the door open.

My father's doing huge lunges across the porch and checking

his pulse by holding three fingers against his wrist. He's also wearing running shorts that are a little too short for my comfort level, a sweat-covered T-shirt, and a smiley face bandanna. I did not make that last part up. He's actually wearing a smiley face bandanna.

"What are you doing?" I ask.

"Cooling down," he says between deep breaths. "At my age you've got to stretch to keep from tightening up."

I think about adding a tip that at his age he should also rethink the concept of short-shorts, but there's not time. I check my watch and it's exactly eleven o'clock. Ben's going to be here any second.

"Do you have to stretch here?" I ask.

"I guess I could do it in front of the Bakers' house, but I think that would look a little strange."

"Spoiler alert: It looks strange anywhere," I say as I scan the neighborhood for Ben. "And why are you wearing a bandanna with a smiley face? Did you lose a bet?"

Dad stops for a moment and gives me a confused look. "Is there something going on that I should know about?"

"No, there most definitely is not," I say. "Now, would you please get inside before you ruin it?"

At first he's completely baffled, but then a look of comprehension comes over him.

"Too late." He nods down the block to where Ben is walking toward our house. "I think I figured out why you're stressed. His name is Ben, right?"

"Why do you want to know?"

"Howdy, Ben!" he calls out.

Howdy? Seriously? When did we become cowboys?

"Howdy, Mr. Lucas," Ben says as he reaches the walkway. "Hi, Izzy."

"Hi," I respond, trying to smile at him while simultaneously giving my dad the cue to disappear.

Dad doesn't seem to get the hint, because he's continuing to stretch and has now moved on from lunges to deep knee bends.

"Just ignore me," he says, as if that were possible. "I have a whole stretching routine I have to do after I run."

"Me too," Ben says. "It drives my teammates crazy."

"Teammates?" my dad says.

"I run cross-country at my school."

"What a small world!" Dad says. "I coach cross-country at PB High."

Do you ever wish that life were like a DVR? I do. That way I could hit pause and rewind this in hopes of it playing out a different way.

"We should run together," Dad suggests.

"That would be great," Ben replies. "I signed up for a 10K next month and I need to train for it."

"The Rocket Run?"

"That's it."

"I'm running it too," my dad says. "We can train together and then keep each other company during the race."

I mean, this is seriously not how I had envisioned the day unfolding. But just when I think it can't get any worse, Ben says three words that break my heart.

"It's a date."

When he said it to me about our day together, I took it to

mean that it was an actual *date*. But now I'm beginning to wonder if it's just something he says.

Finally Dad finishes stretching and asks, "So what do you two
have planned for today?"

"A major makeover," Ben says. "Izzy's going to teach me the ways
of Pearl Beach. She's going to help me blend in with the natives."

I am totally ready for Dad to finish me off with some joke
like "How would she know?" But that's not what he says.

"So you're a runner . . . and you're smart," he says. "That's a
good combination. You guys have fun."

It may sound hokey, but in person, in the moment, it's sweet.
Once Dad is inside, Ben turns to me and rubs his hands together
in anticipation.

"So where do we begin?"

"That depends," I reply. "How much of a transformation are
you looking for?"

"Total witness relocation program," he says. "Wardrobe, attitude, everything."

"Well, then," I say with a smile, "we better get some ice cream."

*T*he Islander has been serving ice cream on the boardwalk for
as long as there has been a boardwalk. It has entrances on both
the beach and street sides, and there is a double counter in the
middle of the shop that faces each way. This counter looks like
an island, which is how the shop got its name. But because PB
actually is an island, locals co-opted it and they like to wear the
shop's "Islander" T-shirts as a sign of civic pride.

I order my usual, a waffle cone with two scoops of mint chocolate chip, and Ben gets a junior sundae with hot fudge and whipped cream on rocky road. There is a row of booths against the wall, and we take the one in the middle.

"I'm always up for dessert," he says. "But I don't see how a sundae is going to give me insight into Pearl Beach. You know, we actually have ice cream back home in Wisconsin. That whole 'America's Dairy Land' thing isn't just for the license plates."

"We're not here because of the ice cream," I say.

I turn sideways so that my back is pressed against the wall and stretch my legs out on my side of the booth. He gets the hint and does likewise. Now we're looking right at the counter.

"We're here for the view," I explain.

"What's so special about a view of an ice cream counter?"

"There are two sides to Pearl Beach," I tell him. "The tourist side and the local side. You can't have one without the other. We need the tourists and the tourists need us."

"Okay," he says. "That makes sense."

"But our beach and their beach are different," I say. "They're coming here for something they've seen in movies and on postcards. It's kind of like the theme park version and not the real one."

"You're starting to lose me."

"I'll give you an example. Have you been to the candy shop down by the arcade?" I ask. "The one with the big mixer machines that twist taffy?"

"Yeah," he says. "I went in there when I was handing out posters. It's really cool."

"Did they offer you a sample of the saltwater taffy?"

"Two," he says with a guilty smile. "They were delicious."

"Do you know why they call it saltwater taffy?"

He looks at me like it's a trick question. "Because it's made with salt water?"

"No," I say. "It's just regular taffy made with fresh water."

"Then why do they call it that?"

"Because over a hundred years ago there was a candy shop on a boardwalk in New Jersey that got flooded in a storm. All the taffy got seawater on it, so the man at the counter joked that it was now 'saltwater' taffy. He was *joking*, but when people heard about it, they started buying it up. They figured saltwater taffy must be something that you can only get at the beach. And from that point on all boardwalks are expected to have saltwater taffy."

"So you're saying that the beach is full of con artists taking advantage of tourists?"

"Hardly," I reply. "You like the taffy. It's delicious. And people expect it to be here. They want to come to the beach and see the pretty candy being made in the big machines. They want to buy a decorative box of it to give to their grandma. There's nothing wrong with that. But while tourists think of it as something to do with the beach, we think of it as something to do with tourists. It's fake. That's true of almost everything on the boardwalk."

"So the locals don't come down here?" he asks.

"Not much. Some of the kids do when they're scamming for a quick summer vacation romance, but for the most part, the locals only come down here for two things: work and . . ."

"Ice cream," he says, putting it together.

I nod.

"The Islander is just that good. Now, if you look toward the boardwalk entrance, most of the people you'll see coming off the beach are tourists. But if you look toward Ocean Ave., you'll see the locals. This table is where the worlds collide. It is the perfect place to study them side by side and see how they're different."

Ben takes it all in and understands what I'm talking about.

"Okay," he says, turning toward me. "This is kind of brilliant."

"And don't forget the ice cream is *amazing*."

He takes a spoonful and nods his agreement. "Yes, it is."

We spend a half hour people watching, and Ben quickly picks up on some of the basic differences. He starts off with the obvious ones, like clothes and sunburns, but eventually starts to pick up on the more subtle things, like attitude.

"All right," he says. "I get the thing about the shoes and socks."

"Sophie will be so relieved."

"But here's one thing I don't get." He nods toward the beach side. "All of these people are on vacation." Then he nods to the street side and continues. "But these people all seem more relaxed."

I couldn't be prouder. This was the reason we started here.

"You've got it," I say as I stand up. "You've figured out step one. That means it's time to move on."

I start walking out toward the boardwalk and he follows me.

"But I haven't figured out anything," he says. "I just noticed the difference. I don't know why they're different."

We keep talking as we snake our way through the clumps of people on the boardwalk. "You don't have to know why. You just have to know that it's true. We all have different theories on why."

"Really? What's yours?"

"My theory is unimportant," I tell him.

"Maybe so," he says. "But I want to hear it anyway. I don't just want to figure out what the beach is about."

"What do you mean?"

He looks at me. "I'd like to figure you out too. I find you . . . *intriguing*."

I worry that this makes me blush, so I look down as I smile.

"Okay," I say. "Come over here and look out at the ocean."

We walk over to the railing that overlooks the water.

"I think it's because tourists are like waves. But maybe that's just me. I always think everything is somehow related to surfing."

"How are tourists like waves?"

"When a wave comes at the beach it looks like the *water* is coming toward the land."

"Isn't it?"

"Not really. It's mostly an optical illusion. The wave is a force of energy that travels through the water and makes it rise and fall. It also pitches forward and falls back a little, but the actual seawater basically stays in the same place. And once the wave is gone, the water is all back where it started. Tourists do the same thing. They come rushing toward town and it's all so very exciting, but they're not here for long. That means they have to squeeze everything into that short period of time. They're so rushed that they're willing to go into a gift shop and buy shells with real money when all they have to do is walk along the beach and pick them up for free. That's loony tunes. So to me they're like waves that come crashing on the shore, and we're like the water. They have fun. They rise and fall. But it's not relaxing. And once they're gone, we go back to normal, like nothing ever happened."

"That's . . . deep," he says, taking it all in. "Are you always so philosophical?"

"Hardly. I just spend a lot of time thinking about waves."

"Okay, so what's our next stop?"

"Next we are going behind enemy lines," I say as we start walking down the boardwalk again. "But you have to promise me that under no circumstances will you buy anything while we're there."

"If it's another ice cream shop, I might not be able to resist. That junior sundae just triggered the hunger without fully satisfying it."

"It has nothing to do with food, but I mean it. You *have* to promise."

"All right, I promise not to buy anything," he says. "But where am I not buying anything?"

Just saying the name brings a scowl to my face. "Surf City."

Surf City is huge. It's a surf shop on steroids. And like steroids, everything about it is phony, especially the girls. Their boobs are big, their tank tops are small, and their knowledge of surfing is comically inept. Take for example the girl at the door who greets us in Hawaiian. You know, because even though we're five thousand miles away from Hawaii, it just sounds so surfy.

"*Mahalo!*"

Of course she has no idea that *mahalo* means "thank you" and not "hello."

"Ma-hello to you, too," I say back, with a tinge of snark as I shake my head.

I lead Ben up to a second-floor landing so we can fully survey the landscape. The lower level is filled with swimwear, clothing, and accessories while the upper has surfboards in every color of the rainbow. Every inch of it's gleaming, and everywhere you look there's another walking, talking Malibu Barbie.

"Welcome to the belly of the beast," I say as I look out over it. "Pure evil."

Ben takes it all in for a second and turns to me. I can tell he's conflicted about something but doesn't know how to say it.

"What's wrong?" I ask. "Spit it out."

"You love surfing, right?"

"More than you know."

He looks out across the store again and then back at me. "Then why isn't this your favorite place on earth? I mean, the name says it all. This is Surf City."

I don't reply with words so much as I emit a low growl.

"Okay, let me rephrase that," he says. "I know this place is like the worst place in the world, but since I'm just a cheesehead from Wisconsin, could you help me develop the right vocabulary to fully describe how awful it is?"

"I'd be happy to. First of all, it's owned by a faceless corporation and only exists to make money. It just happens to be that they make it selling surfboards. There's no love of the ocean or surfing in its DNA. I mean, just look at the boards. They're arranged by color, like that's the most important feature. It's like if you went into a bookstore and all the books were arranged according to how many pages they had.

"No one's concerned about matching customers with the right one. They just want you to buy any of them. And to be honest, the boards are mostly here to create an artificial atmosphere so they can sell you overpriced swimsuits, Hawaiian shirts, and sunglasses. Or, best of all, a bunch of Surf City T-shirts with their logo everywhere so you can go back home and become a human billboard as you tell everyone about your 'radical adventure hanging ten and riding gnarly waves.'"

When I reach the end of my rant, I realize that it was a little more passionate than I had intended. But Ben takes it all in stride and makes a joke out of it.

"So, you're saying you *don't* like it?"

"Yes," I say with a laugh. "I'm saying I don't like it. But it's not about what I like or don't like. It's about showing you how to blend in among the locals. And if you look around, you'll notice that there aren't any here. Only tourists. See the fanny packs and the sunburns?"

"And the white socks."

"Pulled all the way up," I add, shaking my head.

"I wish you told me yesterday before I went and bought all those Surf City T-shirts."

He's joking, but I still give him my "don't mess with me" look. And, while I don't like to brag, my "don't mess with me" look is quite impressive.

"But you said that they're *evil*. How is any of this more evil than selling saltwater taffy? That's just as fake and you're okay with it."

"Seven dollars for a decorative gift box of candy is a lot different from seven hundred for a longboard," I say.

"Seven hundred dollars?" he says with a comical laugh. "You can't be serious."

"Take a look."

We walk over to a row of blue longboards, and he looks at the price tags. He shakes his head in disbelief.

"And the worst part isn't even the money," I say. "This is way too much surfboard for a beginner. But they'll never tell you that. They'll just let you walk out the store and totally bomb in the water. They'd never tell you that you can get a used fish for about seventy-five bucks that's much better to learn on."

"A used fish?"

"It's a type of surfboard," I say. "But we'll save that lesson for later. We're still taking baby steps."

He laughs and we start to leave (escape?) when we pass the store's Wall of Fame. It features action photos of some of the surfers who make up the Surf City Surf Team and a display case full of their trophies.

"Impressive," says Ben.

"Yeah. As much as I hate to admit it, their team is amazing," I concede. "They win most of the tournaments in the state."

"Like King of the Beach?" he says, referring to the annual Pearl Beach tournament.

"How'd you know about King of the Beach?" I ask.

"It's sponsored by Parks and Recreation," he says. "I will be working there later this summer."

"Surf City has won both trophies," I say. "That one's for the top team and that one's for the grand champion. Bailey Kossoff has won the grand champion trophy two years in a row."

"Is he a local guy?"

I shake my head. "No. They sponsor guys from around the state. That's how they make sure to win."

"Does Surf Sisters have a team?" he asks.

I shake my head. "There's no money for it. These guys are like the New York Yankees. They can sign anyone who's really good."

"I bet they can't sign you."

"Well, no, they couldn't, but since I don't surf in contests, it doesn't make much of a difference."

"Why don't you?"

"It's just not my thing," I say. "I like to keep my surfing between me and the ocean. No spectators, no judges."

He raises a skeptical eyebrow but lets the topic slide.

So far the day seems to be going great. I still don't have any idea if he's into me or if he's just looking for a friend, but I feel more comfortable with Ben than I've ever felt with a guy. He laughs at my jokes, and when I try to explain why I think tourists are like waves and Surf City is evil, he doesn't look at me like I'm a lunatic or something. But now it's time for the big test.

Now we're going to Surf Sisters.

$\mathcal{S}$urf City is owned by an evil, faceless corporation," he says as we walk along Ocean Ave. "But you said there's actually a pair of sisters who owns Surf Sisters, right?"

"Mickey and Mo. They're the best."

"Mickey and Mo sound more like surf brothers than sisters."

"That's because the guys they used to beat in all the surf contests thirty years ago were too embarrassed to say they were getting waxed by Michelle and Maureen."

"So, unlike you, they were willing to compete in contests?"

I give him a look, and he holds up his hands in surrender.

"Anyway," I say, changing the subject back, "their dad was a legendary lifeguard and surfer."

"Steady Eddie," he says.

"That's right, Steady Eddie. Lifeguarding doesn't pay much, so he started up Steady Eddie's Surf School to give lessons to people staying at the hotels along the boardwalk. Mickey and Mo's mother wasn't in the picture, so they were always part of the deal. They were the first girls in this area to make names for themselves as surfers, and they were determined to make sure it was easier for the next generation."

"Which is why they opened the shop, right?"

"It just seemed like the logical next step. They turned their house into a shop, and when Steady Eddie passed away, they kept the surf school going to honor his memory. It's part business, part civic duty, part family memorial."

"So the shop was actually the house where they grew up," he says. "Okay, I see why that beats some corporate megastore."

"I was hoping you would."

Sophie and Nicole are both working today, but they've sworn to be on their best behavior when we arrive. Sophie's on register while Nicole's walking around making sure all the customers are finding what they're looking for. Both seem to be keeping an eye on the door as we enter.

Even though they saw Ben when he first came to the shop and again when he was with the campers, they've never officially met him, so I take care of the introductions.

"Ben, meet Sophie and Nicole," I say. "Guys, this is Ben."

They exchange hellos, and when I see Sophie about to talk, I panic for a millisecond that she might revert to her normal self and say something outlandish just to see how he reacts. But she keeps her promise to behave.

"What brings you to the shop today, Ben?" she asks.

"I want to get some new shoes and socks to wear on the beach," he says. "Maybe knee-high socks and something in a boot. Is there such a thing as a beach boot?"

The girls both laugh, and suddenly any potential awkwardness is gone.

"Actually," he continues, "I'm getting some hard-core beach tutoring from Izzy, and I think that means I need some wardrobe adjustments."

"Looking for anything in particular?" asks Nicole.

"I'm guessing I need some new trunks."

They both look at each other in total confusion.

"Board shorts," I say, translating. "They speak a different version of English in Wisconsin."

They laugh some more, but Ben doesn't seem to mind.

"You don't say 'trunks' either?" asks Ben. "It's like 'pop' all over again."

Because the shop is a converted house, it has a homey feel that's very different from Surf City. The staff even picked up Mickey and Mo's habit of referring to the different rooms by what they once were. That's why surfboards are in the garage, women's swimwear is in the family room, and accessories are in the kitchen, where the counter and shelf space are perfect for displaying everything from sunblock and sunglasses to key chains and waterproof wallets.

"We're going to the dining room," I tell the girls.

"We're eating again?" Ben asks.

"No," I tell him. "The dining room is where we put everything that's on sale."

"That's good," he says. "Despite its obvious glamour and prestige, the Parks and Recreation Department doesn't pay particularly well."

"Don't worry," says Sophie. "We've all got employee discounts."

"Yeah," adds Nicole. "We'll take care of you."

I smile because this makes me think that he's passed his first test with them. This is confirmed about fifteen minutes later when Ben carries an armful of clothing into a fitting room and Sophie and Nicole rush over to me like football players about to tackle a quarterback.

"We approve," Sophie says with a firm whisper.

"Definitely," adds Nicole. "By the way, you look really cute today."

"Thank you."

"You owe me so bad," Sophie adds. "Not only am I the one who made you eat with him, but I'm also the one who swapped shifts with you for the rest of the summer. Don't forget about that."

"I already paid you back. Don't forget who bought your ticket at the movie."

"I think this is worth more than a movie. This deserves—"

She's interrupted when Ben comes out of the fitting room wearing a pair of navy blue board shorts. They look great, but we're all a little distracted by the fact that he's shirtless and—surprise, surprise—his muscles and abs come fully loaded. (Thank you, cross-country.) The three of us are literally speechless, a reaction that he mistakes for disapproval.

"They don't look good?" he asks, pointing at the shorts.

"No," I say with a cough. "They look . . . great."

"Yeah," Sophie adds. "Nice trunks."

The mention of trunks makes him smile, unleashing the dimples again. "I know, I know. I promise I'll get the hang of it all."

He is totally oblivious to his current overall hotness factor, which only makes him that much more appealing. He goes back into the fitting room, and the others turn to me and we're speechless again.

"She's right," Nicole finally says. "That's worth way more than a movie."

It takes everything we've got not to bust out laughing. I can honestly say I have never felt the way I feel at this particular moment. I know it sounds pathetic, but it's making me a bit dizzy. I'm having trouble processing the whole thing.

By the time we're done, he's picked up another pair of board shorts, two Surf Sisters T-shirts, and a pair of inexpensive but comfortable flip-flops.

"Give us some catwalk action," Sophie says. "Let's see how it plays."

Ben goes along with this and walks back and forth in front

of the register, accenting it with some goofy fashion poses. When he's done, he turns to the three of us and asks, "So what do you think?"

"I'd believe he was an islander," says Nicole.

"It won't be official until he loses the tan line from his socks," adds Sophie. "But he's definitely getting there."

"I can hardly believe it," I say.

He takes it to mean that I can't believe how well he's got the look down. And while that's true, it also means that I can't believe this is happening to me. The cynic in me is waiting for the bubble to burst.

After we leave the shop, we head down to the beach and walk barefoot along the waterline. I point out some shells and a shark's tooth, but for the moment the lessons are over. I just want to enjoy . . . this.

Whatever "this" is.

It is the most romantic moment in my life, which is a bit of a problem because for all I know I'm just his shopping buddy. I mean, he really seems to like me and we've spent the day together, but I don't know how to know for sure. It would be great if he held my hand as we walk along the beach, but his hands are full because he's carrying two Surf Sisters shopping bags.

I decide to add a little stop.

"Let me teach you something," I say. "Stop, look out at the water, and wiggle your feet like this."

I wiggle my feet side to side and they start to sink into the wet sand. He does the same, and we both settle in about ankle deep.

"I like it," he says.

"It's cool, isn't it?" I reply. "I always love to do that when I'm walking along the water's edge."

We spend a quiet moment looking out over the ocean. It's peaceful and nice, but inside my head I'm going a million miles a minute. Finally I snap and blurt out, "So, do you have a girlfriend back home in Wisconsin?"

It is very unsmooth and made worse by the fact that it is not followed with a quick denial. His face looks a little pained, and I wish I could erase the question.

"I'm sorry," I say. "It's none of my business."

"I don't mind," he says. "I don't have a girlfriend . . . anymore. I did for a long time. For over a year. But we broke up during spring break."

That sounds pretty recent considering they dated for so long. I should stop asking questions, but I can't help myself. "Did you break up because you were coming here for the summer and she didn't want to try long distance?"

"That may have been part of it," he says. "But there were a bunch of little things. I think a lot of it has to do with my parents. I mean, I always thought they were a perfect couple, happy and in love with each other. Then it turned out that they weren't. It made me realize that things aren't always how they seem. I started to question what was going on with Beth and me, and eventually I decided that we weren't right for each other either."

Beth and Ben. Ugh. They even sound perfect together.

"I'm sorry. It really isn't any of my business."

"No, it's okay," he says. "Actually, it's kind of nice to have someone I can talk to about it. Things were so crazy at home, I didn't even tell my parents until a month after it happened. And my guy friends were useless. They don't usually have much to offer when it comes to relationships."

I have killed the mood and totally lost control of this conversation. I have done the boy-girl version of pearling and it's my own fault. Yet I can't seem to make myself pull out of it. I just have to know whom I'm competing with.

"What's Beth like? I bet she's pretty."

"She's really pretty," he says, in an automatic way that I could never imagine a guy saying in reference to me. "And smart. And funny. Everyone thought we were perfect together."

I would like to go on the record here and declare that I completely hate Beth.

"But that's history," he says with a trace of melancholy. "She's in Wisconsin and I'm in Florida."

Izzy Lucas, door prize.

I really have no idea what to say next, so I just stand there and try to imagine how I can possibly compete with the girl he just described.

"It's easy to talk to you," he continues. "You're the kind of girl I can just be myself with. That's nice."

And the final verdict is in.

"Easy to talk to," "kind of girl," and "nice" are all codes I know how to decipher. I'm the confidante, the girl he feels comfortable talking to about the girl he really likes. Unfortunately, this falls into the category of "been here, done this." My heart feels like it's sinking into my stomach just like my feet sank into the sand.

*T*hat's it?" an exasperated Sophie exclaims when I finish recapping my day with Ben. "That's the end of the story?"

"That's it," I say.

We're sitting in a booth at Mama Tacos sharing a plate of nachos.

"You bailed too early," she says.

"I hung in there as long as I could," I reply.

Nicole has an order of chips and guacamole and slides into the booth next to me.

"I still think he's totally into you," Sophie says.

"He sees me the way *every* guy sees me," I say. "As the one who makes for a really good friend and has a great personality. Besides, I think his parents getting divorced has turned him against the whole concept."

"The concept of what? Marriage?" Sophie asks. "I'm not saying he wants to settle down for life, but I think he's interested. And if he is spooked because of what's going on with his parents, then you're going to have to be superbrave like my girl Nicole over here."

She nods toward Nicole right as she chomps down on a huge guac-and-salsa-covered chip.

"What makes Nicole courageous?" Then it hits me. "Wait a second—did you talk to Cody?"

Nicole grins and nods as she finishes the chip.

"I want details!" I say.

"It's not that big a deal," she says.

"Liar, liar, skinny jeans on fire," says Sophie. "It's a huge deal."

"Tell me," I say. "What finally inspired you to break out of your years-long silence?"

She looks me right in the eye and says, "You."

"How's that?"

"I've never seen you as happy as you looked with Ben," she says. "I thought maybe that could happen for me. So I just called him up and asked him if he wanted to catch a movie. Just like that. No plan. No script. No stalking."

My cheeks hurt from how much I'm smiling. "Oh my God! What did he say?"

She almost blushes at the answer. "Yes."

I really am happy for Nicole. She has liked Cody forever, and it is amazing that she had the courage to ask him out. But I'd be lying if I didn't say that a part of me was dying inside. I inspired her because I looked so happy, but the happiness was all based on hope. Not reality. I was happy because I didn't know better, and that makes me feel like some tourist who just bought a surfboard for seven hundred dollars.

Over the next two weeks I see Ben twice for summer camp. I'm polite, but I try to keep the conversation to a minimum. I just can't shake the sting of the conversation we had. Normally, I don't mind being the confidante, but with Ben it's different. I need more.

At the surfing class he comes up to me before we stretch and asks, "Do you think we can do another lesson this week? I still feel like a fish out of water around here."

I shrug and tell him, "It's hard to say. I've got a lot going on with my parents this week."

"Okay," he replies, sounding a little disappointed. "Maybe next week."

"Sure, we'll see."

I continue using my evasive skills the next week, however, and when he makes a joke about calling something by the wrong name, I just give a halfhearted laugh.

"Right. That's funny."

I feel like a total drama queen about it, but it's just so hard. I like him so much and am utterly embarrassed by my inability to navigate these waters. At the end of the lesson I almost go over to him to talk, but I notice that he's talking to Kayla and I hear her invite him to a party. I've lived here my whole life and have never been invited to one of the cool-kid parties. I take it as the final sign that we belong in different circles and that I should just move along.

That's what I'm thinking about on the last day of June as I paddle out on my board. It's early and beautiful and I am safe here, in my special place, with no one around to get in the way. These waters I can navigate perfectly.

The waves are great and it is liberating to ride them one after another. It's like the surf gods are trying to make up for my heartbreak. My last ride in is perfect, and when it finally dies out, all I have to do is step off the board into the shallow water. I am fully relaxed.

And then I hear clapping.

"I knew you were good, but I didn't know you were that good."

I look up at the beach and see Ben sitting there. He stands up, and I have no idea how long he's been watching me.

"I really think you should compete in some of these contests," he continues. "I know it's not your thing but . . . wow."

"How long were you there?"

"For about forty-five minutes," he says.

How did I not see him there? I wonder as I walk up toward him. "What are you doing here?"

"I've got seventy-five dollars," he replies, holding up his wallet. "I want to learn how to surf. I thought you might help me get—what did you call it—a used fish? Is that right?"

"Yeah," I say. "That's what it's called."

"Great. Where do we find one?"

"You could check online or I can ask around at the shop to see if anyone knows of one for sale."

He walks right up to me and stops. "Did I do something wrong?" he asks. "Because if I did, I'm sorry."

"No," I say curtly. "You're perfect."

"Then why are you avoiding me? I thought you were going to teach me about the beach. I don't want to look online for a surfboard. I want you to help me find one. I want you to teach me how to surf. I want to hang out with you."

I close my eyes tightly and can feel the burn of the salt water. "I can't do that."

"Why not?"

"Because . . . I'm busy. I've got work . . . and—"

"I'll work around your schedule," he offers. "Besides . . . I thought we were friends."

"'Friends,'" I say. "Why does that sound so impersonal? Friends."

"I take my friendships very seriously," he replies.

"Of course you do," I say. "Friends are the kind of people you talk to about other girls, right?"

"Is that what this is about? I'm sorry I talked to you about Beth," he says. "But if you remember, you were the one who asked me about her. I never would have brought her up, but you asked and I'm not going to lie to you."

"And what about your new friends, like Kayla?" I ask. "I heard her invite you to a party. Did you go?"

"Yes," he says. "For about thirty minutes, just to be polite."

"Is that what this is?" I ask. "You're being polite?"

"No, this is me trying to figure out why you keep avoiding me. I don't understand."

"I know," I say. "It doesn't make any sense. I'm really sorry, but I have to head back home so I can go to work. I'm opening the shop today."

Luckily I'm still dripping wet from the ocean, so he can't tell that there are tears mixed in with the water on my face. I force a smile and start to walk past him toward my street.

"I knew it was a boogie board," he blurts out.

"What?"

"When you held it up at camp. I knew it was a boogie board. But I always give a wrong answer so that the kids don't feel bad if they don't know something."

"Then why did you act like you didn't know later on?"

"I was flustered. I wanted to have an excuse to talk to you," he says. "I figured if I looked pathetic enough, you might feel sorry for me and help."

"You were flustered?" I say. "Because of me?"

"Wasn't it obvious?"

"No. I'm not very good at picking up signs."

He turns right to me and says, "Let's see if you can pick up on this one."

Even though I'm dripping wet and carrying a surfboard, he wraps one arm around my waist and the other around my shoulder and kisses me. To say the least, I'm caught off guard, but I drop my surfboard and start to kiss him back.

It is the first kiss of my life, and on a scale of one to ten I'd have to rate it at least a fifteen. I know I don't have much to go on, but I have spent a great deal of time thinking about it and it far exceeds my wildest hopes.

There's a cool breeze coming off the water, the sky is bursting with color and light, and my feet sink into the sand as I lose myself in his lips. I feel like I have caught the longest, sweetest wave, and I want to ride it for as long as possible before it crashes against the shore.

July

$\mathcal{I}$t's Tuesday morning and in about fifteen minutes Ben and the summer campers will arrive for their weekly lesson. This will be the first time the kids are going to try to stand up on their boards, and I've recruited Nicole and Sophie to help me demonstrate good technique. It will also be the first time I've seen Ben since the kiss, so I'm hoping they'll help me with that, too.

Since we've already established that I'm useless at picking up signs, I figure it can't hurt to have my own signal-deciphering support staff. Of course that means I have to tell them about the kiss, which I haven't done yet. I drop that bomb while we're carrying all of the gear down from the shop to the beach.

"By the way," I say as if early morning romantic encounters on the beach were just part of my every day. "Did I mention the passionate kiss I had with Ben?"

At first they think I'm joking, but then they see the expression on my face.

"Seriously?" Sophie says with total disbelief. "That seriously happened?"

I nod.

"When?" asks Nicole. "This morning? Last night?"

"Yesterday . . . *morning*," I say sheepishly.

"And we're only hearing about this now? We were with you all yesterday afternoon. How did it not come up?"

The truth is I didn't tell them yesterday because I wasn't sure what to make of it. I'm still not. I know it was awesome and wonderful and the most romantic moment of my life. But it almost feels like it was part of a movie I saw and not something that actually happened to me.

"Details," Sophie says, more as a demand than a request. "Right now."

"Okay," I respond. "But we have to keep setting up. The kids *and Ben* will be here soon."

I tell them everything as we lay a dozen soft boards out on the sand. After a day to analyze and obsess over every detail, it's refreshing to actually tell the story. Hearing it aloud reinforces the fact that it really did happen and wasn't just my imagination. I tell them about catching the last wave and walking up onto the beach. They both eat up the part about Ben sitting in the sand clapping.

"Cute, cute, cute," Nicole says with a broad smile. "So very cute."

And although I'm somewhat embarrassed by the melodramatic tone of my conversation with him, I give them an honest recounting of what was said. By the time I get to the kiss, they are eating out of the palm of my hand.

"And . . . ," Nicole says when I finish.

"And what?" I ask.

"And . . . what happened next?" Sophie asks.

"You heard the part where we kissed, right? That was kind of the big finish."

They look cheated.

"There's got to be more!" Sophie claims. "Did he just vanish into thin air? Didn't you say anything?"

"I'm sure I said something, but my head was spinning way too much for me to remember what it was. I do seem to recall that we were both in a sort of stunned 'I don't know what to make of what just happened' silence during the walk back up from the beach to my house."

"Was there any sort of follow-up moment?" Nicole asks hopefully

I think about it and nod. "There was a part when I sort of manipulated the situation so that we could kiss again."

"And yet you left that out?" Sophie asks, frustrated. "You know you're terrible at telling this story."

"How did you manipulate it?" asks Nicole.

"When we reached the house, we went around into the back-yard and I asked him to help me put my board back on the rack. I told him it had to go on the top pegs but had trouble reaching that high by myself."

Nicole laughs. "Why did you tell him it needed to be up there?"

I am almost too embarrassed to answer.

"I said it needed to be in direct sunlight to keep any conden-sation from contracting the foam core."

They both look at each other and then back at me.

"That doesn't make any sense," Nicole says. "It's like you just made up words."

"I know that and you know that, but he doesn't know that,"

I explain. "It's not like I could say I wanted him to do it because he's tall and I was looking for an excuse to brush up against him."

"Did it work?" asks Sophie. "Did you brush up against him?"

I smile at the memory and nod. "It was electric. I turned and looked up at him, and I was just about to kiss him again when . . ."

". . . yeah . . . ," they say eagerly.

". . . my dad came out from the house to go on his morning run."

They sag. "Argghhhh."

"That's when it got awkward. Dad said something like, 'Hey Ben, what are you doing here?' And I sort of panicked."

"Oh my God," Sophie gasps. "What did you say?"

"I told him that Ben had stopped by so the two of them could go running together."

Sophie and Nicole both laugh out loud.

"You did not," says Sophie.

"No, that's exactly what I did. Because, you know, I'm so smooth."

"And Ben went along with it?" asks Nicole.

"He didn't really have much of a choice. They ran eight miles. By the time they got back, he had to go chaperone the campers on a field trip to the Kennedy Space Center and there was no chance to follow up."

"So you haven't seen him since it happened?" asks Nicole.

"The first time will be in a few minutes when he arrives here. I figure it should be a very romantic follow-up. What with all the screaming kids and of course my favorite person on the planet, Kayla McIntyre."

"Forget about Kayla," Sophie says. "He's already picked you

over her. She lost. You won. Game over. You're his summer romance."

"It was one kiss," I say, trying to maintain some semblance of reality. "In my world one kiss is a huge deal, but in the regular world I don't know that it qualifies as a summer romance."

"Do not sell yourself short," says Nicole. "You always do that. It was a kiss with purpose."

"It was a kiss that he had to run eight miles for," I reply. "How bad is that?"

"No," she says. "It was a kiss that he thought was worth running eight miles for. How *awesome* is that?"

"The tall girl makes a valid point," says Sophie. "He likes you. And when you didn't get the signs he was sending, he built you a billboard."

"Okay, maybe he does like me," I concede. "But he's just broken up with a longtime girlfriend, and he's all freaked out about his parents' divorce. I'm not sure he's looking for a full-fledged summer romance."

"Well, whatever he's looking for," Sophie says, pointing toward the beach access, "we're about to find out."

I turn and see Ben marching the kids our way. He's acting like his normal goofy self, which is a good start, but while he's wearing his sunglasses I can't really read his expression.

"Do not sell yourself short," Nicole reminds me just before they get within earshot. "You are totally worthy of long distance running."

I appreciate the pep talk, but I'm still in full panic mode right up until the moment he reaches us and flashes that smile.

It's a huge relief. I realize that part of me was worried that he completely regretted what had happened and that he was going to act differently around me. I still don't know what there is between us, but at least now I know there's nothing awkward about it, so that's a big step.

Kayla is her normal self, gorgeous and obnoxious (gorbnoxious?) all at once. She's got a new bathing suit that truly showcases her (not so) secret weapons, but today I have a secret weapon of my own—Sophie. Wherever Kayla goes, Sophie is right by her side acting like they're BFFs, roommates, and sorority sisters all rolled into one. This makes it impossible for her to flirt with Ben. When we line up to stretch, Sophie slides in front of Kayla so that she obstructs Ben's view of her. And when it's time to pick demonstration partners, Sophie latches on to her arm and exclaims, "We have to be partners, Kayla! We just have to!"

Despite all the subterfuge and mental distractions, the big news of the morning is the lesson. We keep the soft boards—large, padded surfboards—on the sand and practice our paddling and pop-up techniques. Then we hit the water and put them into practice. I can't express how exciting it is to see the kids' faces light up the first time they get up on their feet and ride a wave. Even though we're only in three feet of water, it's exhilarating for them.

My favorite is Rebecca, the shy girl I noticed the first day. She has continued to come out of her shell a little more each week. Today she stays up on the board the longest of anyone, and I can see in her the same spark I had when I was her age at this camp.

Throughout it all, Ben and I exchange quick glances and

whispered comments. Our hands touch a couple of times as we help kids get up on their boards, and once when I'm not looking his way, he uses a boogie board to splash me, which gets a big laugh from everyone. Even with my compromised sign-reading ability, it all seems kind of flirty.

We finally have a brief moment right after the lesson when the kids are taking an orange slice and bottled water break. I look over and see that Kayla is still dealing with Hurricane Sophie, which means she won't be able to drop in on me again like she usually does.

"They did great today," I say.

"*You* did great today," he replies. "The way you love it so much connects with them. They want to feel the same way because it's so real."

There's an awkward pause, so I just jump headfirst into the situation.

"Speaking of real . . . ," I say, unleashing the worst segue in history, "did that *really* happen yesterday?"

He smiles and nods. "It did. In fact, I think it was maybe going to happen again when we were interrupted."

"By 'interrupted' you mean when you had to take an eight-mile detour with my dad?"

"Kinda, yeah," he says. "I have to say I did not see that coming. I was hoping that maybe we could talk about it. . . . You know, without so many people around."

"That can be arranged."

"How about after work?"

"Sure. My shift ends at six thirty."

"Great, I'll meet you at the shop," he says. "You're not going to make me go running with your dad again?"

I shake my head. "I promise."

"Good, 'cause I'm planning on wearing my flip-flops so I blend in with the locals. And those things really make you blister around the three-mile mark."

Our eyes linger for a moment, and I say, "See you at six thirty."

"See you then."

He rushes off to make sure the kids pick up all their orange peels and water bottles, and I start stacking up the surfboards to carry back up to the shop. I see Kayla finally break free of Sophie and head our way, but she's too late. Today's score is Dolphin 1, Shark 0. And the dolphin is now in it to win it.

Although Sophie and Nicole seem to think that all the signs they saw on the beach were positive, I'm still approaching the situation with total caution. All I really know is that Ben's coming to talk with me after work. Maybe he's planning to say that the kiss was a mistake, or that while he likes me, he doesn't *like* me like me. It's all so hard to figure out.

I spend most of the day watching the clock, and at 6:13 I'm in the middle of my "do you see yourself as a shark or a dolphin?" routine with a girl looking for a bikini when Ben comes into the store. He smiles and waves, and since I don't want to be rude to the customer, I respond on the sly with a half smile and a raised eyebrow that I hope looks cool and not like a nervous twitch.

"Which do you like best?" the girl asks, holding up two swimsuits.

I give her my undivided attention, consider both suits, and point to the one in her left hand. "That one."

She scrunches up her face. "I think I like the other one better."

I resist the urge to say, "Then why did you ask me?" and instead go with, "That one looks cute too. Why don't you try it on?"

She heads for the changing room, and I turn back to look for Ben. Only now he's gone. I scan the shop and half worry that maybe I'm just imagining him now. (Imaginary boyfriend—that does kind of sound like me.)

Sophie sees my distress as she walks over. "Badger Ben just went out to the garage," she says, referring to the room where we keep all the surfboards.

"'Badger' Ben?"

"You shot down all the dairy nicknames, so I thought I'd try something else. In addition to being America's Dairy Land, Wisconsin is known as the Badger State. I figure Badger Ben has alliteration and a nice ring to it."

I don't pretend to understand what it is with Sophie and nicknames, but I'm a little too anxious at the moment to get into it. "How did he seem?"

"Like he was about to break your heart," she says. "He's probably going to tell you that he never wants to see you again and he's running off to marry Kayla."

I gasp before I realize she's joking.

"You might want to turn down the nervous knob," she says,

with a friendly pat on the shoulder. "Listen to the music. I picked this playlist specifically to help you mellow out."

In the shop we usually play a steady blend of beach, Hawaiian, and reggae music, and after a while you stop hearing it and it disappears into the background of your brain. But now that I listen, I realize that Bob Marley is singing one of my favorite tunes: "Don't worry about a thing, 'cause every little thing gonna be all right. . . ."

"Okay," I say after I get the hint, and take a couple of deep breaths. "I'll calm down."

"Good, because you're much better when you're relaxed. You're not one of those 'performs well under pressure' kind of girls."

"Gee thanks, Coach. Good to know I can always get a pep talk."

"I'm just keeping it real."

"By the way," I add, "'Badger Ben' is a no go."

She shrugs. "I knew it the second I said it, but you gotta try these things out to be sure."

Fifteen minutes later my shift is over and the girl has finally decided on a bikini. It goes without saying that she picked the first one I had recommended. I remind myself that it's important for her to be comfortable with her purchase, so I don't mind the other five we had to go through before we got back to it.

Once she's made her purchase, I am free to go and head over to the garage. It's been my favorite part of the shop ever since I was a kid and I'd come to look at all the boards and try to figure out which one was made just for me. We don't have nearly the number that Surf City has in its inventory, but all of ours are choice. About half of them are custom made in the area. These cost a little more, but they are beyond sweet.

Personally, I'm saving up to buy my very own M & M, which is what we call the boards that Mickey and Mo shape themselves. They only make about a dozen a year, so they're pretty hard to come by.

Speaking of Mo, when I get to the garage, I see her in back talking to Ben. She's in her midfifties, but she looks much younger than that. A life spent surfing, swimming, and kayaking has kept her extremely fit. It also keeps her hair wet a lot of the time, which is why she usually just pulls it back in a ponytail.

Of the two sisters, I'm closer to her. This is no knock on Mickey; it's just that Mo and I have more in common. Mickey's loud and in your face like Sophie, but Mo hangs around the edges like I do. We surf alike too. Both of us favor a long, smooth style rather than a more athletic and aggressive one.

She's showing Ben a display case that serves as a tribute to Steady Eddie, her father. It has all sorts of artifacts including surfing trophies, a lifesaving medal, and even his torpedo buoy, which is the big float that lifeguards carried back in the day.

"He won every surf contest in the state," she says, beaming with pride.

"What about King of the Beach?" Ben asks, referring to our local contest. "Did he win that one too?"

Mo laughs. "Seven times—more than anyone."

"Awesome," says Ben. "Where's the trophy for that?"

"At Surf City," she says. "It always goes to the current champion."

"That's kind of unfair," says Ben.

"I don't know," she replies. "It's in their store, but Dad's name is on it seven times. Mickey and I think of it as covertly advertising our store over there."

"Why don't you ask her who's won it the second most times?" I say, interrupting.

"We're in the middle of a conversation, Izzy," she says, deflecting the comment.

"Go ahead and ask her," I say again.

"Who won the second most times?" he asks.

She's reluctant to answer, but Ben and I wait her out, and she finally concedes, "Mickey and I have each won it four times."

"You were King of the Beach?" Ben asks.

She nods.

"The only two girls to ever win it," I add, because I know that Mo won't.

"That means between you two and your dad, you guys have your name engraved on it fifteen times."

"I never thought of it that way, but I guess so." Mo is uncomfortable receiving praise, so she redirects the conversation. "Ben, why don't you show Izzy what you learned?"

"Oh, yeah. Watch this, Iz." One by one he points to a row of surfboards, identifying each one by type as he goes. "This is a shortboard, this is an egg, this is a fish, and this one . . . is . . . a gun?"

"That's right, a gun," Mo says. "Now which one is the quad?"

"The fish," he says, pointing toward it. "Because it has four fins."

"Perfect."

"Very impressive," I say.

Feeling good about his surfboard IQ, he turns to Mo and adds, "I can do more than identify. I also know that you have to keep them in direct sunlight so that the condensation doesn't contract the foam."

Mo starts to correct him, but I shake her off and she lets it slide. Instead she turns to me and says, "I understand you're going to be teaching Ben the fine art." She always refers to surfing as "the fine art."

"Yes, I am," I say.

She gives us the once-over and nods her approval. "Good choice."

I don't know if she's saying that I'm a good choice as a teacher for him or if he's a good choice as a guy for me. Knowing Mo, it's probably a combination of both.

"I'll be happy to take any pointers that you may have too," he tells her. "After all, you are a four-time King of the Beach. Or is it Queen?"

"King works," she says with more than a little pride. She thinks about it and says, "My advice is that you should remember to fall in love with your heart and not with your brain. . . ."

I start to stammer something about it being way too early to use the *L* word, but catch myself when she continues.

"So pick a board that speaks to you right here." She taps him in the center of the chest. "And always listen to what Izzy tells you. The girl has the gift."

"I'll do that," he says.

Mo smiles and leaves us in the garage. For the first time since my dad interrupted us yesterday morning, we are alone. I look at him. He looks at me. And I realize I have no idea what to say. You'd think that since I've been obsessing over this moment for the last six hours, I might have come up with an opening line.

"Hi." (Clever, huh?)

"Hi," he says. "Is your shift over?"

"Yep," I say. "Although I do have to be home for dinner in about an hour."

He thinks this over for a moment. "An hour, huh? That doesn't really leave us enough time to run the eight miles I was hoping to get in, so do you want to just go out on the pier and look at the ocean instead?"

"It's one of my favorite things in the world."

*T*he Pearl Beach Fishing Pier is rare in that it's equally popular with tourists and locals alike. It stretches out from the southern end of the boardwalk and is exactly one quarter mile long. When Ben and I get there, it's low tide and the beach is at its widest. That means we have to walk nearly a third of the length of the pier before we're actually over the water. There are people fishing from both sides for most of the way, but none at the far end. There's also no railing at the end, which allows boats to tie off and lets us sit down on the edge and dangle our feet over the water.

"It's pretty," Ben says, looking out at endless ocean.

"It's better than pretty," I say as I close my eyes and feel the sea mist against my face. "It's perfect."

There's that word again—"perfect." It's the same word I used to describe him yesterday morning, and I wonder if he makes the connection.

We're both quiet for a little while, and I can tell he's thinking of what to say. I decide to beat him to the punch.

"I'm pretty sure I know why you wanted to talk," I offer. "And I'd just like to apologize for all the melodramatic baggage I laid on you yesterday. I also want to apologize for giving you the cold shoulder lately. You deserve better."

"First of all, you don't need to apologize for anything," he says. "And secondly, that's not what I wanted to talk about."

I take a deep breath. This is it.

"What do you want to talk about?"

"You've told me great things about the beach and surfing. You've told me where to eat and how to dress."

"But . . . ," I say. "This sounds like it's leading to a 'but.'"

I open my eyes and turn to him. He's looking right at me.

"But," he says, "you've told me almost nothing about *yourself*. So, if you don't mind, I'd like to talk about you."

This catches me off guard. Completely off guard.

"What do you mean?"

"I mean you know all kinds of things about me. You know about my parents getting divorced. You know about me breaking up with my ex-girlfriend. You know about my school and my uncle and that I run cross-country. But the only thing I know about you is that your favorite ice cream flavor is mint chocolate chip."

"That's probably the most interesting thing about me."

He shakes his head. "You should think more of yourself, Izzy. I'm sure there are an endless number of interesting things about you, and I'd like to know some of them."

I rack my brain trying to think of any worth telling, but I come up blank.

"I'm sorry. It's all just so . . . ordinary."

"That cannot be," he protests.

"Okay, I'll prove it. You've met my parents and I'm an only child, so that means you know my entire family. I get good grades at school, but I'm pretty anonymous when I walk through the halls. That's partly by choice and partly due to the high school version of Darwin's natural selection. I haven't told you about breaking up with my ex-boyfriend because I've never had a boyfriend. So, now you're all caught up."

"You've never had a boyfriend?"

I find this particular bit of information to be supremely embarrassing, so I turn away and look back at the water as I answer. "No."

"Why not?" he asks. "What's the problem?"

"I guess I'm just a loser," I say sharply.

"No. I mean, what's the problem with the boys in this town? How is it possible that you've never had a boyfriend? Does the salt water get in their brains? Does the sun make them stupid?"

"You've seen Kayla," I say. "My school is loaded with girls who look like that."

He thinks about this for a moment. "Okay, I'll admit that Kayla is hot—"

"You think?" I say sarcastically.

"But she's not in your league. You're smarter, funnier, and way more interesting."

"All things that a girl wants to hear. I'm sure she goes to bed every night cursing my really good personality."

"You do have a really good personality," he says. "But if you want me to be shallow, I'll point out that you're also better looking than her."

I give him the look. "That's completely untrue and you know it."

"That's funny, because I don't know that," he says. "I do know that she asked me to go to a party tonight. And I know that I turned her down so I could hang out with you."

I'm not sure if I'll ever have another such opportunity in the future, so I savor this for a moment before I respond.

"Really?"

"Really, and I'll prove it," he says, throwing my line right back at me. He covers his eyes with his left hand. "Ask me to describe Kayla."

I'm skeptical of where this is going, but I don't have much choice. "Describe Kayla."

"Big boobs. Long legs. Great hair."

I haven't mentioned it yet, but he's right—Kayla's hair is spectacular. "Okay," I reply. "You're kind of proving my point."

He shakes his head but still keeps his hand over his eyes. "Now ask me to describe you."

I don't really see how this can turn out well, so I don't say anything. He doesn't let that stop him.

"You have a wrinkle in your chin," he says.

"Wow, a chin wrinkle sounds way better than big boobs."

"You have this *amazing* wrinkle in your chin," he says, ignoring my sarcasm, "that only appears when you smile. It's so irresistible that I keep telling stupid jokes just so that you'll laugh and I can see it again."

I reflexively run my finger along my chin.

"And your eyes defy description," he continues. "When I met you, I thought they were blue. Then, when we went to Luigi's, I could have sworn they were brown. And yesterday morning . . . I'm certain they were green. Every time I see you, the first thing I look at are your eyes so I can see what color they are."

Let me reiterate that this type of conversation is new to me, and it has me feeling a little breathless.

"And when you get embarrassed your cheeks turn red." He uncovers his eyes and looks right at me. "Like they're doing right now."

Of course the fact that he says this makes me blush that much more.

"The first time I saw it was when I asked you how the poster looked and you started to say 'awful' but tried to change it to 'awesome,' and it came out 'awfslome.'"

"You noticed that?"

He nods. "I notice everything about you."

"Well, I can't help but notice that all the things you just pointed out—wrinkly chin, inconsistent eye color, and the oh so sexy blushing—are in fact flaws. So again I say that you're kind of proving my point."

"You cannot believe that," he says. "You know they're not flaws."

"Well, I admit that you manage to present them in a way that's kind of amazing, but—"

"Maybe this analogy will work for you. Before you got to the garage, Mo showed me all the different types of surfboards. She really opened my eyes. Who knew there were so many?"

"I knew," I joke, but he ignores it.

"Girls like Kayla are like factory boards. Shiny. Smooth. Pretty. They look great but they look alike."

"And girls like me?" I ask.

"There aren't *girls* like you, Izzy. There is *a girl* like you, singular. You're like this custom board that Mo showed me. She shaped it herself, and it has all these little details and indentations that make it special and unique. They're features, not flaws."

I look at him and am totally speechless. On the list of the greatest things that anyone has ever said to me, this is the entire list. Nothing else is even close.

"I don't know what to say."

"Well, you could say something about who you are. For once don't make me do all the talking."

"I'm really not trying to be difficult; I just can't think of anything."

"Tell me why you won't surf in a contest."

"I already did. It's just not my scene."

"Sorry, wrong answer," he says as he makes a game show buzzer noise. "There's got to be more to it than that. Is it because you're shy? Is it because you think you'll lose?"

"Maybe . . . but there's more to it than that," I try to explain.

I think about this for a moment, and he waits patiently for an answer. I look out at the water and try to put it all into words.

"For me surfing is completely pure. It's just me and the water and my board. It's almost spiritual. Actually, it *is* spiritual. There's no one watching, no one judging. It doesn't matter who's popular or who's pretty, and it's not about being better than anybody else. It's just about the quest for perfection."

"And what do you mean by perfection?"

"Think about everything that goes into creating a wave: the gravitational pull of the moon, the wind and weather thousands of miles away in the middle of the ocean, the contours of the ocean floor. It's an amazing cosmic event that is hidden from sight until the last possible moment. The wave only breaks the surface for such a short period of time, and perfection is the tuning fork that rings in your heart when you catch it the moment it comes to life and ride it until the last bit of it disappears. It's the feeling of knowing that the forces of nature all came together and you were there to fully appreciate every last bit of it."

He considers this for a moment, and this time I wait patiently.

"Was that perfection yesterday morning?" he asks. "When you caught that last wave?"

I close my eyes and think back to the wave. "Absolutely."

"And did it ruin it for you when you found out that I saw you do it? Did my being there make it *im*perfect?"

"No," I answer. "Of course not."

"Then why would other people ruin it? I think you should get over this fear. Better yet, I think you should compete in the

King of the Beach contest. It's not like girls don't enter. Mickey and Mo both won it. Why not you?"

"Because," I say, as though that alone were enough of an answer.

"That's it? 'Because'? That's not a good enough excuse."

"It should be," I reply a little prickly. "You wanted to know something about me and I told you. And the first thing you're doing is telling me to change that thing. It's not a fear. It's just the way I'm wired. You watching me surf is different from a crowd of people watching me. It's the most personal thing I can share. I don't think you understand that."

"I don't think you have any idea how great it is to watch you. I don't even understand surfing and I think it's amazing. Yesterday morning, watching you, that was mind blowing. Without a doubt it was the best forty-five minutes I've had since I've gotten here."

"Really?"

"There is nothing I can do as well as you can surf. When I first got here, I thought surfing was a hobby. Then, after a few weeks of talking to you, I began to think of it as a sport. But yesterday, when I was watching you, I realized that it's an art. You're an artist, Izzy."

You can now add this to the list I just mentioned of the most amazing things anyone's ever said to me.

"You think so?"

"I know so."

"Okay," I say shyly. "Then that's one thing that you know about me. But I'm not looking to share that with the world, okay?"

"Okay," he says. "I'll stop pushing you."

We both share a smile, and he reaches over and slips his hand into mine. I feel a charge crackle through my body. Neither of us says anything for a moment, and I give his hand a little squeeze in return.

"Now I want you to tell me something," I say.

"Anything."

"Why did you kiss me yesterday?"

He thinks about it for a moment before he answers. "Because I was tired of imagining what it would be like. I just had to know."

"You'd been imagining it?" I ask. "Imagining kissing me?"

He nods. "Big time."

"Since when?"

"Since I met you."

"Right," I say with a laugh. "When I had the guacamole stain on my shirt?"

"I like guacamole and I respect a girl who can pull it off as a fashion statement."

I turn to look at him, and the sea breeze blows my hair in every direction. He reaches up and gently moves it out of my face, and I tuck it between my neck and shoulder.

"And what was it like?" I continue. "Kissing me?"

He flashes the smile I see in my mind whenever I think about him.

"Even better than I had imagined. Which is saying something, because I had set the anticipation bar pretty high."

"Do you . . . maybe . . . want to try it again?"

"I . . . do," he says, but with some hesitation. "I . . . really . . . do."

"Why do I sense another 'but' coming up?"

"It's already July first and I go back to Wisconsin on August twenty-fifth. That's—"

"Fifty-five days," I interrupt.

"Wow, you came up with that quickly."

"I've already done the math. All of it. Fifty-five days, seven weekends, six more summer camp classes." I shrug. "You're not the only one who's been imagining."

This makes him smile.

"I want to kiss you very much," he says. "But if I do, I know that it will hurt unbearably bad fifty-five days from now. Maybe worse than anything's ever hurt before. And that makes me wonder what I should do."

Now I turn my whole body and lean forward so that I am just inches from his face. "What *you* should do? Don't I have a say in this?"

"Of course you do," he answers. "What do you think we should do?"

"I think it's like a wave," I say. "But that's just me. I always think everything's like surfing."

He has a perplexed look on his face. "How is it like a wave?"

"Consider all the cosmic forces that have brought us to the end of this pier. Your parents, my job, your uncle, summer camp. All of these unseen forces have led us here, and the chance that we have is only going to last for a brief period of time. Just like a wave. I say we catch it as soon as we can and ride it until the very last part dissolves into the sand. I say that we shoot . . . for perfection."

I don't wait for him to respond. Instead I reach around, put my hand on the back of his neck, and pull him gently toward me as I begin to kiss him. I can taste the salt air on his lips, and when I close my eyes I lose myself in those lips. It is wonderful and exciting. It's more than I ever would have dreamed could have happened. But no matter how hard I try, I can't ignore the clock that starts in my head. Even as I kiss him I can hear it ticking away.

Fifty-five days and counting.

I want you . . . to name which five members of the Continental Congress were selected to write the Declaration of Independence."

I blink, rub the sleep out of my eyes, and try to refocus. Much to my horror I realize that it's not a nightmare. Uncle Sam really is accosting me in the kitchen. Okay, it's my father in an Uncle Sam costume, but it's still pretty nightmarish.

"What?" I mumble with a sleepy yawn.

"I want you," he says, exaggerating the pose to look like the famous Uncle Sam poster, "to name which five members of the Continental Congress were selected to write the Declaration of Independence."

Normally, I make it a rule to ignore my father when he's in costume. And you'd be surprised by the frequency with which I have to invoke this rule. But that's impossible at the moment because he's blocking my access to the refrigerator.

"I just want to get some milk for my cereal," I moan. "Why does there have to be a quiz?"

"Because it's the Fourth of July and your father's an American history teacher," he says, as though that were a reasonable explanation. "C'mon. Give me the names."

I can tell that he's not giving up, so I rack my brain. "I'm pretty sure one was Thomas Jefferson."

"Yes," he says, no doubt perturbed that I'm only "pretty sure."

"And you've gotta figure that Ben Franklin was there, right?"

"He was."

He waits for more, and all I do is shrug.

"That's it?"

"It's seven in the morning and I'm in the middle of summer vacation," I say. "You should be happy that I got that many."

He shakes his head in total disappointment. "That's two out of five. That's only forty percent. Do you find forty percent acceptable?"

"I'm only getting two percent milk, so yeah," I say with a wicked smile. "That leaves thirty-eight percent for later."

Rather than continue our back and forth history lesson, I wedge my way past him, grab the milk and orange juice, and head for the table.

"John Adams, Robert Livingston, and Roger Sherman were the others," he says. "In case you were wondering."

"Thanks," I answer as I pour the milk over my cereal. "But I wasn't."

Despite my current—and I would argue quite defensible—lack of excitement, Fourth of July is a huge deal in Pearl Beach. It's the busiest day of the year for tourists, and we really give them their money's worth. The celebration starts off in the morning with the Patriots Parade, continues all afternoon with live music at the bandshell, and concludes with a huge fireworks display over the pier.

I don't want to be a buzz kill for my dad, so I try to engage in some conversation. "Is your band marching in the parade this year?"

"Yes," he says with glee, unwilling to let my mood dampen his enthusiasm. "And we're playing the two o'clock set at the bandshell."

I swallow a spoonful of cereal and chuckle. "You love saying that you're playing a 'set,' don't you?"

"I almost said that we had a 'gig,' but I thought you might give me a hard time about it."

"I definitely would have."

Every year on the Fourth of July my dad and a bunch of other guys he knows form a band they call the Founding Fathers. It's perfect not only because he gets to dress up as Uncle Sam, but also because it blends three of his greatest loves: music, American history, and bad puns.

"Are you going to sing my song?" I ask, giving him my best doe eyes.

My song is "Isabel," an old country song by John Denver that my father used to sing to me when he'd put me to bed.

"I don't know," he says, playing hardball. "Our set's only for thirty minutes and we've got a lot of songs."

"Seriously? That's your answer?"

He nods and we have a little stare off before I finally relent.

"Massachusetts, Connecticut, New York, Pennsylvania, and Virginia."

"And why are you suddenly listing states?"

"Because those are the colonies that John Adams, Roger Sherman, Robert Livingston, Ben Franklin, and Thomas Jefferson represented in the Continental Congress."

"You knew all along."

"Of course I did. You've only made me watch *1776* about a thousand times."

"Then why'd you act like you didn't know?"

I give him a look. "Because I don't want to encourage you to give me pop quizzes every morning."

He smiles broadly. "That's my girl."

"Now what about my song?" I ask.

"I guess you'll have to come and find out," he answers. But as he walks out of the kitchen I can hear him start to sing, "Isabel is watching like a princess from the mountains . . ."

Today would be the perfect day to hang out with Ben, except we're both busy for huge chunks of it. He's marching with the campers in the parade and working at the bandshell during the concert. Meanwhile, I'm going in early to help set up at Surf Sisters and working the late shift tonight. If I'm lucky, I'll get out in time to catch some of the fireworks. I'm pretty sure our paths will cross a few times during the festivities, but there are no guarantees as to when.

I ride my bike to the shop, and when I get there, I'm surprised to see Nicole standing in the parking lot wearing her band uniform.

"You know I'm all about seeing you in the funny hat, but shouldn't you be lining up for the parade?"

"I've got about twenty minutes," she says.

I lock my bike to the rack and reply, "I'm sure we've got the inventory all covered. You should go hang out with the drum line. And by drum line I mean you should go hang out with Cody."

"I will," she says. "But Mickey called me first thing and asked me to come in. She said that she wanted to talk to the whole staff."

Mickey and Mo must be concerned about something, because the Fourth is our biggest sales day of the year. I assume they want to make sure that everyone's ready. But when I walk into the shop and see them talking in hushed tones, I begin to worry that something's wrong. Typically they're upbeat, but there are no smiles today.

Mickey steps forward first and does a quick head count to make sure we're all here. Including the two of them, there are ten of us in total, and while I'm closest to Sophie and Nicole, I think of everyone as my extended family.

"We really hate to do this today," Mickey says. "The Fourth is such a big day for the beach, and we know how much of a zoo it can be. But there are some developments that are about to become public, and we want to make sure that you hear them from us first."

Now I am really worried. Mickey is getting teary and has trouble continuing, so Mo puts an arm around her and picks up where she left off.

"After thirty-three years of doing what we love . . . we are sorry to announce that . . . this is going to be the last summer for Surf Sisters. We're closing down the shop at the end of September."

She continues speaking, but I literally do not hear another word while my mind tries to process what she has just said. I know this sounds melodramatic, but I can't overemphasize how important the shop has been to me. I look around and realize that everyone else is equally stunned. This is our place. This cannot be happening.

"What are you talking about?" Sophie blurts out.

"Like I said," Mo continues, "we didn't want to tell you like this, but you're family to us, and word has leaked out and we're sure you'll hear about it."

"How is this even possible?" one of the girls asks. "I know we don't get the crowds that Surf City does, but business seems like it's been good."

"It's more complicated than that," Mickey says, clearing her throat. "A developer is going to build a new resort, and the bank sees this as a chance to make a lot of money. We've tried everything we can think of, but there's really nothing we can do about it. We will, however, do everything we can to help you all find new jobs."

We sit there in stunned silence for a moment, and an idea comes to me.

"What about Luigi's Car Wash?" I say. "Luigi's was able to stay open because it had been here so long. Doesn't the same law protect us?"

They share a look and turn back to us.

"We thought the same thing," Mo says. "We even got our lawyer to file paperwork with the city. But it turns out we opened four months too late to qualify."

I can't believe this would happen at the very moment I was happier than ever before. It's like if one part of my life goes well, then another has to go off the rails. I look around the shop and suddenly years' worth of memories start to flood through my mind. I can't even begin to imagine what this is like for the two of them. They grew up here. They've spent their lives building a business here. And it's going to become some ridiculous hotel.

"What can we do?" I ask.

"I'm glad you asked that," Mickey says. "We know there's a lot of sadness about this, but we don't want our last memories of Surf Sisters to be sad. We want to have an incredible last summer. And you're the key to that. We have accepted that this is going to happen, and we're going to have fun. We want you to have fun too. If you can't have fun at the beach during the summer, then you're really doing something wrong."

"And that fun starts tonight," Mo says. "We're closing a couple hours earlier than planned, and we're going to set up beach chairs on the roof so we can watch the fireworks, just like we used to with Dad. You're all invited."

Suddenly I think about Ben, and I must make an expression, because Mo notices it.

"What is it, Izzy?"

It seems inappropriate to ask, but I don't know what else to say. "I was just wondering if I could bring a date."

For the first time all morning, there are smiles around the room.

"We would love it if you brought a date."

*I*n the world of parades, ours is on the homemade end of the spectrum. We don't have giant balloons like the Thanksgiving Day Parade in New York, and our floats aren't lush and intricate like those in the Rose Parade on New Year's Day. Instead we've got some marching bands, people from different civic groups, old guys in antique cars, and about a dozen pickup trucks pulling flatbed trailers decorated with plastic fringe, chicken wire, and tissue paper. The grand finale is the high school drama teacher dressed as George Washington waving from the back of a fire truck with all its lights flashing. It is beyond corny, and I wouldn't miss it for the world.

Sophie, my mother, and I stake out a spot right at the corner where the route turns off Seagate and onto Ocean Ave. This is the halfway point of the parade as it makes its way from the high school parking lot to the bandshell, and because they have to slow down and wait at the turn, most of the bands play a full song here.

While we're waiting for the parade to begin, we tell Mom about Surf Sisters, and she's almost as bummed as we are. This funk hangs over us until we catch sight of Dad's band coming our way. The Founding Fathers are playing some Dixieland jazz number, and what they lack in precision and synchronicity they more than make up for with enthusiasm and ridiculous costumes.

My dad plays trombone, and I swear he picked it because it's the goofiest looking instrument. He exaggerates his marching when he sees us, and it's impossible not to laugh at him. We all shout and wave, and he responds with a wink and a long, drawn out blast from the trombone.

"Has he always been like that?" I ask my mom.

"Always," she says. "He did the exact same thing when I waved at him during this parade back when he was in the high school band and I was your age."

Sophie and I laugh at this, but as I watch Mom watching him, I can tell she's flashing back in time for an instant. She smiles and I notice her cheeks have the same blush that Ben described in mine. It dawns on me that there was a time when my mom felt exactly the same way about Dad that I feel about Ben. I wonder if she had as many questions as I do or if she was one of those girls who had all the answers.

Our next highlight is when Sophie's little brother marches by with the Cub Scouts. Unlike my father, there's nothing silly about him. He's the pack's flag bearer and takes his responsibility with full patriotic seriousness.

"Way to go Anthony!" shouts Sophie.

He looks over at us and gives us a very grown-up nod. We respond with wild applause and cheering, and he can't help but break into a little smile.

Behind the scouts is a group of Shriners in miniaturized sports cars. The tassels from their fez hats flap in the wind behind them as they race by and make figure eights in the street.

Next up is my least favorite float. It's sponsored by Surf City and features Bailey Kossoff, the reigning champion of the King of the Beach surf contest. He's sitting on a throne next to a fake palm tree, wearing board shorts, a royal cape, and a king's crown.

I've got nothing against him. I think he's an amazing surfer, but I could live without all the Surf City bimbos in their bikinis who surround him and wave to the crowd. Of course Kayla is one of the girls, and when my mother sees her, she says something completely unexpected.

"I know I'm a teacher and I'm not supposed to talk about a student," she says. "But since this is summer vacation and it's just us girls, let me tell you something. I cannot stand that girl."

This is completely out of character for Mom. I don't think I've ever heard her say anything negative about a student in front of me.

"I'm serious," she says. "Her mom was the same way when we were growing up. I tell you, the broom does not fall far from the witch tree."

Sophie eats it up. "I've missed hanging out with you, Mrs. Lucas."

"I've missed you, too, Sophie," Mom says with a smile. "We should do this more often."

I wonder if Mom made this unprecedented move because she has somehow become aware of my current situation. I don't doubt that Kayla's going to keep flirting with Ben, and my mother probably wants to give me a little boost. Before I can give it much thought though, we hear the sound of approaching snare drums.

"Here comes our girl!" Sophie says, pointing at the band.

Nicole may not always like the fact that she's six feet tall, but it sure does help us pick her out of crowds.

"Check it out—she's right next to Cody," I say, noticing the lineup. "Maybe there's something to be said for intervention-worthy stalking."

Mom gives us a look but decides not to ask.

The band marches to the cadence from the drums until they come to a stop right in front of us. They are about to play a song, and since they've played the same six or seven songs at every football game we've ever attended, Sophie and I try to predict which one this will be.

"'Hawaii Five-O,'" she guesses.

"'A Little Less Conversation,'" I counter.

We only have to hear the first few notes before I'm flashing a broad smile and basking in the glow of victory. "Nailed it."

The Pearl Beach High School Marching Panthers have been playing "A Little Less Conversation" for as long as anyone can remember. I wouldn't be surprised if they began playing it the day after Elvis released the song. This is not a complaint, mind you. They play it because they completely knock it out of the park every time.

Just as we do at football games, we all sing along. It builds to a climax when we shout, "Come on, come on! . . . Come on, come on! . . . Come on, come on!" That's when the trumpets reach their crescendo and the whole band starts marching again at our urging.

I really kind of love everything about Pearl Beach, if you haven't noticed.

This is the first time I've seen Nicole perform since she switched to drums, and you'd never know that she hasn't been playing them her whole life. She is so focused she doesn't even notice us jumping up and down waving at her.

There are more Shriners—this group is on tiny motorcycles— and then the mayor rides by waving at everyone from the back of an antique car. Next we see Ben and the kids from summer camp marching alongside the float for the Parks and Recreation Department.

The kids are wearing various athletic uniforms and carrying sports gear to represent the many activities that the department sponsors. Apparently, though, some of them have gotten tired and handed their gear off to Ben. At the moment he's carrying a surfboard, a baseball bat, a football helmet, and a bag of golf clubs. Considering that they're only halfway through the route, you've got to wonder how much more he can carry.

"He's going to pass out before the end of the parade," jokes my mom.

I don't know the proper protocol when your boyfriend (can I call him that? I think so) marches past you in a parade, so I just smile and do a coy fingers only wave when I see him. He's trying to say something to me, but I can't hear him over the revving engines from the tiny motorcycles.

"What?" I ask.

He rushes over to us, short of breath and frantic. "I need your help. Can you take this?" he says as he hands me the surfboard.

"You want me to take it to the shop and hold it for you?"

He gives me an incredulous look. "No, I want you to carry it alongside me and march in the parade."

"You want *me* . . . in the parade?"

He looks desperate. "Yes!"

"You really don't get the whole 'introvert' thing, do you?"

Before he can answer, he has to chase after a kid dressed as a football player who's wandering off in the wrong direction.

I stand on the curb frozen by fear. I'm totally mortified by the idea of marching in a parade in front of, you know, people. That's when I feel a hand push me from behind and make the decision for me. I stumble out into the street and it's too late—I am in the parade. I turn around expecting to see that it was Sophie but am surprised to discover that it's my mom.

"He asked you to help and he's really cute," she says. "Have fun."

Fun?

I'm a little bit like a deer caught in the headlights until I see Rebecca, the shy girl from the surfing class. She's dressed in a soccer uniform, holding a ball in one hand and waving to the spectators with the other.

"Hey, Izzy," she says when she sees me there. "Isn't this great?"

I'm not sure, but I think I just got schooled by the nine-year-old version of me.

"You bet," I say. "Why don't you walk with me?"

Rebecca and I walk together for a couple of blocks and I begin to feel less self-conscious. Once that happens, I help Ben corral the kids, and we start doing a little routine in which we stop, stutter step, and start marching again all in unison. They get a kick out of it, and it stops them from wandering off so much. By the time we reach the bandshell, we've got the step down and I'm actually enjoying myself.

"Thank you," he says as we reach the parking lot. He just drops all the gear that's been handed to him.

"You're welcome," I say.

I give him a moment to catch his breath, and once he does, I ask, "Do you have time for lunch?"

He looks around at the mass of kids. "I need to wait here until their parents pick them up."

I think it through. "How about if I get the food and meet you back here? Hopefully by then you'll be free."

"That sounds great," he says.

I head over to Angie's Subs. Luckily Angie's daughter is a friend and she helps me sidestep the mob. I order a foot-long Italian Special with extra Peruvian sauce (I don't know what's in Peruvian sauce, but wow!), and twenty minutes later Ben and I are splitting it in the arctic chill that is the Parks and Rec office. He clears off some space at the end of his desk, and we set up our little dining area.

"What would you like to drink?" he says as he holds up two bottles of water. "Water or water?"

I play along and scratch my chin as I consider my choice. "Water, please."

"Excellent choice." He hands me one of the bottles and sits down across from me. "So what do you think of my fancy desk?" He raps the metal top with his knuckle.

"I like it," I say. "It's not only cheap, it's also messy."

"It's not messy," he says defensively. "This may look disorganized, but all of these stacks mean something to me. That one's for summer camp. That one has all the permission slips, and those two are for the King of the Beach and the Sand Castle Dance.

"By the way, in case you change your mind"—he takes a sheet of paper off one of the piles and dangles it in front of me—"here's an application for the King of the Beach."

I know he's trying to be supportive, but the thought of

competing in the King of the Beach is simply terrifying to me. I wish he'd stop pushing it. The Sand Castle Dance, however, is a completely different matter.

"Enough with the King of the Beach," I say, ignoring it. "You have a better chance getting me interested in the Sand Castle Dance. It's kind of like our summer prom and a pretty big deal for us."

He nods as he swallows a bite of his sandwich. "I know. I hope I can get a good date. You think Kayla would go with me?"

"That's not even funny," I say as I slug him in the shoulder.

"Ow, ow, ow," he says, rubbing it. "I was only joking."

"Well, now you know better than to tell stupid jokes."

He rubs it some more, and I realize I packed a harder punch than I had intended.

"Do you know why I am working so hard preparing for the Sand Castle Dance?"

"No," I say. "And I'm not sure I care."

"You should care. I'm working so hard because I made a deal with my boss. If I take care of all the prep—which includes finding the band and arranging the decorations—then I don't have to work that night. I get to spend the whole evening at the dance with . . . wait for it . . . *my girlfriend*."

I just let that word linger in the air for a moment. It's got kind of a musical ring to it.

"How do you know I want to go?" I say. "The word on the street this year is that it's being planned by a guy who doesn't know what he's doing. It's probably going to be lame."

He gives me a look. "I'm going to let that slide. But only because you got this incredible sandwich."

"Speaking of dates," I say, trying out yet another unskillful segue, "what are your plans for fireworks tonight?"

"Some oohing, some aahing, nothing special planned," he says. "I thought you had to work."

"About that . . ."

I tell him all about Surf Sisters and the surprise announcement. He seems truly upset that the store's going to close, and I can tell he's trying to figure out a solution. He's not going to come up with one, but he wins points with me for trying. I also tell him about the plan to watch the fireworks from the roof of the shop.

"So, you wanna be my date?"

"You and me on a date?" he says playfully. "In front of all the girls at Surf Sisters?"

"Yes."

"Gee, that doesn't sound the least bit intimidating. Isn't there somewhere we could watch where I'd feel less out of place? You know, like in a pit of wild panthers or something like that?"

I lean across the desk and wag a finger in his face. "I just marched in a parade for you. A parade through crowds of people! Don't even get me started about feeling out of place."

"Okay, okay," he says. "I'll do it."

I hear a new band being announced at the bandshell and I panic.

"What time is it?"

"Two o'clock," he says.

"We gotta go."

"I've still got ten minutes for my lunch break," he replies.

"The Founding Fathers are playing," I reply. "I don't want to miss my song."

We hurry out of the office and get to the bandshell just as they start to play it.

"Isabel is watching like a princess from the mountains . . ."

Ben smiles when he realizes what's going on. "Very nice," he says. "Your dad has a good voice."

We listen for a while, and even though I've heard it countless times, this is the first time I take notice of one particular line.

"With a whisper of her sadness in the passing of the summer . . ."

As a girl I'd always focused on the princess line, but now the idea of sadness and the passing of summer has new meaning. That's in the future though. Right now, I'm just going to focus on enjoying it.

*D*uring my shift at Surf Sisters I have moments of nostalgia, sadness, laughter, and anger. We all do. It's just impossible for us to believe that such an important part of our life is coming to an end. Mickey and Mo try to keep our spirits up, but it's hard to separate the job part from the surfing and the friendship parts. In a way we're lucky that it's the Fourth because we're so busy dealing with customers, we don't have much time to dwell on the negative.

Ben arrives right before closing. He's made a point of going home and switching out of his work clothes and is now rocking the whole islander look with a pair of khaki shorts, a graphic tee, and flip-flops.

"Badger Ben sure doesn't look like he's from Wisconsin anymore," Sophie jokes with a friendly nudge.

I give her a look. "I thought we decided 'Badger Ben' didn't work."

She nods. "I just thought I'd give it one last try."

He walks over to me, does a double check of everyone in the room, and whispers conspiratorially, "I'm the only dude here. Are you sure this is okay?"

Despite his best efforts to keep these concerns quiet, Mo has overheard him. She comes up from behind and whispers into his ear, "She's sure."

Startled, Ben turns around to see her smiling.

"We always like to have a couple guys around," she continues, "just in case any menial jobs come along."

I think this is Mo's way of testing him. A lot of boys might get defensive or feel intimidated. But Ben just goes with the flow and plays along.

"Well, if that's the case," he says, "I think my vast experience doing menial chores for Parks and Rec makes me more than qualified. Do you have any playground vomit that needs cleaning up?"

"No," she says, pleased by his response. "But the night's still young, so you might want to check in with me later."

Despite this confidence, I'm sure Ben feels a little more comfortable when a few more guys show up. This includes Mickey's husband and—surprise, surprise—Nicole's longtime crush, Cody Bell.

"Did Nicole invite him?" Sophie asks.

"She must have," I say. "Probably today at the parade."

Sophie beams with pride. "Aren't my girls growing up?"

I shoot her a look and hope that Ben hasn't overheard. Sophie, meanwhile, walks over toward Nicole and Cody. From past experience I know that's she going in as a wingman to make sure that Nicole doesn't get too nervous.

"What was that about?" Ben asks.

"Just Sophie being Sophie," I say before I quickly change the subject. "Wanna see the roof?"

"Sure."

I guide Ben into the storeroom, where I pull a set of folding stairs down from the ceiling. A generation ago these led to the attic, but the roof has been remodeled and includes a full wooden deck with a wraparound railing and spectacular 360-degree views.

"I get to go up here every two hours to update the surf report," I tell him as we reach the top and open the door to the deck. "My reward is the view."

"Okay, wow!" he says when he steps out and sees what I'm talking about.

Night has fallen over the ocean; the lights along the boardwalk and the pier are coming alive as the moon casts a silvery wash across the water. It is incredibly romantic, and when I see that we are all alone, I sneak a quick but meaningful kiss.

"That's why you wanted to be the first ones up?" he says.

My smile confirms my guilt, although I admit to nothing.

"I don't know what you're talking about," I say. "So what did you think of Independence Day Pearl Beach style?"

"Different from Wisconsin, that's for sure."

"How do you guys celebrate up there? Milking cows? Churning butter?" I joke.

"I'm going to ignore that because today you came to my rescue," he says. "I know you're not a big fan of being in the spotlight, so marching in a parade could not have been fun."

"Fun? No, it was not fun. It was *terrifying.*" I'm only half joking, but we both laugh.

"I do appreciate it."

Pretty soon everyone else makes their way up onto the roof, and we all enjoy some yummy teriyaki chicken skewers that Mickey's husband picked up at Chicken Stix, a kebab shack a couple blocks down the beach. As you'd expect from a Surf Sisters get-together, it's pretty low key and mellow. The funny thing is that no one is talking about the one thing that's on everybody's mind. Then, a few minutes before the fireworks are scheduled to begin, Mickey takes a sip from her glass of wine and addresses us all.

"We'd like to thank you for coming tonight. Back when Mo and I were young girls—way before there was an actual deck up here—our dad would bring us out on the roof every Fourth of July. We'd lie with our backs against the wooden shingles and watch the fireworks go off. We thought we had the best view on the island, and I think you'd have to agree that we were right. So, as we celebrate this tradition one final time, I'd like to propose a toast to the man who started it."

She holds up her glass, and everyone else holds up whatever they're drinking. (For me it's sweet tea.) "To Steady Eddie."

"Steady Eddie," everyone says with enthusiasm.

"King of the Beach," adds Mo.

It's the last part that punches me in the gut. I think about the Surf City float in the parade with its King of the Beach sitting on a throne surrounded by Kayla and her friends. It represents the opposite of everything that Steady Eddie embodied. The opposite of everything I believe in. This is the thought that nags me as we watch the fireworks.

The show lasts for about twenty minutes and really lives up to its billing as *spectacular*. I love the way the colored lights reflect off the water. Standing on the roof, I see that the boardwalk sparkles almost as much. It's great, but even still, I can't get rid of that nagging feeling.

"What are you thinking?" Ben asks toward the end.

"That it looks beautiful," I respond.

"No, I mean, what are you thinking about?" He gives me a look that says he knows something is on my mind. "Be honest—is it a problem that I'm here?"

Apparently, I'm not only bad at reading signs but also at giving them.

"Absolutely not," I say, trying to speak loud enough so that he can hear but soft enough so that no one else can. "It's amazing that you're here. Amazing."

"Are you sure? 'Cause it doesn't look like it."

"I'm more than sure. It's just that I'm upset about all of this." I gesture to the others on the deck with us. "I wish there was something I could do."

He goes to say something, but then he stops himself. Instead, he just looks at me and smiles. Then he puts his arm around my shoulder and squeezes me in closer for a moment.

Maybe it's the nostalgic display of fireworks, or maybe it's the wonderful realization that I, shy Izzy Lucas, am cuddling with my fabuloso boyfriend—I still can't believe that part—that makes me wonder what it would be like if I actually was the type of person who had the courage to compete in the King of the Beach. Better yet, what if all of us girls entered and shredded the waves as one last great send-off for Surf Sisters?

"What are you smiling about?" Ben asks.

I didn't realize I was smiling, but I dare not even say it aloud. Instead I answer, "Nothing . . . everything."

Moments later, the grand finale starts to blanket the sky with color and light, and the noise drowns out any possibility of him pursuing the subject further. Surprisingly, I can't shake the daydream of all of us competing. As a team. As Surf Sisters.

"Hmmmm," I say out loud for no particular reason.

As I look at the fireworks, my mind keeps turning it over. Then, when the final ribbons of color fade into the night and the smoke and smell of powder waft over us, I wonder if this is something we should do. I have found a boyfriend. I have marched in a parade. Could I possibly compete in the King of the Beach? Could all of us? We could go out with a fight. Our very own grand finale.

The party has reached its end, and people are beginning to hug one another and say good-bye. I start to breathe faster as I wage an internal debate. There's no way to go to the register to get a verdict on this one. I have to make this decision all on my own. And as it is with most decisions you dread, the difficulty isn't so much figuring out the answer, which is obvious, but deciding if you can face the consequences.

"Wait!" I say as the others start to leave. They all stop what they're doing and all eyes turn to me. I freeze for a moment as I reconsider my decision one last time.

"What's the matter, Iz?" asks Mo.

"What's the matter?" I say, incredulous. "The store's closing. That's the matter."

Her eyes are watery and consoling at the same time. "I know, sweetie."

"We can't just let it happen," I say. "We can't just keep coming to work and act like we're happy as we count the days until it's over. It's not fair to Steady Eddie and it's not fair to you."

Mo wraps me in a hug as tears run down her face. "I don't know what else we can do," she says.

"I know," I say with a deep breath. Then it hits me. I want to do this for Surf Sisters, but I also want to do it for me. I'm tired of standing off to the side. I'm ready to be noticed. "We can win the King of the Beach and get your trophies back."

*O*ver the next week I develop a new routine in my daily life. Today fits the profile perfectly. It starts in the morning when I wake up early and head to the beach with my surfboard under my arm. This may not seem like a change, considering that I surf most mornings anyway, but now my approach is totally different. First of all, these sessions are not about finding my Zen place and becoming one with the ocean. They are full-out training sessions. I'm working to build endurance and strength.

I'm practicing technique and I'm challenging myself to develop the moves I'll need to do to get the judges to notice me.

Secondly, I've started to surf the pier. Every break, which is what surfers call a specific location, is unique. The more you surf it the better you know its secrets. The King of the Beach is held at the pier, and by the time the contest begins, I want to know each and every inch of it. The problem with surfing there, however, is that it's the most popular break on Pearl Beach. This means there are always other surfers there, even in the early morning hours, and I have to work on my "surfs well with others" skills.

The other girls from the shop are coming down to the pier too, but we are keeping our plans on the down low. One thing—the only thing?—working in our favor is the element of surprise. Surf City has walked away with the team championship every year for more than a decade. On the morning of the competition, their only concern will be figuring out which one of their guys is going to win the individual crown. We don't want them to be just overconfident about the team title. We want them to think it's automatic.

That means we don't arrive together. We don't wear any Surf Sisters gear. And we never talk about the contest. In fact, we don't really talk much at all. Well, except for one of us.

"So," Sophie says as we sit side by side straddling our boards and waiting for the next set. "Have you told Ben that you love him yet?"

I don't even dignify this with so much as a glance in her direction.

"It's obvious that you feel that way," she continues. "You love, love, love him."

"Stop it," I say, still trying to ignore her.

"Have you said that you can't imagine being without him and that you're going to follow him back to Wisconsin so you can live on a big dairy farm together?"

"Do you mind?" I say, finally turning to her. "I'm trying to surf here."

She nods. "And I'm trying to make you better at it."

I flash her my skeptical eyes. "How does annoying me make me better?"

"I'm not only annoying you, I'm also teaching you the importance of not letting anyone distract you. You know . . . like I just did."

"What are you talking about?"

Before I even finish my question, she has turned and is paddling. By the time I figure out what's happening, it's already too late. There's a beautiful wave coming, and she has completely shut me out and stolen my position. Normally I surf by myself or with my dad, and there are no distractions. That won't be the case during the King of the Beach, as Sophie reminds me fifteen minutes later when we're back in the lineup.

"There's no margin for error," she says. "Wave selection plays a big part in who wins and who doesn't. You can't afford to miss any good ones because you're distracted."

I nod my agreement and remind her that we need to keep the talking to a minimum.

After my morning session I go home and crash in my bed for a power nap. Of course, before I do that I check to see if I have any texts from Ben. Even when he's working with the campers, he usually manages to send off a steady stream during the day.

After my nap I head in to Surf Sisters and work my shift. Mickey and Mo have put me on the same shift almost every day. They said it was to help me establish my workout routine, but I think secretly they're trying to have my hours line up with Ben's as much as possible. (See what I mean? They totally rock.)

The vibe at the shop is completely different from the way it was a week ago. Everyone is excited about Surf Sisters competing in the King of the Beach. I think the important part is that it gives us something positive to think about and takes our minds off the fact that the store is closing. Even the fact that we're keeping it a secret gives the whole thing a spy vs. spy feel.

There is one massive problem, however, that nobody's talking about. I know I'm certainly not going to bring it up. But . . . even though I'm the one who came up with the idea and I enjoy our secret sisterhood and backroom plotting, I don't see how we can possibly win the contest.

The Surf City team isn't just good. It's amazing.

Consider this little nugget. Surf City sponsors ten of the twenty highest rated surfers in the state. A team can submit up to eight surfers in the competition. That means two of the best surfers in all of Florida won't even make it on their team. Meanwhile, Mickey and Mo are the only people on our team who have even been in a tournament before. And, while I don't doubt their greatness, the two of them are over fifty and haven't competed in decades.

It is this sobering thought that's going through my mind as I pull down the folding stairs and climb up onto the roof of the store. Every two hours I'm responsible for updating the surf report we put up on our Web site and on the sign that hangs outside our door. That means I get to go up on the roof with my binoculars, check the waves, and read the thermometer and wind gauge. It's like I'm a TV weather girl, except without the hair spray and a perky nickname.

I'm looking through the binoculars when I hear a voice.

"How's it looking?"

I turn around and see that Mo has followed me up.

"Not great. The waves are one to two feet, ankle to knee high. Small, clean lines crumbling through. The wind is five to ten knots north-northeast."

"Oh, to live in Hawaii," she says, bringing a smile to both of us. "But I guess the struggle makes us appreciate it that much more."

She's talking about the fact that Florida waves are nothing compared to their relatives in California and Hawaii. I love it here, but if you want to surf in the Sunshine State you have to work at it and learn how to make a lot out of a little.

"My dad and I have talked about going out there as a graduation present," I say. "The plan is basically to live in a tent on the North Shore of Oahu and surf until we drop."

"You gotta love dads who teach their girls to surf," she says with an appreciative nod. "But don't forget that these waves gave the world Kelly Slater." Born and raised in Florida, Kelly Slater is considered by many to be the greatest surfer of all time. I've got his poster on my wall.

"What brings you roof-side?" I ask.

"The view," she replies, "and you."

"Why me?"

It dawns on me that we're in virtually the exact same spot that we were standing on the night of the Fourth, when she had tears in her eyes and I got the ball rolling on this whole competition thing.

"The last few days I've been out on the pier watching you girls practice," she says.

"Really? I haven't seen you there."

"We're supposed to be keeping it on the down low, so I've been hiding out," she says with a shrug. "But there's one thing that can't be hidden—your talent. I don't think you have any idea how good you are."

"Really?"

"Really," she says.

"How good do you think I am?"

"Beyond slamming. Way better than I was at your age."

I give her a skeptical smile. "Nice try."

"What do you mean?"

"You're trying to build me up for the contest," I say.

She shakes her head. "No, I'm trying to make sure you appreciate your talent. That you understand that it exists."

Praise like this coming from Mo means a lot. Other than my father, she's taught me more about surfing than anyone.

"That's hard to believe, but thanks," I tell her. "You don't know how much that means to me coming from you."

"That's the part I thought you'd like hearing," she says, changing the tone of the conversation. "Now I'm going to tell you something that you won't."

I brace myself.

"In a few months Surf Sisters will no longer be here. But you will still only be sixteen years old. You have a future in this sport."

"What's the part that I don't want to hear?"

She pauses for a moment before saying it. "Surf City doesn't have a single ranked girl on their team. Once they see what you've got, they'd be fools not to jump at the chance to sponsor you . . . and you'd be a fool not to take it."

I cannot believe what I'm hearing. This is like Santa Claus coming down your chimney and telling you that there's no such thing as Christmas. Mo cannot be telling me to join up with Surf City.

"There's no way I would ever do that. Not with them. The only reason I'm even competing in the first place is because I want to beat them."

"Well, that's too bad," she says. "You shouldn't be surfing because of them. And you shouldn't be surfing because of us. You should be doing it for you. I've been watching you and I've noticed a complete evolution in your style. You've found a spark and you should see where it takes you. You know what I think about their store. But there's no denying that their team is outstanding . . . just like you."

"You're right," I say, more confused than anything. "I don't want to hear this."

I don't wait for a response. I just walk past her and head back down the stairs.

*I*t was completely out of left field," I say as I tell Ben about my conversation with Mo. "In a weird way it felt like she was dumping me."

"Don't be ridiculous," Ben says as he tries to scrape the wax off an old surfboard. "Mo loves you. The last thing she'd do is dump you."

Despite my mood regarding Mo and our conversation, this brings us to the best part of my new daily routine. If I'm not training or working at the shop, then the odds are pretty good that I'm with Ben. We've done something together every night this week. We've gone bowling (I was pathetic), played putt putt (I beat him on the last hole and was surprisingly obnoxious about it), and just hung out and watched TV. (He's already got me hooked on British mystery shows.)

We've also started basic surfing lessons. For the first few he borrowed Black Beauty, which is what my dad calls his favorite shortboard, and now Ben's purchased one of his own. It's an old quad fish that he dubbed Blue Boy in keeping with my dad's naming tradition. It's been a while since Blue Boy has been in the water, so I'm teaching him how to strip off the old wax and start anew. He's got it lying across two sawhorses and is bent over, hard at work.

"How's this?" he asks as he scrapes the last bit.

"Good," I say, inspecting it. "Very good."

I hand him a bar of Mr. Zog's that I picked up at the shop.

"Now start to apply the base coat. Make straight lines from one rail to the other directly perpendicular to the stringer." The rails are the side edges, and the stringer is a thin strip of wood that runs down the center of the board and makes it stronger.

"Like this?" he asks as he carefully rubs the bar of wax across the board.

"Exactly," I say.

I like watching him work. He does this little thing where he bites the left side of his lower lip when he concentrates, and it's beyond cute. It's also a sure sign that he is trying to do it perfectly. It's a total contrast to the goofy way he is around the kids during camp.

"You know Mo was just looking out for you," he says. "She doesn't want you in denial. She wants to make sure you can move on after the summer."

When he says this I realize why the conversation with Mo is bothering me so much. It's not just the fact that she thinks I would represent Surf City. It's the fact that she is already encouraging me to find something new after the summer. She's trying to make it all right for me to replace Surf Sisters. And the problem is, if she can persuade me, then so can Ben.

"Is that something you can relate to?" I ask pointedly.

He starts to answer but stops when he realizes that I've set a trap.

"They're two very different things," he says, choosing his words carefully. "But, yes, I can relate to worrying about you in September."

I put my hand on his hand to stop him for a moment, and he looks up at me.

"When the time comes for you to go back home, do not be like Mo. Don't encourage me to meet another boy and replace you. I knew what I was getting into when I kissed you on the pier. I'm a big girl and I know that September will come. But we said this was going to be like the perfect wave. We're going to ride it until the very end and not worry about the next one."

He stands upright and carefully looks at me. I can tell he's debating what he should say next. In my brain I know that he will go home and find someone new. And, theoretically, I know that I will also find someone. But, in my heart, I can't bear the thought right now.

"Okay," he says quietly. "I promise I won't."

Then, completely out of nowhere, I start to cry. Not big sobs, but steady tears that slide down my cheeks one by one. The fact that I'm embarrassed about this emotional display only makes me cry that much more.

We're on opposite sides of the surfboard, so he reaches across and holds my hand as he navigates his way around the sawhorse and wraps me in his arms. I cry a little harder as I bury my face in his chest, and he gently strokes my back. I start to apologize for being such a drama queen, but he just shushes me and holds me tighter.

"It's okay, baby."

Just hearing him say that fills me with this warmth. In a weird way I've never felt worse and better at the same time. I close my eyes and listen to the sound of his heart beating.

O kay, I'd like to officially apologize for *whatever* that was earlier," I say as we walk along the beach a few hours later. There's only a sliver of a moon hanging over the water, but stars fill the night sky and it's stunning.

"You don't have to apologize," he says. "You're allowed to show emotion. That's part of the package."

"Well, it was both unexpected and unprecedented," I explain.

"Although I will say that there was a sort of emotional cleansing quality to the whole thing."

"Is that your way of saying you feel better now?" he asks.

"Well, if you want the SparkNotes version, yes."

"I am perfectly happy with the SparkNotes version," he says. "But also more than willing to go into greater detail if that makes you happier."

I stop and put my hands on my hips in mock protest. "Are you saying that it doesn't matter or just that you don't care?"

"Neither," he answers as he skillfully snakes a hand through my arm and pulls me closer to him. "I'm saying that I'm here for you however you need me to be."

I give him a playful nod and counter, "You're a slick talker, Ben Taylor. You always seem to say just the right thing."

"And is that a problem?"

"It kind of is."

"Let me get this straight," he replies, looking down at me. "Are you now criticizing me for *not* saying the wrong thing?"

"The female mind is quite the riddle," I joke. "Besides, I'm not criticizing you. I'm just keeping you on your toes."

"How about I keep you on your toes instead?"

He wraps his arms around my waist and lifts me ever so slightly, so that now I'm on my tiptoes—the perfect kissing height. At first I think it's going to be a peck, but our lips linger and I close my eyes. The instant it's over, I pick up the conversation where I left off.

"See what I mean? You always say the right thing. That's suspicious, don't you think?"

I break free from his arms and sprint ahead of him.

"Where are you going?"

"I thought you were a runner," I call back. "Yet I'm the one winning the race to the lifeguard stand!"

Up ahead of us is a lifeguard stand. It looks like a giant high chair that's twelve feet tall and made out of bright orange two-by-fours. I've got a good head start, but he quickly closes the gap and we both get there at the same time.

"I won," I say, catching my breath.

"Hardly," he laughs. "It was a tie and you cheated more than a little bit."

"That's not what I meant. I won because I got you right where I want you," I say as I climb up into the seat. It is big and roomy enough for a lifeguard to sit with all of his gear. Or, in other words, it's the perfect size for two people to squeeze into.

"So this was your plan all along," Ben says as he climbs up and slides in next to me.

"Bwahahaha," I reply with an evil master villain's laugh. "And you, Ben Taylor, were just my puppet."

This high up, there's a cool night breeze that makes it perfect for snuggling. I've known that couples do this and I have always imagined what it would be like. (Spoiler alert: It's awesome!) Ben puts his arm around me and I slide up next to him, and we just snap together perfectly like pieces in a jigsaw puzzle.

"Are we even allowed to be up here?" he asks.

"Of course we are," I say. "It's for lifeguards during the day, couples at night. It really fits right into the whole 'reduce, reuse, recycle' philosophy that we encourage here at the beach. Very multipurpose and good for the environment."

I rest my head on his shoulder and look out at the sea. More than a minute passes without either one of us saying a word. We just listen to the slow and steady music of the waves washing up on the beach and then pulling back into the ocean. Everything at this moment is perfect. So of course that means I have to screw it up.

"Can I ask you something?"

"There's an ominous beginning," he says.

"Whose idea was it to break up?"

"What are you talking about?" he asks. "We're not breaking up."

"No. I mean between you and Beth. Whose idea was it to break up?"

He lets go of me and turns so that his back is against the side of the chair. I may not be fluent in body language, but I can tell he's not thrilled with the question. "Why would you even ask that? Everything about this moment is perfect. Excuse me, *was* perfect."

"I know."

"So why would you ask that?"

"I told you. The female mind is complex."

"It's not a joke, Izzy."

"And I'm not joking. I know it doesn't make sense to you, but this is all new to me. I've never had a boyfriend. Nothing even close to one. That means you know every single thing about my past relationship history. So when we're sitting like this and everything's perfect, you know what's going on in my mind."

"Trust me when I say that I have no idea what's going on in your mind."

"Okay, that's a fair point," I answer. "But all I know about Beth is that she was beautiful and wonderful and everyone thought you two were a perfect couple."

"And after I told you that, you ignored me for two weeks," he says. "In fact, just a few blocks up from this very spot you told me that you couldn't be the girl I talked to about other girls."

"Things are different now," I reply. "And to be honest, since the only things I know about Beth are how wonderful she is, a little part of me could stand to hear how it ended."

I really don't know what it is about me that takes perfect moments and twists them into psychodramas, but I can't help it. I am who I am.

There's just enough moonlight on his face for me to tell that he's biting the left side of his lower lip. He's in deep thought mode, so I stop talking. Finally, after what seems like forever, he responds.

"It was my idea. We were out by the lake. She was talking about the prom and how important it was and how it would be this signature moment in our relationship. I mean, I know it's a big deal, but it is just a dance. She was obsessed with what table we were going to sit at, where we were going to go for photographs, and I just couldn't get excited about it. Maybe it's because I was in a pissy mood about my parents, but I just couldn't. Then, somewhere in the middle of it all, I just knew it was over."

He stops for a moment and takes a deep breath.

"Some of my friends said that I should've just hung on until it was time for me to come to Florida, but I couldn't do that to her. She didn't deserve to be strung along. So I told her that I was really sorry but I couldn't go to the prom with her and that we couldn't see each other anymore."

"You dumped her right before the prom?" I say, almost feeling sorry for her.

He nods. "I know. I'm a terrible person."

"You're not a terrible person," I say. "The timing was unfortunate, but if that's how you felt, you did the right thing."

"Just for the record, Beth did not agree with your take on it. She made sure everyone knew how much it was not the right thing. I can't blame her, I guess. Somehow she did manage to bounce back and find a guy who was more than happy to sit at the right table and smile his way through God knows how many pictures. He's a good guy, actually. I hope it works for them."

There's a pause. Which means of course that I have to keep pressing the issue.

"How did you know it was over?" I ask. "You said that in the middle of it all you just knew."

He turns his head to the side and shakes it in disbelief. "You really want me to tell you this stuff?"

I nod. "I know. I can't help it."

"Somewhere in the middle of all the discussion it dawned on me that it really was more than a dance for her. She sounded like my sister did when she was planning her wedding. And that's when I realized that Beth was actually in love with me. We weren't just dating. It wasn't just some high school thing. She loved me."

"And you weren't in love with her?"

"No," he says. "I might have been in love with the idea of her. I might have loved the attention. But I didn't love her, and it seemed incredibly unfair for me to let someone love me when I didn't feel the same way in return."

Now here's a problem.

I have no doubt that I am completely in love with Ben. Not the idea of him. Not the concept of him. Him. I've even wondered if I should tell him. But now I think the smart thing to do is to keep that secret to myself. Instead, I lie to him for the first and hopefully only time.

"Lucky for us we don't have to worry about that," I say, trying to sound convincing. "We both know that this is just for the summer."

He doesn't really answer. Instead he just kind of nods, and I lay my head on his shoulder again. It takes a moment, but he puts his arm around me.

It's quiet for a while and we just sit there. I can't help but think I'm doing everything wrong in this relationship. I don't know why I asked about Beth, but the truth is I really felt like I needed to know that stuff. I put my hand over to rest it on his chest, but he pulls back, and I worry that he's about to tell me that I'm just not worth the headache. But instead, he says something completely unexpected.

"Is that a body?"

"What?"

"Over there," he says, pointing down the beach about a hundred feet. "I just saw that dark shadow move. I think it might be a body."

I look, and when I see it, I know instantly what it is.

"Ooh, ooh, ooh, it's not a body," I say, trying to contain my excitement. "Follow me."

I quickly climb down the lifeguard stand, and he's right behind me.

"I just saw it move again," he says as he tries to keep up. "What is it?"

I stop and turn to him. "A turtle!"

I grab him by the hand and we race down the beach together until we get close. We slow down and stop when we're about fifteen feet away from where a massive sea turtle is slowly dragging herself across the sand. She's three feet long and weighs nearly two hundred pounds.

We keep our distance, and I put my finger over my lips and say, "Only whisper, and don't cross her path."

He nods and replies, "She's huge."

"She's a loggerhead coming ashore to lay her eggs."

A bank of clouds drifts by and reveals the moon, its light dancing across the turtle's red and brown shell.

"She's going to lay them over there," I say, pointing toward the sand dunes. "Don't disturb her and don't let her see any lights, like your phone; it can confuse her."

"Okay."

We spend the next thirty minutes watching her. It's a lumbering crawl up onto the edge of the dunes, and you can't help but marvel at her determination. When she starts to scrape away an area with her front flippers, I tug on Ben's hand and we quietly loop around to get a closer look. She uses her hind flippers to dig a nest and then fills it with dozens of ping-pong-ball-sized eggs.

"Oh my God!" Ben whispers, being careful not to disturb her. "It's amazing."

I nod in agreement.

Once she's done laying eggs, she uses her flippers to cover the nest back up, and then she begins the laborious task of dragging herself back to the ocean. We keep watching, but we move far enough away so that we can talk at regular volume.

"She was born here in Pearl Beach," I say.

Ben gives me a skeptical look. "How could you possibly know that?"

"Because sea turtles always come back to the same beach where they were born. It's in their DNA."

He thinks about this for a moment and then says, "Like me."

"What do you mean?" I ask.

"I came back to the beach where I was born too."

I laugh. "That's true. You did."

"What will happen with the eggs?"

"In about six weeks they'll hatch, and the little turtles will poke out of the sand and look for the moon. That's the key."

"What do you mean?"

"That's how they find their way," I explain. "During hatching season all the houses on the beach keep their lights off. That way the babies can find the reflection of the moon on the water and know where to go. Then they'll scramble back toward the ocean and disappear."

"That sounds amazing," he says. "We've got to come and watch."

"Will you still be here then?" I ask.

I didn't mean it as anything more than a basic question. But, given the conversations of tonight, it carries some emotional baggage.

"Yes," he says quietly. "That should be my last week."

I've already been enough of a drama queen for one night, so I decide it's time for me to put on the brave face. I take his hand in mine and our fingers intertwine.

"Perfect," I say. "We'll come out and watch them together. You're going to love it."

I'm a total moron," I say as I slip on a blue cami and look at it in the fitting room mirror.

"You're being too hard on yourself," Nicole calls out from the next stall. "I'm sure you're exaggerating."

"I don't think so," I reply. "I cried. I grilled him about breaking up with his girlfriend. Twice. It was basically a horror movie."

"And then you were saved by a sea turtle," she says. "Now there's a twist on the normal environmental dynamic."

"No kidding. Who knows how much damage I could have done if she hadn't rescued me?"

"Let me see the outfit," she says.

I step out and she looks it over. I'm wearing a lace shirt over the cami and a pair of white jeans.

"It's nice," she says. "But I like it more with the skirt than the jeans."

"That's a relief. I was worried the jeans would look better and then I'd have to make it through a whole meal without spilling anything on them."

"But it's okay to spill something on the skirt?" she asks with a raised eyebrow.

"No, but the white denim is just asking for it. That looks amazing on you, by the way."

Nic's trying on a floral baby doll dress with black leggings that really take advantage of her height.

"You sure? They're not too tight?"

I shake my head. "You know what Sophie says."

"There's no such thing as too tight," we both answer in unison.

The one drawback of life on Pearl Beach is that the nearest mall is almost an hour away. The two of us have made the trip because we've found ourselves in an unexpected situation. Namely, for the first time in our lives we have boyfriends. As a result we're both looking for a little wardrobe pick-me-up. Of course we don't have much money to spend, so we're only looking on the sale racks.

"It was a lot easier when I stuck to dark colors and solids," Nicole says. "You know, in order to blend in while I stalked him."

"Good times," I say as we head back into our stalls. "Speaking of which, how are things now that you and Cody actually talk?"

"Way more fun," she says. "Although we're taking it kind of slow. We only go out once, maybe twice a week."

"Are you okay with that?"

"Absolutely," she says. "The slow helps because it's all so new to me. I feel like I need relationship training wheels."

"That makes two of us. I don't think I can count on that turtle rescuing me every time I start to spiral out of control."

"Yeah, not so much."

We step back out and now she is wearing a graphic tank top and a high-low skirt that looked like nothing special on the rack but incredible on her.

"I should never shop for clothes with you," I say.

"Why?"

"Because of the whole six-foot-supermodel thing. I feel like Stumpy McGee."

"Who's Stumpy McGee?" she says with a laugh.

"I don't know. I just made her up. But he cannot pull off any of the looks that you've been rocking."

"Well, you're not Stumpy McGee because everything you've tried on looks adorable. Besides, I could never get away with wearing those," she says, pointing at the pair of boyfriend jeans I'm trying on.

"Sure you could," I say. "Except on you'd they'd be capris."

We both laugh and I realize that this is the beauty of having a lifelong best friend. You can give each other garbage, boost each other's confidence, and look out for each other all in consecutive sentences.

I remember learning how to ride a bike, and I'm still learning how to drive. (I've got my permit, but I do not feel a rush to get my license.) But I don't remember learning how to surf. It was too long ago, and that's a shame because if I did remember, it might help me teach Ben. Today is his first lesson on his new board, and he wants to make it memorable.

"It's time we go out where the grown-ups surf," he says.

Up until now, he's been using my dad's board and I've done the same lessons with him that I do with the summer campers. We've stayed in shallow water, and he's only caught waves after they've broken. It's a great way to learn, but now he's ready to go out beyond the white water. At least, he thinks he's ready. Just in case he's not, I'm right alongside him reminding him of each step along the way.

First we wade out into the water until it's waist deep, and then we lie out on our boards and start paddling. The part that surprises people the most is how hard it is to paddle. It looks like it should be easy, but it's not. You have to get used to balancing, and you have to work hard to go against the tide.

"Don't forget to duck dive," I tell him.

Duck diving is what you do when you paddle into a wave that's coming right at you. The way you're supposed to do it is to speed up right until you're about two feet away and then push the board down under the water and let the wave pass over you. If you forget, the wave slams your board into you.

Apparently he didn't hear me, because he forgets.

"My bad," he says. "I was supposed to do something there, wasn't I?"

"Duck dive!" I say, louder this time as another wave approaches. Now he picks up speed, and although it's not particularly graceful, he manages to get under the wave and pop out on the other side.

"Like that?" he asks.

I ignore the lack of grace and focus on the positive. "Yes. But next time try holding the rails tighter and push down with your whole body."

"Got it," he says.

We dive under a couple more waves before we get out beyond the break to where the water is calm. The look on his face is priceless. He is loving it.

"Now you need to straddle your board like this," I say, demonstrating.

"Do I look at the ocean or at the beach?" he asks.

"Did you not listen to any of the lessons I gave you?"

"I tried," he says. "But it's hard to pay attention because you're so pretty."

This makes me laugh. "You look out at the ocean until you see the wave you want. Then you turn and start paddling."

"Got it," he says.

I look over at him and see that he's struggling to find the right balance. His butt keeps sliding from one side of the board to the other and he overcorrects to keep from falling off.

"Don't worry. You'll get the hang of it."

He squirms a little more and then finally settles into position. Kind of.

"This is . . . what's the word you use . . . 'radical'?"

"I think they stopped using that a couple decades ago," I say. "But I know the feeling. Now remember, you don't have to stand up the first couple times. You can catch the wave and ride it lying down. It's good practice and helps you get the hang of it."

"Are you kidding me?" he scoffs. "I did not rescue Blue Boy

from some old garage just so I could ride him lying on my stomach. We are ready to hang ten."

"Do you even know what hanging ten means?" I ask with a laugh.

He shakes his head. "Come to think of it, I don't. But there's not enough time for you to tell me because I believe this wave is for me."

It's a great dramatic moment. Or at least it would be if he successfully turned and caught the wave. Unfortunately, all he does is turn and slide off the board. Six times in a row. Once he finally gets the turn down, he goes through a brutal thirty minutes in which he tries to catch wave after wave only to watch each one pull away and leave him behind.

"What am I doing wrong?" he asks.

"The moment the wave lifts your board, you're natural instinct is to lean back, but you should actually lean forward."

He nods. "It's harder than it looks."

"Much harder," I say. "Do you want to take a break? We could paddle in and rest or maybe practice some more in the white water."

He shakes his head defiantly. "I am not paddling back. I am riding in."

"Okay . . ."

"I mean it," he says, trying to psych himself up. "I'm going to ride in . . . standing up."

Fifteen minutes later he actually catches a wave for about ten seconds. When he loses it, I worry that he'll be frustrated, but the opposite happens. He's more jacked than ever.

"That time I really felt it," he says. "I think I've figured it out. I did what you said and it worked. I just have to force myself to commit to it. I have to force myself to continue leaning forward."

That's what he does on the next wave and I am beyond thrilled as he catches it and takes off toward the beach. There are a couple times when he almost loses it, but I can see the exact moment when he latches on for good.

It's a thing of beauty.

And then he tries to stand up. Which is not a thing of beauty.

He actually makes it farther than I would have guessed. He's wobbly but he manages to find his balance, kind of like a baby when it's taking its first steps and keeps its butt real low. Then he tries to straighten out his legs and stand all the way up, and when he does, he leans too far forward and pearls. The tip of the board digs into the water and throws him into the air. He slams face first into the ocean and disappears for a moment before standing up in shallow water.

I instantly catch the next wave and ride it right to him.

"Are you okay?" I ask anxiously.

"I'm not okay, I'm great," he says.

Then he turns and I see his face. There's a gash under his right eye that's bleeding and makes me gasp.

"What's wrong?" he asks. "Is my nose broken?"

"No. Your nose looks fine," I say. "But you've got a bad cut under your eye."

"Cool," he says, oblivious to any pain. "Did you see that ride? It was wicked fun. I totally get why you're addicted to this. Let's get back out there."

"Maybe we should, you know, take care of the cut first."

"Really? Can't we stay just a little bit longer?"

"Oh my God," I exclaim.

"What is it?" he asks.

"You're already hooked."

I hear the knock and I bolt into action.

"I've got it!"

I hurry down the hall, but before I open the door, I pause, take a breath, and run my fingers through my hair. It's important not to seem anxious and frantic. Especially at times like this, when you *are* anxious and frantic.

"Hi," I say as I crack the door open to reveal a smiling Ben.

"Hey," he says in his superspecial dreamy way. The swelling in his cheek has gone down, and I no longer worry that I've destroyed the masterpiece that is his face.

I lean out and whisper, "You know you don't have to do this. It's not too late to run away."

"I want to," he says. "Besides, I brought these."

He holds up a small bouquet of flowers, and I fling the door open.

"You got me flowers?" I'll admit it. There's a hint of giddy in my voice.

"Actually," he responds with a cringe, "they're for your mother. I wanted to thank her for inviting me to dinner."

"Hmmm," I say, with raised eyebrows. "So that's how you're going to play it. And here I thought you always knew the right thing to say."

We walk down the hall toward the kitchen.

"Ben's here!" I announce. "He brought flowers."

"For me?" Dad says, looking up from the pot of spaghetti he's stirring.

"No," I respond. "They're for . . . Mom."

Dad cocks his head to the side and wags a wooden spoon at us, splattering some red sauce across the stove. "You better watch it, son. That woman's married and she'll break your heart."

My mother comes in from the dining room shaking her head. "Would you two give the boy a break? Sometimes I feel like I live with wild animals."

Without missing a beat, Dad and I both do jungle animal noises, which only makes her shake her head that much more. She ignores us and takes the flowers from Ben.

"Thank you, Ben. They're lovely."

"Thanks for inviting me," Ben says.

She motions to Dad and me. "It certainly would have been understandable if you had declined. How's that cut?"

"Better," he says. "Thanks for that, too."

Mom was the one who treated the cut when we got back to the house. She checks to make sure it's healing okay.

"Needless to say, living with these two has made it necessary for me to develop basic first aid skills."

Dad and I do the jungle noises again, and Mom just shakes her head.

Even though Ben's been hanging out at the house on a regular basis and has eaten with us on multiple occasions, this is the first time he's "officially" been invited for dinner. My mother has some old school South in her, and she wants to make sure he knows that he's welcome in our house. She's even insisting that we eat in the dining room instead of the kitchen like we usually do.

At first I didn't get it, but judging by the flowers and the fact that Ben wore nice khakis and a button-down shirt, I think that she may have been onto something I missed. Once we put the flowers in the vase and finish setting the table, I have to admit that it does feel special.

Ever the English teacher, Mom asks him, "Have you had to do any summer reading for school?"

I start to answer no for him because I haven't seen him near a book, but he surprises me.

"I just finished *The Grapes of Wrath* a few nights ago. It was great. Steinbeck's my favorite author."

"I didn't know that," I say.

"Which part? That I just finished *The Grapes of Wrath*? Or that Steinbeck is my favorite author?"

"Either."

He shrugs. "You never asked."

"I love Steinbeck too," says my mother. "Although I prefer *Of Mice and Men*."

"That book's too sad for me," he says.

"You don't think *The Grapes of Wrath* is sad?" she asks.

"Incredibly sad," he says. "But somehow it has a sense of hopefulness about it."

I look across the table at my mother, and the only way to accurately describe her reaction is to say that she is actually swooning.

"Why, yes it does," she says, with a glow to her cheeks. "There certainly is a lucky English teacher up in Madison, Wisconsin."

"Did I miss the memo about book club?" I ask.

"No," says Dad. "It's not really book club. He's just kissing up to your mother."

Ben shoots Mom a look. "I'm not kissing up. I really do like Steinbeck."

"I know," she says. "We can talk books later."

"Great," he says.

The conversation continues, and a few minutes later Ben finishes a bite of spaghetti and goes to say something but stops.

"What is it?" I ask.

"I was going to say how great the spaghetti is, but then I realized your dad would just think I was kissing up to him, too."

"No, no, no. Feel free to compliment the spaghetti," Dad says. "That's totally different."

"How is that different?" I ask.

"Because unlike the collected works of John Steinbeck, the epic greatness of my spaghetti sauce is indisputable. Go ahead, son, kiss away."

"I want to make it when I go back home, so can you tell me what jar it comes in?"

My mother and I burst out laughing, and Dad's eyes open wide in horror.

"A jar? You think I make spaghetti sauce out of a jar? I'll have you know my mother was born in Italy. And not the one in Epcot. The real one."

Dad loves giving people a hard time. He calls it "bustin' their chops," but I refuse to use that term because I'm not some high school boy in the 1980s. But the truth is, he loves it even more when someone is willing to bust his right back.

"I'm just kidding," Ben says. "It's delicious. Is it your mom's recipe?"

"Actually, no," Dad says, bursting with pride. "I invented it."

"I think 'developed' would be a more appropriate usage," the English teacher across the table from me says. "'Invention' usually implies some sort of groundbreaking shift or advancement."

"Like I said," Dad replies with his booming voice, "I 'invented' it."

Mom and I laugh because we know that Dad has just begun. He could talk about his sauce for hours.

"I've spent years perfecting it. It is perfect, don't you think, Ben?"

"'Perfect' is exactly the word I would use."

"And I've never written the recipe down. I keep it all up here." He taps his right temple. "I make it for my team the night before every big race."

"Then let's hope it pays off tomorrow."

"It most definitely will."

While the inspiration for the meal may have been good manners, the menu selection was all about carbo-loading. Tomorrow Ben and Dad are driving to Cocoa Beach for the Rocket Run, a 10K road race whose name was inspired by the nearby space center. They've trained together a couple times a week and have turned it into some sort of male bonding thing.

"The trick is that you have to make sure the sauce is not too heavy. My mom's sauce is great, but if you ate it the night before a race, it would slow you down. This is light but still has enough kick to make it worthwhile."

"Too bad it doesn't come in a jar," Ben says after another forkful. "I'm sure my team back home in Madison would love it."

"I can teach you to make it," Dad says out of the blue. "You've just got to promise not to tell anyone else. We'll keep it between you and me."

"I promise."

Ben's happy. Dad's happy. I, however, am . . . not happy.

"Excuse me?" I say.

"What's the matter?" asks my dad.

"When I asked you how to make it, you said that I couldn't be trusted."

"That's because you're terrible with secrets," explains my father. "But I trust Ben."

I know this started out as a joke, but there's a part of me that is semi-offended here. I really did ask him to teach me, and he really did refuse.

"What makes you so sure you can trust him?"

Dad looks at me as if it should be obvious. "Well, I've already trusted him to take care of the thing that I love the most in the world. I think he can handle a spaghetti recipe."

I'm glad that my dad loves me so much, but seriously. "I'm not just some *thing* you trusted him with. I'm your daughter."

The three of them are quiet for a moment, and then I hear Ben trying to hold back a laugh. He fights it for as long as he can, but then it finally erupts.

"What's so funny?" I ask him.

"I don't think he was talking about you, Izzy."

I look at their faces and can tell that he's right.

"Then what was he talking about?"

"His surfboard. He trusted me with his surfboard."

"Black Beauty is the thing you love most in the world?" I say, with all the outrage I can muster while laughing.

"I'm sorry, baby," Dad says. "I thought you knew."

Now Ben is really losing it, and I realize that I've never seen him laugh this hard. He's like a kid having a good time, and it dawns on me that this is the thing he's been missing. Maybe it's even the thing he thought he'd never get again. His family is breaking apart, and there will never be any dinners like this where his mom and dad are sitting around the table telling jokes and giving him a hard time.

The rest of the meal is filled with funny stories and new insights. For example, I learn that in college he's hoping to major in English—another swoon from my mother—and that he's terrified of roller coasters—more chop busting from my father.

Originally I was thinking we might go out after dinner to catch a movie, but instead I suggest he get a taste of the über-competitive cage match that is our family game night.

"The game is charades," Dad says as we move to the living room. "Lucas-style charades."

"What's Lucas-style?" Ben asks me.

"Lucas-style is when your parents are both teachers and they like to take everything that's fun and turn it into something that's educational and maybe a little less fun. Like at my fifth-grade birthday party, where instead of Pin the Tail on the Donkey, we played Pin the Beard on the Civil War General.

"It was one of those big bushy beards," Dad tries to explain to Ben. "But it just didn't translate."

"No, it didn't," I say.

"And how do you do Lucas-style charades?" Ben asks.

"The categories have more of an Advanced English and AP American History vibe," I answer him. "Instead of TV shows and celebrities, we've got categories like Underappreciated Authors, Historic Battlefields, and my personal favorite, Politicians of the Nineteenth Century."

"Those were good clues," Dad says rehashing a sore spot from a past game. "I was pretending to 'fill' the cups and get 'more' of them. Fill . . . more. Millard Fillmore."

"Those clues are only obvious to you," I say.

"Well, today you don't have to worry about my clues," Dad says. "That's because this is a battle of the sexes—Mom and you against Ben and me."

And, then, as if gender supremacy wasn't enough, he raises the stakes just a little bit more and says, "Winning team picks what flavor ice cream we get from the Islander."

"You're on!" I say, in a growl that would make a professional wrestler proud.

Ben lights up as we break up into teams, and I can tell he really needs some family time. When it's time to play, I'm up first, and I pull "William Shakespeare" out of the hat.

"We got this," I say to Mom as I get into position.

Dad hits the stopwatch and signals me to go.

I do the signs for "writer" and "second word" and start shaking side to side. Ben and Dad laugh hysterically, but I ignore them.

My mom starts shouting out answers. "Twist. Shimmy. Shake."

I signal that she's right with "shake" and move on to the next part of the word. I pretend to throw a spear, and it takes her a moment to figure it out, but then she gets it.

"Shake . . . spear. William Shakespeare!"

Dad hits the stopwatch and announces our time. "Twenty-three seconds."

Mom and I high-five. We feel pretty confident, and I can already taste the mint chocolate chip ice cream I plan on selecting.

Ben's up next and draws a name from the hat. Since I'm the timekeeper, he shows it to me, and I see that it's "J. D. Salinger."

"This round's all ours," I assure my mom. "No way they'll beat twenty-three seconds."

"Ignore that," Dad says, trying to encourage Ben. "I trust you with my recipe and I trust you with my clues."

Ben thinks for a moment and finally decides on his plan. "Okay," he says. "I'm ready."

I signal him to go. He does the sign for writer and then squats like a baseball catcher and holds up his glove.

"J. D. Salinger!" screams my dad.

I hit the stopwatch and look down at the number.

"How fast?" asks Dad.

I shake my head. "Seven seconds . . . but it doesn't count."

"What do you mean, 'it doesn't count'?" asks Dad.

"You cheated," I say.

"How did we cheat?" asks Ben.

"I don't know how, but I know you did."

"What do you mean?"

"All you did was squat. How is that J. D. Salinger?"

They both look right at me, and at the exact same moment say, "*The Catcher in the Rye*."

That's when I realize that they didn't cheat. Even scarier, they're totally in sync with each other.

"Oh my God," I say, turning to my mom.

She says exactly what I'm thinking. "We've created a monster."

What follows is the most intense game of charades I've ever played—and, in my family, that's saying something. Ben and Dad make a great team, but Mom and I keep it close. We finally lose it with Politicians of the Nineteenth Century. That category always kills me. I draw a blank trying to act out "Ulysses S. Grant," and Ben somehow gets "Zachary Taylor" from my dad pretending to sew.

"It's a Taylor, like a tailor," he says, trying to explain.

Even though we play competitively, we don't really take it seriously, and I feel a deeper connection with Ben than I did before. I never realized how important it was for me that he get along well with my family.

"As the champions, we get to pick the ice cream flavor," Dad announces. "And as our MVP, you get to make the decision for us, Ben. What flavor do you want?"

Ben thinks about this for a moment and says, "Mint chocolate chip."

"No," Dad says, as though he's just suffered the ultimate betrayal. "You're picking that because it's Izzy's favorite flavor."

"It is?" he says, playing dumb as he shoots me a wink. "I'm picking it because it's my favorite flavor."

"The whole point of winning is so you can rub the loser's nose in it after the competition," says Dad.

"It really is hard to believe they let you coach children," says my mom. "Come on, let's go get the ice cream. I'll let you be as obnoxious as you want the whole car ride over."

"You will?" says Dad. "That's really sweet. That Zachary Taylor hint was amazing, wasn't it?"

Mom and Dad leave and, for twenty minutes at least, I get to be alone with Ben.

"So now you know what game night is like," I say.

"It was a lot of fun," he says.

I walk over to him and wrap my arms around his waist. "I guess you deserve a victory kiss."

"I would think so," he says.

We kiss for a moment and everything seems good. Unfortunately, that moment does not last.

"I need to tell you something," he says, pulling back. "I didn't want to do it in front of your parents, but I got a call from my mother right before I came over here."

"Is everything okay?"

He shakes his head. "The divorce is getting uglier, and now they're arguing about custody rights. My mom wants me to be with her all the time, but my dad wants to split custody so that I'd go back and forth between them."

"Well, that's good that your dad still wants to be part of your life, isn't it?"

He thinks about it for a moment and seems sadder than I've ever seen him. "Maybe if that were the reason. But he doesn't really want me around. I think he just wants to make sure she doesn't win and to make it so that he won't have to pay as much in child support."

Once again I am so grateful that my parents are happily married.

"Anyway," he says, "the judge wants to talk to me."

Now it dawns on me.

"What does that mean?" I ask.

"I have to fly up to Wisconsin," he says. "I leave on Sunday."

Now I really panic. "You're coming back, aren't you?"

"Yes."

I breathe a sigh of relief and ask, "How long will you be gone?"

"A week."

Even though we never talk about it directly, I always know exactly how many days there are until Ben's supposed to leave at the end of the summer. At the moment I have exactly thirty-one days. My plan is to use each one of them carefully, and now I am going to lose seven just like that.

"Seven days . . . ," I say softly.

"I know," he says.

"That's not fair."

I look at him and realize that I am being totally selfish. He's losing seven days too, but during that time he has to meet with a judge and pick one parent over the other.

"But even worse, it's not fair to you," I say as I give him a hug. "I'm sorry you have to go through this."

He rests his head against my shoulder, and I think I hear the faint whispers of him crying.

I swap my Saturday shift with Nicole so I can go watch Dad and Ben at the Rocket Run, and then on Sunday I get Sophie to drive Ben and me to the airport. His uncle was going to do it, but I'm trying to get all the time with him I can. To say the least, my mood is a little down, and there are extended quiet periods on the ride.

"The surf contest is just a few weeks away," says Sophie, trying to generate any sort of conversation. "We're going to get a lot of practice in while you're gone."

I expect Ben to respond, but he doesn't. He just bites his lower lip, lost in thought. He's concentrating, but I have no idea about what.

"Is something wrong?" I ask.

He turns to face me in the backseat. "Parks and Rec is sponsoring the surf contest," he says.

"Right?"

"And I work for Parks and Rec."

"Okay."

"It wouldn't be right if I used that position to give you an advantage. Ethically, I mean."

"Of course not," I say.

Sophie raises her hand partway. "Are we sure about that?"

"Yes," I say, slapping her hand down. "Of course we are."

"I was just checking."

"We don't want you to cheat for us, Ben," I tell him.

"Right," he says with a smile. "But it wouldn't be cheating if I told you that it is a good idea to read the rules. I tell that to everyone when they pick up an entrance form."

Sophie shoots me a look in the mirror, and both of us are wondering where this is going.

"And since you know that I am a lawyer's son and was taught to read everything carefully—and, by everything, I mean . . . every . . . single . . . word—then unlike other people who just ignore it, you might take that advice to heart."

He stops there and we share a look. I have no idea what he's getting at, but I do know that he's trying to give us a little help. I also know that, for the moment at least, that's as far as he's willing to go.

"Well, my boyfriend is going out of town," I say. "So I have plenty of free time this week, and I was planning on reading through the contest rules very carefully."

He smiles and nods. "And you're going to do that before you turn in your entrance form?"

I nod. "Absolutely."

The car is quiet for a moment.

"Okay," Sophie says. "That was . . . weird . . . but we're here. So why don't I drop the two of you off? Izzy, I'll come back around and pick you up in twenty minutes."

"Thanks," I say as I reach forward and clasp her on the shoulder.

"I know, I know, I'm amazing," she says, and although she's joking, it's completely true.

Ben and I get out and things are pretty quiet. He doesn't have to check his bag, so once he picks up a boarding pass, we walk over to the security line. It's killing me and he's only going away for seven days. I can't imagine how it will be in four weeks when we come back here and he'll be going away permanently.

We stand there for a little while and just silently hold hands. Then, when it's time for him to go, he gives me a kiss and a hug that linger longer than I expect.

"Good luck," I tell him. "I'll be thinking about you the whole time. Especially on the day you see the judge. It's going to be all right."

He nods and gives me another kiss.

"I'm going to miss you so much," he says.

One more hug and then he walks away and gets in line.

"I meant what I said," he says as he turns back. "Read every word."

"I will," I say, trying to put on a brave face.

I watch him walk away, and although I know he can't hear me, I just have to say it aloud, so I whisper.

"I love you."

August

$\mathcal{I}$'m pathetic.

I know this. But knowing it and being able to do something about it are two totally different things. It's been five days since Ben left, and no matter where I go, I'm constantly reminded of him. Right now we're closing up the shop, and as I lock the front door, I notice the poster he brought in the first day we met. Just the sight of it makes me want to cry, so you can guess how much fun I've been to be around. Nevertheless, Sophie and Nicole have not wavered in their repeated attempts to lift my spirits. You have to love their tenacity.

"Ladies, the dance floor is ours," Sophie announces as she turns up the volume on the sound system. "Let's crank it."

Sophie is obsessed with nineties dance music, and she loves to blast it while we clean up. As a result, she's gotten Nicole and me hooked too. The first song on the playlist is another example of how she keeps trying to make me smile.

> Right about now, the funk soul brother
> Check it out now, the funk soul brother

Despite the fact that it is basically just the same two lines repeated over and over and that its name is completely baffling,

I love "The Rockafeller Skank." I know, it makes no sense, but the beat is irresistible. Which is no doubt why Sophie is leading off with it.

Sophie sings along behind the counter as she sorts the day's receipts, and Nicole busts a shoulder shimmy and dances with the push broom while she sweeps the floor. I, however, maintain my groove-free status as I mope and restock the clothing racks.

"Who's up for Mama Tacos tonight?" Sophie asks, raising her voice but still moving to the beat. "I could destroy some nachos."

"Count me in," says Nicole. "How 'bout you, Iz?"

I shake my head and mumble some excuse that gets drowned out by the electronic rhythm.

"What?" she says, this time raising her voice.

I try again, but they don't hear me.

Finally I just blurt out, "No thanks!"

Sophie presses stop. The room goes quiet, and suddenly our fun little surf shop becomes one of those cop show interrogation rooms.

"Why not?"

"I'm just not very hungry," I say defensively. "And I've got to get up early to train."

"Which is it?" asks Nicole.

"What do you mean?"

"You gave us two excuses," she says as she stops sweeping. "Which one's the real one?"

"First of all, they're not 'excuses.' They're answers. And both happen to be real."

Nicole turns to look at Sophie; they share a brief psychic-twins moment. Then she turns back to me and says, "You're shutting us out, Izzy. I don't know why, but you are."

"Just because I'm not in the mood for nachos? That means I'm shutting you out?"

"Now you're 'not in the mood.' That's excuse number three. Who are you trying to convince? Us or you?"

She walks over until she's standing just across the rack from me. "You haven't hung out with us once this week. We get that you're busy when you're with Ben. We'll cut you that slack. But since he's out of town, we thought the three of us would do some stuff together."

"Yeah," says Sophie. "We kind of figured we could cheer you up."

"I don't need cheering up," I say curtly. "I'm fine."

Nicole goes to reply, but instead she just shakes her head and resumes sweeping. "Whatever."

"What is it?"

"I've known you forever," she says. "Whatever this is, it's not *fine*."

"Well, you're entitled to your opinion."

She looks at me and nods. "And you disagree?"

"Very much so."

"Then why don't we take this to the register."

I cannot stress how much I am not in the mood for having my love life taken to the register. "Let's not. The last thing I need right now is the two of you ganging up on me."

"Excuse me," says Sophie. "You feel terrible. We understand that. But if you think we would 'gang up' on you, then we've got real problems, because that's not who we are."

I know she's right and I regret saying it, but the truth is there's nothing they can say that will make me feel better. Plus, I worry if I tell them *everything* that's on my mind, it will only make things worse.

"It was a poor choice of words," I offer. "I apologize."

"It's *us*," says Nicole. "You don't need to apologize. You just need to talk."

I don't respond. I just keep rehanging shirts that were left in the fitting rooms. I figure they'll give up, blast some music, and let me get back to my mope-a-thon. But they wait me out. There's no music or questions, just the sound of the hangers as I slide them on the rack. Finally, I give in.

"You really want to know what's bothering me?" I say.

"We really do," says Sophie.

"He's only been gone for five days and I'm fully mental. What happens a month from now when he's gone for good? And what happens a month after that when this shop closes? What am I going to do? Where am I going to go? I can't just sit in my room and cry all the time."

"Is that what you've been doing, sweetie?" asks Sophie. "Have you been crying in your room at night?"

"Maybe," I grudgingly admit. "But I'm serious. What should I do? I can't figure it out."

I look at them and wait for answers. I can see that Nicole is carefully considering her words before responding, "I don't know."

I wait for more, but she doesn't say anything else. "'I don't know'? That's your answer?"

"That's the truth," she says. "I don't know what you should do. But I do know that whatever it is, you're going to do it with me. You'll be with me at school and wherever it is that we decide to hang out once this place is gone, and we'll figure it out together."

"It's awful," Sophie adds. "Ben's great and he's totally into you. You're such a cute couple, so we get that it's not fair. But don't forget that you were already awesome before he came into your life. And you'll still be awesome after he goes back home. Maybe even more so because he's opened up parts of you that we've never seen."

I raise a skeptical eyebrow. "Like what?"

"Like the fact that pre-Ben Izzy would never have entered the King of the Beach," says Nicole. "She should've, but she wouldn't have. Ben gave you confidence. He made it so you believe in yourself."

This is something that I had not thought of. "You might be right about that."

"Of course we are," says Sophie. "We're your best friends. We know things about you that you don't even know about you."

"Is that so?" I ask, amused.

"Yes, it is," she says. "Like for instance, right now I know that you've still only told us part of what's bothering you. We already knew that you missed him and were unsure about the future. This is not that kind of moping. This goes deeper. What else is it?"

Somehow the vibe has gone from interrogation room to confessional. They really are great friends, and I know that I can tell them anything. Still, I have to take a couple of deep breaths before I can say it.

"I love him."

They raise their eyebrows at this announcement, but neither says anything, so I continue.

"It's not a crush. I don't just like him. I am *in love* with him. And I know that I have no experience and don't know what I'm talking about. But I also know what I know. I love him and I can't even tell him."

"Why not?" asks Nicole.

"He broke up with his last girlfriend because she was in love with him and he didn't feel the same way in return. He said he didn't think it was fair to her. I can't take that chance. It's bad enough that I'm going to lose him at the end of the month."

It's amazing how relieved I am to have that off my chest. I can't tell Ben, but I can tell the two of them. Saying it out loud makes it seem real and not just something floating around in my mind.

"If you really feel that way, then I think you should tell him," Sophie says. "You should at least give him the chance to say it back to you. But that's for you to decide, not us. That's well beyond the powers of whoever controls the register."

"Does that mean you're ruling in my favor?" I ask.

"You're guilty of shutting out your best friends. There's no doubt about that. But I'm going to let you off with a warning and a reminder that we're your biggest fans. All we ever want to do is make things better."

"Okay, I know that. I won't forget." I'm relieved to have shared my secret and relieved that she's not going to make me do something stupid. "I also appreciate the fact that you resisted your recent trend of overstepping your bounds when you're on the register."

"I'm not done yet," she says.

I shake my head and turn to Nicole. "I knew it was too good to be true."

"This court also finds you guilty of another crime, and I'm afraid it's one that cannot simply be ignored."

"And what is that?" I ask.

"Failure to dance to 'The Rockafeller Skank.'"

This makes me laugh for the first time all week. "Please tell me it's another warning."

"Oh, no, no, no," she says. "We are going to stay here until we see . . . the Albatross. And don't just go through the motions. We want to see it performed with the passion and pageantry it deserves."

The Albatross is a goofy, over-the-top dance we came up with one night when we were doing inventory. It involves strutting around while holding your arms fully extended like wings. It's exactly the type of thing that you do when you're being silly with your friends, yet under no circumstance would you do anywhere else.

Sophie presses play and the music starts blaring again.

They just stand there with their arms crossed, looking at me expectantly.

"No way," I say. "You can stare at me all you want," I continue. "Because I am not going to do this."

They turn the music up even louder.

That's it. I can fight it no longer.

At first I just tease it a little and bounce my knees, then I bust out a big smile and the arms extend as I start the strut. They clap and holler, and pretty soon the three of us are grooving. It's fun and a great emotional release. I get so into it that I even close my eyes, which is dangerous when performing the Albatross.

We're startled out of our little moment when the music shuts off abruptly. We look to the counter and see Mo standing by the sound system. I'd totally forgotten that she was working in the garage.

"Sorry to interrupt your party," she says, clearly enjoying the moment, "but I need you guys to come out to the garage."

We follow her outside and are surprised to see that Mickey is there too. Today was her day off, which means she must have come in through the back door while we were busy.

"What's up?" asks Sophie.

"The King of the Beach is coming up," says Mickey, "and we thought we should have a team meeting."

Even though there can be as many as eight competitors on a team, so far the Surf Sisters squad is just the five of us. None of the other girls at the shop really surf much, and despite my attempts to secretly recruit during my practice sessions at the pier, so far I have struck out.

"That's a good idea," I say. "You want to go over practice schedules?"

"Actually, we thought we might start off by giving you guys some M&M's."

"None for me," answers Nicole. "I try to eat just a few, but then I start craving more, and before you know it I've polished off an entire family-sized bag. It's not pretty."

The sisters share a look and chuckle.

"We're not talking about the candy," says Mickey.

It takes a moment, but I'm the first one to figure it out. "Oh my God! Oh my God! Oh my God!" I say as I begin to tremble with excitement. "Do you mean . . . ?"

Mo looks at me and nods. "We figure it's the least we can do. We may not have the best team at the contest, but you can bet we're going to have the best-looking boards."

Now I notice that there are three gift-wrapped surfboards lined up against the back wall. They're giving us hand-shaped, custom made Mickey and Mo—M & M—surfboards. (This is me hyperventilating.)

"Those M&Ms?" Sophie says, pointing at them and practically crying. "You mean those M&M's?"

The sisters laugh even more, tickled by our excitement. "Consider them your bonus for years of hard work and dedication."

Nicole's the last one to catch on, but when she does, her reaction may be best of all. She doesn't say a word. She just squeals as she runs over to them, her long arms flailing in excitement.

"We wanted you to have them for the contest," Mickey says. "But we figured you'd need some time to break them in."

"Go ahead," says Mo. "Open them up."

We tackle the wrapping paper like human paper shredders and unveil three gorgeous and gleaming surfboards. Each one has an original design and color scheme. Sophie's is cosmic seventies psychedelic, perfect for her retro tastes, while Nicole's has a pattern that looks like a stylized sea turtle's shell, no doubt because she's our most ardent environmentalist. They're both beautiful, but mine . . . mine is the prettiest of them all.

"I absolutely love it," I say. "It's breathtaking."

My board has a swirl of colors that radiate from the center like the fingers of a hurricane. The colors look like little tiles in a mosaic and alternate between shades of green, blue, and brown. The phrase "The Eye of the Storm" is written in the center.

"I'm particularly pleased with how that one turned out," says Mickey. "I took a couple of pictures for our portfolio."

I look up at her and shake my head in awe. "It's a work of art, Mickey. How'd you come up with the design?"

"I didn't," she says with a smirk. "It was your boyfriend."

"Ben? Did this?"

"He actually wanted to buy you a custom board," Mo starts to explain. "He asked if we could work out a payment plan because he said he wouldn't have enough money until the end of the summer, but that he really wanted you to have it in time for the contest. He said he even knew what he wanted the design on the board to be."

I look over at Sophie and Nicole, and they smile warmly at the thought of Ben doing this.

"We told him that we had already planned on giving you boards for the contest," adds Mickey. "But we were curious to see his design."

"That's when he handed me this," Mo says as she holds up a sheet of paper with the design sketched out on it. "I thought it was great."

"I wonder why he wanted this design in particular," I say.

She shrugs. "So do we. He told us that you would know."

I have no idea.

I look down at it. It is mesmerizing. It seemingly changes color depending on how you look at it or how the light hits it. That's when I realize what it is, and I'm so caught off guard that I reach up and cover my mouth.

"What?" asks Nicole.

I shake my head. "I can't. It's too . . . mushy."

"That means you have to tell us!" Sophie says. "We could stand some mushy."

I look at them and say, "It's the color of my eyes."

I have a love-hate relationship with video chatting. I love, love, love the fact that I can see Ben even though he's 1,347 miles away. (Yes, I figured out the exact distance between our houses because, well, you know.) But I'm not particularly fond of seeing myself in the lower left corner of my computer screen as I talk to him.

Tonight is the second time we've tried it. The first time had mixed results. Halfway through the conversation I noticed that my eyebrows bounce up and down when I get excited and that there's some strange sniffle flare that happens with my nostrils while I'm in deep listening mode. When I tried to correct these things, I overcompensated, and by the end of the conversation I felt like I was having some sort of bizarre face spasms. It was like the time I tried to examine everything I do when I surf and it made me pearl over the front of my board. I've solved the issue by taping a small piece of paper over the image. Now all I see is Ben.

"Hi," I say. "How ya doing?"

"I'm okay, I guess," he says. "Better now that I see you."

Tonight is especially tricky. I'm still walking on air because of the incredibly romantic gesture Ben made with the surfboard design, but he spent half the day in a courtroom talking to a judge about his parents' divorce. My goal is to keep things positive and be as low maintenance a girlfriend as possible.

"I love my surfboard! The design is . . . perfect."

"I can't wait to see it," he says.

"You don't have to wait. I brought it for show and tell."

I pick up the surfboard and try to hold it in front of the computer so he can get a look. The problem is, because I've taped over the part that lets me see what he's seeing, I have trouble telling if it's in the right spot or not.

"I'm going to try it out first thing in the morning," I say. "I want to break it in before the King of the Beach."

"Speaking of which," he replies, "have you read through the rules like I suggested?"

"Yes," I answer. "We all have."

"And?"

"And . . . the truth is . . . none of us can figure out what you're talking about."

Ever since the trip to the airport, Sophie, Nicole, and I have read and reread the rules of the King of the Beach. Ben seems to think there's some great secret hidden in them, but we've given up finding it.

"It all seems pretty cut and dry," I continue. "We enter a team. Every surfer earns points based on how well he or she finishes in the individual competition. The team with the most points wins the title."

"Yes, but . . ."

There's a pause on the other side, and I try to read the expression on his face. I can't tell if he's angry, frustrated, or something else.

"I'll just tell you," he says, with a distant tone to his voice. "If there's one thing I've learned this week, it's that my ideas of fairness and cheating are outdated."

The divorce proceedings must be going even worse than I thought. He's never said it outright, but I've gotten a strong indication that his father cheated on his mother. I don't want to get lumped in with that vibe.

"Stop right there," I say. "Your ideas of fairness are no different from mine. I don't want you to help us by cheating. Never in a million years would I ask you to do that."

"I know, I'm sorry," he says. "It's just been . . . bad up here. It's kind of shaken my confidence."

"Well, in two days you'll be back down here," I say, trying to boost his spirits. "And we are going to have an amazing time. You can be confident about that."

There's a brief pause, and I wonder if he's about to deliver some bad news. I've secretly been worried that because it's so late in the summer, his parents might just have him stay up there and not come back at all. Instead he says, "I've missed you even more than I thought I would. And that's saying something, because I thought I'd miss you a lot."

I let this sink in for a moment and smile.

"I miss you . . . so much," I say. "And, I would never want you to go against your sense of right and wrong. I promise you, if there's something to be found in the rules, I will find it."

We talk for a little bit more, but I can tell he's worn out, so I wish him sweet dreams and blow him about a thousand kisses. When we end the call, there's a brief moment when the image on the screen freezes and the look on his face kind of breaks my heart. He seems so troubled, and I want to be able to ease that pain but have no idea how. Then it disappears, and I'm left staring at my computer screen.

I begin to obsess over the call the instant it's over. I'm not sure why, but I feel uneasy about it. Everything he said was positive. Not only does he miss me, but he misses me a lot. And he can't wait to see me again. Still, there's a knot of uncertainty in my stomach. I give myself a little mental pep talk and pull up the Parks and Recreation Web site and go to the link for the King of the Beach. It's just past midnight and I am determined to find whatever he thinks is important in the rules.

There are more rules than you'd expect. The King of the Beach is part of what's known as the Summer Series. There are contests held all over Florida, and surfers earn points by competing in those contests, which count toward the series championship as well. Because of that, there are twenty-three pages of rules I have to scour through. They address everything from eligibility to how each surfer is judged to guidelines set by the series sponsor and ones specific to the contest in Pearl Beach. I read them as closely and carefully as I can, but nothing strikes me as important.

At 12:45, I decide to print them out, and I then arrange them across the floor of my room. By 1:15, I'm convinced that because Ben doesn't know much about surfing, he thinks something is more important than it is. I'm going to call it a night and go to bed, but then I see my new surfboard.

The Eye of the Storm. It's pretty awesome and inspires me to dig some more.

At exactly 1:47 I see three words that catch my attention. I check the page numbers to make sure I have them in the right order. Then I reread the rule a few times. I go back to the Parks and Rec Web site and make sure the rules I printed are the most up to date. By 2:03, I am convinced. Those three words aren't just significant.

They change everything.

What's so important that we had to meet before the shop opens?" Sophie asks. "On my day off, I might add."

"Three words," I say.

"If those three words are 'I love you,' do not expect a hug."

I have called an emergency team meeting, and despite Sophie's attitude, I can tell that I have at least caught the attention of the others.

"What three words?" asks Mo.

I hold up a copy of the King of the Beach rules, all twenty-three pages, and wave it in the air for emphasis. "'From . . . all . . . divisions.'"

"Now you really shouldn't expect a hug," says Sophie.

"There are four divisions in the contest," I continue. "The most important one is the Main Event. Whoever wins the Main Event is named the King of the Beach. But there are three other age group contests: Menehunes for kids twelve and under, Teens for thirteen- to nineteen-year-olds, and Legends for anyone over forty-five."

"Yeah," says Nicole. "Why is that important?"

"Because every year the people on the Surf City team, and all the other teams for that matter, only enter the Main Event. They all want to compete for the individual title."

"I still don't see your point," says Sophie.

"Listen to the rules for the team competition." I read from the rule book. "'Competitors will be awarded points based on their finish in their individual competitions. The team championship will be awarded to the team whose members accumulate the most total points . . .' And here's the tricky part, because the sentence starts on this page but continues on this one," I say as I flip to the next page. "'. . . from all divisions.'"

I let this sink in for a moment.

"I still don't get it," Nicole says.

"You can earn points for your team in any age group," I say. "But none of the other teams ever do it. If we enter surfers in Menehunes, Teens, and Legends, we could earn a lot of points. We could build a really big lead before the Main Event even starts. We might even be able to win this thing."

Now I see the expressions I was hoping for.

"Are you sure?" asks Mo.

"Look for yourself," I say as I hand her the rules.

"Most teams are just made up of young guys at the peak of their skills. So of course they all enter the Main Event. It never occurred to anybody to make up a team that spanned different age groups."

Mickey flashes a big smile. "At least not until now."

"I think I've changed my mind," says Sophie. "I deem this hug worthy." She wraps her arms around me and squeezes so much that it lifts me off the ground.

"Sophie, you and me in the Teens," says Nicole, thinking aloud. "Mickey and Mo in Legends. That leaves us with three spots. Who else can we get? We need some Menehunes."

"I've been thinking about that," I say as I break free from Sophie's hug. "Rebecca and Tyler are the two best surfers in summer camp. I bet they'd do it."

"Those two make seven," says Sophie. "We can add one more."

"I know who would be perfect!" says Mickey with a Cheshire grin.

"Who?" I ask.

"Your dad," she says. "Is he over forty-five?"

"By six months," I say excitedly.

"He'd be great," Sophie says. "He's really good."

"Oh my God. He'll pass out when I tell him."

"That gives us three Legends, three Teens, and two Menehunes," Nicole says. "If everyone does well—"

"It still won't be enough," Mo says, interrupting.

We look over to where she has the rules spread out on a surfboard. She's writing numbers on the back of one of the pages.

"Why not?" I ask.

She scratches out some more math and looks up at us. "The points count from all the divisions, but the point values are bigger in the Main Event. There's a very real chance that Surf City will sweep that, and if they do, it doesn't matter how well we do in the others. We'll still fall a few points short."

She holds up her paper to show us the math.

We all think about this for a minute and try to figure out a solution.

"We have to have someone in the Main Event who finishes high enough to score points," Mickey says. "Those will count double because not only will we be adding them to our score, but we'll also be subtracting points from their total points. That could put us over the top."

"Considering we've got two past champions on our squad, I still like our chances," I say. "One of you can surf in the Main Event and the other in Legends with my dad."

Mickey shakes her head. "I'm afraid it will have to be one of you three."

"Why?" I ask. "You've both won it before. You've got the skills."

"Our skills have faded," says Mickey. "We can do some damage in the Legends, but it would be a miracle if either one of us made it out of the first round in the Main Event."

"She's right," says Mo. "It needs to be one of you."

"And if we're going to be honest," says Nicole, "I'm not in the same league as Izzy and Sophie. So it shouldn't be me."

I feel my pulse pick up pace as Sophie and I lock eyes on each other.

"That means it's got to be you," I say to her. "You're much better at cutbacks and tricks than I am. You can earn a big score. You can do this."

Sophie laughs. "You know that's not true. You know that I am nowhere near the surfer you are. This is your time to be bold. This is your moment."

"Well, it's got to be one of you," Mo says.

"How do we decide?" I ask.

Mickey smiles at me. "That's easy. The same way we always decide disputes at Surf Sisters. We're going to go to the register."

"But we're not open yet," says Sophie. "No one is working the register."

Mo nods. "I know that. But since Izzy is the one who first came up with the idea of competing, and since she's the one who found this wrinkle in the rules, we'll say that she's officially on register. We'll let her decide."

I breathe a sigh of relief. Bullet dodged.

"That's not fair," says Sophie. "You know I'm right and you just gave her a way out."

Mo looks at me with an intensity that's unnerving. "I don't know about that. There's a lot of responsibility that goes with being on the register. If you take the tradition seriously, you don't just make the easy choice. You make the right choice. I think Izzy takes things seriously. I think she'll make the right choice."

That last bit gets to me. I do take tradition seriously. I look at them one by one, and each one stares right back at me. I think about the contest. I think about the summer.

Back in June the idea of me competing in the King of the

Beach would have been laughable. But so much has happened. I'm definitely not the same girl I was then. I'm not even the same girl I was on the Fourth of July. Then I start to think about the girl I want to become. No one rushes me. No one says a thing. They just wait for me to respond.

"Okay," I say. "I'll make the decision."

"Who's it going to be?" asks Mickey.

There is no hesitation in my voice. "Me."

*B*en's first day back in Pearl Beach doesn't follow any of the romantic comedy movie plots that have played out in my imagination. There is no indie pop love song playing as we rush into each other's arms at the airport. (I have to work so his uncle picks him up without me.) I don't walk out of the shop after my shift and find him waiting for me across the street as he sits on the hood of a sports car. (His flight's delayed two hours, so he's still not back when my shift ends.) And we don't go on a picnic and have it ruined by a sudden rainstorm only to kiss passionately after we take cover beneath an abandoned gazebo. (Okay, so I was pretty certain this one wouldn't happen but, man, how cool would that be?)

In fact, Ben's first day back in Pearl Beach doesn't even include me until it's almost over. I still haven't heard from him by ten o'clock, so I try to call and it goes straight to voice mail. I figure (at least I hope) that it's because his battery is dead and not because he hit ignore when my picture popped up on his phone. Without really thinking it through, I ride my bike over to his uncle's house and knock on the door. I regret this decision the moment I see his face.

"Hi," I say as he opens the door.

He smiles, but it feels forced. "Hey." I can tell that he's exhausted both physically and emotionally.

"How was your flight?" I ask.

"Long . . . like the week."

There's an awkward silence, and I'm not getting any encouraging signs, so I decide to cut my losses.

"Well, I was just riding home from Nicole's and wanted to make sure you got back okay. I'll see you tomorrow."

I turn around and try to speed walk over to my bike, but he runs up behind me and takes me by the shoulder.

"Wait a second," he says. "Why are you in such a hurry?"

I turn around and try to read his face, but it's hard in the darkness.

"I don't know. I figured you'd be happy to see me. But you don't seem happy. So I thought I should leave."

"I *am* happy. It's just that I'm tired and I have to get up early for work."

("You gave two excuses. Which one's the real one?" I think as I remember what Nicole said to me just a couple of nights ago.)

"I completely understand. Let's just act like this never happened. We'll see each other tomorrow and run into each other's arms."

I really could use a laugh right here, but he looks serious.

"Why don't we go for a walk?" he says. "So we can talk."

All these signs are worrisome. I start to breathe heavily, but I try to hide it as Ben tells his uncle that he'll be right back.

I'm not sure how to describe the vibe as we walk down to the beach. Our chemistry feels completely different. The problem is that I don't know if this is because things have changed between us or if it's because he's tired and I made a mistake by coming over this late. I'm also a bit concerned by the fact that he said he wanted to talk, but he's keeping awfully quiet.

I decide to take charge of the conversation.

"If you want to talk about what went down with your parents and the judge, you know that I'm more than happy to listen," I tell him. "But if you just want to forget about that stuff, that's fine too."

He thinks for a moment. "Maybe another time, but right now I'm just happy to be away from it."

It's night, but it's still too hot and humid to snuggle as we walk down the beach together. We hold hands, but there's a formality to it.

"I hope you got to have at least some fun while you were up there."

"There was a big party at the lake, and I saw a lot of my friends from school," he says with a faint smile, "so that was fun."

I can't help it, but the first thing I do when I hear this is wonder whether or not his ex-girlfriend, Beth, was at the party. Amazingly, I resist the urge to ask him and instead let my crazy worrying stay in my head.

"What did you want to talk about?" I ask, not sure I really want to hear the answer.

"I really missed you," he says.

"I really missed you, too."

"But in a couple weeks I'll be going back for good and . . . I wonder if we should—"

I put my finger up against his lips to quiet him.

"Why don't you stop right there," I say. "We both know that September's coming. But I don't think we should talk about it. I think we should just enjoy the moment."

He takes a deep breath and considers this. "It's just—"

"I don't even want to talk about surfing," I say, cutting him off again. "I just want to hold your hand and walk along the beach."

"Okay," he says reluctantly. "We can do that."

We don't say much after that. We just walk, and as we do I hold on as tightly as I can.

The next few days aren't much better. Ben and I both smile and say all the right things, but there's a definite distance between us. He even cancels on me twice. Yesterday he backed out of lunch because there was a problem at work, and today I was supposed to give him another surf lesson, but he bailed at the last moment. He said that he had to go listen to a couple bands he was considering for the Sand Castle Dance. I offered to go along with him, but he said that since it was work, he really shouldn't bring anyone along.

I'm pretty sure he was about to break up with me on the beach, and now I wonder if I should have just let him do it. Rather than sit in my room so I could stress and obsess, I call Sophie and ask her to meet me at the pier for some intensive training.

"What's wrong?" Sophie asks when she sees the expression on my face.

"I don't really want to talk about it," I say. "I just want to work."

She nods. "Okay. Let's work."

I haven't mentioned it yet, but my new surfboard doesn't just look amazing. It is amazing. Mo told me that because our styles are so similar, she knew just how to shape it. (We'll call that the understatement of the year.) It's perfect in every way and feels like an extension of my body whenever I'm in the water. At first I was worried that it had too much curve to it, but that curve has opened up my ability to attack my cutbacks. That's what I'm working on today and the reason I called Sophie. She's great at them.

The cutback is probably the most important surfing maneuver of all. As the energy of the wave pushes you forward, you can get too far in front of it. When that happens you have to turn, or cutback, into the wave and go against it until you're closer to the power source. It lets you ride the wave longer and gives you the power to do bigger and better turns and maneuvers.

If you do a cutback right, you look like you belong in the Bolshoi Ballet. If you do it wrong, you look like my Uncle Barry doing the chicken dance at a wedding reception. After thirty minutes I'm looking more like Barry than Baryshnikov. I think this is partly due to the fact that I'm trying to add some flair to the maneuver in order to look good for the judges, but also because of my Ben funk.

"So tell me," I ask Sophie as we sit on our boards in the lineup, waiting for the next set of waves. "What am I doing wrong?"

She gives me that Sophie smirk and asks, "Are we talking about surfing or Ben?"

I think about it for a moment before answering. "Surfing."

"I think you're trying too hard. The thing that's so great about your technique is how smooth it is. But today you look uncomfortable, like you're fighting the waves."

I nod as I make mental notes.

"When you drop down into that turn, try leaning back more, right up to the point where you feel like you're going to fall into the wave. And then picture big round circles in your mind as you start to whip around. It will make the move more fluid and help you pick up speed. No wasted energy."

I think about this for a moment. "Okay," I say. "That all makes sense. I think I can do that."

"I know you can do it," she says, with just the right amount of enthusiasm in her voice.

We look back at the ocean and all we see are pancakes. There are no real waves coming our way, so we just bob quietly for a few moments until I break the silence.

"All right," I say with a smile. "What am I doing wrong with Ben?"

She thinks about it for a moment. "The same thing. I think you're trying too hard. You look uncomfortable."

"It's not just a look," I say. "I *am* uncomfortable. It used to be that when we walked on the beach our hands fit together like pieces of a puzzle. It was just perfect. But ever since he came back from Wisconsin, there's been a distance between us. Physical and emotional. I keep hoping it will go away, but it doesn't."

"Do you think it's because of what happened when he went home?" she asks. "Is he freaked out because of his parents' divorce?"

"Maybe." I shrug. "I have no way of knowing. He doesn't talk about it, and I'm too scared to ask."

"I understand him not volunteering it," she says. "But you can't be scared to ask him something. If you're a couple, you should be able to ask him anything you want. Don't be shy. You know what happens to timid surfers?"

"They wipe out."

"You bet they do. It's the same with boys. If you're timid, you wipe out. Now show me that cutback."

I see a set of waves coming right at us and pick out the one that's just for me. I catch it, and as I ride along the shoulder just ahead of where it's breaking, I think about the advice that Sophie gave me. I lean back farther and farther. At first it feels like I'm going to fall off the surfboard, but instead of falling I start picking up an amazing amount of speed. I shoot out in front of the break and do a wide sweeping turn known as a roundhouse. I can hear Sophie squealing with delight and cheering in the distance. After another hour of practice it's almost second nature.

By the time we're done, I'm exhausted. The practice has taken my mind off Ben, and the fact that my cutback has improved so much at least gives me something positive for the day.

"You own that move," Sophie says as we carry our boards back toward the shop. "You need to be that bold with Ben."

"I'll try," I say honestly. "But that's easier said than done."

"All the great things are."

Throughout the week I try my best to be bold with Ben. It's not my default setting, but I'm determined to do whatever I can to make things right. It works best one morning when I convince him to come out for another lesson. At first he's reluctant, but I'm able to fill the lulls in conversation with surf talk. Then the instruction starts to pay off, and he catches a few waves in a row. This is without a doubt the happiest I've seen him since he's come back from Wisconsin. And best of all, he doesn't pearl and end up with a bloody face this time.

I try to extend this emotion when we finish, so I tell him that I'm taking him out for lunch to celebrate his success. When he says that he really should get to work, I say, "I won't take no for an answer."

This is me being bold. This is also me being stupid, because he really does have a lot of work to do. We're only a few bites into our pizza when he gets an angry phone call from his uncle, wondering why he's late for work. Lunch ends abruptly and this blah vibe carries over into everything we do for the next few days. I pick a movie for us to see and it's terrible. I arrange a picnic on his lunch break and we get rained out. And unlike the movies, there's no romantic gazebo to hide under. Karma is doing everything it can to keep us apart.

On Tuesday we hit rock bottom.

Ben arrives at Surf Sisters with the summer campers, but we can't let any of them in the water because there's a rip current. It's hard because everything looks fine on the surface of the water and the kids don't understand. This makes them cranky, and when I try to convert the lesson so that it works on the beach, it all falls flat. Their bad mood boils over into mine, and I wrap up the lesson a half hour early.

"We're done?" Ben asks.

"Yeah," I say. "I've stretched it out as much as I can without going in the water."

"What am I supposed to do with them?" he asks. "The van won't be here to pick them up for another thirty minutes."

I'm sure that I will look back on this moment as a lost opportunity. But my funk keeps me from coming up with any creative solution to the problem. So, instead of saying, "We can go shell hunting," or something like that, I say, "I'm sure you'll figure out something."

He shakes his head and asks, "Why are you being this way?"

"Because I can't change the ocean current," I snap. "And I can't magically put kids in a good mood. And I sure can't seem to make you happy about anything."

It is totally irrational, and I can't believe it as I hear the words come out of my mouth. But that's what I say. I can't really read Ben's reaction. I'm not sure if he's angry or just confused, but I am totally off the rails. Luckily, Sophie has come down to help with the lesson, and she distracts the kids before they get to watch me break down.

"Who do you think can build a better sand castle?" she says. "The boys? Or the girls?"

The kids all shout, and within thirty seconds Sophie has them split into two groups who are happily building away. Fearful that I might start crying in front of everybody, I say a quick good-bye and head up to the shop. This is strategic on my part because I know that Ben can't leave the kids, so he won't be able to follow me.

I hide out in the shop's storeroom for about twenty minutes and make it back down just as they're finishing. The sand castles look great, and the kids are having a wonderful time. I'm really disappointed that I acted the way I did. I feel like I let them down. Ben walks up to me, and I still can't read his face.

"I'm really sorry," I say, convinced that it's too little too late.

"Me too," he replies.

There's an awkward silence.

"Do you want to do something tonight?" I ask, half prepared to hear him say that he doesn't ever want to do something with me.

"Sure," he says. "Whatever you want."

I am so not good at this. Considering my current track record of bad ideas, I decide to stop with the boldness.

"I want you to pick," I say. "None of my ideas seem to be working out too well lately."

He gives me a little smile. "The picnic almost worked out."

"You mean except for the thunderstorm."

"Yeah, but the sub sandwich tasted good. Wet . . . but good."

It feels nice to joke, even a little bit. "Still, I'll let you pick. Surprise me."

He nods. "I'll pick you up at eight."

*T*he ultimate surf maneuver is to ride inside the barrel or tube of a wave. It's super difficult, especially here in Florida where there aren't usually waves big enough, but when you do it, you are surrounded by water collapsing on you from all sides. Your only hope is to keep aiming for the light at the end of the barrel where you come back out again. That's how I'm feeling about things with Ben. Everything is collapsing around me, but I'm still aiming for that light, still hoping to ride this wave all the way in to the shore.

Since I don't know what he's got planned for us, I'm not sure what I should wear. I decide to turn a negative into a positive. Rather than worry about what's appropriate, I just pick out the cutest outfit I can find: a navy skater skirt with a white tank and a sleeveless plaid shirt. I like how it looks, but just to play it safe I text a quick picture to Nicole, and she responds with a row of smiley faces. The most important smiley face, though, is the one Ben shows me when I greet him at the door.

"You look great," he says.

"Thanks," I reply. "Is this appropriate for where we're going?"

"That all depends. Can you dance in it?"

Dancing. I like it already. I should always let him decide what we're doing.

"I can dance in anything," I say with some surprising confidence. "Where are we going dancing?"

"There's a party down the beach."

Suddenly my mood drops.

"Whose party?"

"I'm not exactly sure," he says. "Kayla promised that it was going to be huge and fun."

"Kayla?" I say, trying to control my anger. "Seriously?"

He looks utterly confused by my reaction. "Is that a problem? She invited us to a party, and I thought it would be fun."

"Kayla didn't invite *us* to a party. She invited *you* to a party because she likes you. She saw me have a breakdown today at camp and probably figures she's in the perfect position to swoop right in."

"No," he says, completely oblivious. "She knows you're coming with me. I thought you would like this."

"Why on earth would I like this?"

Is it possible that he doesn't know that Kayla and I are mortal enemies?

"You said you never get invited to these parties. I thought you might like to go to one and meet some new people."

I'm trying to keep my voice down so my parents don't hear, and as I take a deep breath, I realize why he went for this.

"Is that what this is about? You want me to *meet* people?"

"I don't see why that's a bad thing."

"I don't want your charity," I reply. "I don't need you to find people for me to hang out with once you're gone."

"It's not charity."

"Did it ever occur to you that I have in fact met all of these people? It's not that big an island. I've grown up with them, and they never became my friends. That's not going to magically change because they see me arrive at a party with you. They might be nice to me while you're around, but they'll be making fun of me the second we leave."

None of this has occurred to him, and I see him trying to make sense of what I'm saying.

"It's just a party," he says. "You said you wanted me to surprise you."

"Well, you certainly did that."

"We can just drop by and then do something else."

"You still want to drop by?" I reply, incredulous.

"I don't want to be rude. I told Kayla I'd go."

"Oh, yes. Let's make sure we look out for her feelings and not mine."

"Fine," he says. "We won't drop by. We can do something else."

"No," I say. "I don't feel like doing anything. You go to the party. You have fun. Meet all the people you want. I just want to stay home. Alone."

It's at this point that I think we might be breaking up. It is excruciating and painful and more than I can bear.

"Okay," he says. "I really am sorry."

There is a hesitation, and for an instant I think he can save the moment. I don't know what he could do, but I know I don't want it to continue this way. I look at him with sad eyes and wait for him to say something. Anything. But he doesn't. He bites his lower lip for a second, and then he turns and walks away.

I don't start to cry until I'm back in the house with the door shut. I don't know how I made it this far, but once I'm clear of the outside world, the tears start to fall. My mom comes down the hall toward me, and from her expression I can tell I failed miserably at making it so my parents didn't hear me. I bury my face into her shoulder. She doesn't say a word. She just puts her arm around me and hugs me tightly as I sob uncontrollably.

*I*zzy."

A hand grabs me by the shoulder and tries to wake me.

"Izzy, get up."

I am completely disoriented as I wake up from the deepest sleep. My eyes are still sore from last night's extended crying jag, and they're also bleary due to the early hour. I squint and look out the window and my fears are confirmed. It's still pitch-black outside.

"Dad? What time is it?"

"Five oh seven," he says.

My head slumps back onto the pillow. "Leave me alone. I need to sleep."

He yanks the pillow out from under me, and my head plonks down on the bed.

"Oww!"

"We'll take the pillow with us," he says. "You can sleep in the truck."

Now I am completely confused. "Where are we going?"

I'm finally able to focus on him as he flashes a huge grin.

"Sebastian!" he says. "It's going to be epic."

Now I'm starting to wake up. Sebastian Inlet is the best surf spot for over a hundred miles.

"How epic?" I ask.

"There are two hurricanes in the Caribbean, and according to the surf report the waves might be as big as we've seen in years."

I let this sink in. "We better get going."

Dad has an orange and blue Ford Bronco that was old when he got it back in college. It's not much to look at, but it's weathered decades of salt air and sand, and is the ultimate surf vehicle. We load our boards into the back and minutes later pull out onto A1A, the highway that runs right along the Florida coast. It's going to take us about an hour and a half to reach Sebastian, so I tuck my pillow against the window and fade off to sleep.

At the halfway point we pull off for a pit stop at a hole in the wall diner that serves amazing breakfast burritos. They have egg, peppers, chorizo sausage, and salsa all rolled up in a homemade tortilla. Dad and I stop here whenever we get the chance.

"That is so good," he says as he savors his first bite.

I'm still too tired to talk much, so I just nod my sleepy agreement and smile before taking another bite. We sit there silently eating for a moment until Dad catches me off guard with a comment.

"Despite what you may be thinking," he says, "Ben really cares about you."

I continue to eat in silence, but I flash him the expression that says I'm not interested in having this conversation.

He totally ignores it.

"He's probably not great at expressing it, but he's heart-broken about his parents. It makes him doubt everything."

I swallow another bite of my burrito and look right at him. "I don't want to talk about it, okay?"

He nods. "Okay. I just know you're hurting."

"I'm serious, Dad. I don't want to talk about it."

"All right, my mistake. Let's finish these in the Bronco and get back on the road."

We climb back up into the truck, and after silently finishing my burrito, I resume my sleeping position. I'm not actually sleeping this time, but I figure it's the best way to keep him from trying to talk about Ben.

When you drive along A1A, you can see the ocean in between gaps in the sand dunes, and with the sun rising over it, it all seems kind of magical. I think about what Dad was saying in the diner, and after about twenty minutes of mulling it over, I ask him, "How do you even know?"

"Know what?"

"That Ben cares about me? Parents just say that stuff to make their kids feel better. You can't know that."

"You're wrong about that," he says. "I can know it. I see it in the way he looks at you and in the way he talks to you. But I also know it because he's told me so."

Now I sit up and look right at him. "When?"

"We run together three times a week," he reminds me. "What do you think we talk about?"

"Sports?"

"No," he says. "Well, sometimes we do. But mostly we talk about life and things. He talks about you a lot."

"What does he say?" I demand. "I want specifics."

Dad shakes his head. "I can't tell you that. It wouldn't be fair. Just like I wouldn't tell him things you told me in confidence. But I can tell you that he cares about you more than he's cared about anyone in his life. You mean the world to him, Iz."

"It sure doesn't seem like it," I reply.

He smiles the same smile that he's smiled at me my whole life. "I know, baby. Being a teenager can be really confusing, can't it?"

"You're not kidding."

"Just remember that sometimes it can be amazing."

"Like when?"

"Like right now," he says as we pull in to the parking lot

and look out at the surf. The sun has just broken over the horizon, and there's enough light to see that the waves are amazing.

"You weren't kidding," I say, referring to his prediction. "Epic."

We spend hours surfing the inlet. It's crowded, so you have to wait your turn, but the wait is more than worth it. These are the biggest waves I've ever surfed, and the fact that I'm sharing them with my dad makes them even more special.

We're both working on specific skills to help at the King of the Beach. I'm still trying to be more aggressive, and Dad is practicing his carving. Carving is what you do when you make turns and dig the rail—the side of the surfboard—into the wave and send water spraying.

"You've gotten so much better," he says while we wait in the lineup. "It's unbelievable."

"Really?"

"Really," he says. "I bet you're ready to try an aerial."

"Come on. There's no way."

An aerial is when you ride up the face of the wave, launch into the air, and then come back down and land on the same wave. It's an incredible move, and not only have I never done it, I've never even tried it.

"The waves are big enough," he says with a wink. "You can get the speed."

I shake my head as though it's a ridiculous idea, but in my mind just a little part of me considers it. Completing an aerial would be awesome. I remember the first time I saw one. My dad and I were watching a DVD of surf highlights, and seemingly out of nowhere Kelly Slater just rocketed right off the wave. I couldn't believe it. I made Dad pause it and go through it frame by frame. Last year Bailey Kossoff did one during the King of the Beach, and that's the moment I knew he had it won.

"Just try it once," Dad says. "For me."

I give him another skeptical look, but I don't completely reject the idea. Am I good enough to land an aerial? I guess there's only one way to find out.

The next wave I catch is my biggest one of the day. I am flying across the face, and I pass up some prime turning opportunities to look for just the right spot. I see it on the lip and shoot right up into the air.

For an instant I feel like I'm flying. It's breathtaking.

I reach down and grab the rail with my right hand to keep the board from separating, and then I land back on the wave. Or rather, I try to land. I come in awkward and fall off the back, slamming hard into the ocean. It takes my breath away, figuratively and literally. That doesn't take away from the experience one bit. I try it a few more times, and each time I come close but struggle with the landing and wind up eating a face full of ocean. By the time we climb back into the Bronco, I am battered, bruised, and exhausted. I'm also inspired.

"So, what do you think?" asks Dad as he pulls out of the parking lot and back onto A1A.

I know he's asking me what I think about the day in general, but my answer is much more specific.

"What do I think?" I reply with a big grin on my face. "I think I can land it."

Dad cackles as we start to glide down the highway. "That's my girl."

As I blend in with the tourists near the bandshell, I watch the summer campers get picked up by their parents outside the Parks and Rec office. None can leave without sharing a high five or a supersecret handshake with Ben. Kayla's there too, which complicates things, but luckily she heads off in the opposite direction and doesn't see me. Once Ben is alone I walk over to him.

"Hey," I say quietly as we make eye contact.

"I tried to call you yesterday, but you never answered."

"Sorry about that. My dad and I went on a day trip that was kind of sudden."

There is an awkward pause before I ask the question that has been eating away at me for the last forty hours. It's one that I have to ask in person.

"Did we break up? The other night on my porch, was that what happened?"

He shrugs. "I don't know."

"Neither do I," I reply honestly.

We stand there for a moment, and I can tell that he's in real turmoil. I certainly don't want to be the cause of that.

"Can we maybe grab a bite at Mama Tacos and try to figure it out?" I suggest. "I promise there will be no drama. No raised voices. No tears."

"Sure," he says. "That sounds good."

Mama Tacos is at the other end of the boardwalk, so we hop into his truck and drive down Ocean Ave. I don't know what to say, so I just fiddle with the radio.

"Where'd you go?" he asks. "With your dad?"

"Sebastian Inlet. It's a great surf spot, and the waves were really good because of a couple storms out in the Caribbean. It's kind of our special place. We go there every once in a while but never with anyone else. It's always just the two of us."

"That's nice."

We arrive at Mama Tacos between the lunch and dinner rushes, so we're able to get a quiet booth in the back. Once we place our order, there's no one around to hear us talking.

"First of all, I want to apologize for how I acted the other day," I say. "In fact, for how I've acted a bunch lately."

"You didn't do anything wrong," he says. "I've been a mess. I'm trying to figure things out, and you keep getting caught in the cross fire."

"What are you trying to figure out?" I ask. "I'm not sure if I can help, but I'd like to try."

He picks up a tortilla chip and studies it for moment as he tries to think of what to say to me.

"We were a happy family when I was growing up," he says. "At least I thought we were. We took trips together. We had fun together. Everything seemed perfect. Well, the last few years weren't perfect. I knew my parents were arguing, but I still thought they loved each other. But the people I saw when I went home—I can't believe they ever loved each other. Not the way they acted."

"I'm so sorry," I say.

"You and your dad have . . . What's the name of the place where you went surfing?"

"Sebastian Inlet."

"Right. Sebastian Inlet. It's your special place. I bet just seeing it on a map makes you think of him and smile, right?"

"Yeah."

"My parents had that. There's a place in Michigan called Mackinac Island. It's beautiful, with old Victorian buildings. Very romantic. They went there when they were dating and liked it so much they had their wedding there. They even went back a few times for their anniversary. It was their special place."

"It sounds really nice," I say.

He looks up at me, and I see tears welling up in his eyes. "When we were going through everything with the judge, I found out that Dad already took his new girlfriend there. They even stayed in the same bed and breakfast where he and Mom got married. Why would he do that? I mean seriously, how messed up is that? Isn't it enough that he broke her heart? Isn't it enough that he has totally ruined everything? He has to go back and ruin the past, too?"

I reach across the table and take his hand, gently rubbing my thumb across his fingers.

"I wonder if she wishes that she never saw Mackinac Island in the first place," he says. "At least then it wouldn't hurt so much."

The conversation stops when the waiter brings our food, and I feel terrible for Ben and how he's feeling. Once we're alone again, I ask him a question.

"Do you wish you hadn't come into the shop that day to give us the poster?"

He doesn't hesitate at all. "Of course not."

"Neither do I," I tell him. "Even though I know it's going to hurt when you go home, I would not trade this summer for anything in the world."

He looks deep into my eyes. "Really?"

"Not one second of it . . . Well, maybe the meltdown on the beach the other day . . . and the fight on the porch . . . but other than that, not one second."

For a moment I think he's going to cry, but he holds it off and smiles.

"Neither would I."

"We don't have to put a label on this. We don't have to say that we're girlfriend and boyfriend. But I still want to spend as much time as I can with you before you go home. I've been a better version of me ever since I met you."

Now he reaches across and takes both of my hands.

"Me too."

*O*n Saturday I have him over to the house, and for the first time since he returned from Wisconsin, he seems like the old Ben.

"Are you ready for a surprise?" I ask as I greet him at the door.

"I guess so," he answers cautiously.

I get behind him and cover his eyes, which is not easy considering how tall he is. I guide him down the hallway and through the kitchen, and we only run into two chairs along the way.

"Happy Birthday!" I yell as I pull back my hands and reveal my miniature surprise party. There's a cake, a pizza, and three presents.

"This is surprising," he says with a crooked smile. "Especially because . . . it's not my birthday."

"I know that," I answer. "But tomorrow is the King of the Beach and we're both going to be really busy, so I thought we'd celebrate a day early. Besides, Mom and Dad are out, so I get you all to myself. No charades. No parents liking you more than they like me."

"You got me presents?" he says.

"And I baked a cake. There are a couple cracks on the top layer, but where other people might see that as a negative, I see it as a place to hide bonus frosting."

He leans over to give me a kiss, but it's just a peck. Our relationship is undefined, and at this point I'm determined not to push it any.

"Everything has a special meaning," I say as we sit down. "The pizza's a Big Lu from Luigi's Car Wash. . . ."

"In honor of our first meal together."

"Exactly."

"And the presents . . . They have special meaning too?"

"Why don't you open them and find out?"

First I hand him a flat, rectangular box. I have a slight panic attack as he starts to unwrap it, because I've never bought anything for a guy who isn't named Dad. I'm not sure if I found the right mix.

"Saltwater taffy!" he announces. "That means you—"

"Yes. That means I went into the wilderness that is the board-walk."

"With all those tourists?" he says, as though they were dangerous animals.

"What can I say? I'm dedicated. The taffy is to remind you of the differences between the tourist beach and the locals' beach. It was also my sweets backup in case the cake didn't turn out."

He unwraps a piece of candy and pops it in his mouth. "I know you say it's a scam, but I still stay it's delicious."

"I'm a little nervous about this next one," I tell him. "If you don't like it, you can return it. I promise it won't hurt my feelings. But if you like it, it's the final stage in your wardrobe makeover."

"I can hardly wait," he says as he opens the package.

It's a wool beanie with a Surf Sisters logo on it.

"I love it!" he says, much to my relief.

"I hear there's snow up in Wisconsin. So I wanted to make sure you can stay warm and have a little beach with you at the same time."

He tries it on and turns his head from side to side to model it for me. "How's it look?"

"Very nice," I say, in the understatement of the night. "Now, this last gift was hard to get. Consider it a birthday-slash-graduation present."

"Graduation from what?"

"Summer school," I say as I hand it to him. "You asked me to help you blend in, and after months of hard work, well . . . you'll see."

Even in the wrapping paper you can tell that it's obviously a

T-shirt, but he plays it up, holding it next to his ear and shaking it as though he were trying to figure out what it is.

"I have no idea what it is," he says. "It could be anything, but I hope it has Surf City written on it."

I slug him in the arm. "Another joke like that and you're going to have that cake all over your face."

He opens it, and when he sees what it is, he has the exact expression I was hoping for.

"I thought these were only for the locals," he says as he holds up an Islander T-shirt from the Islander Ice Cream Shop.

"I had a long talk with the owner," I explain. "Sophie and Nicole were there too, and we convinced him that you were a legit local. It helps that you were born here."

"I love it so much," he says as he holds it up to look at it closely. "I promise to wear it only on special occasions."

He turns to look at me, and for the moment at least, most of the distance that has been between us lately is gone. And it's not because of presents or anything superficial like that. It's because we've reconnected with the special moments from the summer. It's like the cutback; I turned and went back to the power source of our relationship.

Now, if only I could figure out exactly what that relationship was.

I take it as a good sign when we walk down to the beach to check on the sea turtle nest. We hold hands, and once again it feels natural and easy. There's no sign of activity around the nest, but the ocean seems more turbulent than usual. There's another tropical storm in the Caribbean, and it's sending bigger waves our way.

"I hope those keep up for the King of the Beach," I say.

"Are you nervous about it?" he asks.

"What? Nervous about competing against the best surfers in the state? Just a little."

"You can't let them intimidate you."

"It's pretty hard not to," I answer.

He thinks for a moment. "You should do that thing they tell you to do in order to relax before you give a speech. You know, you're supposed to imagine that everyone's in their underwear."

"They're already going to be in bathing suits," I point out. "Underwear's not that different."

"Good point," he says as he tries to think of a different tactic. "Then you should imagine they're in grass skirts and coconut bras."

This makes me laugh. "Well, that might do the trick."

"I like it when you laugh," he says. "I get to see that wrinkle in your chin. I've missed it."

I hold my chin up in the moonlight for him to see it.

"I'm sorry about everything," he says.

As he says this, he gives my shoulder an extra squeeze. I think back to what Sophie said, about telling him that I love him and giving him a chance to say it to me. Instead, I decide to fight that urge as we continue walking on the beach. It's taken a while, but I'm beginning to learn that sometimes it's best not to say anything at all.

*B*rrrrrrrrppppppppp!

The blast of an air horn rattles through the house, waking me from a very enjoyable sleep. Either I've traveled in a time machine back to World War II and we're under attack, or my dad is being totally dadlike.

Brrrrrrrrppppppppp!

Yeah, it's Dad.

"Good morning, sunshine," he says as he pokes his head in my door. "It's King of the Beach Day!"

"I thought Mom confiscated all of your air horns," I say as I wipe the sleep from my eyes.

"I had this one hidden for special occasions!"

He sticks his hand with the horn through the door, and I cover my ears just in time before he sounds another alarm.

Brrrrrrrppppppppppp!

"Can't I get a few more minutes of sleep?" I ask.

"Sure," he says. "But your bacon pancakes will get cold."

That wakes me right up. "You made bacon pancakes? You should have led with that and not the stupid air horn."

My dad makes amazing pancakes that have pieces of bacon mixed in with the batter. This lets you get the full spectrum of breakfast tastes in every bite. He makes them for me every year on my birthday. He's obviously stoked about the contest.

"Steady Eddie taught me how to surf," he says between bites. "I can't believe I get to compete on his team. This is a huge day for me."

We discuss strategy about picking the right waves and what we think the judges will be looking for. Then, after breakfast, we load the boards into the back of the Bronco and drive over to the pier.

All of the competitors are required to attend a meeting before the contest begins. It's held in a giant tent, where we have to sign in and pick up an information packet. Ben's working and I'm competing, so to make sure no one thinks there's any favoritism we keep the contact professional.

"Isabel Lucas," I say when I reach the front of the line.

"Which division are you competing in?" he asks. I can see that he's anxious to hear my answer.

"Main Event."

He flashes a broad smile.

"Excellent," he says as he checks my name off a sheet. "You are competitor number twenty-seven. Please sign here and pick up an information packet."

We both smile at our little charade. When I'm done signing, he adds, "Good luck today."

"Thank you."

I look down at the sign-up sheet and see that there are more than seventy competitors in the tournament. Over half of them are in the Main Event. Only the top eight finishers earn points, and that suddenly seems a whole lot more difficult.

Ben's uncle Bob, who is the Parks and Recreation director, addresses everybody at the meeting. He introduces the five judges and explains the basics of the competition. He goes into detail about how the surfers will be scored. Basically, each round lasts twenty-five minutes, and while you can ride up to six waves, only your top two scores will be counted. This was part of my strategy discussion with Dad. The important thing is to get two solid scoring rides in early. That way you have a chance to take some bigger risks on the final waves.

Once he's gone over all of the basics, Bob announces, "I need at least one representative from every team to stay, but everyone else can leave."

Even though I'm not the captain, I hang around to keep an eye on what happens next. The next five minutes could be the most important part of the day. There are a total of five teams in the team competition. In addition to Surf City and us, there is a team sponsored by a surf shop in Cocoa Beach, and two made up of friends who have joined forces.

Mickey is our captain, and she's the one representing us in the meeting. She stands away from the others and I don't know if this is her way of trying to protect our strategy or her way of avoiding Morgan Bullard. He's the manager and captain of the Surf City team and—surprise, surprise—he's a total jerk.

"I need everybody to turn in your final team rosters to the young man behind the table," Uncle Bob says, pointing to Ben.

Once again Mickey lags behind the others, trying not to show our hand.

"Why don't you save yourself some trouble, son, and start engraving these names on the trophy," Bullard says with a cocky wave as he slaps the Surf City roster on the table in front of Ben. "Everyone else is competing for second place."

Ben looks over the roster as Bullard starts to walk away.

"Excuse me, sir," he says, calling him back and making me cringe. "You have eight people registered for the Main Event."

"That's right," he says. "And I guarantee you that one of those eight is going to win."

"I want to make sure that you've read the rules," Ben says. "All of them."

I don't know where this is going, but I'm a little nervous. Mickey shoots me a raised eyebrow look.

"Surf City has won this trophy twelve years in a row," Bullard scoffs. "I'm pretty sure we've got the rules down."

"Then why did you forget to sign here?" he says, turning the roster back to him. "It needs your signature for the roster to be finalized."

Bullard is beyond annoyed as he scratches his name across the bottom of the paper. "I wrote nice and big to make sure you could read it," he says. "Are you happy now?"

Ben looks up to him and smiles broadly. "Extremely, sir."

Mickey is the last one to turn in a roster, and when she does, Ben looks it over carefully. He is obviously delighted, and I can tell that we've done what he was hoping we'd do. I linger around after the others leave and talk to Ben for a moment.

"Did any of the other teams enter surfers in all the different divisions?"

"No," he says. "Everyone on the other teams is entered in the Main Event. Surf Sisters was the only team to figure out the advantage of entering all the divisions."

I smile. "Let's hope it pays off."

A horn sounds, and I worry that it's my dad bringing his special brand of crazy to the beach, but Ben tells me that it's the ten-minute warning for the first competition.

"That's Menehunes," I say. "I'm going to go give Rebecca and Tyler a pep talk."

"See you later!" he says as I go in search of my junior surfers. "Remember to picture them in grass skirts and coconut bras!"

"I will," I call back to him.

Surf Sisters has staked out a chunk of beach for the staff and our families to cheer us on. Even though there would be big sales, Mickey and Mo decided to close the shop for the day so that everyone could come down and turn the event into a party atmosphere.

"Thank you for making this happen," Mo says as I walk up.

"What do you mean?"

"Competing in the King of the Beach was all your idea," she says, pointing to our cheering section. "You gave us something positive to think about. You saved the summer."

She gives me a huge hug.

"Well, here's hoping that we bring back a trophy to put up in the store."

She shakes her head. "I don't care if we finish last. This is a win. A huge win."

I know what she means, but I can't think that way. "Maybe so. But I have no intention of finishing last."

I walk down to the water with Rebecca and Tyler.

"Are you guys nervous?"

"Nope," says Tyler.

"No way," says Rebecca.

Their confidence takes me by surprise. "Not even a little?"

"Why should we be nervous?" Rebecca says. "We've practiced and we're ready. We're going to go out and do our best. If we win, we win. If someone beats us, then they probably deserve it. There's no shame in that."

Just like back in the Fourth of July parade, I think I just got schooled by the nine-year-old version of me.

"I like that."

"Besides," she continues with a confident gleam in her eye, "no one's going to beat us."

"Come on, Bec," Tyler says as they head out into the water. "Let's show 'em how it's done."

They wade into the ocean, and I am blown away. Sophie's been coaching them, and more than a little of her confidence has worn off on them. They back it up with their actions. Tyler rips off a couple of long rides to finish second, and Rebecca shows off the skills of someone at least four of five years older and wins the Menehune title going away.

They are swarmed by our cheering section when they come back up to the beach. After I give each of them a hug, I head over to the scoreboard and wait for the fireworks. Our secret is about to get out, and I want to be there for any reaction.

When Rebecca's and Tyler's scores are posted by our team name, we're moved up into first place in the standings. It takes about a minute or so before we see Morgan Bullard hotfooting it through the sand straight toward the scoring tent.

"How is it possible that Surf Sisters already has points on the scoreboard when the competition hasn't even started yet?" he bellows at Ben's uncle.

"The competition *has* started," Uncle Bob replies calmly. "We just completed the Menehune event, and the competitors from Surf Sisters took the top two places."

"Menehune?" he asks. "What do a bunch of little kids have to do with the King of the Beach?"

"According to the rules, a team can earn points in *any* division," Bob says.

"That's ridiculous," Bullard says.

"No," says Bob. "That's the rules."

Bullard thinks for a moment and realizes his vulnerability. "Does Surf Sisters have anyone in the other divisions?"

Bob turns to Ben, who hands him the roster. Bob looks it over and then turns back to Bullard. "The Surf Sisters team has competitors in each of the divisions."

I look up at Mickey and Mo and both of them are smiling.

"This is not right," Bullard replies. "I want to move some of my boys into the Teens division then."

"You can't."

I look over and see that Ben has entered the conversation.

"Your roster was finalized the moment you signed it," he says. "You can't change divisions."

Now Bullard is really putting things together, and he's not happy about it. He points an angry finger at Ben. "This boy is trying to rig this," he says to Bob. "He did not tell us about this rule!"

"Actually," Uncle Bob says, coming to the rescue, "this morning when he tried to make sure you knew the rules, you mocked him and treated him with disdain."

There's really nothing that Bullard can say in response to that, so he storms off. As he does, he passes right next to us and stops in front of Mickey and Mo. "Think you're clever, huh? It won't matter. My boys are still going to win this contest, and you are still going to be out of business once the summer's over."

The sisters don't even reply to him. Instead, they just bust out laughing, which only makes him angrier. He walks away, and they turn to me.

"Well," Mo says. "I think this is going to get pretty interesting."

*T*here are more than twenty competitors entered in the Teens division, and even though none of them are on the Surf City team, the group is loaded with talented surfers. Sophie and Nicole stand out because there aren't many girls, and Nic even more so because of her height. To keep the waves from getting too crowded they only go out in groups of six surfers at a time. Sophie's in the first group, so I stand with Nicole to watch.

"Look at Sophie," I say, pointing at her as she takes off on a wave.

The judges are looking for maneuvers that demonstrate speed, power, and flow. Sophie rips off a ride that demonstrates each as she attacks her wave with a series of cutbacks that show off her athleticism. It's a ten-point scoring system, and she gets sevens and eights across the board. She tops that a few minutes later, and by the time the buzzer sounds ending the session, she has the second highest score in her group. She's almost certain to make it into the finals.

Nicole doesn't go out until the last group, which is a shame. The waiting around has made her stiff, and seeing surfer after surfer post good scores has made her nervous. I try to calm her nerves before she goes out.

"Don't worry about the score," I say. "Just dominate the wave and the score will take care of itself."

Sophie and I join the rest of the group to cheer her on. She has twenty-five minutes, and despite some promising swells, she lets the first dozen waves go by without catching any.

"What's she doing?" Sophie asks. "Why does she keep letting them pass?"

"You know Nic," I say. "She's waiting for the perfect wave."

"She better not wait too long," she says. "She's only got fifteen minutes more."

Just then Nicole pops up on a beautiful wave. Normally, her height works against her, but she has such a smooth ride it just makes her look that much more elegant. She does a beautiful roundabout cutback, and as she rides it up the face of the wave and attacks the lip, a cheer erupts from our group.

Moments later the judges flash a series of eights and nines, one of the highest scores of the day.

"Okay," Sophie says, a bit relieved. "That was awesome."

Unfortunately, when Nic paddles back out there's a lull, and we start to worry that she'll run out of time.

"She needs two scores," Dad says. "She knows that, right?"

"She knows," I answer, without taking my eyes off her.

Even from this far away I can tell she's keeping calm. She knows the situation and she's not going to panic. Another wave comes, and even though it's not big, she paddles along and catches it. There's not much to work with, but she gets the most out of it, and we all feel relieved that she's going to post a second score.

And then the horn sounds, marking the end of the session.

Sophie's still riding her wave, which means she didn't complete it in time and that the judges don't give it a score. Despite the big number on her first wave, she's disqualified.

She stands up in waist deep water and hangs her head, waiting for a few moments before she slowly begins to wade in. Sophie and I rush down to console her.

"I'm so sorry," she says, as tears stream down her face. "That's incredibly stupid. I can't believe I did that."

"It's okay," says Sophie. "Thirty seconds more and you would have had it."

"We're still doing great," I say, trying to boost her spirits. "We are going to win this thing."

The good news is that Sophie did qualify for the finals, which means she's guaranteed to earn some points for the team. As the eight finalists stand side by side to pose for a picture, Sophie's size and gender are impossible to ignore. Not only is she the only girl, but the guys on both sides of her are nearly a foot taller.

You can tell they think they can intimidate her, which is funny if you know Sophie. A few minutes later, they're all out on the water and one of the tall guys tries to drop in on a wave that she's already riding. It's a total breach on his part, but rather than pull out, she keeps her line without flinching. To avoid a collision he has to bail, and Sophie ducks under his flying board and pops back up to ride the wave to its finish.

The Surf Sisters crowd goes wild, and the judges reward her with straight nines. She finishes in third place, a great showing in such a strong division. The team is definitely in the running.

*T*he Menehunes and Teens were both exciting, but I get goose bumps when the horn sounds to start the Legends. Mickey and Mo had both retired from competition before I was even born, so I've never gotten a chance to see them in this type of environment. With my dad thrown in, it's almost more than I can handle.

Right as they're about to start, I make eye contact with Ben. We're keeping our distance during the competition. Still, he smiles at me, and I can tell he's excited for this too.

"What am I looking for?" my mother asks me as we watch Dad paddle out to the lineup. She is the one member of the family who knows nothing about surfing. "How do I know if he's doing well?"

"It's all about showmanship," I say. "If he makes a long ride and manages to show off a little, we should be good."

Mom smiles. "Showing off is his specialty."

The girls and I laugh in agreement. "It sure is."

The first one of our Legends to catch a wave is Mo. She cuts a long, elegant line across the face and looks like she was born to surf. You'd never guess she was in her fifties, especially toward the end of her ride when she does something that no one else has done all day. She gets air.

It's not particularly high, but she rides up the face of the wave and launches. She doesn't even reach down and grab the rail. The board stays with her like it's glued onto her feet, and when she lands it, we are all in stunned silence.

"Did that just happen?" Sophie exclaims. "Did that really just happen?"

"Fifty-three years old and she pulls off an aerial," I say in amazement.

"Your dad's not going to do that, is he?" Mom asks, with more than a hint of worry in her voice.

"I don't think so, Mom. But up until a few seconds ago I didn't think Mo could do it either."

Mickey comes right behind her and floats along the top of the crest before pulling a fins-free snap, a sharp turn where the fins slide off the top of the wave.

As I watch her, I wonder what's going through her mind. I imagine she's channeling all of her emotions about the shop into this ride. Steady Eddie would be proud if he saw his girls today. They are something special.

"Here he comes," Mom squeals as Dad catches his first wave. "Don't fall, honey!"

We all laugh again, but Mom couldn't care less.

When we went to Sebastian, Dad practiced carving, and now it's really paying off. He is, to use the eighties lingo he loves so much, totally shredding the wave. Mom's squeals continue all the way until the judges post their scores of sixes and sevens.

"Is that good?" she asks me, uncertain.

"You bet," I say. "That's definitely going to put him in the top eight."

When the horn sounds ending the round, I'm happy because of how well they did, but a little sad that it's ending. It was great watching the three of them out there. They wade in together with big smiles on their faces. Mom wraps my dad in a huge hug that leaves her dripping wet. She couldn't care less.

"Not too shabby for a bunch of senior citizens," Mickey says as we all greet them. "Not too shabby at all."

It's no surprise that Mo and Mickey take first and second, and Dad is more than pleased with his fifth-place finish.

"My first . . . and last . . . surf contest," he says. "Fifth is more than I could have hoped for."

With the exception of Nicole's misstep in the Teens division, our plan has worked perfectly. We've picked up points in each division and have a big lead. That's the good part. The bad part is that Surf City is ready to dominate the Main Event and I'm the only one we've got left.

With so many people entered in the Main Event, there will be six different preliminary groups. The top sixteen will make the semifinals, and then the top eight will compete in the finals. I won't go out until the fourth group, so I try to relax while I wait my turn.

I watch the other competitors to get an idea of what types of moves and tricks they're doing, but mostly I try to visualize the waves and think about what I'm going to do. In the middle of this, Ben comes out of the scoring tent and walks over to me. Nicole and Sophie come over too, so they can hear what he has to say.

"How does it look?" I ask.

"You're still in it," he says. "But just making the final eight isn't going to do it. You won't have enough points."

I see the disappointment on Nicole's face and love it seconds later when Sophie puts a reassuring arm around her shoulder.

"How high do I have to finish?" I ask.

"It depends on how many from Surf City make the final, but I think you're going to have to finish in the top five for the team to win."

Gulp.

When it's time for my group, I paddle out just like I have every morning for more than a month. The pier feels like my surfing home now, except for the fact that it's filled with spectators. I try to block them all out and focus on the waves. I wash all doubt out of my mind.

When the first one comes along, I am amped and ready. The strategy is to get a solid score out of the way. I'm not going to do anything showy. I'm just going to surf smart.

I start to paddle along, and I can feel the wave grab hold of my board. I pop up and feel a surge of confidence as I race across the face of it. There's a moment of hesitation when I'm trying to decide if I want to carve or do a cutback, and it's in the middle of that hesitation when I pearl like a grommet, which is what we call a new and inexperienced surfer. The tip of my board digs into the water and sends me flying over the front. I slam face forward into the water.

Everything's in slow motion as I rag-doll underwater. I cannot believe it. This was supposed to be my safe ride and I don't even put up a score. I'm already behind. I instantly panic about time. I can't let it run out on me like it did on Nicole. I get back on my board and paddle back to the lineup.

The other surfers smirk when they see me. It's obvious to them that I have no business in the Main Event. As I wait my turn I feel like I have let everybody down, and I start to hyperventilate. Then one of the guys says something to me.

"What's up with him?" he asks as he points toward the pier.

Sophie warned me about getting distracted, so I ignore him. I'm straddling my board and looking for swells. But then I hear a laugh. And then another. The other surfers are all looking at the pier, so finally I look over too.

It's Ben.

He's standing at the end of the pier wearing a grass skirt and a coconut bra. It's just like he described to me and it makes me laugh. Sophie and Nicole are with him, and the three of them are all doing the hula.

This cures my panic attack. My friends know me well.

I take a slow breath. I see a wave coming, and now I am confident that I am dialed in. On the next wave I combine a floater, where you ride along the top, with a snap, when you shoot down off the wave, and then a roundabout cutback that is as pretty as any I've ever done. I finish by pumping across the wave, which is a showy form of carving, and finally end it by smacking the lip.

When I go back out to the lineup, the smirks are all gone. I can tell they wonder why they've never seen me before.

"What's your name?" one of the guys asks me.

"Izzy Lucas," I say as I straddle the board and catch my breath.

"Sweet ride, Izzy," he replies.

"Thanks."

$\mathcal{M}$y tenth-place finish in the first prelim easily puts me in the semifinal, but it's going to take more than that to make it to the finals. We go out in two groups of eight, and I am in the second group. This is good because it lets me rest a little and work up a strategy.

"What are you thinking?" Dad asks as he comes up to me.

"You know what I'm thinking," I tell him.

I can tell by his expression that he does. I thought I'd try the aerial in the final, but now I think I'm going to have to do it just to make it into the final eight.

"Don't forget that you have to post two scores," he says.

"Don't worry. I know what I'm doing."

I love the expression he gives me. It is one of total pride and confidence.

I let that confidence build inside me when I paddle out for the semifinals. Bailey Kossoff, the defending champion, is in this group. He's quiet and focused, and I study him to see what he's doing. He's the first one in the group to catch a wave, and he sets the bar high with an aggressive run that flows as easy as water.

"Damn," one of the other surfers says. "We're just playing for second."

I take off on the next wave, and even though I'm looking for a chance to get air, the wave doesn't really play out that way. Instead, I execute a flawless floater along the top, then I drop down and do what's called a vertical backhand snap. You build up as much speed as you can and then stick the board up off the top of the wave and whack it back down.

I feel good about it, but I still think it's going to take something bigger to get me into the finals. I'm determined that it be an aerial. I try to get air on each of the next two waves I catch, and even though I'm close to landing it, I fall off each time.

I paddle back out and am concerned about the amount of time I've got left. I've only posted one score, and if I try the aerial again and fail, I might not get another chance.

I can't think that way. I know I can do it, so I'm going to give it everything.

I catch the next wave and keep things basic with some carving while I look for the perfect spot to launch. It comes to me like a vision, and the wave unfolds perfectly. I take off into the air, and this time I don't reach down and grab the rail. I trust the board and fly. And fly. It feels like I'm up forever. My legs buckle a bit when I land it, but I stay on the board and feel a rush of adrenaline charge through my body. I do another cutback and finish my ride.

I'm too exhausted to go back, and even though there's a little bit of time left, I decide to call it for the round. If I have not posted high enough scores with those rides, it's just not going to happen. I wade up to the waterline and plop down on the sand.

"When did you learn to do that?" Sophie asks as she sits down next to me. "When did you learn to catch air?"

"Just now," I say with a laugh. "That's the first time I landed it."

"Well, you picked a pretty good first time," Nicole adds. "You really got up there."

Once I catch my breath, I get up and head over to the Surf Sisters crowd. My dad is beaming.

"I told you you could land it!"

I smile at him, but I'm still a nervous wreck.

We have to wait a few minutes for the scores to be tabulated, and when they are, I am in the final. I've climbed all the way up to sixth place, but that doesn't matter now, because all the scores are reset at zero for the finals.

Before we go out, all the finalists pose together for a picture beneath the King of the Beach sign. Not only am I the only girl in the group, but I'm also the only one who's not competing for Surf City.

I start walking over to Mickey and Mo to get some last second pointers when Morgan Bullard suddenly cuts me off.

"Morgan Bullard," he says, extending his hand to me. "Surf City."

"I know," I say. "I was there earlier when you were yelling at everybody."

He doesn't let this faze him one bit. He just chuckles and says, "What can I tell you? I'm passionate about surfing."

"Is that what you call it? Passion?"

"You were . . . impressive out there. Izzy, is it?"

I nod my head yes, my eyes wandering for Mo, wondering if she had anything to do with Morgan Bullard taking time out of his precious life to talk with me.

"I just wanted to introduce myself and say that there might be a spot on our team for you in the future. It's a sad thing that Surf Sisters is going to close, but I hope you'd consider joining up with us next season."

"That's very nice of you to offer," I say, mustering all the politeness I can.

"Well, it's not an official offer, not yet," he says. "I just want you to know it's a possibility."

"Of course," I say.

Bullard leans in to me, his lips mere inches from my ear. Considering that sharing an entire miles-long beach with this overly tanned "my surfboard don't stink" sellout is borderline unbearable, it takes each and every drop of my Zenlike calm to bare his intrusive stance.

"Think about it," Bullard whispers, turning to leave as Ben comes to my rescue, ready to give me the latest on scoring.

"You're amazing," Ben says. "When you flew up in the air, I had chills. I am so proud of you."

"Thanks," I say, trying to shake my run-in with Bullard and keep my focus on what's still to come. "What's the magic number? How high do I have to finish?"

"Third," he says, and I feel the air race out of my lungs.

"Really? Third? I thought you said top five."

"That was before Surf City took all of the seven other spots in the Main Event final. Fourth would tie it, but Surf City would win the tiebreaker. You're going to need third to get the trophy."

At this point my strategy is simple. I have to surf better than I ever have in my life to get to third place. I need to post two monster scores. There's no value in getting a couple of safe scores out of the way like in the earlier rounds. I've got to go for as much as I can get.

I come out swinging and nail an aerial on my first ride. I don't know how far I get into the air, but Bailey Kossoff high-fives me when I get back to the lineup. I have another great run during which I pull several moves in quick succession, each one flowing directly into the next. In a weird way they all play like music in my head, as if I'm riding from note to note.

I feel good about my rides, but it doesn't feel like third. I need one more and I need it to be epic. As the clock winds down, the only two people left in the lineup are Bailey and me.

"It's all yours," he calls out as a wave comes. I start to paddle, but then I pull off. I don't think it's going to be any good. He smiles and takes it instead. A part of me worries that I just blew it.

I know I'm short on time, but there's something I've learned coming out here every day. The pier is an odd break, and a lot of times after there is a set of good waves, there will be one stray wave that comes along even better. I look down at the board for a moment and see the Eye of the Storm design. It gives me focus. Then I look back at the water and see the stray wave I was hoping for.

"There it is!" I say, even though no one is around to hear me.

I lie flat on my stomach and paddle with all I've got. I try to flush everything out of my mind, but I can't. Except, instead of thinking about the wave and surfing, I think about everything else. All these images shoot through my mind: meeting Ben, teaching the campers, the kiss on the end of the pier, waving good-bye to him at the airport, the look on Nicole's face when we got our surfboards. It's like I'm watching ten televisions at once.

A wave is a cosmic event, and this one is more than just the gravitational pull of the moon and the force of the ocean. This wave is the result of a summer like none I've ever had before. My ride is almost dreamlike. And before I know it I am surrounded by water on all sides. I am in the barrel of the wave, and everything is collapsing around me as I shoot for the light at the end of the tunnel.

I can imagine how nuts they're going up in our little cheering section, and when I burst back out of the tube and ride up the face of the wave, I feel invincible. I snap back and turn and ride until the last bit of it dies off. That's when I step off into the shallow water. It's like I'm asleep, and then the horn sounds and wakes me up. Time's up. I finished with only seconds to spare, but I finished in time.

The first two to greet me are Nicole and Sophie, who wrap me in a hug so violent that we end up crashing into the water.

"That was awesome!" Sophie screams. "Awesome!"

It's strange because, other than when I rode through the tube, I'm not really sure how it went. I just kind of did it all by instinct.

"Oh my God, Izzy!" Nicole says as she kicks water on me. "Oh my God!"

I pick up the board and we walk up onto the beach, where I take off my leash and sit on the sand to catch my breath. I can see a lot of activity in the scoring tent as they add up the final scores, and I get up and walk over there.

"Sweet ride, Surf Sister," Bailey says as I walk by him. "Very sweet."

"Oh, and Bailey!" I shout after him. He turns around, swiping away the wet hair sticking to his forehead. "Tell your fearless leader thanks, but no thanks." With a deep breath, I try to take it all in. The beach, the sound of the ocean, the amazing feeling rushing through me. "I can't surf for him. I won't."

Bailey smiles. "I'd hope not. Till next time, Surf Sister," he says, joining his team, already congratulating him.

Mo breaks free from the clutch of people in the scoring tent and walks over to me. Her eyes are red, and I think she's about to cry. My heart sinks.

"Did I make it?" I ask. "Did I finish third?"

She quietly shakes her head. "No, sweetie. You didn't."

Heartbroken, I lower my head forward onto her shoulder. She puts her arm around me and pats my back. And then she whispers something into my ear that I never imagined I could possibly hear.

"You won."

*T*he Surf Sisters victory celebration starts on the beach and migrates to the shop, where it turns into a full-fledged party with music and food. There are more celebratory hugs and kisses than I can count, and at one point I even cry when Mickey and Mo have me pose for a picture with the King of the Beach trophy in front of the original STEADY EDDIE'S SURF SCHOOL sign.

Hours later it still hasn't sunk in. I cannot believe that I won. I don't know how I did it. I've heard various descriptions of the final wave, but I still don't remember most of it. But that's more than okay right now as I slow dance with Ben on the roof of the shop. It seems an appropriate location considering this was the place where I challenged everyone to try to win back the trophy from Surf City. But never in my wildest dreams did I see us actually doing it.

"If you're the King of the Beach, what does that make me?" asks Ben. "The First Dude? The Royal Boyfriend?"

"Boyfriend?" I ask with a raised eyebrow. "Is that a label we're using?"

He hems and haws for a moment.

"I win King of the Beach and suddenly we're boyfriend and girlfriend again?"

Now he looks horrified, and I bust out laughing.

"I'm just kidding," I say. "You pretty much sealed the deal as my boyfriend the moment you put on the coconut bra and danced the hula. That saved me. I was panicked and flustered, but when I saw you out there on the pier, I realized that everything was going to work out. And not just in the contest. Everything."

"The end of the pier's been pretty good for us," he says.

"It most definitely has."

He leans over and gives me a quick kiss.

"You know, at some point, we're going to have to have the talk."

I look up at him as we sway to the Hawaiian music wafting from the sound system below. We have not talked about how all of this comes to an end. There haven't been any discussions of attempts to make something work long distance. It's so complicated. But I'm still not ready to say it all out loud.

"I've got ten days left in the most amazing summer of my life. I know it's going to end, but there's nothing that I can do about that. So I'm going to make the most out of every one of those days."

"You certainly did that today."

I allow myself a moment of pride as I flash a big grin. "I did, didn't I?"

"Okay," he says. "We'll wait and have the talk the night before I leave."

"At the end of the pier," I say. "But for now we just dance."

He gives me a little look. "I didn't realize you were in charge."

"You didn't? We're on the beach and I am the king. I've got a trophy over there to prove it."

He laughs some more and holds me tighter. I press my ear against his chest, and we continue to move to the mellow music. I feel completely different than I have ever felt in my entire life.

*E*arlier in the summer I had expected that these last days would be the worst. I thought I'd be filled with dread as the clock kept counting down toward August twenty-fifth. Oddly, that's not the case. I don't know if it's because I'm living in some sort of denial and will be a total cry factory on the twenty-fourth, or if I've somehow come to accept that I can't control the things I can't control. This is not to say there aren't moments when I get in a funk or wallow in a momentary flurry of self-pity. But for the most part these are just quick and they pass.

The last day of summer camp is memorable because all of the kids celebrate our victory in the King of the Beach. As members of the Surf Sisters team, Rebecca, Tyler, and I are presented with cardboard crowns that we wear for most of the class. Normally I wouldn't, but the kids really want me to, and I can tell that it drives Kayla crazy. Ben has a special little waterproof camera that he uses to shoot video of all the kids surfing. Then he pulls out a surprise and shows them how good he's gotten at surfing too. At the end of the class, we have a graduation ceremony where Mickey and Mo present them with their official surf-plomas and we all pose for a group picture.

Every night Ben and I walk on the beach and check on the turtle's nest. Sometimes we just sit there in the sand for over an hour looking at the nest and talking about anything and everything, except for the future. Then one night we're about to get up when I notice the sand above the nest shift ever so slightly.

"Check it out," I whisper. "I think it's time."

The sand begins to drain down and we see a tiny loggerhead, less than two inches long, pop his head up from underground.

"He's so tiny," says Ben. "How does he grow to be so big?"

There's a flurry of activity, and one by one little turtle heads start popping up from the sand as the hatchlings use their tiny flippers to crawl out onto the beach. Within thirty seconds, there are nearly a hundred of them.

"Look at them all!" he says in total amazement.

"They're going to follow the moonlight," I remind him. "The reflection of the moon on the ocean is their guide."

"This is the most amazing thing I've ever seen." Ben looks over at me in the moonlight and adds, "Well, maybe the second most amazing thing."

"Is that so?" I ask. "What's first?"

He gives me a coy shrug, then gets up onto his feet and follows behind the hatchlings as they scamper to the sea.

I follow too, and once the last turtle reaches the water, I hug Ben from behind and press my cheek up against his back.

"What's the most amazing thing you ever saw?"

"There was this girl," he says. "And she had a wrinkle in her chin."

"And eyes that seemed to change colors?" I joke.

"That's right," he says. "And a big old guacamole stain on her shirt."

He turns around to face me, but I still keep my arms around him.

"You're never going to let me live that down, are you?"

"Well, I'm certainly never going to forget it."

"You also better not forget that I have pictures of you . . . on the beach . . . in shoes and socks, coach's shorts, a belt, and a tucked-in shirt. I'm talking photographic evidence that can be enlarged and printed."

He pulls me even closer. "I only dressed that way to get your attention. I knew that you'd have to rescue me."

I stand up on my tiptoes and give him a kiss. I close my eyes when I do and let my lips linger on his for a moment.

"You know, I haven't officially asked you to the Sand Castle Dance," he says.

"I was wondering when you'd get around to that," I say. "And I think it was a big oversight on your part."

"Is that so?"

"Earlier in the summer I'm sure I would have jumped at the chance to go with you. But now that I'm King of the Beach, I've got other offers to consider."

He looks down at me, and I can see the moonlight in his eyes.

"Don't even joke like that," he says.

I give him an apology kiss. "I'm sorry."

"Isabel Lucas, would you like to go to the Sand Castle Dance with me?"

"More than you can possibly know."

He kisses me again, and then we walk back down the beach. There are three days left of summer.

*F*or more than fifty years the Sand Castle Dance has signaled the end of the summer season as the locals come out to the bandshell to dance the night away. Nicole and I have been many times, but this year is significant because it's the first time we'll be going with dates. We're at my house and I'm putting on the finishing touches.

"You look amazing," Nic says when she sees me in my dress.

"Really?"

"Absolutely."

"So do you," I say.

I'm wearing a white summer dress with floral lace over a soft interior layer. I'm hoping to strike a balance between cute and comfortable that will still look good after hours of dancing outside on a hot and humid night. A tall order indeed.

Officially Ben and I are doubling with Nicole and Cody. Sophie's boyfriend, from Florida State, is coming, but they're going to meet us there.

"Can you believe this summer?" I ask her. "I mean seriously."

"It's been a whirlwind," she says. "Starting with Sophie's first day back at the shop."

"That's the day I met Ben."

"And the day you sentenced me to talk to Cody."

I smile. "That turned out to be a good day for us."

She looks at me, and I can tell that she's concerned. "Are you going to be okay?"

I nod. "I'm going to have to be."

"Have you told him?"

I shake my head. "No."

She goes to say something else, but there's a knock on the door.

"They're here!" I say as I get up and start to walk down the hall to the front door.

Nicole comes right behind me, and before I answer it, she takes me by the shoulder. "Tell him how you feel. You owe it to him and you owe it to yourself."

I nod.

Both of us take a breath and we open the door. Ben and Cody are standing together on the porch. In keeping with tradition, each one is wearing board shorts, a short sleeve button-down shirt, and a tie.

"Okay . . . wow!" Ben says. "You look sensational."

"You look pretty good yourself," I say, trying not to blush too much.

The dance is great. The band, which Ben picked out, is fun and plays covers of music from all different eras. This is important because the dance is for all ages. There are couples who have been married for more than fifty years dancing right next to teenagers like us.

"I know our big talk isn't until tomorrow night," I say while we're slow dancing. "But there is something that I kind of need to tell you tonight."

"Sure," he says. "What is it?"

"I lied to you."

He looks down at me with deep concern in his eyes. "When?"

"The first time we climbed up into the lifeguard stand. I asked you about Beth and why you broke up."

"That was a fun conversation."

"Anyway, you told me that you broke up with her because she loved you and you didn't feel that way toward her. Then I said—"

"'Lucky for us we don't have to worry about that,'" he says, quoting me from that night. "'We both know that this is just for the summer.'"

"So, you really do remember," I say, surprised.

"I really do," he says.

"It was a lie," I say.

"I know."

This catches me off guard. "What do you mean, you know?"

"I knew it was a lie that night. You were worried that if you told me that you loved me, then I might break up with you, too."

I stop dancing and look right at him. "You knew that I loved you?"

He nods.

"But you didn't break up with me."

He shakes his head.

"Does that mean . . ."

"That I love you too?" he says. "Yes, it does. I've loved you from the beginning, Izzy. I am hopelessly, helplessly in love with you. Don't you know that?"

Tears stream down my face. "Well, I do now."

Luckily there are a couple more slow dances in a row, which gives me a chance to compose myself.

"Very nice, Ben," Sophie says as we go back to a table and meet with the others. "You have organized a very nice Sand Castle Dance."

"Why, thank you," he says.

The boys head over to the snack bar to get us some sodas, and Nicole sees the tears in my eyes.

"You told him, didn't you?"

I nod.

"And?" asks Sophie.

"And," I say, "he loves me too."

This is the moment it hits me. This is the moment I realize what's really been bothering me. I haven't been worried that he didn't love me. I've been worried that he did. Because that makes what's about to happen all that much worse.

"He's loves me and he's leaving."

"You're going to be okay," Nicole says. "You really are."

I nod. "I know. It's just hard to imagine."

I try to compose myself again as I see the boys come our way. Then the most unexpected thing happens.

"'The Rockafeller Skank'!" I shout as the music blares from the speakers.

The band has taken a break and a DJ has taken over.

"Did you do this?" I ask Sophie.

"No, I didn't," she says, laughing.

The boys reach the table and I turn to Ben. "Did you pick this song?"

He nods. "I picked all the music. You like it?"

I smile. "You could say that."

I look at each of the girls, and we know exactly what we have to do.

"All right, boys," Sophie says. "Try to keep up."

The three boys have no idea what's about to happen, but Sophie, Nicole, and I all head out to the dance floor, turn to face them, and do the once unthinkable. We unleash the Albatross in full public view.

The shy girl that was once me is no longer.

*A*ugust twenty-fourth is Ben's last full day in Pearl Beach. Unfortunately, I'm not the only one in his life, and I have to share this day with others. He has a shift at Parks and Recreation, and they take him out to lunch. He also has to eat dinner with his aunt and uncle. That means I get a little bit of time with him in the afternoon, and then we're meeting on the pier after dinner.

Judging by the tears that started falling at the dance, I'm beginning to worry about how emotional that conversation will get, but I'm determined to keep things light and happy in the afternoon when he comes to say his good-byes at Surf Sisters. That is, *if* he comes by. At the moment, he's forty-five minutes late.

"Stop looking out the window," Sophie says. "He'll get here when he gets here."

"I know. You're right."

The phone rings and I see that it's him.

"Hey," I say. "Where are you?"

"I'm sorry," he replies. "I got held up at work. Is either Mickey or Mo there?"

"Mo's off today, but Mickey's here. Why?"

"I need to talk to her," he says cryptically. "It's important."

This all strikes me as odd, but I take the phone to Mickey and they have a brief conversation.

"What's all this about?" I ask when I get back on the call.

"I'll explain it when I get there."

And just like that he hangs up.

Twenty minutes later, Mo arrives with a man I don't know, and the two of them meet with Mickey in the garage.

"What's going on?" Nicole asks.

"I have no idea," I reply.

Finally Ben walks into the shop. He smiles when he sees me and gives me a huge hug and a kiss.

"Sorry I'm late," he says. "Where are Mickey and Mo?"

"In the garage," I answer. "Why?"

He smiles again. "Come on. I'll tell you when I tell them."

Luckily there aren't many customers, so Sophie, Nicole, and I are all able to follow Ben into the garage.

"I'm sorry I've been so cryptic," Ben says, addressing us. "But I've been trying to come up with a really great good-bye present for Izzy, and I think I've done it."

We're all confused.

"What's your present?" asks Mo.

"I think I've figured out how to save the shop."

Mickey and Mo both gasp. The three of us girls are equally breathless.

"What are you talking about?" asks Mo.

"It's the best present I could think of," says Ben. "Izzy loves this place, so I thought that I should try to save it. You see, my dad's a pretty awful husband, but he's an amazing attorney. We'd always talk about the cases he was working on, and he taught me how to look for loopholes."

"Like the team loophole in the King of the Beach?" I say.

"Exactly."

"And you found a loophole that helps us?" asks Mo, trying to contain her excitement.

"I hope so," he says. "Is this the attorney you told me about?" He motions to the man with them.

"Yes," the man says.

Mickey and Mo are practically glowing with excitement.

"What's the loophole?" asks Mickey.

"Luigi's Car Wash," says Ben.

It takes a moment to set in, but everyone in the room, except for Ben, deflates. He doesn't realize that they've already pursued this option.

"Luigi's Car Wash is protected because of the laws that were in effect when it first opened," Ben says, continuing. "Luigi can't be forced to sell his property and neither can you."

"Actually, we can," says Mo, her hopes dashed. "Surf Sisters opened four months after the new law was passed. We're not protected."

"No," Ben says. "Surf Sisters isn't protected." He unzips his backpack and pulls out a large file. "But Steady Eddie's Surf School is."

He hands the file to the attorney and continues. "Part of my job this summer was turning old paper files into digital ones. I had to scan thousands of documents that the Parks and Recreation Department has accumulated. Among those files were contracts for Steady Eddie's Surf School to teach surfing and water safety to the summer campers. These contracts go back more than twenty years before Mickey and Mo founded Surf Sisters. The address on all of those contracts is his house, which I believe is the building we are standing in right now."

I look over and see Mickey and Mo are on the verge of tears.

"Even to this day, Steady Eddie's Surf School is listed in the contracts. That means that the same business has been operating out of the same building for more than fifty years, which more than meets the standards of the law."

Mo is the first one to reach him. She wraps her arms around him and gives him a huge hug. Mickey is right behind.

"How did you do this?" Mo asks.

Ben shrugs his shoulder. "What do you mean?"

"I mean, what made you come up with all of this?"

"That's easy," he says. "Izzy loves you . . . and I love Izzy."

*T*he full moon hangs over the ocean and floods its light across the waves. I walk down the pier and try to think of what I can possibly say to Ben. He has just given me the most amazing summer of my life, and tonight I'm going to have to say good-bye to him. Technically, I'll say good-bye tomorrow at the airport. But there will be people there and a plane to catch. This will be the real good-bye. Just the two of us on *our pier*.

I look ahead and see that he is already waiting. His back is turned to me as he sits on the end of the pier, and even though he is only a silhouette in the moonlight, I know every inch of him.

Wordlessly, I sit down next to him and take his hand.

He turns to me and starts to talk, but I press my finger against his lips so I can speak first.

"I've thought about it, and even though people say that long distance doesn't work, I'm not about to let you walk away forever. We can video chat and call and write. Certainly you'll come down and visit your uncle, and I'm already saving up money to fly to Wisconsin. You can show me Madison just like I showed you Pearl Beach. And we're only a couple years away from college. For all we know, we might end up at the same school."

He shakes his head ever so slightly, and I feel my heart sink.

"I don't think that will work."

"Why not?"

He reaches over and touches my cheek with his hand. "It turns out that my mother wasn't exactly honest with me."

"How do you mean?"

"When she told me that she wanted me to spend the summer down here to protect me from all the arguments, that wasn't the only reason she wanted me to come here."

"What was the other reason?"

"She wanted me to see if I liked it here," he says. "She's planning on moving back to Pearl Beach to start a new life after the divorce is final. The only question is whether she's going to do it now or after I graduate from high school."

"When did you find out?"

"Tonight at dinner. She flew down to surprise me and talk to me about it. If we decide to stay, she's going to start looking for a new job."

My heart races.

"How will she decide?"

"She told me that it's my decision," he says. "She knows it's hard to move in the middle of high school. And all of my life is up there. . . . Well, almost all of it."

"Don't move here because of me," I say.

"What?"

"It's not fair to you and it's not fair to me," I say. "I would love for you to live here. But if you move here because of me, then anytime that something goes wrong, it will be my fault. You'll end up resenting me. If you really love me like I love you, then we'll figure out a way to make the distance work. But if you move here, it has to be because you think that this is home."

"I know," he says. "I came to the same conclusion. Which is hard because you're a big part of everything that's here. I've spent the last hour debating back and forth, trying to figure out the right thing to do."

"Good," I say.

He stands up and looks out over the water. I stand up next to him.

"Actually," he says, "I spent fifty minutes of it trying to figure out the right thing to do . . . and ten trying to figure out how to tell you."

That sounds ominous, but oddly I feel strong enough to hear it, even if it means he's heading home. He turns so that he's looking right at me and his back is toward the ocean.

"Okay," I say. "I'm ready. Whatever it is."

He has a strange look on his face, and it takes me a moment to realize that he's slowly falling backward. By the time I do, I reach out to grab him, but it's too late. He plummets toward the water fifteen feet below and lands with a big splash.

I let out a surprised squeal as I look down at him. "What on earth are you doing?"

"First of all, it's not on earth, it's in the sea," he calls up. "And it's just what all good loggerheads do. I'm following the moonlight into the ocean."

I look down and see that smile, that amazing smile, as he looks up at me from the dark water.

"What's your decision?"

"You're going to have to come down here to find out."

"How's the water?"

"How do you think it is? It's awfslome!"

I empty my pockets, take off my sandals, and without so much as a second thought, I jump. I feel a charge rush through my body, and I close my eyes to brace for the impact, ready to splash into the water and see where the current takes me.

STEADY EDDIE'S
SURF SCHOOL GLOSSARY

aerial: when a surfer rides up the face of a wave, launches into the air, and comes back down, landing on the same wave

barrel: a breaking, hollow wave, also called a tube

boogie board: also known as a body board; used in order to ride waves lying flat on the belly

carving: turning on top of a wave

cutback: turning back into the wave, closer to the wave's power source

duck dive: paddling under a wave that is coming straight at a surfer

fin: the curved piece underneath the surfboard

fins-fee snap: a sharp turn where the fins slide off the top of the wave

fish: a short and thick surfboard used to ride smaller waves

floater: when a surfer rides along the top of a wave

grommet: a new and inexperienced surfer

hang ten: riding a surfboard with the toes of both feet hugging the front edge

Kelly Slater: born and raised in Florida; considered to be the greatest surfer of all time

leash: the cord that attaches a surfer's ankle to the surfboard

pearl: when the nose of the surfboard digs under the water and propels the surfer over the front of the board

rail: the side edge of a surfboard

rash guard: a swim shirt worn to protect one's skin from the wax and sand on the surfboard

rip current: a strong current flowing from the shore out toward the sea

roundhouse: turning one hundred and eighty degrees

snap: when a surfer shoots down the top of a wave

soft board: a beginner's surfboard with a soft, foam top

stringer: a thin strip of wood that runs down the center of a surfboard, making it stronger

shred: term used to describe a person surfing well

vertical backhand snap: when a surfer builds up as much speed as possible before sticking the board up off the top of the wave and whacking it back down

SWEPT AWAY

For Tom S.

Who possibly knows everything.

And definitely knows more than I do!

June

Why do lupine flowers have to be such an old-lady color?"

I open one eye, then the other. I squint at my best friend, Cynthia Crowley, who stands in front of the full-length mirror hanging on the back of her bedroom door. She fluffs the grayish-bluish-lavenderish skirt of her formal dress.

She isn't all wrong. If you've ever been to Maine, you've seen lupines. They're the tall, spiky, green-leafed plants that kind of look like corn on the cob on top, but with flowers instead of kernels. They're everywhere. Standing proud like soldiers in gardens, marching along the roadside, reproduced on tea towels, souvenir mugs, and postcards. Even T-shirts—though I don't think any Mainers wear those, just tourists.

Lupine flowers are all kinds of purple in real life. Translated into Cynthia's gown, the color somehow ended up pretty fusty. But that's what happens when the Ladies of the Lupine Festival League sew the dress themselves.

I shut my eyes again and fling my arm over my face to block out the morning light streaming through the bay window. "Why does the Lupine Queen have to begin her reign at the crack of dawn?" I moan.

I hear the rustle of chiffon and fake flowers and know Cynthia is about to pounce.

"Good morning, good *morning!*" she belts out in her "I'm going to be a Broadway star" voice. The song is from one of her favorite old movie musicals, one with lots of singing and dancing, and I can see why she likes it. I guess I kind of like it too. I actually prefer blockbuster action films, but Cynthia thinks they're "juvenile."

I roll away from Cynthia just as she lands on the bed. She bounces on her knees the way we used to in third grade, jostling me so much I grab one of the poles of her four-poster bed to keep from rolling off. The bright blue canopy flutters above us. *Everything* in Cynthia's room is a bright color—and usually bejeweled, appliquéd, or fringed, too.

"Your dress!" I scold. "You'll ruin it!" Only I'm laughing so hard I doubt she understands me.

I pull myself up to a sitting position and lean against one of her many jewel-toned pillows. I rub my face. "How come we both got zero sleep," I grumble, "and you're already dressed and looking camera ready?"

Cynthia gives me one of her coy "li'l ol' me?" looks. "Just the kind of girl I am," she quips in a babyish voice.

She isn't wrong about that, either. When Cynthia wakes up, she's ready to start the day. All energy, enthusiasm, and blond hair. It's why she's had boys pursuing her since they stopped seeing girls as cootie carriers.

Me, not so much. Sure, I've had boys ask me out sometimes, but mostly as a way to penetrate Cynthia's inner circle, since I'm the innermost ring. At least, that's how I figure it.

Cynthia climbs off the bed in a flurry of chiffon. "Seriously,

Mandy," she says in her normal voice. "I have to be there at nine for the kickoff at ten. You've got to get ready."

"I can't believe you're abandoning me for the summer for musical-theater camp!" I pull a bejeweled pillow onto my stomach and punch it. Then I tuck it behind my head and add sulkily, "Even though I'm very happy for you."

I really *am* happy for her. Mostly. I know how much going to camp means to her. She's taken tap, ballet, jazz, and hip-hop dance classes since she could walk, along with voice lessons that were a whole hour drive away. Since I've known her, Cynthia's been itching to get out of "Rock Bottom" (her name for Rocky Point) to pursue her performing-arts dreams. I wish I had such direction. My mom wishes I did too.

I force myself up off the bed and cross to the window. If I get into the exact right position, I can see the lighthouse peeking out of the morning fog, overlooking the restless sea. Red stripes circle its white three-story tower, so everyone calls it Candy Cane. The skinny strips of Maine's jagged coastline reach out like tentacles, as if they're trying to grab the many islands that pepper the waters, with Candy Cane the striped fingernail on the finger that is Rocky Point.

Before there was even a real town here, there was the lighthouse. It was decommissioned long before I was born, another sign, according to Cynthia, of how unimportant Rocky Point is to the rest of the world.

This, she isn't exactly right about. The Coast Guard built a newer, more modern one on Eagle Island farther out into the water back in the 1940s. We can hear Eagle Island's automated foghorn and see the red-light flashes. But Candy Cane is one of the few reasons tourists come to Rocky Point. So maybe it's the *only* important thing about Rocky Point to the rest of the world.

I turn away from the window. I'll be seeing far too much of Candy Cane this summer. Mom roped me into working for the Historical Preservation Society, and the lighthouse is their star attraction. "Working" in the sense I have to show up, not in the sense that I'll be getting paid.

Whomp! One of Cynthia's pillows whacks me in the face. Luckily, it's a fringed one, and not one covered in tiny mirrors.

"Hey!" I complain, tossing the pillow onto the bed. "What was that for?"

"Stop looking so dire!" she scolds. "You'd think *you* were the drama diva, not me!"

I fling a hand across my forehead and clutch my chest. I stumble across the room to gaze piteously at our shared reflection. "I don't know what's to become of me!" I wail in a terrible Britishy accent. "Trapped in the tower as a servant to an evil witch."

Cynthia giggles and flicks me with her stretchy headband. I snatch it and twist it around my wrists. "Save me," I beg, dropping to my knees and holding up my bound hands. "I'm a prisoner! The witch kidnapped me when I was a mere babe. She absconded with me—"

Cynthia raises a honey-blond eyebrow at me. "Absconded? Working on your SAT vocab already?"

"Absconded," I repeat, raising my own dark eyebrow back at her. She gestures magnanimously for me to continue.

"*Absconded* with me to a land where buildings are made of candy canes."

Cynthia's mouth twists as she tries not to laugh. "She used her powers to trap you inside a kiddie board game?"

"Not Candy Land," I admonish her. "A *land* of *candy*."

She holds up her hands in surrender. "I stand corrected." She goes back to frowning at her dress, studying it from every possible view.

I slump against a bedpost. "At first I loved all the fudge, saltwater taffy, and caramel. But soon my stomach hurt all the time, my teeth rotted, and the peppermint scent of my prison gave me awful headaches. Now I desperately await the arrival of a prince with a serious sweet tooth to free me."

Cynthia gives up searching for the elusive angle that would make the dress passable and turns to face me. "You done?" she asks, reaching for her headband.

"For now." I unwind the headband and give it back to her.

She slips it over her head and pulls her hair back from her face. "Maybe one of the summer boys will rescue you."

I snort. "Yeah, right."

"Could happen," Cynthia says. She picks up her signature bubblegum lip gloss and points it at me. "So. Could. Happen," she repeats, using the lip gloss to punctuate each word.

"Are you kidding me?" I flop back onto her bed. "Like who?"

Cynthia narrows her eyes, considering. I can practically see her flipping through her mental file labeled "Summer Regulars." "Someone new," she concludes.

"Would have to be," I say. "Since not a single Regular is even remotely an option."

Rocky Point doesn't have the long, sandy beaches that some

of the coastal communities in Maine have, and isn't close to the big towns with loads of things to do. So we have people who come for the whole summer, mostly because they have ties to the area: They're here visiting relatives, or they grew up here or nearby and keep a cottage as a summer place. They generally come year after year, so we've watched the kids in those families grow up from toddlers to our age.

The only "true" tourists we get are usually on their way somewhere else. They break up the drive by spending the night at one of our two bed-and-breakfast inns because they have the charm and romance missing from the land of suburbia. Or so I figure it. Sometimes we get groups on a Lighthouses of Maine tour visiting Candy Cane since it's the subject of a famous painting featured on Maine postcards. There are also Artists and Artisans tours. Every Maine schoolkid can rattle off the names of the famous artists who painted here: Edward Hopper, Winslow Homer, N. C. and Jamie Wyeth among many others. So tourists check out the art galleries and our genuinely showstopping views that inspired so many paintings, then go on their touristy way. Still, it's Candy Cane that's the star attraction.

Satisfied with her makeup, Cynthia slips off the headband and refluffs her hair. "Your mom's not an evil witch, ya know."

"Not to you, maybe," I grumble. "And now she's my boss. As if she's not on my case enough already. And with Justin gone for the summer . . ."

"Why would anyone *voluntarily* take summer classes?" Cynthia shakes her head.

"I know! Mr. Overachiever Double-Major just makes my

grades seem even more pathetic. Even though they were actually better this past year." I sigh. "I can't believe he's staying at school all summer."

Cynthia gives me a sympathetic look in the mirror. Now that my brother and I have outgrown our childhood attempts to kill each other, I kind of adore him. Mom certainly does. They practically *never* fight. And while Justin was away at college this year, Mom and I got into it more than ever.

Can my summer get any worse? No Cynthia. No Justin. That means no baby steps into the ocean until Cynthia yanks me under with her. No nightly trips to Scoops to try every flavor at least three times before voting for Best New Flavor at the Goodbye to Summer Festival. No action flicks with Justin to relieve the frustration of the third-straight day of rain. And no outings to local theaters to watch Cynthia perform.

Nope. This summer is going to be all me, Mom, and Candy Cane.

"Your mom can't hang around the lighthouse," Cynthia points out. "She has her job at the library."

"She'll find a way," I groan.

"I've done all I can." Cynthia lifts and releases the overskirt in one last attempt to make the dress turn into something wearable, and concedes defeat.

"Aren't you going to freeze?" I ask, frowning at the strapless gown.

Even though the Lupine Festival is the "official" start of summer in Rocky Point, Maine, our first day of summer is chillier than the last. Most of the Summer Regulars haven't even started arriving yet, so it's like one big party for the locals. That's why I like it—there's lots to do, but it's still super low-key. The calm before the summer season storm.

Cynthia picks up a gray-blue-lavender chiffon shawl and drapes it around her shoulders. "I've got this lovely item, to complete the grandma look." She pouts at her reflection. "I can't believe they expect me to wear this to the Lupine Dance tonight too. It will be everyone's last memory of me."

"You're not dying."

She waves a hand dismissively. "You know what I mean. This is how everyone will picture me while I'm away."

"Not with all the selfies you post," I tease.

She sticks out her tongue and goes back to arranging the shawl, before shouting, "Would you puh-leeze get up already!" She tosses my clothes onto the bed. "I have to be there in less than half an hour."

"Okay, okay." I get up, grab my bag with my toothbrush and toothpaste in it, and slump across the room to the bathroom. "But I expect you to keep your eyes peeled for my prince."

*M*y nose wrinkles at the full-on assault. The only downside of the Lupine Festival is that it's a serious fish feast. Last year I couldn't get a decent order of French fries for a week because they tasted like fried clams. My mom swears they don't fry them in the same oil, but I don't believe her.

It's hard to be the only person in Rocky Point who hates seafood. Maybe the only person in all of Maine. It's not just weird;

it's practically sacrilegious, since fishing is a major component of the Maine economy. My English teacher's husband is a fisherman, the Brownie troop leader's son is a fisherman, the Little League coach is a fisherman, my neighbor owns the marine supplies store on the wharf . . . Long story short, fishing isn't only a way of life here, it's *the* way of life.

Music blares from the little stage set up on the commercial pier where a band called the Rock Lobsters performs passable covers of classic songs. I turn away from the food booths on the public pier and keep my face to the ocean. Still briny, but the salty air blowing off the water helps tone down the fish smell. It's a little biting, with a slight chill still in the air, but I love the wide-awake feeling the ocean spray gives me.

I wave at some kids I know from school who are handing out flyers for Whistler's Windjammers cruises. The only takers today are the people with houseguests; locals don't go on the high-priced cruises since a lot of them have boats of their own, or have friends who do. I scan the crowd but don't see anyone to hang with, so I start over to the nonfish booths. At least they had the good sense to separate them this year.

Cynthia will know exactly where to look for me. Salivating in line waiting for my first fried blueberry pocket of the summer. Yum. That's a booth where I can trust the oil is lobster- and clam-free. Pure. Nothing but pastry dough in that grease.

I'm blissfully Mom-free for the festival, so no lectures today on how many are too many pockets. Right now she's standing at the foot of the circular staircase that leads up Candy Cane's tower. I can picture her there wearing her 1840s-style dress that could have been worn by Katharine Gilhooley, the wife of the first lighthouse keeper. Thanks to James and Katharine's large family, the keeper's house beside the lighthouse is pretty big. About ten or so years ago, the historical society did a fund-raiser to turn the house into the Keeper's Café and Gift Shop.

The Keeper's Café is closed for the Lupine Festival but has a booth on the pier with all the others. Mostly for publicity, since their menu is woefully limited. As I pass it, I notice Celeste Ingram selling lemonade. Smart move hiring her. Judging from the boys hanging around the booth, the café might actually draw some local customers this summer.

Celeste is back from her first year at college. Even Cynthia— who can pretty much start a conversation with anyone—has never spoken to Celeste. There's something, well, *celestial* about her. As in, out-of-this-world beautiful, and sort of untouchable. She has flowing white-blond hair in the summer that only darkens a tinge the rest of the year, and wide blue eyes, broad cheekbones, and a sharp, tiny nose that gives her the appearance of an elfin queen.

"Hi, Mandy," Vicki Jensen says as I get in the blueberry-pocket line behind her. "Where's Cynthia?" Vicki and I have had a bunch of classes together most years, but she's more Cynthia's friend than mine.

"Stashing her tiara," I reply. Cynthia's changing into something less formal until the dance, now that she's been crowned and sashed, and has declared this year's Lupine Festival officially open.

"How'd it go?" Vicki asks. "I only got up a little while ago."

"You mean you slept in? Like a normal person the first week of summer vacation?" I pout with envy. "Cynthia insisted I be there with her at the opening ceremony."

"Yeah, I figured." Vicki grins. "What best friends do, right?"

I grin back. Silly as it might seem, it's always nice to hear myself acknowledged as Cynthia's best friend. Once we hit high school, Cynthia roared into the popular crowd, and I worried that our bestie status since elementary school had ended its long run. But Cynthia proved me wrong.

"Hello, Mandy." Our next-door neighbor, Mrs. Jackson, has her twins—rambunctious eight-year-old boys—with her. I get as far away as I can from those two the moment they're armed with pastries. Blueberry stains are impossible to get out.

But Maine is the blueberry capital of the world, which means blueberry stains are an inevitable part of Rocky Point summer life—just like grease spots, fish smells, and mud. I may be considered a traitor for not liking seafood, but no one can fault me on my Maine bloob (my *personal* term for blueberries) loyalty.

"Hi, Mrs. Jackson. Hi, guys," I say, scanning my possible escape routes post–pocket purchase.

"I've been dreaming about these for *months*!" a familiar New York accent cries up ahead of me in the line. Joanna Maroni and her family have been coming to Rocky Point since we were in seventh grade. Cynthia and I usually hang with her and another Regular, Patti Broughton from Boston, all summer long. Cynthia'll be gone, but at least I'll still have Joanna and Patti. But I know it just won't be the same.

When I finally arrive at the front of the line, I reach for the luscious deep-fried fruity treat. A hand suddenly snatches it away.

"Hey!" I spin around, ready to smack the pocket thief. Instead I fling my arms around the culprit.

"Justin!" I crow. This is the first I've seen my brother since he came home for spring break in March. He must have arrived last night while I was at Cynthia's for our sleepover.

Justin grins at me, flecks of piecrust on his lips and purple smudges on his chin. I take a step back and punch his arm. "That was mine! You owe me a pocket!"

"Mmm-mm!" He takes another big bite and rolls his eyes heavenward. "My first pocket since last summer!" He licks his lips. "As good as I remembered."

"It was supposed to be *my* first pocket of the season!" I scold him.

"Watch it!" Justin grabs my arm and yanks me out of the path of a pocket-wielding eight-year-old. The twins are waving their treats around in delight.

"Boys," Mrs. Jackson scolds. "Those are food, not flags."

Justin and I move away from the line, now stretching all the way back to the lobster roll booth. I narrow my eyes at Justin. "Just because you saved my hoodie from the twins," I tell him, "doesn't mean you're off the hook. I want my pocket."

Justin swallows the last bite. "Where's Cynthia?"

That seems to be the first thing everyone says to me if they ever find me without Cynthia by my side.

"She's ditching the gown till later," I tell him. "And you're avoiding the subject. You. Back on line. Now. Must. Have. Pocket!"

He frowns, puzzled. "Gown?" Then he nods. "Oh, right. Lupine Queen. I forgot."

I look up at him, surprised. "You used to be all gaga for the Lupine Queen."

"Don't remind me. I can't believe I'd actually get up at the crack of dawn just to be at the front of the stage for the opening ceremony." He shakes his head at the memory of his younger self.

"So now you think this is all, what"—I gesture vaguely to indicate the whole festival—"dumb?"

"Not dumb at all," Justin says. "The queen thing, though. You've got to admit it's kind of dorky."

"And you're not particularly interested in high school girls, now that you're a big college man."

He grins. "Something like that." He wipes his mouth, then tosses the napkin in a nearby trash can. "Come on, let's get back in line."

"You're the one who should wait in line," I protest.

He grabs my arm and drags me along, and I let him. It will give us a chance to catch up. We stroll along the length of the line, greeting neighbors, classmates—and then I see *him*.

I have no idea who he is. I have definitely never seen him before. I would have remembered.

He's studying the festival schedule, and the first thing I notice is that he's nearly as inappropriately dressed for early summer in Maine as Cynthia was.

He stamps his sandaled feet and shifts from side to side, giving me the impression that he's already regretting the Hawaiian-print board shorts and vintage-looking sky-blue bowling shirt. I figure any minute now he'll admit he's cold (why don't boys ever want to do that?) and untie the dark blue sweatshirt knotted around his waist.

The next thing I notice is his shaggy brown hair, with bangs long enough to flop over his face as he gazes down at the paper in his hands. Then he tips his head back to swing the bangs aside, and sticks his sunglasses on top of his head.

I suddenly stop noticing anything at all.

Anything, that is, other than the lips that look soft and full enough to be a girl's; the high, wide forehead; the sharp chin that seems to be pointing at the schedule in his hands; and his sun-tinged skin that tells me he's come from somewhere a lot warmer than Rocky Point, Maine. And twinkling blue eyes—or are they green?—that suddenly lock onto my own dark ones.

Busted.

I quickly glance away, grab Justin's arm, and breathlessly say, "Come on, slowpoke. They might run out before you get me my pocket."

"The booth's only been open an hour," Justin protests as I practically trot him toward the back of the line. I can't help risking a peek over my shoulder at the mysterious sun-kissed stranger, but he's gone back to studying his festival schedule. Only a tourist would give it such careful consideration.

Is he here for just the day? Or is he—oh please, please, please—a new *Regular*?

I spot Cynthia arriving at the pier, scanning for me, flanked by Joanna and Patti. "There's Cynthia," I tell Justin. "You get me my pocket and come find us. We'll probably be over at the arts and crafts."

Justin shrugs. "You know they're best right out of the fryer," he says.

"Just do it," I order. I weave my way through the snaking lines radiating from the booths. This time I manage to keep from swiveling my head for another peek at Surfer Boy.

I stop dead in my tracks midway to Cynthia, paralyzed by the *worst* idea. He probably thinks Justin is my *boyfriend*! I literally smack my forehead. *How stupid am I?*

I stand there still as a statue, forcing the hungry throngs to swerve around me. Luckily, on Lupine Festival day everyone's always in a good mood, so no one seems to mind. My brain spins on overdrive trying to think of a way to remedy the situation as I watch Patti, Joanna, and Cynthia approach.

Patti looks thinner and for once isn't carrying one of her ever-present bags of chips. Maybe she kept her vow to "eat healthy." The hamburger, two hot dogs, and a lobster roll, along with mounds of potato and crabmeat salad at our Labor Day picnic at the end of last year's season nearly did her in.

The big surprise is Joanna's hair. A spiky short cut dyed a color not found in nature has replaced her long dark mane. Fuchsia is the closest I can figure.

If I wasn't already frozen by my possible gaffe with Surfer Boy, her dye job would have stopped me. All the years the Maronis have been coming to Rocky Point, Joanna and her three sisters have always dressed in the same ultraconservative uniform: pastel sundresses or khakis and polo shirts. Their hair was often styled identically—French braids or pulled back with skinny headbands. Did her sisters dye their hair too, to keep with the matchy-matchy? That I'd have to see to believe!

"Don't worry," Joanna says, holding her sandwich away from me. "We'll stay downwind."

"Thanks." I grin, happy that she remembers my fish aversion. Sometimes it takes a while for us to get back in the swing of things after being away from each other for a year. It's nice to know that my quirks and I don't just vanish, like that town in the musical *Brigadoon*. Cynthia and I have watched the movie a bunch of times—it's about this town in Scotland that appears only for one day every hundred years. Sometimes I feel Rocky Point is like that to anyone *from away*—the term Mainers use for someone who isn't from Maine. To them we exist only while they're here and then vanish back into our famous Maine fog.

"Your summer's going to be great," Patti says to Cynthia. "I know how much you love being in shows."

Cynthia nods, her eyes bright. Every time she talks about going to the Vermont Performing Arts Summer Workshop she gets the same slightly dizzy look—like the very idea makes her head spin. "It's going to be awesome," she says, bending forward from the waist to make sure no mayo falls onto her top from her overloaded lobster roll.

"Yeah, you must be stoked to be getting out of here," Joanna says, just as her front jeans pocket buzzes. She pulls out her phone and reads the text. She types something back, then sighs. "I begged my parents not to drag me here, but no. They want to torture me."

"Torture?" I repeat. Rocky Point hardly qualifies as a method of torture, and for all the summers I've known her, Joanna has loved it so much she cried when she had to leave. Maybe the fuchsia hair dye has affected her brain.

She waves her cell phone around. "I think they did it just to break up me and Sam. He's back in Brooklyn with our friends, and I'm stuck here."

"But you come here every summer," Patti points out. "It's not some new stunt they pulled."

Another buzz, another text. While Joanna's eyes are on her phone, Cynthia and I each give Patti a "what's up with her?" look. Patti shrugs.

Justin appears with my bloob pocket. "Don't say I never did anything for you, Sneezy," he says, holding it out to me. Sneezy is his nickname for me, thanks to my allergies.

"You *didn't* do anything for me," I counter. "You repaid your debt."

I take the paper-wrapped treat from him and tentatively flick it with my tongue to test the temperature. You have to be careful with pockets. They can be treacherous, luring you in with their homey, acceptably hot pastry, then spurting steaming blueberries that scald the roof of your mouth. But this one is perfect. Still hot, but not at a dangerous level. I take a bite, shut my eyes, and inhale deeply, which is the only way to eat a pocket.

"Hi, Justin," Patti says.

"Hey," he replies. I can tell he's trying to place her. Maybe to Justin the Regulars live in Brigadoon, and *we're* the real world.

"You remember Patti," I say, rescuing them both from potential embarrassment. I can be magnanimous now that I have my bloob pocket. "She lives in the green cottage on the bay side past

Second Time Around but before Scoops," I explain, listing two of Rocky Point's favorite spots.

"Oh, right," he says. I know he still has no idea who she is.

I also realize from the way Patti is twirling her hair and smiling that she's into Justin. But she's not even a blip on his radar.

"See you later, Sneezy," he says. "I told Mom I'd fill in for her at the lighthouse so she can grab lunch."

"Great," I grumble. "Suck up to Mom so I seem like an even worse child."

"You *are* the worse child," he teases.

I scrunch my nose at him, since my mouth is too busy with the pocket to bother with a retort. Patti laughs way too loudly, and Joanna never raises her head from her cell phone.

"Are you going to the dance?" Patti asks Justin.

"Gotta see Cyn here dolled up in her Lupine Queen gown, don't I?" Justin winks at Cynthia.

"Ugh." Cynthia shudders, then licks the glob of lobster that fell out of her sandwich off her wrist. "I'm never going to live it down."

"Exactly why I have to see it." Justin salutes us. "Ladies."

I swallow the last bit of pocket and say, "You're going to look lovely in Mom's Mrs. Gilhooley costume."

"Ha-ha," he says, then jogs away.

"Make sure Mom gives you the bonnet, too!" I call after him. I roll up the paper the pocket came in and wipe my face.

"Does he have a girlfriend?" Patti asks, still twirling her hair.

There must have been a lull in the texting because Joanna pipes up, "Forget it, Patti. Why get involved with someone you'll leave at the end of the summer?"

"I think it would be romantic," Cynthia says. I shoot her a look, and she quickly adds, "Not with Justin. I mean, he's a nice guy and everything, but he's like my big brother. Only better," she adds, "since I don't have to share a bathroom with him."

"Yeah, that does suck," I say.

"You really think having a thing with someone who is here only for the summer is actually a good idea?" Joanna presses.

"Why not?" Cynthia says, studying her lobster roll. I know she's trying to decide if she can just pop the last of it into her mouth in one piece. "Sometimes knowing a thing is temporary makes it beautifully tragic." She makes up her mind and in the sandwich goes.

"Ever the drama queen," Joanna says.

"Well, I'm ready for something nice and simple, and a summer fling seems exactly in order," says Patti.

"Forget Justin," I tell Patti. "He's only here for a few days. Then he goes back to the University of Maine for a summer semester."

"I'd imagine a two-day fling is too short for even the ever-adventurous Patti," Joanna teases.

"Two days would hardly qualify as a *romance*," Patti scolds. "And it's romance that I'm after."

They continue debating various definitions of romance as my mind wanders back to the dark-haired boy I saw earlier.

"Ready to buy some mismatched coffee mugs?" Cynthia interrupts my thoughts.

We turn away from the food booths and stroll along Water Street to Main. The Square, as everyone calls it, is the literal center of Rocky Point. The grassy plaza lies halfway between the harbor and the bay. It's also midway between the pointy tip where Candy Cane stands to the south and the beginning of the woods to the north. Mom's library anchors the south side, the middle school the north. Our high school is a few blocks away from the library.

Today's flea market is set up in the parking lot of the middle school. That means we can check out the Artists and Artisans tent in the town square on our way there. We cruise by the shops with sale racks and tables outside.

People sprawl on the benches lining the Square. They're busy eating fried clams out of cheerful red-and-white-striped cardboard cartons from booths on the pier, or sandwiches from Taste To Go, the take-out place on Randolph Street. Kids drip ice cream and giggle or drop ice cream and wail. Mostly they're kept out of the Artists and Artisans area because no parent wants to be forced to buy hand-painted chiffon scarves covered in ice-cream fingerprints or historically accurate sailboat models with suddenly broken masts.

Cynthia and I breeze past the section where framed pictures hang on chicken-wire walls. Candy Cane is a favorite subject, though none of the paintings has the evocative feeling of the one on the postcard. Maybe because those displayed by the amateur artists all depict her (I always think of Candy Cane as a "her") on a bright sunny day, and the painting on the postcard is of the lighthouse in the gloom. To me, that's a more accurate image. Rocky Point's sunny days are nowhere near as common as the rainy, foggy, or cloudy ones. The anonymous artist knew Rocky Point like a local.

"What do you think Brad Ainsley came up with this year?" Cynthia asks. We stroll past tables with handblown glass vases and goblets.

"Something bizarre, I'm sure." Brad Ainsley lives up by the Canadian border and does the whole arts-festival circuit in Maine. The sculptures have some kind of theme each year that's only clear to him.

"Nautical," Cynthia surmises as we study Brad Ainsley's latest creations.

"Ya think?" I deadpan. The sculptures appear to be in two categories: those whose stuck-together pieces create a ship shape, and those made of actual ship or fishing materials.

I lean forward, about to press a button placed on the shoulder of a figurehead, wondering what craziness it will unleash, when I let out a gasp and grab Cynthia's arm.

"What?" she asks. "Did something bite you?"

"No," I squeak. I step in front of her, my back to Surfer Boy. I force myself to speak in a calm, low voice. "Don't look, but there's a boy over by the sculpture with the broken blue mast sticking out of the upside-down hull."

Cynthia's eyes flick from mine to a spot over my shoulder. I know she spotted him when her jaw drops. "He's new."

I nod. "I saw him before when I was in the pocket line."

Her eyes return to mine, and she takes my hands. "We need a plan."

My eyes open wide and my body goes cold, then hot, then cold again. It's some weird combination of fear, exhilaration, and anticipation.

Cynthia's eyebrows rise expectantly. But my usually over-drive brain is on strike. Total blank.

"Uh . . ." is all I can come up with.

Cynthia gives me a little shake. "Don't get stage fright now! This is our chance!"

"What if he's from up the coast and is only here for the festival?" I say weakly, disappointment washing through me as I realize this is the most likely scenario.

Cynthia grins. "Then we just have an awesome day of flirting!" She drops my hands and gives me a hip check. "We could use the practice."

Her hip check jostles an idea loose. "I got it!" I declare. "Follow my lead."

We edge our way around some of Brad Ainsley's more lethal sculptures as our target moves to the last one in the row. I hoped we could position ourselves opposite him, but he's standing right where the tent is tethered to the ground. We'll have to settle for sidling up beside him. Which we do.

Surfer Boy doesn't even look up. He's intensely focused on a piece that I can only describe as Ship-nado. Dozens of small model boats—dinghies, canoes, schooners—swirl around in a chicken-wire funnel.

My plan is to start talking about super-interesting things so that he can't help but check us out. Only now I can't speak. Complete mental freeze.

My eyes flick to Surfer Boy. He's kneeling and peering up inside Ship-nado. I wonder if that's how Brad Ainsley wants us to view his work.

Cynthia keeps nodding her head toward him in sharp little jerks and widening her already wide-open eyes in strange rhythmic bursts, like reverse blinking.

I clutch her hands. "Ask me something," I whisper hoarsely. "Something interesting. It will make him look."

She stops blinking, tilts her head the way she does when she's thinking, then gives a sharp nod. She clears her throat and says loudly, "I think it's wonderful that you're helping the very important Historical Preservation Society with one of its most prized landmarks."

I'm about to give her an "are you kidding me?" glare but then realize if he's from away, he might actually be interested in our little lighthouse. So I quickly turn my glare into an approving "good one" expression.

"Oh yes, Candy Ca— I mean, the Rocky Point Lighthouse is such a great—"

I break off as our target stands up, brushes the gravel from his knees, and strolls away.

Cynthia and I stare at his back. "Can you believe that?" Cynthia fumes. "It was as if we weren't even here!"

My brow furrows. "You know, I think he really didn't have any idea that there were humans around. He was so into this sculpture." I peer at it again. Now that I'm up close, I can see that the ships aren't empty. Teeny-tiny people are inside. It's kind of great and kind of creepy at the same time.

Cynthia shrugs. "Probably just a Summer Snob."

Summer Snobs are a subgroup of Regulars who come here every year but don't want anything to do with the locals. They give parties for each other, browse the art galleries, and visit the antique stores and the weekly farmers' market, but wouldn't be caught dead at Louie's Lobster Pound eating a shredder with their bare hands—even though everybody knows that's the best way to eat your lobster. If you like lobster, of course.

I watch Surfer Boy approach a table of antiques. Once again he's mesmerized. He strikes up a conversation with the woman at the table. I give him one last look as Cynthia and I leave the tent to head for the flea market behind the school. We gave him a chance to talk to us, and he didn't jump at it. Cynthia always says that if a guy doesn't take a little hint, don't bother giving him a bigger one.

I shake off my disappointment and get into my flea market groove. I love flea markets. Not only are the items in my price range, but it's fun to poke through other people's stuff. It's like sneaking into their house and spying on how they live.

I know it's silly, but there's a little part of me that feels bad for the odds and ends, and I always hope they'll find new owners to appreciate them. Sometimes I buy things that I figure will never get bought. Mom just sighs when I show her my latest "pity purchase" and then says, "Well, at least these are the only kinds of strays you bring home." Mom has a strict "no pets" rule.

"Snob sighting just to starboard," Cynthia murmurs.

I look up from the chipped pig-shaped mug that is going to join my wacky mugs collection. Two tables over Surfer Boy gazes intently at a pile of lobster traps. Then he does the same thing at a table selling knot art and handmade fishing lures.

"You know, I don't think he's a Summer Snob," I tell Cynthia, formulating a theory. "I think he's an alien from a planet where no one fishes."

"If the aliens all look like him, you should move there," Cynthia teases. "You'd get to avoid all seafood *and* be surrounded by hunks."

"Definitely not from Maine, that's for sure." It's not just the tan and sandals. His curiosity about pretty much everything on sale at the flea market tells me these are things he's never seen up close before. Things that are part of daily life here.

Then the unthinkable happens.

Blue eyes—yes, they are definitely blue, not green—suddenly meet mine.

And I can't do anything but look back.

I'm as mesmerized by those eyes as he was a moment ago by a tiny ship-in-a-bottle. The weird thing is, I don't do any of the things I thought I would when confronted by the steady beam of a handsome boy's gaze. I don't blush; I don't giggle; I don't faint; I don't anything.

I don't even move.

But weirder? Neither does he.

I have no idea how long we stand like this, both frozen. It feels like forever, until I realize that Cynthia has only just finished paying for her floppy sun hat. In the time it took for Cynthia to pull out her wallet, count out the bills, and hand them over to the ninth-grade algebra teacher, Suzanna Hughes, who's manning the table, something shifted in me. Or rather, *not* shifted. It felt as if I was caught in a fishing net, unable to move, but not wanting to try.

Maybe thirty seconds at most.

Then it's over. Cynthia says something to me, something distracts Surfer Boy, and our eyes drop. Life picks back up, and we each return to our separate worlds.

"You okay?" Cynthia asks, adjusting the hat so that the brim doesn't make it impossible for her to see.

"He looked at me," I whisper.

Cynthia's head swivels, and she spots Surfer Boy down the row. Now he's studying an old sailor's manual.

"And when I say *looked*," I continue, "I mean took in every detail, almost as if he could—" I'm about to say "see into my soul" but luckily realize before the words come out how ridiculous they'd sound.

"As if he could . . . ?" Cynthia prompts.

"As if he had X-ray vision and was checking to see if my brain was still in my skull."

Cynthia laughs. "Well, is it?"

"Not so much," I admit.

Cynthia tips her head back so she can examine my face from under her floppy brim. "Wow. Boy made an impact, did he?"

"He did."

"And you're saying he actually made eye contact."

"And held it," I confirm. "Unless he has such super vision that he was actually trying to see the price tag on the ironing board for sale behind me."

"Well, that bowling shirt *could* use a quick pressing . . . ," Cynthia jokes. She knocks into me with her shoulder. "So . . . go get him."

"I—I . . ." I slump and look down at my feet. One of my sneakers is untied, and I have a big splotch of blueberry on the other one. That's in addition to the blueberry trail down my shirt. I *thought* that pocket was a little understuffed. Now I see where some of the filling had gotten to. "For all I know he wasn't looking at me because he's interested. He could have been staring at my blueberry stains. Or thinking how weird I am for buying a pig mug."

"Hang on." Cynthia grips my arm.

The sudden change in her tone makes my head instantly pop back up. She's openly staring in Surfer Boy's direction, and she looks seriously stunned. I glance over and my jaw drops.

"What is he doing talking to old Freaky Framingham?" I gasp. "And Freaky Framingham is talking back!"

"It's hard enough to wrap my brain around Freaky Framingham being here at all," Cynthia says. "I think my head's going to explode, putting him and Hottie McHottie together."

Freaky Framingham has lived in Rocky Point as long as I can remember. He's that guy whose house you avoid, which isn't hard to do, since it's in a deeply wooded area. The path to his house from the road is just a narrow strip of dirt without a sign to mark it. But everyone in Rocky Point knows exactly where it is. Each year on Halloween kids dare one another to knock on his door.

There are rare Freaky Framingham sightings. He'd usually be in his battered blue pickup. But he'd never wave to pedestrians or other drivers at our few stoplights, like everyone else. He just keeps his hands firmly on his wheel. Though his face is hard to see behind the cracked windshield, we all assume his expression conveys how much he hates everything and everyone. He'd be at Main Street Goods, picking up groceries, and someone would greet him and he'd just grunt. Or he'd mutter under his breath and stalk out.

And now he's standing two tables over, and Surfer Boy is showing him the sailor's manual. Surfer Boy doesn't look nervous or afraid talking to our town grouch. Framingham looks almost presentable for a change. Normally he wears ratty paint-spattered overalls with flannel shirts washed so many times it's hard to believe they're any warmer than wearing tissues. His gray hair is wild and long, and he has the weather-beaten skin of many old-time Mainers, the result of a life lived mostly out of doors, battered by high winds, powerful sun, and cold weather.

Today he's still wearing overalls, but they're cleaner than usual, and the shirt looks close to new. His hair is brushed and pulled back into a low ponytail. He looks almost . . . normal.

"That is seriously freaky," I murmur.

"No lie," Cynthia says, equally mystified.

We watch as if it's some kind of mystery show on TV, and we're looking for clues to explain how these two people wound up talking to each other.

"Do you think ol' Freaky has, I don't know, been to therapy or something?" Cynthia suggests.

"Hard to picture, but something has happened," I say.

"Maybe he decided to strike up a conversation with the only person here who wouldn't know him."

"Could be," I say doubtfully. "But don't they seem like they know each other?"

Freaky's usual dour expression hasn't changed. He just stands there frowning, stroking his stubbly chin while Surfer Boy shows him things in the book. Then Framingham does something totally bizarre. He pulls a wad of bills out of his back pocket and pays for the book. Mr. Cooley, the guy who sells secondhand books at Second Time Around over on Berry Street, looks as shocked as Cynthia and I feel. He takes a minute to register that this is really happening, then accepts the dollar. Freaky Framingham strides away from the table, and Surfer Boy scurries after him.

Cynthia and I turn to face each other, wearing identical "huh?" expressions.

"How could they possibly know each other?" I ask.

"Why would anyone voluntarily spend time with Freaky Framingham?" Cynthia says. "I mean, that boy, that serving of yummy cuteness, just followed him. On purpose."

Our heads turn simultaneously to catch another glimpse of the strange sight.

I don't know if it's because he could feel us staring in complete and utter disbelief, but just at that moment Surfer Boy looks back.

And I'm mesmerized all over again.

Because this time he doesn't just stare at me. He smiles. And lifts his chin in a teeny-tiny itty-bitty greeting.

But it's big enough to make me bang into Cynthia. And that's without even moving. I guess I kind of went a little lopsided. If she hadn't been standing next to me, I might have fallen over.

Cynthia slings her arm across my shoulder and brings her face next to mine. "Seems you made an impression on him, too."

The ginormous smile I feel on my face reminds me of how not-cool I am. There is no way I can play coy, or haughty, or any of the other ways I've seen girls act around the boys they like.

It's just right out there: *I like you*, in screaming neon on my face.

He turns and jogs to catch up with Framingham. Proof that he actually is with the old coot. If he wanted to escape, he could have, since ol' Freaky hasn't slowed down a bit and is now out of the parking lot.

"I need a bloob pocket," I murmur. "For strength."

"Do you really want to get back in that line?" Cynthia asks. "With all those eavesdroppers? We have some planning to do!"

Happily, the usual table piled with drinks and baked goods donated by the middle school sits again at the exit. The money from these sales goes to the school, so I feel virtuous as I buy a blueberry muffin, an oatmeal-blueberry cookie, and a tall lemonade. Once we have our purchases, we leave the tent and cross the Square. I sit cross-legged on top of a picnic table, and Cynthia lies on the bench, her floppy hat protecting her face from the sun. She says something, but it's too muffled to understand.

I reach down and flip off her hat. "What?" I ask.

She sits up and swivels around to face me. "I said, I just can't figure it out."

"I know!" I gnaw on my lower lip.

"You know what I think?" Cynthia says impishly. "I think just like you're trapped in a candy tower to be a witch's servant, he's under a spell. A spell that can only be broken by a kiss from an innocent year-rounder."

I duck my chin so that she can't see the flush creeping up my neck. I fiddle with my shoelaces, my mouth twisting as I try to keep the smile from spreading. A kiss. A soft, tender brush of those lips on mine.

I haven't had much experience in the kissing department. Last New Year's Eve, Kenny Martin suddenly laid one on me in the middle of a party. I yelped—not exactly the reaction he'd been hoping for—and banged into Cara Michaels and Evan Lawrence when I stumbled backward in surprise. They weren't exactly pleased when I interrupted their dance-floor lip-lock. And there were a couple of awkward good-night kisses when Johnny Carmichael walked me home after a group of us went to the movies. Awkward enough that he stopped trying, much to my relief.

But now . . . I tip my head back and watch the clouds drift. Their soft edges make me remember how soft his lips looked. I'm pretty certain kissing Surfer Boy wouldn't be anything like my previous experiences.

Of course, kissing him would require seeing him again. And talking to him. How am I going to do any of that with Cynthia gone? I'll never have the nerve. If our paths ever even cross again.

"Maybe he'll be at the Lupine Dance," Cynthia suggests.

I brighten at the idea. Day-trippers often stay for the dance. Best of all, Cynthia will still be here to help me get ready, coach me, and provide moral support. A kiss from a day-tripper sounds incredibly romantic. One beautiful night and then just a lovely memory.

I sit glumly at the edge of the pier, my legs dangling over the gently lapping water. The moon's reflection quivers with each rise and fall of the peaceful wavelets, and the little white twinkle lights strung on every pillar and post sparkle in the sea's mirror. It looks like fireflies learning to swim. The DJ's music thrums from the loudspeakers, and even though my back is to them, I can picture my neighbors, my friends, and random visitors dancing their butts off.

Over on the other pier, the food booths are now lit with clip-ons so bright that it looks like a movie set. Beside me two tween girls compare notes on a shared enemy, some boy who spent most of the school year embarrassing them. I want to interrupt and explain that it means he likes them, but then I tell myself to shut up. What do I know about boys?

I hear a rustle behind me and glance up at Cynthia. She has put her Lupine Queen dress back on as required for the Sunset Ceremonies, and now her tiara is askew and her sash is crooked. "Scoot over," she orders the tweens. They oblige without protest. After all, she's the queen.

"Your dress . . . ?" I say as she plops down beside me. The skirt puffs up around her, making her look as if she's rising from a lavender-gray-blue cloud.

"They make a new one every year," she reminds me. "One of the perks of being queen." She lifts, then drops, a fistful of chiffon. "I get to keep this monstrosity."

"Everyone get their blue ribbons?" I ask. One of the duties of the Lupine Queen is to dole out prizes for the various competitions just before the dance.

Cynthia nods. "Lorraine Bartley won for her painting of lobster traps."

I gasp in mock horror. "You mean Candy Cane wasn't a prize-winner?" The lighthouse is always a favorite subject.

"I know. Shocking."

I wiggle my toes, trying to ease the ache in my feet—and warm them up. It's still pretty early to be walking around at night in sandals, and I don't usually wear such high heels.

Our preparations were in vain. The high heels and my favorite red sundress with the scalloped hem and seams that give my somewhat boyish figure a bit more curve. Cynthia loaned me her short fake-leather jacket that hits my waist at just the right spot. She helped me with my makeup, and we even practiced possible opening lines. You know, to break the ice and start a conversation. All for nothing, because the mysterious stranger remains a mystery. He never showed up.

"I just don't get it," I say. "Why didn't he come?"

Cynthia tosses a pebble into the water. *Plink*. "I guess he was a day-tripper after all."

"Then why would he be with Freaky Framingham?"

"Good point."

I turn to face her. "He wanted to avoid me."

Cynthia twists her face into her "you're being ridiculous" expression. I know it well. "Why would he want to avoid you? He doesn't even know you. And that smile definitely implied he'd actually *want* to get to know you."

I kick my feet together lightly, still trying to warm them. "Maybe he really *is* an alien," I muse. "And aliens have been experimenting on Framingham all these years."

"That could explain why Freaky is so freaky," Cynthia says.

"Now the alien sent here disguised as a surfer has beamed them both up to the mother ship. Only an alien would dress like that in June in Maine."

Cynthia nods. "Someone got their intel on infiltrating humans wrong."

"Or," I continue, the tale spinning taking my mind off my cold, aching feet and my disappointment, "maybe Framingham used his terrible powers to turn Surfer Boy into a lobster." Ol' Freaky being an evil sorcerer is a pretty common Halloween story. "Then he chopped him up and served him in one of the lobster rolls."

Cynthia smacks my arm. "That's just gross."

I giggle. "But you have to admit, it's kind of so bad it's good."

"I like the alien theory better," Cynthia says. "Add it to the archive."

The "archive" isn't really an archive, or any actual place. It's just what Cynthia says after I spin a particularly good story.

Cynthia yawns. "I am so beat. Being a queen really takes it out of you. How do the royals do it?"

"They have things like household staffs," I say.

"Oh yeah. Forgot."

"And," I add, stretching, standing, and then holding my hand out to help Cynthia up, "they don't have to worry about getting in the middle of a knock-down-drag-out over at the pie contest."

Cynthia stands clumsily, nearly tipping over into the water when her foot catches on her hem. I right her, and we step carefully away from the edge. "No lie. Mr. Carruthers and Ms. Lynch glared so hard at each other I thought their eyes would fall out of their heads."

The rivalry between Mr. Carruthers and Ms. Lynch over their blueberry baked goods is legendary.

"That's a definite plus to queendom," Cynthia says as we make our way along the periphery of the dwindling dancers. "I get to sample the contenders."

In spite of myself, my eyes still scan for the mysterious stranger. By the time we reach the end of the pier, I have resigned myself to having tortured my toes for no good reason. A wave of sadness washes over me.

Snap out of it, I order myself. This is ridiculous. I'm feeling all this disappointment over a boy I had never seen before and will probably never see again.

*P*ostcard rack? Filled. Brochures about joining the historical society? Neatly displayed beside the cashbox. Xeroxed copies of *The Lighthouses of Maine* map stacked on the table by the front entrance? Done! The oversize lighthouse bank with the neatly lettered sign DONATIONS WELCOME! not very subtly placed? Yep. I've been at my post at the lighthouse for a whole ten minutes, and I'm already bored. How am I going to get through the next six hours? How am I going to get through the next two and a half months?

Cynthia headed off to camp yesterday morning full of anticipation, and all I have to look forward to is imprisonment in Candy Cane. *She'll be back in August,* I reminded myself when I arrived and yanked open the heavy wooden door, years of humidity making it stick.

I survey my domain. In the dark entryway there's a wooden bench, an umbrella stand, and some pegs on the wall. Visitors rarely hang up their coats, but the pegs are used to hang stray scarves, hats, and gloves they sometimes leave behind.

The reception lobby is in the attachment that connects the keeper's house to the lighthouse. Originally the keeper had to leave the house in freezing rains and gale-force winds to tend to the lighthouse, sounding the foghorn, keeping the lanterns lit. So sometime in the 1870s, after enough complaining, the attachment was built so that he could be protected from the weather and still get the job done. Thanks to the distance to the tower from the house, the room is pretty big. There's even a second floor that once housed sailors who'd been rescued, reached by a rickety, narrow staircase in the alcove behind my desk. Now it houses exhibits.

The lobby holds long glass display cases, the reception desk (really just an old table), and the souvenirs I'm supposed to sell. On one side is a door to the original keeper's house, where the café and the gift shop are, and another upstairs exhibition room, though that's closed this summer. On the other side is the entrance to the lighthouse tower. People can climb the three-story circular stone stairs to the top. The actual light was removed when Candy Cane was decommissioned, so there's room up there for three people. It's the spot where people love to take photos. It has an amazing view of the harbor, the bay, and on clear days, the ocean.

I amuse myself briefly by skimming the totally lame jokes in the very slim paperback *Wit and Wisdom from Down East*, then rearrange the souvenir T-shirts. That doesn't take up more than a minute, since we only sell three styles: one with a lobster on it, one with a lighthouse (not Candy Cane), and one with the word "Maine" on the front. On the back it says "Vacationland," something that can be found on a lot of Maine license plates. The *real* gift shop is in the café. Mom had the idea to sell a few things here just in case a visitor doesn't bother going into the café. Since it only takes me one minute to switch the T-shirt order, I switch them back again.

In desperation I start reading the captions of the photos displayed on one of the walls.

"Huh," I grunt. I never knew that the second Candy Cane lighthouse keeper was the son of the first.

I hear the door open behind me. *Unbelievable!* Mom's checking up on me already! I knew she'd never be able to resist "stopping by" on some pretext.

"I'm totally fine," I snap as I whirl around.

Only I'm not anymore.

"Whoa," Surfer Boy says, a startled expression on his face. "No one said you weren't."

I blush all the way from my multihued toenails (leftover from the sleepover with Cynthia) to the crooked part in my hair. If it could, I think my loose braid would go from dark brown to bright red with embarrassment.

"I—I'm so sorry," I sputter, my hand rising involuntarily to fluff my bangs. "I—I thought you were someone else."

"Ooo-kay," Surfer Boy says. Now he goes from startled to

puzzled. He's staring at me like he's trying to place me. Either that or he's deciding whether or not he should just back away slowly and run away.

Or maybe I have something on my face. My hand once again moves on its own, this time to my mouth for a quick subtle swipe. I give it a furtive glance. No crumbs, no stains. I run my tongue quickly across my teeth, feel nothing sticking, and lick my lips. Determining that I'm bloob free, I smile. Big. I need to make up for my rudeness. Hopefully he doesn't think I'm a hostile psycho.

Then I remember: He has been seen in the company of Freaky Framingham. Compared with that curmudgeon, my greeting was as warm as could be.

My smile must have triggered something, because instead of making a quick escape, he smiles back. "You were at the Lupine Festival yesterday."

Ohmigod, ohmigod, ohmigod. He really *did* notice me. It wasn't just my imagination. I finger the tags dangling from the T-shirts on the rack beside me. The plastic hangers make little clicky noises as they bang lightly against each other. "Yeah. Were you?"

Inwardly I wince. Why am I acting as if I wasn't mesmerized by those exact blue eyes? I don't have to admit to the mesmerized part, but I can at least acknowledge I saw him, too!

If he was insulted by my super-cool response, he doesn't show it. He nods and grins. "Great intro to Rocky Point."

My heart speeds up. This is the perfect opening to grill him for information. Why oh why isn't Cynthia here with me?

"You visiting?" Am I only able to speak in two-word sentences?

"Got here a few days ago," he says, finally taking his first real steps into the reception area. He perches casually against a long display case holding odds and ends that were found in the keeper's house during the renovation, things the original keepers had left behind. He crosses one foot over the other at the ankle, and leans on his elbow. I know I'm supposed to tell him not to put weight on the display case, but he looks too cute like that.

"From where?" I ask. Okay. Two-word sentences will have to do for now.

"California."

"Ah." *Seriously, Mandy?* my inner voice shrieks. Now I'm down to syllables.

California explains the tan, the board shorts, and the sandals. I notice today he's far more suitably dressed for early summer in Rocky Point. Dark jeans, flannel over a tee, and sneakers complete with socks.

"So, are you open?" He gazes around at the displays.

"Yes! We are. I mean, I am." *Get a grip!* "That is, yes, Candy Ca— The lighthouse exhibit is open."

He nods and straightens up.

"Here for the summer?" I blurt. "I mean, that would be kind of a long trip for just a few days."

He ambles to my little desk where I sell the tickets. "Yeah," he says, fishing out his wallet. "My mom and me—we're here visiting her dad. I haven't seen him since I was really little and he was out in California."

I take his twenty, give him his change, and try to think of a way to keep this conversation going. Happily, he does that for me.

"Maybe you know him," he says, slipping the wallet back into his pocket. "John Framingham? His house is a bit out of town, back by the . . ."

I never hear the rest of the sentence because my mind is spinning. Freaky Framingham is related to this totally gorgeous, totally normal-seeming hunk of cuteness? His *grandfather*? How is that even possible?

My fingers itch to grab my phone and text Cynthia. But I don't. Mom lectured me on giving the right impression since I'm representing the historical society (and—though she didn't say this—her). Being on my cell isn't proper greeter behavior.

He's looking at me expectantly, and I realize that he has given me information in the form of a question. Which I should answer. "Of course I know him. Everybody in Rocky Point does." I manage to stop myself from saying "he's the town weirdo." I very cleverly finish up with "He's lived here, like, forever."

"Not exactly forever," says Surfer Boy aka Cutest Boy I've Ever Seen aka Freaky Framingham's Freaking *Grandson*. "But close. I'm Oliver, by the way."

That might be the most adorable boy name I've ever heard. I don't know anyone named Oliver. It sounds quirky and old-fashioned and sort of hipster all at once. Special. Not like my name.

"Mandy," I say, wishing it was something more unique. Less bland. It's not even short for anything. Not Amanda. Not Miranda. Not Mandolin or Mandible. Not that I'd rather be named for an instrument or a jawbone.

"So, Mandy," Oliver says, "do you have to stay here at the desk, or can you take me on a tour?"

Suddenly I wish I'd read the mountain of info Mom piled on me about Candy Cane's history. But I'm not going to let a little lack of knowledge force me to pass up this opportunity.

I'm not actually supposed to leave my desk, but it's not like I'm expecting a truckload of tourists to arrive. That never happens, and even if it does, it won't be until after the Fourth of July weekend.

I give him a big smile, and just as I'm coming out from around the desk, I can see that someone's struggling to get the door open. *Really? Now?* I stare at the door, willing the person to give up, to assume that we're not open, anything to get them to go away.

No such luck.

The door gives suddenly, and a tubby man stumbles in, his hand still gripping the knob. "Whoa," he says, righting himself. He straightens his rain slicker. He's dressed as if he's well acquainted with Maine. "That door puts up quite a fight, doesn't it?" he says with a smile.

"Um, yeah," I say. I glance at Oliver. He slips his hands into his pockets and peers at the photos above the display case. *Maybe I can take care of this guy quickly, and then give Oliver a tour*, I think.

"Just one?" I ask cheerfully, already picking up the ticket book.

"Just a second," the man says. He steps back out, carefully propping the door open with his foot, and hollers, "They're open! Come on!"

I watch in dismay as a passel of people pour into the lobby. There isn't parking at the lighthouse, so I had no warning that three SUVs just unloaded three blocks away in the public lot. There are fifteen in all: two sets of parents, three random adults, and eight kids ranging from toddlers to teens.

By the time I sell them their tickets, answer multiple questions, and field various requests for bathrooms, drinks of water, and suggestions for other nearby attractions, Oliver has vanished. Who could blame him? I wish I could have disappeared too—though preferably with him. Did he go upstairs to the second-floor display area? Into the lighthouse?

More important—will I get a chance to talk to him before he leaves?

He's here all summer! The idea blasts through my bad mood like it's the Eagle Island foghorn.

The family group splits up, some going into the Keeper's Café, others checking out the lighthouse. They seem in constant motion, and the various side doors keep banging open and shut. I finally remember to slide the stopper under the front door to hold it open so that visitors won't have to struggle with it, and—my mom's big fear—assume we're closed.

After the noisy family finally departs, and I write down their purchases in the ledger book (one lighthouse magnet, one lobster-shaped teething ring for a baby), I pull my cell out of my bag. I figure if I hold it in my lap and someone walks in, no one will notice that I'm texting.

Freakiness with Freaky just got freakier!

I wait for Cynthia to respond. I know that once she's actually at camp she probably won't be able to text very much, but right now she's still at her grandparents' place in Vermont. It doesn't take long.

Tell tell tell!!!!!!!!

How can I boil it all down into texts? How adorable he looked leaning against the display case, all casual and comfy as if he's been here a million times before. That when he paid for his ticket, I got a whiff of salt air and sunblock, and even though that's how everyone smells in Rocky Point, there was something different about his scent, as if the California air still clung to his clothes. That his smile revealed one front tooth an infinitesimal smidge shorter than the other. That his hand, when he took the ticket from me, has a faded scar on the back of it.

Wow. I had no idea I noticed so much about him.

I decide to stick with the headline:

He's Framingham's grandson.

And then follow that doozy with the really big news: **He's here all summer!!!!**

Barely a second passes:

OMG!

Then:

OMG SQUARED!!!!

As I'm trying to figure out what to text next, she writes back: **How did you find out?**

Me: He came to check out Candy Cane.

Cynthia: I guess you're not so mad about that gig anymore!

Me: No lie!

I don't get to read the next text because Mrs. Gallagher comes in. I'm glad I kept the phone under the table. "Hi, Mrs. Gallagher," I say, quickly hitting vibrate so that the phone won't ring or beep. "What can I do for you?"

"Do you think it would be all right if I leave flyers about the Fourth of July events here?" she asks, holding up a sheaf of bright red paper. Mrs. Gallagher runs the community center and is always looking for a way to spread the word about the summer festivities.

"Oh, sure," I say, then frown. It's not like there's much counter space. "Leave them with me, and I'll find a spot where they can go."

She smiles indulgently at me, that look adults get when they're about to make some pronouncement about you. "You're all grown up. With a job and everything."

I'm not sure this qualifies as a job, and don't know what she means by "and everything," but I just smile as I'm expected to and say, "Yup. Looks that way."

"Well, I don't want to keep you from your work."

We both look around the empty lobby. Mrs. Gallagher smiles again and says in her always-chipper voice, "Hope you'll enter the boat parade this year. Toodles!"

Once she leaves, I riffle the stack of papers, scanning for a spot to put them. I finally just shove them under the cashbox. At least they won't blow away if a gust comes through the open doorway.

I slip one out and look at it. I've always kind of wanted to enter a boat in the Fourth of July boat parade. It's not any-thing fancy: homemade floats on any nonmotorized boat—rafts, canoes, kayaks, dinghies. Some are as simple as a rowboat strung with Christmas tree lights along the gunnels with costumed kids rowing. Others are far more elaborate, their builders hoping to win one of the prizes.

I slip the flyer back under the cashbox and allow myself to indulge in some serious crushing. "Oliver," I murmur dreamily. I picture us in a cute montage doing all those things summer sweethearts supposedly do: taking romantic walks on moonlit beaches, sharing a lemonade with two straws, riding together on a single carousel horse . . .

Carousel horse? I snort. Where did *that* image come from?

I stand and pace the lobby. My only ideas about romance come from books and movies. I have nothing to draw on but my twisted (Cynthia's word) imagination.

Creaking overhead alerts me to the presence of a visitor upstairs. Then footsteps. I stare up at the ceiling. Those are definitely footsteps up there.

I swallow and tell myself it must be a straggler from the massive family that just left. But I could have sworn I counted fifteen enter and fifteen leave.

Then who . . . ?

I lower myself into my seat, thinking about the ghost of Anna Christine, the sad widow of the lighthouse keeper who was swept away in a storm. She was said to still haunt the lighthouse, waiting for her true love to return. On Halloween there are always a few people dressed as poor Anna Christine.

I grip the edge of the table, ears perked, ready for the piercing wail or deep moan, or whatever goose-bump-raising sound ghosts make.

"Are you open every day?"

I nearly fall off my chair when Oliver comes around the desk. "You've been here this whole time?" I ask.

He smiles sheepishly and shoves his hands into his jacket pockets. "I—I know. I—I'm impossible."

Impossibly adorable.

"Wh-what do you mean?" Are we both actually *stammering*? Is that cute to the nth degree, or are we both so uncomfortable with each other that we can barely get the words out?

He hunches his shoulders in an apologetic shrug. "I drive my friends nuts. That is, the ones willing to go to museums with me. I read every single label, look at every single object. Often more than once."

"That's why you were here for so long," I say. "You're a 'completist.'"

He looks baffled, so I quickly explain. "It's someone who has to own, say, every issue of a particular comic. Or is compelled to absolute thoroughness in a museum. It's what my brother Justin calls our cousin Randy. A completist."

One eyebrow rises. "Oh yeah?"

I grin. "Don't worry. I think there's a twelve-step program for it."

He smirks. "Oh, I don't know. If being a 'completist' is wrong . . ."

"You don't want to be right." I finish the song lyric. Our parents must play the same dorky music.

We smile at each other, and I desperately try to think of something clever to say, something to keep the conversation going, some way to get him to ask me out, to stick around, anything—but my mind is a total blank.

"So, uh . . . ," he begins, but before he can get the sentence out, I see someone in the entrance and abruptly stand. Startled by my sudden movement, Oliver takes a step back.

She's backlit by the bright noonday light, but even without actually being able to see her face, I know exactly who it is. "Mom!"

She steps out of the shadowy entryway. Her eyes flick to Oliver and hold for a moment, and then back to me. "How is everything going?"

"Fine. Great. Splendid." *Splendid?*

She looks at me for a moment then turns to Oliver. "Is this your first visit to the Rocky Point Lighthouse?" she asks.

I can tell her wheels are turning. She's trying to decipher exactly what's going on. Is this boy a distraction? A paying customer? My secret lover?

Ha! I actually snort out loud at that one. Her head swivels back to face me. I look down at the desk and rearrange the souvenir pens and pencils in their holder.

"It's my first visit to Rocky Point, period," Oliver says. "It's very cool." He looks around the lobby. "And this place . . ."

His whole face lights up, as if the photos on the walls, the objects in the display cases, the cheesy gift shop items, fill him with a kind of joy. I watch, fascinated. What does the world look like from inside his bright blue eyes? "Well, it's just great."

My mom smiles, and the lines on her face seem to vanish. *Make Mom's day,* I think. She's looking at him as if she just discovered a long-lost best friend.

"You think so?" She gazes around the lobby fondly. "It certainly holds a special spot in my heart. I'm always glad when someone else sees how special this place is."

I roll my eyes and sit back down. I really hope she isn't going to launch into how much she loves Candy Cane.

"See, Mandy?" she says to me. "This young man doesn't think Rocky Point is boring."

Oliver looks at me, surprised.

"I don't think the lighthouse is boring," I say defensively.

Now Mom looks at me with the same surprised expression as Oliver. "This very morning you said—"

"Isn't the library open?" I ask, cutting her off.

"I thought I'd take my daughter to lunch on her first day on the job."

Oliver takes this as his cue. "Well, I'll see you," he says.

"Wait," I blurt. He and Mom both look at me. *Now what?*

I grab one of the flyers and hold it out to him. "Um . . . you should check this out."

He takes the flyer, smiles, then lopes out of the lobby, tripping a bit on the way out the door. He glances back at us, his cheeks tinged slightly pink. I smile, he shrugs, then he's gone.

"I love it when younger people take an interest in the history here," Mom says.

I rummage in my bag to make sure I have the lighthouse key, then knock the wedge out from under the door and hold it open for Mom. "Yes, I know."

I grab the GONE FISHIN' sign that hangs on the inside doorknob and slip it onto the outside knob.

"Is he a day-tripper?" she asks as I make sure the door is locked.

"No, he's here for the summer."

"Really? Where's he staying?"

I shrug. For some reason I don't want to let on that he's Freaky Framingham's grandson. She'll probably assume he's just as weird as his grandfather, despite their shared love of Candy Cane. "We didn't really get much of a chance to talk." That's certainly true.

Mom leads the way up the path. We've never gone out to lunch together before, not on our own. It suddenly seems weird.

I don't think something bad has happened. When Mom has to break bad news, her eyes and mouth don't match. She smiles a toothy, tense grimace as if she's trying to project "everything will be okay" no matter what she's about to say. But her eyes won't match her lips—they're shadowed, holding a sadness or worry in them. When she told us about Dad's heart attack, even back then, I had already learned to recognize this contradiction on her face. That day, the disparity was sharp, her smile bright but brittle, and her eyes sunk into her face as if they were in retreat. Justin and I perched on the battered vinyl sofa swing on the screened-in porch, and I knew I didn't want to hear whatever she was about to say. Knew with such certainty that I covered my ears before she spoke.

I sneak a peek at her as we walk the three blocks to where she parked the car. Mom isn't exactly a chatterer so we walk along in silence, accompanied by the familiar sounds of our crunching, shuffling footsteps, the *whump, fwump* of seagull wings, and the soft slap of water against the moss-covered boulders. As far as I can tell, Mom's face forms a coherent whole. Her eyes seem kind of tired, and her mouth has a downward slant, but that's been her usual expression for a while now.

We slide into the car, the seats warm from the sun, and buckle up. Her hands on the wheel, she says, "Tiny's?"

I shrug. "Sure."

Tiny's actually *is* tiny. The owner took the space in the alley between the Laundromat and the hardware store on Main Street and created a thriving take-out place. In deference to the local economy there's always one seafood item on the menu, but otherwise it's vegetarian and vegan. More Summer Regulars seem to frequent it than us locals, though it's often quite busy right after New Year's when people making vows to eat more healthily suddenly remember it's there.

By the time we've gotten our salads (lobster for Mom, of course, greens with feta cheese and watermelon for me) and snagged one of the benches lining the town square, the fog has burned away. It's not hot, the watermelon is weirdly delicious in the salad, and Oliver is going to be here all summer. Things are looking up—I even forgive Mom for interrupting my first conversation with him.

Until . . .

"I know you're disappointed that both Justin and Cynthia are gone most of the summer. But perhaps without the usual distractions, we can spend some time thinking about your junior year."

"Seriously, Mom?" I put the plastic fork back into the take-out container. "Summer vacation just started. You really want to talk about school?"

"Next year is crucial for your college applications," Mom says. "Your grades improved this past year, but . . ."

I sigh, long and loud. "I know. I'm not perfect like Justin."

"Now, Mandy," Mom says, "I'm not comparing you two."

"Of course you are. Just like all my teachers who say '*You're* Justin Sullivan's sister?' as if they can't believe Mr. Straight As could be related to the B Queen."

"I'm sure you're exaggerating. And you got several B-pluses this year."

Here's my thing with school. If it's about concepts, I've got it nailed. So I'm good in English, and even things like social studies. But when it's about stuff that has to be memorized and super detailed, not so much.

Before he died, Dad was the one who used to help me with my homework. The strongest impression that stays with me is how patient he was. Both Mom and Justin would try to help me later, but Justin would get bored (who can blame him?), and Mom just got frustrated.

"Okay, Frowny-face," she says in her teasing tone. It's what she's called me since I was a little girl and would pout. "I get it. It's a bit early to start in on school." She pats my hand. "And you're showing real maturity and responsibility taking on the greeter job at Candy Cane."

Wow. A compliment. I give her a small smile as we pack up our trash and toss it into a nearby receptacle.

After parking in the lot, Mom walks me back to Candy Cane, and as I struggle to get the heavy door to unstick, I hear her sigh behind me. "Another thing to fix," she mutters. The door suddenly gives and I stumble inside. I slip the wedge into place to hold it open, then turn to say bye. She smiles that oh-so-bright smile and says cheerfully, "Just add it to the list."

What's this about? I wonder. Her worried eyes don't match the chirpy tone. *Something* is *wrong.* "Um . . . ," I begin.

She turns slightly so that the breeze off the water stops blowing her hair into her face. She smooths it down with one hand and jiggles the car keys with the other. "I'd better run," she says. "Caroline is alone with the new volunteers, and sometimes having the help isn't any help at all."

"Thanks for lunch," I call after her. She waves without turning around, and I watch her slim back as she heads toward the car. As I take my seat behind the desk, I wonder what she's worried about, then remember that she basically worries about everything. It probably isn't anything specific, just her general "I'm a mom and so I worry" thing.

Other than a completely imaginary return visit from Oliver, no one comes to the lighthouse for the rest of the day. Cynthia must have been somewhere with her family in a cell-phone-free location, because I texted her a few times and never heard back. I played a few games on my phone, one eye to the door at all (okay, most) times in case Mom came back or someone did wander in. I stuck my head out the door to remind myself that the town actually still exists, restraightened every single flyer and brochure, and finally, finally, finally it's four o'clock and I can go home. And look forward to another dull and endless day tomorrow.

The lobster boats are back where they belong in the harbor, the catch unloaded long ago and already being delivered to restaurants or sold to walk-ups right at the dock. People really go gaga for that—fresh off the boat, right out of the trap. Me, I have to look in the other direction. The squirmy, crawling creatures give me the jeebies.

I dismount at the steepest part of Weatherby Hill and push my bike to the top. This isn't going to be big fun come late July and August when the sun beats down and the humidity skyrockets. Hopefully, though, the daily bike ride will get me into better shape. I'm not exactly the most athletically inclined person. I'm more of a couch-inclined person, something Justin and Cynthia rag on me about, sometimes simultaneously.

I'll show them, I think with a grin. I hop back on the bike and pedal hard for about two blocks, and then decide it's just too much work. This is vacation, right?

After dinner I call Cynthia. With all we have to discuss, texting just won't do.

"Don't leave out a single anything," Cynthia says. "How did you find out about the freaky Freaky connection?"

I tell her everything—about Oliver's arrival, how cute he looked, how we were bonding, and how Mom might have ruined it all by almost revealing my lack of interest in Candy Cane, which he seems to love as much as she does.

I flip over onto my back with an awful thought. "He might not come back to the lighthouse. I mean, he already spent all morning looking at what takes most people fifteen minutes. Twenty, tops."

"Because he likes you and wanted to hang around," Cynthia insists.

Sadly, I have to tell the truth. "Not exactly. He spent all the time upstairs looking at those exhibits. I didn't even know he was up there."

"Huh." Now I can picture Cynthia's "working on it" expression. The face she makes when her brain is trying to come up with a solution, a plan, or an explanation for something. "Well, maybe now that he knows you work there, he'll come back!"

"Maybe . . ."

"Come on, Mandy! The way he looked at you at the festival! That was the face of a boy who seriously liked what he saw. It was as if I wasn't even there at all."

I sit straight up at that. She's right! Cynthia was standing right next to me, and *I* was the one he smiled at, who he remembered. A giant grin spreads over my face.

"What is with me?" I moan. "All day I've been mood swinging. Elated. Miserable. Happy. Sad. Panicked. Calm. What is up with that?"

"Hormones," Cynthia says, perfectly imitating her mom. That's what her mother says to explain the inexplicable things Cynthia or her sisters do. Part resignation, part exasperation. Turns out it's a pretty convenient excuse. Cynthia started using it herself to get out of trouble, particularly with her dad, who turns seven shades of pink at the mere mention of hormones. It's become our favorite catchphrase to explain the unexplainable— everything from a teacher suddenly getting strict to extreme shifts in the weather.

"Hormones," I agree, giving the word the same treatment. This sets us both laughing hysterically.

Over my cackling I can hear Mom calling up the stairs. "Hang on," I tell Cynthia. I open my door and pop out my head. "Yeah?"

"Shouldn't you be getting ready for bed?" Mom says from the foot of the staircase. "It's another workday tomorrow."

"Gotta go," I say into the phone.

"Keep me posted," Cynthia says.

I nod at Mom and return to the privacy of my bedroom. "As if I wasn't going to send you hourly bulletins if I ever see him again."

"You will."

That's the thing about Cynthia. Her confidence is contagious. At least for a little while. Long enough for me to go to sleep excited about tomorrow.

As I coast down Weatherby for my second day of Candy Cane duty, the breeze coming off the water blows strands of hair into my face. They keep sticking to my lip gloss, but I'm in such a good mood I don't care. I simply flick them away each time it happens. I just hope I'm not wiping off the Blushing Rose gloss each time I do. I forgot to toss it into my bag, since I don't usually travel with makeup, much to Cynthia's constant annoyance. At least the shadow, mascara, and shimmer face powder won't wear off. I'm not so certain about the shimmer. It might be a little much for sitting in a lighthouse all day, but I can always wash it off once I get there.

Even though I know it's unlikely that Oliver will come back, I took care not just with my face but with the rest of me too.

The jeans that fit great and a cute top Cynthia picked out for me last month to "enhance my assets." Not exactly sure what assets those might be, but whatever. If Oliver really is a "completist," then he might come back today to make sure he didn't miss anything.

I hope!

I open up, humming a sea chantey that had been blasting from the open doors of Ahoy, a swimwear shop on Main Street. Once the season really gets under way, Rocky Point goes overdrive on the fishy and Maine Americana. It's as if summers send Rocky Point back in time, and that's the way the Regulars like it. They seem to come here to get back to the "good old days," but truth to tell, I don't see what's so great about them. How people lived here in the winters before good heating, television, and cars is beyond me.

Today as I look around Candy Cane, I try to understand what Oliver finds so appealing. Is he a history buff? Into lighthouses, specifically? Drawn to all things sea-related? I've met all of those types of visitors, and I guess I'm even related to one, since Mom loves all that stuff. I can't remember if Dad did too, but since all my memories are of them happily together in never-ending conversations, I guess he did.

By noon there have been no visitors, and my stomach is growling. I poke my head out of the lighthouse door. No one. Not Oliver, not a tour bus, not even Mom to take me to another lunch.

That's probably a good sign, I tell myself. It means she doesn't feel the need to check up on me. But it also means that

I'll have to settle for whatever's on the menu at the Keeper's Café. Luckily, I don't have to pay for the overpriced fare since it's a "perk" of the job, but I should really start thinking about bringing lunch.

I hang the GONE FISHIN' sign on the door and lock it. Then I walk around to the main entrance of the café, the one you can enter without having to go into the lighthouse.

The café is supercute, with lots of Maine-related decor and old photos, but the menu's limited to what can be prepared on a hotplate or in a microwave. The idea had been that the café would offset some of the costs involved in maintaining the light-house, but I don't see how that's possible. No year-rounder or even Summer Regular eats there since the menu is so limited and, frankly, pretty bad. And tourists to Rocky Point are only a trickle, not a deluge.

I've only taken a few steps inside when I realize there's some-one sitting at the counter, talking to Celeste Ingram.

Not just someone. Oliver.

I spaz out. I freeze, and the screen door bangs me in the butt, making me yelp and drop the magazine I'm carrying. My scrunchy bag slides down my arm and lands on the floor with a *thwump*. All this commotion makes Celeste look up and Oliver swivel on his stool at the counter.

Invisibility spell now! I plead silently.

"Mandy, hi," Oliver says, a smile lighting up his face.

I give him a weak smile and an even weaker wave. *A wave? I'm waving at a boy just a few feet away?* Oliver seems to bring out the utter dork in me.

"Hey there, Mandy," Celeste says. "You meeting Cynthia for lunch?"

This is even more shocking than seeing Oliver a second day in a row. Celeste Ingram not only knows my name, but she also knows I'm best friends with Cynthia? Not possible! Then I realize that it's more likely she knows who Cynthia is and recognizes me as the sidekick.

They're both looking at me, waiting. Right. Words. They're those things that come out of your mouth. "Actually, Cynthia's away till August," I say, taking a few tentative steps into the café.

"Working today?" Oliver asks.

I nod and keep approaching the counter. Slowly. They don't seem mad about my being there, but I still have the awful fear that I interrupted something. Once a boy has Celeste's attention, his own stays pretty riveted on her.

"Lunch break, huh?" Celeste picks up a menu and drops it onto the counter right beside Oliver. Not that I need the single laminated page. Still, I take this as a sign that she completely expects me to sit there.

I like that assumption.

"You two have met?" Celeste asks.

I slide onto the stool and pretend to study the menu waiting to hear what Oliver will say about our encounter.

"I was in the lighthouse yesterday," he explains.

The bare facts. Oh well. I suppose he doesn't want to admit to the celestial Celeste that we shared some serious eye beams at the festival, too.

"Can I have a veggie burrito?" I ask. "And a lemonade."

"Sure."

Celeste picks up the menu, slips it back beside the cash register with the others, then pushes through the swinging doors into the small kitchen.

Alone with Oliver, I'm stumped for things to say. He seems equally stymied. He just smiles at me. There's no plate in front of him. Did Celeste already clear it away, or did he come here just to see her? The Keeper's Café opens at eleven. Has he been here a whole hour already? Even a completist would have completed checking out the café decor and gift shop by now, since the upstairs exhibit area is closed.

"Here ya go." Celeste returns with the burrito and lemonade. Microwaving doesn't take much time.

I feel Oliver looking at me. I turn to face him as if I'm capable of conversation. "Why are you eating *here*?" I blurt.

Celeste looks at me in surprise. My mom would be so pissed if she heard me bad-mouthing the café to a potential customer. "I mean, it's kind of far for you," I add lamely.

Celeste has a new kind of surprise on her face. This isn't an "I can't believe you just said that" expression. This is a "you already know his deets?" face.

I busy myself trying to figure out the best way to eat the soggy burrito. It may be free for me to eat here, but I am *so* going to start bringing my own lunch.

"I was checking out the grounds," Oliver explains. "When Celeste opened up, I realized it had been a long time since breakfast."

Of course. He took one look at Celeste and followed her inside like a baby duckling after its mama.

A woman with steel-gray hair cut in a short bob pops her head into the café. "Do you know when the lighthouse opens up again?" she asks.

I turn around, still chewing the big bite I took of the burrito, and say, "I can open up if you want."

"Oh, I wouldn't want to interrupt your lunch," she says, but her tone broadcasts she really wishes I'd hurry up already and let her in.

I take a swig of the lemonade and stand. I hastily wipe my mouth with a napkin, wad it up, and toss it onto the plate.

"Thanks," I say to Celeste. I pick up the lemonade. "I'll bring the glass back later."

"Sure. You want me to wrap up the burrito?"

"No thanks."

I start walking toward the woman, who stands half in, half out of the café doorway.

"Hang on, Mandy," Oliver says behind me. "I'll come too."

I spin around in disbelief to see Oliver picking up a sketchpad that he had stashed under the counter. He's going to leave Celeste and come hang out with me?

But once I struggle with the door and take the woman's admission fee, it becomes apparent he's not there to hang out. He's back to visit the lighthouse again. "I thought I'd do some sketching, if that's okay," he says.

"Sure. Just . . . if a group wants to go up to the tower, give them room."

I refuse his five dollars; it seems like a lot to pay since he was just here yesterday, and I'm hoping maybe it will encourage him to keep coming back.

I don't see Oliver—or anyone else—the rest of the afternoon. That's not strictly true. Oliver came down from the tower and then walked around outside, sketching Candy Cane from different angles. What's so fascinating?

When I lock up for the day, he's still outside, sitting at one of the picnic tables behind the Keeper's Café. My heart sinks. Is he waiting for Celeste? He doesn't look up when I cross to the shed to get my bike. Our great romance is over before it begins.

I slam the shed shut and yank the padlock closed. I walk my bike along the gravel path, the tires spitting up little pebbles. In case Oliver looks up, I don't want him to see me awkwardly mounting the bike. I've never quite mastered accomplishing this gracefully. I force myself not to look his way.

"Hey," I hear him call. "You done for the day?"

I glance over. He's standing now, and heading toward me.

"Yup," I say.

"Okay if I walk with you?" he asks.

There go those hormones again: from doldrums to delight. "Sure," I say.

We fall into step, me pushing the bike, him carrying his sketchpad. I'm glad he doesn't have a bike too. I don't want him watching me huff and puff up Weatherby. I'm living proof you can be slim and not exactly be fit.

"I'm meeting my mom at the library," he says. "You know where that is?"

I laugh. "I should. It's where my mother works." Good. I'm managing sentences of more than single words.

"Have you lived here your whole life?" Oliver asks.

I nod. "Have you lived in California all yours?" There. A question about him. That's what the dating guides Cynthia and I pore over say to do to keep a conversation going with a boy.

"In Cali, yeah, but not in the same place. When my parents got divorced, my dad moved to Sacramento, where he works, and Mom and I moved to the suburbs not too far away."

"Was that a big adjustment?"

The instant I ask I want to take the words back. It's such a personal question. Oliver just shrugs. "We were living in the suburbs before, we just moved closer to the city. The divorce part . . ." His voice trails off. I wait. "It was weird that it was suddenly official that dad wasn't living with us. But they had hardly spent any time together for a long time. Mom's job can take her practically around the clock, and Dad often had business trips."

"When did they split up?" It's kind of amazing that he's so open about all this. Maybe it's a California thing.

"A few years back. I think they'd been planning it for a while but wanted to wait until it was time for me to start high school. You know, because of the move."

We start the incline up Weatherby. I nod a greeting at Vicki Jensen and her dad standing outside Second Time Around. Vicki's eyes are huge, taking in the sight of me with a new boy. She makes the universal "call me" sign. I'm glad Oliver doesn't notice. He's too busy watching the ferry chugging toward Hubbard Island.

"So . . . you're visiting your grandfather." Once again I have to stop myself from calling him Freaky. "How come you've never been here before?"

"Partly the distance. And Mom gets antsy if she's too far away from civilization."

"And Rocky Point isn't exactly civilized."

He turns his head to look at me full-on. "I think it's great!" he protests. He stumbles over the curb, turns pinkish, and brings his attention forward again. "Mom, though. She grew up in Cranston and couldn't wait to get out of Maine."

Cranston is a town just a ferry ride away. Or a circuitous drive to the next-door peninsula.

"Like me and Cynthia," I say.

"Who's Cynthia?"

"My best friend. She's away for the summer. She practically has a calendar in her head where she's x-ing out the days until she gets to leave 'Rock Bottom.'"

"This place is so beautiful," Oliver argues. "It's like it says on that sign we passed on the highway." He holds up his hands as if he's creating a banner in the sky. "'Maine: The Way Life Should Be.'"

"The way it should be for a few weeks a year," I counter. "If you were here year-round you'd get insanely bored. There's a reason so many people in Stephen King's books go nuts in Maine."

"Maybe. But this is so much better than the suburbs. Except for the weather." He gives me a grin. "See, I'm not *totally* swept away by all the beauty here."

I blush. I think I know what he really means, but I can't help imagining what he means is me.

"Back home, it seems to be all stress all the time," he contin-ues. "Mom's job is wacky big. Like, millions of bucks at stake."

"What does she do?"

"Matches investors with new tech. So she stays on top of everything that's out there, and tries to nab big money before anyone else can."

"Intense."

"No joke."

"So why now?"

"Why now what?"

"Are things less busy at her job now?"

"She doesn't actually *have* a job. She *is* the job. But, well, some stuff happened that made her want to see her old man. So here we are."

I wait, but he doesn't elaborate. It's probably too personal. I don't care what the reason is; I'm just glad that it brought Oliver here.

We reach the south end of the Square, where I make the turn onto Berry to go home. "Well," I say, "this is where I get off."

Oliver shakes his bangs out of his face, then pushes up his sunglasses. "So, see you around."

I watch him as he walks toward the library. Why doesn't he actually ask me out?

And I'm back down in the doldrums. "The doldrums" is a sail-ing term. It refers to a spot in the Atlantic Ocean where there can be long stretches of no wind. If you're in the doldrums, you aren't going anywhere. Which is exactly how I feel. Going nowhere.

*O*liver is waiting at Candy Cane when I arrive the next morning. That's three days in a row! No one can love a lighthouse this much! He *has* to be here to see me—or Celeste, I remind myself as a way to keep from giggling giddily. I skid to a stop, spitting gravel. I climb off the bike, vowing to practice so that I can do it with ease.

He smiles sheepishly. "I'm back."

"So I see." I smile, then stash the bike. When I turn back around, Oliver's up and waiting at the door.

"Awfully eager," I tease, jiggling the key in the lock. The tumblers turn, but the door doesn't budge. Dang! Stuck. I let out a puff of air to get my bangs out of my face and push harder.

"Let me," Oliver says.

I take a step back. "Be my guest."

Oliver rattles the doorknob, then puts his shoulder against the door. It groans, but doesn't open. Oliver steps back again. "Are you sure you unlocked it?"

"It's sticking worse than usual," I offer. I think maybe he's a little embarrassed that he tried to go all macho and failed. "The humidity."

"Must be it." Oliver runs a hand through his hair. "Okay. On the count of three?"

"Sure." I step up and stand sideways to the door, figuring we'll both have to use our shoulders. Oliver moves into place behind me.

I shut my eyes and feel his warmth against my back, and

sense his chin just above my ear. I smell that scent again, part laundry detergent, part ocean, part something unidentifiable. I grip the knob, afraid I'll lean into him instead of into the door.

"One. Two. Three. Now!" Together we shove hard against the door. It swings open and we stumble through. Oliver grabs my elbow to keep me upright, but our momentum is too much. We land on the floor in a tangled clump.

We're laughing so hard, we just lie there, my arm trapped under his chest, his leg across my hip. Once we catch our breath, we quickly scramble back up to standing, straightening our clothing and not looking at each other. I think we both sensed the moment had gone on a tad too long.

To recover completely, I lean against a display case and cross my arms. "Okay. What is it about the lighthouse you love so much?" I'm genuinely curious, and there's more than a teeny-tiny part of me that hopes he'll say something like "it's not the lighthouse, it's the lighthouse keeper." Mushy I know, but I figure it would sound a lot better coming out of his mouth than rattling around in my brain.

Oliver looks around the lobby, his eyes dancing from one photo to another. "I don't really know," he says.

Not the answer I was hoping for.

"When I was really little, we lived near the water," he goes on. "I don't really remember it, but there are pictures of me dressed as a pirate. Maybe that's when the whole seafaring fixation started."

I smile, picturing him as a little pirate boy. "And continues," I say, remembering the way he studied the model boats in the Artists and Artisans tent at the festival. Now that I know he's a completist, his behavior that day makes more sense.

"You must know a lot of great stories about this place," Oliver continues.

I shrug. "Some, I guess." My mind spins as I try to recall a single bit of lore from Mom's files, but I draw a blank. I never am good under pressure. I don't know how Cynthia manages, getting up there in front of everyone when she performs.

"I love a good ghost story," Oliver admits. "Or just weird history. Lighthouses and places like Rocky Point are great sources. Not like the boring suburbs."

Those things I'm actually into. It just never occurred to me before that maybe Candy Cane qualifies. I gaze around the lobby with new interest. Maybe I'll take another look at Mom's files while Oliver is . . . My face scrunches in confusion. *While Oliver goes around measuring things?* He has pulled out a professional-looking tape measure and eyes the archway that leads to the stone stairs.

"Mind if I . . . ?" He jerks his pointy chin toward the stairs.

"Go ahead."

He smiles, and I wave away his wallet. What the heck is he doing? I can't ask, because a group of kids all wearing bright orange camp T-shirts barrels in, followed by two frazzled teen counselors (the younger sisters of a couple of boys at my school) and two even more frazzled adults. Usually the camps bring kids on rainy days, so I'm surprised to see them.

"Plumbing issue," the chunky older woman in khaki shorts and camp T-shirt explains with a sigh. "We have to find things to do with them all day while repairs are made. We missed the first ferry to Hubbard Island, so we're here until the next one."

That explains the frazzle. "Do you want me to let the café know that there's going to be a group?"

"We brought our own lunches, but thanks."

Too bad. Mom would have been thrilled to have such a crowd so early in the season. "You could always grab a cup of coffee," I suggest.

"That would be great, but these munchkins are a handful," she replies.

She's not wrong. The kids make so much racket that Oliver comes down from the tower to see what's going on. Good thing, too, since several kids make a beeline for the stairs, a teenaged counselor trotting after them. Oliver flattens himself against the wall to let them by.

"Only three fit in the tower at a time," I call after them. I catch Oliver's eye and give him a rueful smile. He gives me a "what can you do?" shrug. He mouths "Later" and leaves, nearly tripping over two kids rushing to the mini-gift-shop area. I'm disappointed but seriously, I can't blame him. It's as if Candy Cane has been invaded.

Once they leave and I've restored order to the lobby, it's time for lunch, which I forgot to pack. It's Keeper's Café again.

And once again, there's Oliver, sitting at the counter, chatting away with the intimidatingly beautiful Celeste. I try to back out before they can see me, but Celeste, perfect in all ways including as employee, looks up immediately. "Hey, Mandy."

Oliver swivels and grins. "Survived the hordes, I see."

"All in one piece. And so are the displays, thank goodness." I hover in the doorway like an idiot, again unsure if I'm interrupting something.

"Meeting someone?" Celeste asks, grabbing some menus.

"Oh! Nah." She must think if I'm still standing at the door I want a booth. Oliver smiles at me, his legs stretched out, one sneakered foot over the other. That's the way he stands, too, one leg slightly over the other, ankles crossed. Must be some kind of laid-back California posture.

"Know what you want?" Celeste knows I can recite the menu as easily as she can.

The burrito was pretty close to awful, so I decide to try something nonmicrowaved. "Salad?"

"Lobster, crab, chicken, or just greens?"

"Chicken, please. And a lemonade."

She slips a tall plastic glass under the lemonade dispenser, then places it next to Oliver. I guess that's where I'll be sitting.

"Oliver said you got a big crowd," Celeste says, placing the rolled-up napkin holding my silverware on the counter as I settle onto the stool. "You think they'll come over here?"

"Sorry," I tell her. "They're a camp group that brought their lunches."

She rolls her green eyes. "Of course they did. Hang on, and I'll get your salad."

"She must be as bored as me," I say as she pushes through the door into the kitchen.

"Not just bored. She's not making any tips if there aren't any customers," Oliver points out. "She's worried about school expenses."

331

So she spilled her woes to him. They're getting close. When he came to the lighthouse, he was so busy measuring and sketching he never really talked to me.

I slouch, letting my hair fall like a curtain, masking the sides of my face. I don't want that flashing neon sign that always reveals what I'm thinking to show Oliver my jealousy. But seriously, why *wouldn't* he be into her? And why wouldn't she be into him?

Although . . . Celeste's in college. Isn't he going into his junior year like me? The thought cheers me up enough to restore the appetite that I lost when I first walked into the café.

I hear that boy Oliver has been spending time with you," Mom says.

My fork doesn't make it to my mouth; it just hangs there, scrambled egg dangling through the tines. Once a week we have breakfast for supper, and tonight's the night.

This was Mom's late day at the library. Even though school's out, the library stays busy. Summer Regulars always run out of books to read because they forget how often it rains here. And the library has the best Wi-Fi in town, and the only truly consistent cell signal.

I shovel the scrams into my mouth, buying some time to get my various reactions under control. Shock that she knows, annoyance that everyone knows everything about everybody in this tiny town, and a teensy thrill at the idea that it's *me* people think Oliver is there to see.

"Not with *me*," I say after I swallow. "He's in love with your lighthouse."

Mom chuckles. "I guess I do kind of think of it as mine." She reaches out and pats my hand. "And now yours."

New thought: Does she know that I haven't been charging him? That would probably bug her more than the idea of Oliver trying to have his way with me up in the tower.

"If he's really interested in the history of the lighthouse, you should send him over to the library."

The historical society's office is on the top floor of the library. The building is her home away from home. I think if she didn't believe a mom has to be present with a teenage girl in the house, she'd happily move there.

"I'll mention it," I say, although I know I probably won't. If he's at the library all day, that means he won't be dropping by Candy Cane as often.

"Do you spend much time talking to him?"

I sigh. "Don't worry, Mom," I say, pouring syrup onto my bacon. "I'm greeting everyone just the way a greeter should."

My tone must irk Mom, because she bristles and says, "Good to know, but that isn't why I asked." She taps a finger on the table, the way she does when she's getting ready to head into tricky territory. "I was wondering if you know anything about him."

Uh-oh. How to play this? Is she genuinely asking me, or does she know already that Freaky is his grandfather? And if she does, would that mean she'd ban me from seeing him, if I ever get the chance? Outside of the lighthouse, that is.

"Not a lot," I say warily. "Do you?" It only just occurs to me that Mom could be a good source of intel.

She takes a sip of decaf, her concession to this breakfast being of the supper variety. "Rumors. You know how Rocky Point is."

Do I ever. "So . . . ," I say as casually as I can. "What have you heard?"

"The one thing that seemed the most unlikely turned out to be true. He's John Framingham's grandson. He's here visiting with his mother."

So she already knows.

One of her eyebrows rises. "You don't seem surprised."

"Actually, he told me. And I saw them together at the Lupine Festival."

"That's right, there *had* been a Freaky sighting."

I gape at her. She smiles. "What?" she says. "The adults find him just as odd as you kids do."

"How'd you find out?" I ask.

"Oliver's mother came into the library. She needed to use our Internet connection. I'm not surprised there isn't one up at the cottage."

"Yeah, somehow the world's crankiest recluse doesn't seem the type to use social media," I say. "So what's she like?"

"A little intense. You know, one of those high-powered types who want everything yesterday. She tried to cover it, but I could tell that our connection wasn't fast enough and that 'relax' isn't a word she's very familiar with. But pleasant enough."

Mom sneaks a piece of syrup-soaked bacon from my plate. "I wonder what it was like to have John Framingham as a father," she muses. "She mentioned she grew up in Cranston, so we may have actually been to some of the same events."

"Framingham didn't always live up on Evergreen, right?" I ask.

"He moved here just around the time you were born, I think."

"Did she say how long they're here visiting?"

"Hard to say. I think the plan is the whole summer, but I don't know how long she'll last. She seemed pretty frustrated by her cell service too. She made jokes about it, but I don't think this is actually vacation time for her."

My heart sinks. I might never get a chance to really get to know Oliver if they leave soon.

*J*ust near closing time Oliver walks into the lighthouse. He no longer bothers to attempt to pay since I always refuse to take his money (don't be mad, Mom!).

I'm doing the end-of-the-week tally: number of visitors, what items were sold, anything we need to restock. Pretty easy since it's been slow.

He holds his sketchbook in front of him, as if it's a protective shield. He looks different. Shy. Insecure. Not the look he usually wears.

"Um. . ." He tosses aside his bangs and clears his throat. He tries again. "Um, so I bet you've been wondering what I've been doing."

"Maybe a little."

He takes another step closer. What's he being so tentative about? I don't really care. It makes him look all cute and vulnerable.

He lays his sketchbook on my desk. "Take a look," he says.

I give him a quizzical glance and force myself not to rip it open. I've been dying with curiosity to see what he's been spending all that time doing.

I'm still not sure. The first page has xeroxed pictures of Candy Cane taped to it. Mystified, I turn the page. Here there's a sketch of Candy Cane with notations and conversions: *1/8" = 1 foot*, that kind of thing. My eyes flick to his face then back to the page. He did these? They're amazing.

Other pages have different views of the lighthouse along with close-up details: the portholelike windows in the tower; the different doorways, both inside and out. There's what looks like a floor plan, along with sketches of the Keeper's Café.

"These are so good," I say.

I get to the last of the impressively accurate and detailed drawings and shut the pad. I'm relieved there aren't any romantic portraits of Celeste. But I don't understand why pictures of our lighthouse make him so shy.

"I figured out the scale, then drew up what I thought would be best," Oliver says.

"Best for what?" Is he planning to build a replica of Candy Cane for his yard back home in California? That would definitely stand out in the suburbs.

"Oh, right. Like usual, I forgot the most important part. Mom says I work up to things backwards."

I still look at him uncomprehendingly. "Are you ready to start from the front?"

"Fourth of July." He taps the red flyer peeking out from

under the sketchbook. The pile is still nearly as thick as when Mrs. Gallagher dropped them off. Business hasn't exactly been booming.

I wait for him to continue, because even though he seems to think he's explained everything, I'm still completely clueless. Whatever's obvious to him isn't at all clear to me.

"The boat parade! We should make a replica of the lighthouse and enter it. Pops already said I could use one of his dinghies. Whaddya think?"

What do I think? Did I actually hear him say "we"? As in *we* should do this together. Oliver and me. Me and Oliver. Sharing a common goal. And spending loads of time together.

My fantasizing comes to an abrupt halt when I see the disappointment on Oliver's face. "Sorry," he mumbles, reaching for the sketchbook. "You gave me the flyer. I—I thought you'd be into it. I shouldn't have assumed—"

"I am! I am!" I slap my hand on top of his to keep him from picking up his pad. "I'm completely interested."

Was that too enthusiastic? I don't care. Our eyes meet, and I feel his hand under mine. I don't want to move it. I get the sense he doesn't want me to.

For one glorious moment we smile at each other, then the nerves kick in and we each back off.

"We'll need to get started right away," I tell him. "We have less than three weeks."

"I kind of already got started," he tells me. "But yeah. The pressure's on. Do you have to work here every day?"

"No," I say. "I'm here four days a week, and Janet Milner is here the other two we're open. And it stays light late, so we can still work after my shift. Right?"

"Right. When's your first day off?"

"Tomorrow," I tell him, never more happy to use that word before in my life.

*I*t's really happening," I whisper hoarsely into the phone. "Tomorrow!"

"What?" Cynthia says. "I can barely hear you. Where are you?"

I pace and glance up and down the street from the screened-in porch. I'm too antsy to sit still. I'm keeping an eye out for Mom; this is a conversation she can't overhear. Neighbors either.

I'm about to do something big—go to a boy's house, a boy I like, without telling my mom. And the reason I'm not telling my mom is the biggest part of the story: The boy's house is actually the home of Freaky Framingham.

"I'm home," I say in a more normal voice. "But this is radio-active news."

"My favorite kind!" Cynthia says. "What's going to explode?"

"Me! And"—I lower my voice again—"possibly my mom."

"Oooh." I hear rustling. I can picture Cynthia getting comfy, settling in for a long session. "Spill."

I pause and wave back at Mr. Martin, who's walking his dog, Thunder. Or more accurately, Thunder is walking *him*. Mr. Martin smiles at me and continues trotting down the street.

"Hello?" Cynthia says. "You still there?"

"Just waiting till the coast is clear."

I tell her every single word Oliver and I exchanged, because of course I have them memorized. For once, Cynthia doesn't interrupt me. "You wouldn't believe how adorably awkward and shy he was leading up to his Fourth of July proposal. I mean, proposition," I correct myself hastily. Wait, that sounds even worse. "I mean, *request* to work together," I finish lamely.

There's a brief silence, then Cynthia says, "Whoa."

"Yeah," I agree. "'Whoa' barely covers it."

"But I don't get the mom part," Cynthia says. "Why can't you tell her? I mean, just because you haven't really dated before doesn't mean—"

"You forgot the critical fact!" I squeak. My eyes dart back and forth, ensuring my solitude. I lower my voice again. "Remember who we're talking about. Who he's *related* to . . ."

I hear a sharp intake of breath. "You're right. That's practically nuclear."

"So you see why I can't tell Mom. She might not let me go. Since we have to build the boat at his house. Since that's where the boat is," I add, though I know I'm stating the super obvious. But since Cynthia forgot the Freaky part of the equation, I figure I'd better spell things out.

More silence.

"Hello?" I check the phone. Not a lot of bars, but that's standard. Certainly enough to still have a connection.

"Just thinking."

Good! I'm counting on her to come up with one of her winner schemes to keep Mom from freaking out and forbidding me from going up there.

"Maybe . . . ," she begins, and then stops.

"Yes . . . ," I prompt.

"Maybe this one time your mom's right."

I blink. Twice. That is so not what I thought she was going to say.

"I mean, who knows what kind of crazy you'll find."

"Oliver isn't crazy," I say hotly.

"That's not what I'm saying," Cynthia says. "But do you really want to be up at Freaky's Haunted House of Horrors with a boy you barely know, where there's, like, no road and no cell reception?"

"You make it sound like an episode of *Supernatural*."

"I'm just saying . . ."

"Framingham may be weird, but he's lived here all of our lives, and there's never been anything really strange happening up there—"

"That you know of . . ."

"Are you kidding me? If they found even a dead mouse on his property, the whole town would know about it."

"There's always a first—"

I cut her off. "It's really mean to call it Freaky's Haunted House of Horrors. He's a person. He has a right to live how he wants without everyone going all judgey."

Now this is weird. I'm standing up for Freaky Framingham.

"Mandy, I'm trying to look out for you. You're so nuts about this Oliver that you—"

"You know, I thought you'd be excited for me. I finally have a boy who likes me. Who I like back."

"Look, I saw him. He's supercute. But—"

I don't want her to finish that sentence. "Mom's coming up the street. Gotta go."

For the first time ever I hang up on my best friend.

As I bike up Evergreen Road toward Framingham's house, Cynthia's voice yells at me in my head. Is she right? No one knows where I'm spending the day. If I disappear, will anyone know where to look?

A twig snaps in the woods off to my right, and I nearly swerve my bike into the bushes. *Get a grip!* I order myself.

How could Cynthia do this to me? I fume. Until that awful phone call last night I was utterly delirious about today. Now I'm completely on edge: nervous about what will happen if Mom finds out; worried that Cynthia's right and that I'm making a terrible, terrible mistake; and actually scared of woods that I've known my whole life.

I had a text from Cynthia this morning—an order to text or call the minute I get home. *If I don't hear from you by 7pm I'm telling your mom.*

Unbelievable.

Though as the woods grow deeper around me, it begins to seem like a pretty good idea.

Framingham's house is on the same side of the peninsula as the harbor, but farther inland, where the woods start. There are winding roads here, so you can't see very far ahead, and it's kind of hilly. Big houses peek through breaks in the pines. Mailboxes

341

line the road to mark where the turnoffs begin. Some mailboxes are super plain—others are pretty hokey. One has a lighthouse perched on top; another is shaped like a big clam.

As I bike up yet another hill, the trees grow more and more dense. The sun's rays hit my face through the small patches between countless trees. The summer warm-up has begun, and I know to be grateful for the shade, but it feels overly symbolic. "If this were a movie," I murmur, then force myself to shut off my overly active imagination.

I round the curve where we gather on Halloween to dare one another to knock on Freaky's door. This is my last chance to back out.

I see movement through the bushes, and I'm so startled I nearly topple off my bike. I right myself, my heart pounding. Then it pounds harder when I recognize the figure loping around the bend.

Oliver.

Over the last week I've gotten to know that loose-limbed gait, the toss of the head to get the bangs out of the way. He smiles and waves, and I pedal toward him, thankful for the dark of the woods that just one minute ago spooked me.

"I thought I'd meet you so you wouldn't get lost," he says as I dismount. "Finding the right road can be tricky. Mom missed it three times when we arrived."

"Thanks." I don't confess that I know the spot well. That pretty much every kid in Rocky Point does.

"Come on," Oliver says. "We have a lot of work to do!"

I push the bike along the rutted path, Oliver strolling on the other side of it. "Is your . . . mom around?" I had been about to ask about his grandfather but switched at the last minute.

"At the house. And Pops is in the shed. He said he'd help."

Help? I'm not sure which is more shocking, that I'm actually going to have a face-to-face encounter with Freaky—a bit like having a conversation with a yeti—or that he's actually on board to help us.

The path isn't nearly as long as it seems on Halloween. Very soon a two-story house with an attic appears through the bushes, Freaky's familiar blue pickup truck parked off to the side of the patchy lawn, a shiny silver car beside it. In daylight it's easier to see how ramshackle the house is—missing shingles on the roof, peeling paint, a sagging porch. It has the look of a place no one really cares much about. I wonder what it's like to be staying here.

"We're set up out back," Oliver says. "Let's grab some sodas first."

I nod, too nervous to speak. I brace myself for whatever I might find: shrunken heads, voodoo candles, stacks of newspapers towering to the ceiling, dust bunnies as big as a T. rex. Heck, maybe even an actual T. rex.

Oliver opens the screen door and I follow him inside, carefully arranging a smile on my face, determined to play it cool no matter what I encounter. I stop after just a few steps. It's nothing like I expected.

The spotless room is large, with just a few pieces of well-worn furniture. A sofa. A big easy chair by the front windows. I realize that this is the first time I've seen the curtains open. There's a low coffee table in front of the sofa with a coffee mug and a newspaper on it. Behind the sofa are a table holding two lamps and some books. There's a fireplace with a large stack of wood piled beside it, obviously well used, judging from how blackened the bricks in it are. Between the front windows is a large oil painting, a gorgeous rendering of what looks like a foggy Rocky Point Harbor. Maybe that's the view Framingham looks at when he keeps the curtains drawn.

Narrow stairs near the front door lead upstairs, presumably to the bedrooms. A doorway minus a door on the other side of the room reveals a sunny yellow kitchen. Not a color I would have expected. There's a door in what looks like a newer wall, some kind of addition, that isn't visible from the front. The original house is so big I wonder why he'd need more space. Maybe that's where he keeps the bodies. . . .

Stop it! I order myself, following Oliver across the room. Still, I can't keep from peeking through the door's window into the addition. All I can glimpse are rolls of what look like canvas.

"Hey, Mom," Oliver says as we enter the kitchen. "This is Mandy."

If the front room surprises me, the kitchen shocks me. The giant old stove taking up a whole lot of space makes sense; it looks like it's been in the house since dinosaurs roamed the earth. But the super-expensive fancy-pants pots and pans do not compute. The cappuccino maker Oliver's mom is using matches *her*, but not Framingham. Does she crave her version of caffeine so badly that she brought it along?

She glances up from foaming and smiles. "Hello, Mandy. Your mom's the librarian, right?"

"That's right." I grin. Oliver must have told her that. Which means he talked about me.

Then it hits me. There are no secrets in Rocky Point. Oliver's mom will mention my being here to my mom the next time she needs an Internet connection.

She spoons the foam into her cup and sprinkles cinnamon over the top. Even with her back to me, I can see what Mom saw. A trim, pulled-together woman who radiates a kind of coiled energy, like she's bursting to do something and there isn't enough to do. If I were wearing her crisp, navy linen slacks and the equally crisp white top, they'd be wrinkled and stained almost as soon as I put them on.

She turns and leans against the counter. "You know, that boat parade has been around since I was a kid," she says. "Are motors still outlawed?"

"Yup," I say. Then I realize I should probably say more. This is Oliver's mom! I want to make a good impression.

"Too bad," she says. "It would be a lot easier to make elaborate floats if you didn't have to worry about rowing."

That problem occurred to me, too. I've seen enough rowboats tip over and oars tear apart decorations to know that rowing will be an issue. It's super funny when Cynthia and I watch from shore. No one ever really gets hurt. Wet and cold, yes, but the parade is too well monitored for anything bad to happen. But now I'll be someone who could wind up in that water.

"I think it's cool," Oliver says, opening the fridge and pulling out two sodas.

"I know. You love a challenge," his mom says, smiling at him. She reaches up and ruffles his hair as he passes her.

"Mom," he complains. He hands me my soda and smooths his hair back down.

"Well, I won't keep you. I know you two have a lot of work to do."

"Nice to meet you, Mrs.—" I stop, realizing that she's divorced now and I have no idea what name she uses.

"Call me Alice," she says. Wow. A grown-up asking me to use her first name? She is *so* not from Rocky Point.

"Well, thanks, Alice." It feels awkward but also very adult.

"There's Pop's leftover lobster mac and cheese, and salad, and cold cuts if you get hungry," she tells us. Then comes the whammy: "Is the library open today?" she asks me.

"No," I reply. Luckily, it's true. Mom's there taking care of historical society business, but the library itself is closed to the public.

Mrs. . . . *Alice* sighs. "I guess I'll be driving over to Franklin. Let me know if you want me to pick up anything."

"Will do," Oliver says.

Made it through round one: meet the mom. I think I passed. Now onto round two: meet Freaky.

Maybe we've all been wrong about him, I muse. *The house is so . . . normal. Maybe Freaky is too.*

We go out the kitchen door. The backyard is much bigger than the one in front, though just as unattended. There's a big shed that's practically the size of a small cottage. A picnic table with benches sits under a shady tree; grass and weeds curl around the table legs. Right in front of the shed stands a worktable with an attached vise and a saw lying on it. I can smell that sweet scent of freshly cut and sanded wood. Sure enough, there are several pristine planks stacked beside the table.

"Pops?" Oliver calls. "You back here?" Oliver starts for the shed as I take a swig of soda and settle onto the picnic table bench.

"Don't need to holler." Framingham emerges from the shed carrying a roll of chicken wire. He squints at me.

"Pops, this is Mandy. She's going to help with the boat."

"Hi," I say.

Framingham just gives a sharp nod, then leans the chicken wire against the shed. "Getting you your materials," he tells Oliver. "That's the way to start. Everything to hand."

"Right, Pops," Oliver says. "We got much more to haul out?" He crosses to Freaky.

"Enough."

They head toward the shed, and I stand and put the soda can on the table. Just as I start to follow them, Freaky calls over his shoulder, "We'll handle it."

"Uh. Oh. Okay." I sit back down. Does he think that because I'm a girl I shouldn't be around tools? Or does Freaky not want me in his shed?

I take another sip of soda. The fog has burned off, and now the outside of the can is sweating. Soon I will be too.

Oliver and Framingham come back out, Oliver carrying a toolbox, with his sketchbook tucked under his arm. Freaky has a staple gun in one hand and coiled wire in the other. Looking at them side by side, I can see the resemblance. They're both long limbed, with narrowish shoulders. Neither would ever be mistaken for a football player. Framingham wears his standard flannel shirt and paint-spattered overalls. Today, maybe because he's been working, his wild gray hair is held back not only in a ponytail but a purple bandanna as well, hippie style.

"I'll leave you to it," he says. "Going fishing. Tell your mother."

"Okay," Oliver says.

Freaky goes back into the shed. Oliver lays the sketchbook on the picnic table and opens to a diagram of the structure he wants us to make. It's a little intimidating.

"So I think I took care of all the math," Oliver begins, but stops when Framingham comes back out with his fishing gear. Now he wears a battered canvas hat and has exchanged the flannel for a T-shirt, revealing muscular and tan arms. Skinny, but muscular. "Sinewy," I guess is the word. The flannel is now tied by the sleeves around his hips. He nods as he passes but doesn't say another word. He goes around the house, and in a few minutes we hear the truck start up.

Oliver fiddles with the pencil he's holding. "Um, so, my grandfather doesn't really talk very much. Don't take it personally."

"I don't."

I wonder if Oliver has any idea of his grandpop's rep in our town. Should I tell him, or will that make him not like me?

"Pops helped me figure out what materials we'll need," Oliver says. "He had a lot of stuff already."

"So how is this going to work?" I ask.

He points to the sketchbook page. "We'll use the planks as the base. Pops already cut them to the right size. We'll build the lighthouse on top of that."

"Out of chicken wire," I surmise.

"Exactly. It's lightweight, so it should work."

"Yeah," I say with a laugh. "It would be pretty embarrassing if a lighthouse made a boat sink. It's supposed to prevent that!"

He grins, then returns to the page. "Once we've got the shape, we'll cover it with papier-mâché and paint it."

"What about the hat?" I ask.

"The what?" His eyebrows knit together.

My cheeks flush. "That's what I call the spot up on top where the light used to be. That would be hard to construct out of chicken wire."

"Oh! The lantern house," he says. "I was thinking maybe balsa wood? It's super lightweight. I use it to make models all the time."

So he's a model maker. It tips him a bit into the nerdy category, but somehow that just makes me like him even more.

"What kind of models?" I ask.

He flushes. "Oh, you know, the usual. Old-fashioned airplanes. Whaling ships. That kind of thing."

"That's what had you so interested at the festival."

"You saw that, huh."

"Kinda sorta," I say, and he grins again. I don't know why, but it gives me a supreme lift being able to make him smile so easily.

Oliver puts the boards on the worktable. "I figured out a scale that will work on the boat but still be big enough to sit inside."

"How will you row?" I ask, trying to understand what he has in mind.

"Who said I'm going to be the one rowing?"

I gape at him. "You roped me into this project so that I can be the one doing the hard work?"

"Kidding!" he says. "Though . . ." He studies the boards. "You'd probably fit better than I would."

"Let's make sure the thing is seaworthy before I even think about volunteering for that job."

He shows me the mini keeper's house he already started making, then we spend the morning working on the lighthouse tower. We hammer the boards together to make an open square, then use staple guns to attach the chicken wire to it. Oliver is very precise about everything, so it takes forever. He had noticed that Candy Cane narrows toward the top and insisted our chicken wire version do the same. It's not easy to do, especially since it's my job to hold the ends together while he checks the measurements and his drawings. The wire digs into my hands, leaving deep, red grooves. He's rapidly going from cute to annoying.

Once we have the basic shape down, Oliver steps back and announces, "We need a break."

"That's for sure." I use my arm to wipe the sweat off my forehead, and open and close my hands, trying to stretch them out. I never knew you could sprain your palms.

"How about we eat down by the river?" he suggests.

"Sounds good." Maybe my cranky will vanish once I'm sitting in the shade and don't have to worry about making sure my nails go in absolutely straight, or that the staples are evenly spaced. And I thought Mr. Forester the science teacher is exacting.

I follow Oliver back into the house. Freaky hasn't returned. The silver car is out front, so his mom is still around somewhere.

"So . . . lobster mac 'n' cheese doesn't really seem like picnic food."

"Not so much," I agree, relieved I don't have to confess my antiseafood stance. I also realize I'm starving. A quick glance at the clock tells me we worked way past my usual lunchtime.

"How about . . ." He rummages in the fridge and pulls out a paper-wrapped packet. "Turkey?" He tosses it onto the counter. Then he reaches in and pulls out another packet. "Or ham." He tosses that onto the counter too. "Or that old classic, PB and J. The J being Maine wild blueberry of course." He pulls out the jars and places them on the counter, then peers into the fridge again. I have the feeling if I don't stop him, he'll empty its entire contents.

"Ham," I declare, just as he holds up several plastic-wrapped cheeses. I cross and take what looks like Swiss from him. "And cheese."

He grins, and in the brightness of his smile all of my annoyance vanishes. "Mustard? Mayo? Lettuce? Cornichons?"

"Cornichons?" I repeat. "Who has cornichons?"

He shrugs as he holds up a jar. "Pops is kind of into fancy food."

"You're kidding me!"

"That's surprising to you?"

"He—he just never struck me as the gourmet type." I frown. "Except this kitchen looks like it belongs to someone who knows food."

"Yeah. He's definitely a better cook than my mom."

"I heard that." We both glance up and see his mom standing in the doorway.

"Uh . . . sorry, Mom."

I notice she has the same twinkly blue eyes as Oliver. "Don't be. I agree with you. He likes cooking; I don't. Though I can't remember him doing any cooking when I was a kid." Her voice changes as she adds, with less warmth, "It was a later interest."

She eyes the counter, now piled high with all the choices Oliver pulled out. "Hungry?"

"Just being a good host," Oliver explains. I can see that he and his mom get along and they like teasing each other.

"Planning on eating the peanut butter with a spoon?" She crosses to the sink and places her cappuccino cup into it.

Oliver and I both look at the counter. He smacks his forehead. "Bread! I knew I was forgetting something."

"That's so something I would do," I tell him. "Including the head smack."

He smiles again, obviously appreciating my mini confessions. It's cool to meet someone I can tell embarrassing things to, and instead of making fun of me (yes, Justin, I mean you!), he thinks they're endearing. At least, that's how it seems.

"How's the project going?" Alice asks.

"We're going to apply the papier-mâché after lunch," Oliver says. So that's what's on the agenda for the afternoon. Excellent! Something I know how to do. And very difficult to screw up.

"Sounds like you've got it all under control."

"Where's the cooler?" Oliver asks. "We're going down by the river."

"Don't track the mud in," she warns as she steps aside and opens a very well-organized pantry behind her. She pulls a Styrofoam cooler from a shelf. "You know your grandfather."

"Outside is outside, inside's in," Oliver says, sounding as if he's quoting a well-worn saying. He takes the cooler from her and tosses in some cool-packs he pulls from the freezer. Only he drops them twice before they land where they're supposed to. I pretend not to notice.

"Exactly." Alice opens a cupboard and takes out a plate, then narrows her eyes at the counter. "I'll wait till you're through in here." She returns the plate to the shelf and once again tousles Oliver's hair as she leaves the room.

Oliver rolls his eyes and smooths his hair back down. "Moms, right?"

"Don't I know it."

We make our sandwiches—ham and cheese for me, turkey with, *ooh la di da, cornichons* for him—then stash them in the cooler. Oliver adds two sodas, a pair of peaches, and some cookies. We head outside, wind around the shed, and take a downhill path Oliver tells me leads to the river.

"I found this spot the first day I was here," Oliver says. "You'll love it."

I glance up at him and watch the cutest blush spread across his face. *That's right, buddy,* I think with pleasure. *I didn't miss that little assumption you just made there. That I'll love it 'cause you do.*

"I mean, I *think* you'll love it." He shifts the cooler to the other hand. "That is, I hope you'll like it."

"I'm sure I will," I assure him, letting him off the hook. "Even if I didn't go for the cornichons, I feel I can trust your judgment."

The woodsy part of Rocky Point has a completely different

feel from the harbor and the bay. Those are wide open places, where sound travels and light glints off the water. On sunny days, anyway. I always want to whisper in the woods; the tree canopy overhead and the dense brambles make it seem like a place for secrets. The smells are different too—not the salty tang of sea-water but a darker smell of damp earth and pine.

"It gets narrower and steeper here," Oliver says. "We should go single file."

He moves in front of me, and I have to say, I do enjoy being able to watch the cute habit he has of tapping the bushes as he passes them, almost as if he's petting them. And the way his T-shirt shifts across his shoulders as he ducks under a low tree limb. Not to mention the curve of his butt in his cutoffs.

I'm paying too much attention to Oliver and not enough to my own feet. I trip over some roots and stumble into him. I fling out my hands to catch myself and wind up with a fistful of his T-shirt. This makes him lose his footing too, and we flail about and then land in the dirt.

"Sorry, sorry, sorry!" I say as he turns to look at me.

"You okay?" he asks.

"I should have warned you. I'm kind of a klutz."

Weirdly, a total look of relief takes over his face. "Seriously?"

"Uh, yeah. Why do you look like I just told you your bout of plague is in remission?"

"It's just—I'm a total klutz too!"

"You are? But you didn't do any dumbhead thing building the tower."

"I'm good on the micro scale," he explains. "But macro? The

only reason I haven't slammed into a tree yet is because I'm concentrating super hard."

"That's great!" I exclaim.

We stare at each other for a moment. It's one of those "I'm seeing you for the very first time" kinds of deep looks. Then I spoil it by bursting out laughing.

"What?" he asks, looking wary, like maybe I was only pretending to be a klutz so that he'd make this confession.

"We're both super happy that we have clumsiness in common. But we're working together on a project that requires us to not just use tools and build something, but to navigate down a river."

He lets out such a contagious laugh that I start laughing again. We shake our heads as we smile at each other, and for a minute I think he might kiss me. He doesn't lean in, though, and I suddenly feel self-conscious. I stand and brush off the back of my shorts. Then I hold a hand out to help him up. He takes it, and I feel the warmth of his hand, its solid palm but slender fingers. It's the hand of someone who can do fine detail work, not the hand of a sports guy or a fisherman.

I drop it the minute I realize I've held it a beat too long. "Lead on," I say in a bright voice worthy of Cynthia in one of her perkier performances. "I promise not to trip you again if you promise not to lead us directly into the river and drown us," I add in my own voice.

He cracks a grin that makes the slightly longer front tooth poke out over his lower lip. Adorableness. "Deal."

He turns back around, and we carefully make our way down to the water's edge. This part of the river is pretty wide, and it moves with the laziness of a turtle. The only noticeable move-ment is where boulders poke up sharply and the water has to slap around them.

I scan the area, searching for a dry place to park ourselves. Like so many places in Maine, there's very little shore, and what there is here consists primarily of muddy grass. We didn't bother bringing a blanket, which suddenly seems like a serious oversight.

"I'll show you my favorite spot," Oliver announces.

He pushes aside the branches of a thick bush, revealing a large flat rock. A large, *dry* flat rock.

"Looks good," I say. He squeezes past the bush, then holds it back so I can make it through without too many scratches.

We settle onto the rock, the surface nicely warmed by the sun, but still cooled by the breeze off the water and the shade of the trees overhead. Oliver unpacks our lunch, and I try to find the most flattering position to sit in. I decide stretching out my legs ensures that there's no awkward possible over-revealing. I really should have checked out my outfit in every posture imaginable. Another thing Cynthia would have helped me with. There's so much that I rely on her for. My heart sinks a little remembering our fight last night.

But then it lifts again. Oliver is kneeling beside me and holding out my sandwich. I take it from him, and he shifts around to grab the sodas. He pops his can open, then clinks mine. He holds up the can like he's making a toast. "To a good morning's work," he says.

"Without any casualties," I add, tapping his can with mine. I wish he'd made a more personal toast, but it's still sweet.

We each take sips, then get down to the serious business of

eating. I'm not one of those girls who pretends she's not hungry when she gets around a boy. Food should never be betrayed that way. Unless it's fish, of course.

"Nice, huh?" Oliver says. He finished his sandwich and is now lying with his arms under his head, gazing up at the treetops.

I swallow the last of mine, then stretch out beside him. "Definitely," I agree. The leaves overhead rustle with the breeze. Each time they flutter, a bright patch of blue sky appears then vanishes again.

"It's funny," I muse. "Each part of Rocky Point is totally different, like there are four distinct towns."

"What do you mean?" He rolls onto his side, leaning on his elbow.

I keep my eyes on the leaves above me, all too aware of the closeness of his face. I also don't want to spoil the moment by becoming *over*aware of the smear of mustard in the corner of his mouth.

"Well, there's here, all woodsy and rivery. Then there's the harbor."

"Where the food booths were for the festival."

"Yup. To me, the harbor is kind of the heart of Rocky Point. The *real*est part. That's where the fishermen work and live and keep their boats. The shops there aren't the touristy kind."

"There's that lobster shack," Oliver points out. "I even read about it in a tourist guide."

"Yeah," I concede. "But it's there even when tourists aren't. It's a super-convenient way for the lobstermen to unload the lobsters that aren't already tagged for restaurants."

"What are the other parts? To you."

"There's the bay side," I continue. I'm enjoying being a tour guide, particularly since I can do it lying down. With a boy. A boy who is not only Cute with a capital C, but also seems to be completely interested. Though I'm still not sure if the interest is in me or in Rocky Point. "That's where you can go for a beach fix with actual sand. It's not very big, but there are beachy shops, beachy views, beachy things to do. Beach houses . . ."

"Beach umbrellas, beach volleyball . . ."

I giggle and continue the game. "Beach dunes, beach grass, beach . . ." I run out of things to add, so Oliver picks up.

"Beached whales. *Beach Blanket Bingo*. The Beach Boys."

I smack him in the chest as I laugh. "And then there's the Square," I say. "The town square," I add, so he knows what I'm talking about. "Around there it's like a small town you might find pretty much anywhere in New England. What makes Rocky Point unique, though," I say, just now realizing that I actually believe what I'm telling him, "is that you can experience all these different Rocky Points in a single day. With just a bike."

He smiles. "You love it here."

I sit up and turn to look down at him. "You know, maybe I do."

He sits up too, rummages in the cooler, then hands me a cookie. I take it from him, frowning as I think.

"Something wrong?" he asks.

"I was just thinking I should thank you."

"For what?"

"For a couple of things, actually. One, for making me see my own town in a different way. Making me realize I don't actually hate it here." I take a bite of the oversize cookie. Oh my. Probably the best oatmeal chocolate-chip cookie I have ever tasted in my entire life.

"Add thank you for this cookie!" I say, spitting crumbs. My hand flies to my mouth. "Sorry," I mumble behind my hand.

"Thank Pops," he says with a grin. "Like I said, he knows his way around the kitchen."

"No lie." I take a swig of soda to wash down the crumbs, regretting washing away the flavor of the cookie as I do. Happily it's a really big cookie, so I'll have plenty more tastes.

"What was the other thing you were going to say before the cookie distracted you?"

"Thank you for asking me to make the float with you. I've always wanted to take part."

"So why haven't you?" he asks, taking a bite of his own cookie.

I shrug. How can I explain it just never seemed right? Cynthia wasn't into it, and no one ever invited me to join a team. He'd think I'm a friendless loser.

I turn away, trying to think of a way to change the subject, and my eye catches something floating downriver. I swing my legs around and kneel for a better look.

"See something?" Oliver asks.

"Just some twigs tangled together," I say. Something about the sticks in the water reminds me of something.

"Doll rafts," I murmur. My throat feels thick, and my breath feels tight, as if someone's squeezing my chest.

"What?" Oliver sits up and scoots beside me. I turn away.

I know these symptoms. I'm about to cry. *So not cool!* I yell at myself in my head.

I clench my jaw and jam my teeth together. I swallow, trying to get the lump to melt.

"What's wrong?" he asks, alarmed.

I don't want to use the "hormones" line on him—that would be more embarrassing than crying.

I shake my head, which, to my horror, makes tears actually drop out of my eyes. I cover my face.

"Mandy?"

I inhale sharply, squeeze my eyes shut behind my hands to wring out any remaining tears, then force myself to face him. "I don't mean to be a total weirdo," I say. "I just—it's just that . . ."

He's looking at me with such soft concern I glance away. Keeping my eyes on a tree limb sticking up against a boulder in the middle of the river, I say, "I had a memory. It snuck up on me."

"A bad one?" His voice matches his concerned expression.

I sigh. "No. A good one. One of me and my dad."

"And that upset you?"

I shut my eyes again and give a little laugh. "Right. You're not from here. You don't know everyone's history from the moment they were born." I open my eyes again and twist to face him. "My dad. He died when I was eight. There was something wrong with his heart."

The concerned bewilderment is replaced by sympathy. "Oh," he says softly. "Sorry."

"Yeah, thanks." I bring up my knees and hug them. Using a twig, I make little trails in the dirt. "Mostly it doesn't get to me.

You know? It's part of who I am. But every now and then a memory jumps out and grabs me."

"And the river pulled a sneak attack?"

"Yeah." I sense my tiny smile and realize the memory now feels good, not sad. "I don't really hang by the river much. I guess being here now . . ." I raise my head, but I'm still not quite ready to look at him, so I glance back to the water. Using the stick, I point at the clump of twigs that set me off. "That bunch of twigs for some reason made me think of the rafts my dad and I used to make. Toy-size. He called them doll rafts because I insisted on putting passengers on them. And then, of course, he'd have to go rescue them because I'd get hysterical when they'd float away."

"Sounds like a good guy."

"Yeah." It comes out as a sigh. I look down at the ground again. "Yeah." I remember something else. "Sometimes he'd make up stories to go with the rafts, usually about someone being rescued by the Candy Cane keeper."

"Wait—like a Christmas elf?"

I laugh. "It's the lighthouse. Candy Cane. Because of the stripes. Not the official name, of course."

He smiles. "I like it."

"I think there was a story he told me so I'd stop being upset about a toy he wasn't able to catch in time. . . ." I try to remember the details, but they don't come. I shrug. "Anyway, being here. It suddenly brought it back."

"It's a nice memory, though, right?" Oliver asks. "I mean, I'd hate . . . I wouldn't like . . ."

"It's a nice memory. Yes." I put my hand lightly on his arm. "Another thing to thank you for."

He puts his hand over mine. "My pleasure."

Something jumps from the shore into the river, making a loud splash. Startled by the sound, we drop our hands to look. Just like that the moment's over. Thanks to a frog.

Oliver reaches up and pulls a leaf off the bush and pulls it into strips. "I miss my dad too. But at least I know if I want to I can call him. See him."

"Was it bad?" I ask. I know some kids whose parents got divorced, and it was sometimes kind of nasty.

"Bad?" He thinks it over. "Not really. It never got ugly. They never fought—at least not in front of me. When they broke the news to me, they said it was a mutual decision, and I believed them. Now Mom says it was because they had each changed."

"What do you think?"

He shrugs. "I just saw them as Mom and Dad. If they were different from when I was a little kid, I never noticed. But . . ." His eyes drift as his thoughts take him somewhere else. I wait, not wanting to rush him, letting him figure out whatever he's figuring out in front of me.

"The way we lived had changed," he says finally. "Around the time I started middle school, Mom got super successful and super busy. We had more money, but I could tell there was more stress."

"How? You said they didn't really fight."

"Not yelling and screaming, no. But now looking back, maybe all that quiet was significant. You know what I mean?"

I nod. My brother's ex-girlfriend Fiona gave him the silent

treatment for a whole week when they were dating. It wasn't pretty.

"Mom says they ended up wanting different things," Oliver continues. "She's actually really happy being this powerhouse. She stresses when she doesn't have enough to do, not the other way around. Her brain's always on overdrive. I think that's part of what drove them apart. Dad's one of those guys who works hard but wants to kick back, too. She didn't come installed with that button."

"Which one are you like?" I ask.

"You tell me," he says.

I study his face. The humor in his bright eyes. The uneven front teeth. The soft-looking lips. "Jury's still out," I say, my voice a little shaky. The close scrutiny unnerves me. "But if I had to guess right now, you're a mix of them both."

"Sounds right." He laughs. "At least, that sounds better than hearing I'm a driven workaholic or a slacker party boy."

"Your dad's a slacker party boy?"

"Nah. But he *is* more into vegging in front of the TV or inviting the whole neighborhood over for a barbecue than Mom."

"Opposites might attract, but then they wind up driving each other crazy," I say.

"Hey, your doll raft floated away." Oliver points to the water.

I swivel my head to look. He's right. The boulder's clear of debris now. "It's on its way to Candy Cane."

"I guess we should get back to work."

I don't want the picnic to end, but I help him pack our trash in the cooler.

He picks up the cooler and leads the way back to the path. We're both quiet, but it's a nice quiet. I'm not trying to come up with things to say, and I don't think he is either. We just feel . . . calm. Relaxed.

Visitors talk about how being by water puts them into a zone. It doesn't matter if it's the bay, the ocean, the river, or the harbor. Something about negative ions. Or maybe it's the hypnotic effect of moving water. Could be there's something to it, and that's why Oliver and I are so comfortable lazily strolling silently side by side. I feel like we're two different people leaving the woods from those who entered. Or at least our relationship is: We know each other better; we've both revealed ourselves a bit more to each other, maybe more than either of us had expected.

Once out of the woods I can tell by the angle of the sun that our picnic lasted a lot longer than we'd planned.

We step into the kitchen, and he drops the cooler on the counter. His mom must have been in the living room, because she pops her head in, a quizzical look on her face.

"There you are. I thought we might have to send a search party after you."

I back up against the door, totally embarrassed. She probably thinks we were making out this whole time. When we never even kissed.

"We were at the river," Oliver says. He rummages in the fridge and pulls out a soda. He holds it out to me. I shake my head no.

He shuts the fridge and pulls the tab on the soda can. I glance at his mom. She's got that look on her face like she's trying to figure out if we've been up to anything. Oliver is totally oblivious, but I recognize it immediately.

Maybe it's a look parents only use on their daughters. Or maybe boys are just clueless about this kind of thing.

Oliver tips back his head to take a swig, and his eye catches the clock on the wall. "Is that the real time?"

His mom crosses her arms. "That's the real time."

He completely misses her tone. Her "this is why I'm curious about what you were doing" tone.

"Oh man." He puts down the soda and rakes his fingers through his hair. "I guess we should call it a day," he says to me. "I didn't realize it was so late. It doesn't make sense to start doing the papier-mâché now."

"Okay," I say. "I should probably be heading home anyway."

"Would you like to stay for dinner?" Oliver's mom asks.

I would, but I should let my mom in on the news that I'm hanging with Freaky Framingham's grandson before I announce I'm already at the house. But there's another reason I have to say no.

"The service here isn't great, right?" I say. "I'd have to let my mom know."

Alice frowns. "That's right. And Pop never put in a landline. Another time, then."

"How about tomorrow?" Oliver pipes up. A worried look crosses his face. "You're coming back tomorrow, right?"

"I have to be at Candy Cane," I tell him, noticing Oliver smiling at the nickname, now that he's clued in. "But I can come after four. If that's not too late."

"Any time you can spare will be great," Oliver says.

"Okay. I'll ask Mom about dinner." I hope she'll let me. In fact, I hope she'll let me out of the house after hearing I spent all day at Freaky Framingham's without telling her.

We walk through the living room. "So what's in there?" I ask, pointing to the door of the addition.

"That's Pops's studio," Oliver says. "He's an amazing painter. He has some things stored there, but it's always where he works when he's not painting *en plein air*."

"Plain what?" I ask, crossing to the door.

"That's what it's called when an artist paints outside."

"Can I see?" I put my hand on the doorknob, but Oliver quickly puts his hand on my arm and stops me from turning it.

Oliver looks nervous. "Actually, no. It's the one room we're not allowed in when he's not here. It's the major rule."

I pull my hand back, disappointed.

"But no one says we can't peek," Oliver adds with a grin. "Take a look."

I step up to the window in the door and crane my neck. By getting into weird positions I can see different parts of the room. I catch the corner of a painted canvas on one side and cans holding lots of paintbrushes on a worktable. I wiggle a bit more and spot paintings stacked against a wall. I step back. "It looks like he's a really serious painter."

"He is." He turns me around and points at the painting over on the wall opposite the fireplace. The one of the harbor in fog that I noticed when I first came in. "That's one of his."

I step up close to it. I don't know how he did it, but he captured the strangeness of fog, the wetness, the way light looks through it. Tiny little brushstrokes in unusual colors that when I step back again form into a very recognizable Rocky Point Harbor.

"That's really good," I say. "Does he sell them?"

Just then Freaky strides through the door, looks at us suspiciously, nods at Oliver, then disappears into the kitchen. He grunts a greeting to Oliver's mom—at least I think that's what the sound is—and then I hear the back door bang.

"Tools!" I hear him yell from the backyard.

Oliver flushes. "Gotta go. Pops is a stickler about taking proper care of his tools. If he's not happy, then he won't let us use them anymore."

"Go, go." I wave him away. "See you tomorrow."

I'm in such a good mood when I get home that I'm not angry at Cynthia anymore. In fact, I'm grateful to have a friend who worries about me. Cynthia is more like a sister than a friend, and this is just another example.

I punch in her number. She answers on the first ring.

"So I guess you're still alive," she says flatly.

Okay. She's still holding on to her mad. I'm not going to let that rile me up. "I know you were just concerned," I say.

"Don't use that mom speech on me," she says.

"I'm not!" I exclaim. "Anyway, *you* were the one doing the mom thing—" I stop myself and start over. "We were totally wrong about Freaky."

"He's not freaky?"

"Well, I wouldn't go that far. He's not exactly bursting with people skills. But his house is totally different on the inside than the outside."

"Yeah?" She's using her interested voice.

"Yeah. He's like this gourmet chef. Your mom would kill for his kitchen."

"No lie?"

"But here's the headline." I pause for dramatic effect. I've learned a lot from Cynthia over the years. "He's a painter. Seriously good. He's got all these canvases stacked up in a studio he built onto the house."

"That *is* headline news."

"So, come on, Cyn. Let's not be in a fight."

"We're not in a fight," she protests.

"I know, let's not go over it again."

"You have to understand—"

"La-la-la-la-la-la-la," I sing over her.

That gets her laughing. "You are such a child."

I can't really fault her on that since it's what we used to do when we were little kids to stop someone from speaking. Though we usually did it to others, not to each other. Still, I say, "No I'm not. I'm just . . ." I pause to let her brain catch up with mine.

"Hormonal!" we shriek at each other over the phone.

And with that, everything's back to normal again.

*S*o, um, Mom, you know that boy Oliver?" We're digging into take-out fried chicken at the dinner table. Have I mentioned

Mom's not so keen on cooking? I have the funniest image of her getting cooking lessons from Freaky Framingham.

"The lighthouse fan," Mom says with a smile.

Good. The first thing that comes to her mind is what she likes best about him.

Just come right out with it, Mandy. "His mom invited me for supper. Tomorrow night."

Mom looks up from her side dish of corn niblets and cocks her head. "When did you see his mother?"

Oops. I didn't prepare for that question. All I've got is the truth without any prep time to figure out the best way to present it. So I just present it. "Oliver and I are working on a project together. For the Fourth of July," I add quickly. She likes it when I participate in community events. "All about Candy Cane," I put in for good measure.

She frowns and puts down her fork. I now have her full attention. I prefer her in her more distracted state.

She folds her hands in front of her. "You're working on what exactly?"

"A float for the boat parade," I respond with huge enthusiasm, hoping to get her on board.

"Where exactly are you working on it?"

Uh-oh. Two exactlies in a row. Bad sign. And here's where the fight will begin.

"Up at, uh, Mr. Framingham's house." I figure it would be better to add the "Mr." this time—help convince Mom how normal everything is with Oliver. "His mom was there the—"

She cuts me off. "Let me get this straight. You went to a

stranger's house. Where there's no cell reception. Possibly not even a working landline. Without a word as to where you were going. Or asking my permission."

"He's not exactly a stranger," I counter, trying to keep my temper in check. A big blowout is not in my best interests.

"Mr. Framingham isn't just a stranger; he's *strange*," Mom responds angrily.

"That's unfair!" Okay, there goes my plan to keep a cool head. But it *is* unfair. "You just know stupid rumors. And that isn't even what I meant."

She raises an eyebrow. At least she's still letting me talk.

"I meant that *Oliver* isn't a stranger. You've even met his mom. You've talked to her a bunch of times this week. That's all you ever ask about when I go anyplace."

This argument actually seems to work. Not bad for an improvisation. Her face changes from her "you are about to be punished" expression to something neutral. That I can't read.

"Let me think about it" is all she says, then goes back to eating her niblets.

I sigh. Well, at least it's not a no.

All day at Candy Cane I replay yesterday with Oliver. I can't believe I got weepy with him! But the most shocking part of this is that I don't feel embarrassed about it. The little crease that formed between his eyes when he was afraid he'd upset me, the soft tone of voice he used—it makes me swoony even now. Between his opening up about the divorce and my brush with tears, there's no denying we are truly getting to know each other.

It's weird, I think as I lock up. This getting-to-know-you thing. I've basically known my friends forever. Even people I'd categorize as acquaintances I've known pretty much all my life. I haven't had to . . . *learn* someone in ages.

Scary.

But deliriously exciting, too.

Mom finally relented. She said I could go to Oliver's to work on the boat and today for supper, but she insisted she drive me over from the library. She claims it's because she doesn't want me riding my bike home after dark. The woods along Evergreen Road are pretty dark, thanks to the thick groves of Christmas trees the road is named for. There's a reason the state flower is a pinecone. But it's *really* so she can check out the situation. Secretly I'm glad. It's a long haul by bike from the tip of Rocky Point where the lighthouse is to Freaky's house in the woods.

I ride to the Square and lock my bike in the rack in front of the library. Mom's as klutzy as me, so she didn't want the hassle of getting the bike into the car. I didn't want to waste time going home, so we compromised. She'll drive me back here tomorrow morning, and I'll bike the rest of the way to Candy Cane. Bonus: It cuts my ride in half.

The library's AC isn't the best, but the dark wood cabinets and high ceilings at least give the impression of being a lot cooler inside. The library is nearly empty. A dad with a baby in a Snugli is trying to convince a toddler that it's time to go. An older woman sits at a computer terminal. A high school boy sits with his head down on a table, obviously asleep. From the curly hair

I identify him as Marshall Beamer. Must have summer school. I flip through some paperbacks in a revolving rack as I wait.

"I'm sorry," I hear my mom saying. "There's just no way we can swing that."

I glance up and see her walking down the stairs with Mr. Garrity, the other historical society bigwig.

Mr. Garrity sighs and takes a handkerchief from his jacket pocket. He uses it to wipe the back of his neck. "I know. We're going to have to take a hard look at the budget. And soon."

I replace the book so that the minute Mom lands on the ground floor we can leave. Oliver's waiting.

"There's my daughter," Mom says, noticing me. "We'll discuss this more."

"I'm sure we will," Mr. Garrity says sadly, then disappears through the STAFF ONLY door.

"Anyone come in today?" she asks as we leave the library.

"Not a single one," I complain.

"No one at the café, either?" We climb into the car.

"Actually, there were some customers," I say as Mom maneuvers around jaywalking tourists. "Guys." I give her a sidelong glance. "Is that why you hired Celeste?"

"What do you mean?" She gets off Main Street and begins the twisty route toward Evergreen.

"So local boys will go to the café."

She gives a little laugh. "No, but if that's a side benefit, I'll take it. We hired her because she's the only one who applied."

I can see why. Everyone knows you don't make much money there. I wonder why Celeste wanted to. "Is she a lighthouse lover too?" This would give her something in common with Oliver. Dang.

It's darker now that we're in the woods, and Mom keeps her eyes straight ahead. I do too, so that I can tell her when to turn onto the right path.

"Actually, I think she needs to make some money but still be able to study. I'm guessing she has plenty of downtime during her shifts. She's doing some kind of online course."

Come to think of it, I did notice thick textbooky books near the cash register at the café.

"This is it," I say when I spot the turnoff.

Mom's eyebrows rise as she navigates the narrow and bumpy path to Framingham's. "Doesn't exactly scream 'welcome.'" Her eyes flick to me. "Did you feel . . . comfortable when you were here?"

"Yes," I say forcefully. Then, so she has no doubt that I'm telling the truth I add, "Not at first. But definitely by lunchtime."

She pulls up to the house, and I see her look of dismay.

"It's totally different on the inside," I assure her, unbuckling my seat belt and opening the car door before she can frantically drive us away. "Wait till you see."

We trudge up the sagging steps, and I open the screen door, then knock.

Alice appears, tossing a dish towel over her shoulder. "Hi, Mandy. Hello, Marjorie. Nice to see you."

That's right, they've met. Good. Even though Oliver's mom told me to call her by her first name, it still would have felt weird to say "Alice, this is my mother, Mrs. Sullivan."

"I drove Mandy over," Mom explains. "I don't want her to bike back in the dark."

At least the excuse sounds reasonable. It would be terrible if Alice knew the real reason was so Mom can make sure they're not a family of cannibals or something.

"Come in, come in," Alice says, stepping aside and holding open the door.

"What time should I pick her up?" Mom asks as we walk inside. Her eyes dart all around, and I hope Alice doesn't notice how surprised she is by what she's seeing.

"You're welcome to stay," Alice offers.

Please say no please say no please say no.

"Another time," Mom says. "I have a lot of paperwork to get done with the Fourth of July events coming up."

"Have enough time for a cup of coffee? Or tea?" Alice asks.

Mom smiles. "That I can do."

"Oliver's out back," Alice says as she leads us to the kitchen. "Hard at work. I was washing up so that everything will be ready for when my dad gets back."

Mom's eyes nearly bug when we arrive in the kitchen. "Mandy wasn't kidding when she said this was state of the art."

Alice gazes around fondly, then pats the giant stove. "I wouldn't exactly call this up to date, but Pop won't hear of replacing it. He's the cook in the family, not me."

"We have that in common," Mom says, leaning against the marble counter. "Mandy's father did most of the cooking in our house."

"He did?" I say.

She slings an arm across my shoulder. "But I'm proud to say you preferred *my* overcooked carrots."

She's not wrong. I liked the burned bits. Still do.

"Where *is* your father?" Mom asks. I can't tell if she's hoping he's home or hoping he's not.

"Grocery shopping. He doesn't trust me to do that, either. Which is fine by me."

The back door opens and Oliver steps in. His T-shirt is soaked with sweat, pebbles and dirt cling to his knees, and his work gloves look too big for him. He's wearing a bandanna Freaky-style across his forehead. Not exactly glamorous, but insanely appealing.

So is the big smile that appears when he realizes I'm here. "Hallelujah! Reinforcements!" he exclaims.

"Oliver, this is my mom," I say. Then I smack my forehead. "D'oh! You already met."

"At the lighthouse," Oliver says. He holds out his hand for a handshake, which seems kind of over the top, then pulls it back sheepishly when he notices the work glove. "So, hi."

Mom has that annoying "aren't children adorable" look on her face. "Hi again. Any friend of the lighthouse is a friend of mine," she says.

"I'm glad to see you decided to listen to me and your grand-father and wear the gloves," Alice comments.

He scowls at his hands. "They make everything even harder."

"Maybe so, but I'm guessing you've cut down dramatically on the cuts and scratches."

"Whatever," he grumbles, and crosses to the fridge. He pulls out a bottle of Gatorade and takes a long swig. I watch his Adam's apple bob with each chug.

"We should get to work," I say. I want to get out of the indulgent-mom-smiles zone. It feels as if we're specimens to be studied. Since I'm still trying to figure out what's going on between Oliver and me, it's extra uncomfortable to have the scrutiny.

Oliver grabs a second bottle of Gatorade and holds it up to me. "You okay with blue?"

I nod, then we traipse out the back door.

"I hope my mom doesn't tell your mom embarrassing stories about me," I say.

"Back atcha," Oliver replies.

I stop and stare at the structure. "You did the windows!"

There are now evenly spaced holes cut into the chicken-wire tower, three on each side, just like Candy Cane. On the work-table I spot a small balsa-wood structure next to the keeper's house replica. "And the lantern room!"

"That was a lot easier than the windows," Oliver says. "Chicken wire fights back."

"So what should I do?"

"How about you tear the newspaper into strips. The papier-mâché is the next step."

"I can handle that." I sit beside a stack of newspapers and begin tearing. Oliver is very organized. He has a box set up for me to drop the strips into so they don't blow away or get dirty. As I rip, I watch him using wire cutters to bend back the edges of the windows.

"I cut them bigger than they actually are," he explains as he works. "That way we can use the papier-mâché to keep the edges of the chicken wire from biting us."

"Biting *you*, you mean," I say. "Remember, you're the one who's going to be doing the rowing." I stop tearing. "What about a door?" I ask.

He keeps working, his back to me. "What door?"

"How are you going to get inside?"

He stops, his wire cutters midair. Without turning around, he finally says, "We'll bring it to the river, you'll lower it down on top of me, attach it, and presto, I'm inside and ready to row."

I'm really glad his back is to me. I don't think he'd appreciate the way I'm looking at him. But my mouth just reacts. "That's crazy!"

He stops what he's doing to face me. "I've worked it all out," he says a bit testily.

"Oh yeah?" I smirk. "You worked it out? Just this minute when I pointed out the fact that there's no door."

He's about to argue, then laughs. "You caught me."

I laugh too. "I thought you were Mr. Precision."

"I am," he insists. "But there's no door in the lighthouse, so there can't be a door in this."

"There used to be," I point out. "Before they built the attachment."

This stops him a moment, then he shakes his head. "No. A door big enough for me to get through won't be to scale. It's supposed to be an accurate replica."

I'm about to argue but zip my lip. After all, this is *his* baby.

Still, my mind works hard as I rip newspaper after newspaper. I have serious misgivings about his plan.

He tosses aside the wire cutters, yanks off the gloves, and wipes his hands on his shorts. "Okay," he declares, turning around. "Time to get messy. I'll get the stuff to make the glue."

When he goes into the house, I stand and stretch. My hands are covered in newsprint. I spot a spigot on the side of the house and rinse my hands.

The spigot is under the window of the addition. When I stand, I see a big painting leaning against the wall inside. It's breathtaking—a boy playing in a river, so focused on his toy boat that he's oblivious to the deer watching him from shore. It's painted in such a way that I can practically feel the cold water on my own toes, sense that it's about to rain and that the boy's playtime is nearly over, and understand both the boy and the deer are equally transfixed. It makes me want to be quiet so I don't disturb them, while also wanting to warn them to take cover. Freaky Framingham is a freaking incredible artist.

Oliver comes back out carrying a gigantic bowl, a sack of flour, and a pitcher of water. He puts everything on the ground beside the chicken-wire structure, then tosses me the apron he had slung over his shoulder. Not a frilly apron, but a serious workman's apron.

"That should take care of most of you," he says. "You're a lot smaller than Pops."

I slip it over my head, then tie the ties. "He's okay if I borrow it?"

"Yeah." Oliver laughs. "Anything to keep us out of the kitchen while he cooks, I think."

My stomach clenches. I haven't mentioned my fish aversion. What if Framingham is whipping up some kind of gourmet seafood dish? Will I be able to get down at least a few bites?

"Hope you like Indian food," he says as he sets up. "Pops said you're probably sick of seafood since you live here."

"I love Indian food!" I exclaim. I'm not even sure if I do, but as long as there's nothing that swam in the water on my plate I'm willing to try.

Oliver mixes the flour and water. "We need to be sure there aren't any lumps," he says. "Have you done this before?"

"Not since grade school, but it's probably like riding a bike, right? Once you learn . . ."

We get to work, dipping each strip into the glue mixture until it's supersaturated. Getting the strip onto the chicken wire is harder to do than you might think. Those suckers like to wrap around things: my fingers, the wrong part of the wire, themselves. Oliver wants us to lay them all in the same direction, but overlapping. This way, he says, we'll know if we've covered each section the same number of times.

It's a gooey and goopy task, and my legs are getting sore. I'm getting in a squats workout from all the bending and stretching.

And the time just zips by.

"'My father was the keeper of the Eddystone Light,'" I sing when it's my turn. We're making the time pass by telling pirate stories (complete with pirate lingo, arrrrgh!) or singing sea chanteys. This is an old folk song that pretty much any kid in Rocky Point knows. Duh, there's a lighthouse in it. "'He married a mermaid one fine night!'"

"'From this union there came three,'" Oliver joins in. "'A porpoise and a porgy and the other was me!'"

I gape down at him. "You know it!"

"Sure! Even us lighthouse-deprived types know songs about the sea."

Oliver is carefully wrapping a strip around the bottom window to help defang the chicken wire. After all three layers are applied, the sharp edges should no longer be lethal.

I crouch by our bowl of flour paste and dip in another strip. Oliver drops down to his knees and sticks in a strip too. I watch our hands swirling the paper, never quite touching, moving as if choreographed. It's how we've been working together too. Like we've been doing it forever, with a matched rhythm. I'll duck under him just as he reaches above me; he'll go one way as I go the other, like we're reading each other's minds.

We pull out our strips and run our fingers along the length of them, squeezing out the excess. Then we both stand and, for the first time all afternoon, bang into each other as we reach for the same spot.

"Oopsie," I say as I carefully peel my strip off his arm. Little white flecks of glue stand out against his tan.

I feel something sticky on my shoulder. That's where Oliver's strip landed. His hand hovers just above it.

"I guess I'm stuck on you."

My head pops up at the husky tone in his voice. He's looking at me so sweetly, the way you might look at a kitten or puppy. I start to say something, but my brain goes blank when his lips are suddenly on mine.

It's a soft, tender kiss, but it shoots through me like a summer thunderbolt.

It's only a moment and then it's over. He pulls back so quickly my eyes have only just closed. I open them slowly, and he's searching my face, wondering, I suppose, if the kiss was welcome.

Before either of us can speak, before either of us can back away, retreat, freak out, or stammer, I place the back of my hand on his cheek, not wanting to get glue on that gorgeous face. I stand on my tiptoes, taking care to not knock over the bowl of glue, and I kiss him.

Me. Mandy Sullivan.

I.

Kiss.

HIM.

And it's wonderful.

July

*T*here are only three days left before the boat parade, and I have discovered something else Oliver and I have in common. We don't work well under pressure.

We're behind schedule. Our classic Maine weather hasn't helped. Luckily, Freaky is a freakishly accurate weather predictor, so Candy Cane Jr. (Oliver's adorable nickname for our float) has never been caught outside, no matter how sunny the weather forecast is on the news. But the rain, the humidity, the general dampness that is Rocky Point slowed down our progress. A lot.

We're supposed to wait twenty-four hours between layers of papier-mâché, but it stayed sticky longer than that. And until that's dry we can't paint it.

But don't worry. We found ways to fill the downtime. That first flour-paste-covered kiss changed everything.

Kisses. Kisses that last forever and not long enough. That keep me occupied in my daydreams and as I drift off to sleep. I don't even text Cynthia. It's as if the kisses exist in their own perfect world. A world so private, so delicate, I'm not ready to share it with anyone. Not even her.

I've never had a single experience—certainly not one this big—that she hasn't in some way been part of. We dissected, analyzed, and categorized everything together down to the most minute detail. As exacting as Oliver is with his measurements.

This is different. For once I don't want to overthink. I just want to . . . be. To . . . discover. To find out what this bright and shiny new energy is.

It's not that I'm keeping a secret from her. It's that I have no words to describe how I'm feeling. What our time together is like. The expression on his face when he confesses what he misses about predivorce days. How he holds my hand without a word and just lets me talk about Dad. Complain about Mom. How we make the work go faster by making up ridiculous sea chanteys or impossibly complicated stories. What it's like to have him casually sling his arm across my shoulder as he points at something on Candy Cane Jr. as if of course that's exactly where his arm is supposed to be. The way I just as casually slip my hand into his back pocket, lean into him, and just listen, happy to be exactly where I am.

Is this what it's like to fall in love?

Only I'm not feeling a whole lot of love today. For the past week stressing over Candy Cane Jr. has made us pretty snippy with each other, and after yesterday's not very successful work session, I'm mostly irritated, annoyed, and exasperated. I thought this project would bring us closer together, but if things keep going the way they have, it might actually make us stop being friends—or whatever—altogether!

The rain outside completely matches my mood. It's also brought in more Candy Cane customers than normal, so I'm actually a little bit busy. Also good, otherwise I'd stew all day long.

I finish counting out the change for one adult, two kids' admission prices, then as the visitors move away, I spot Lexi Johnson hovering at the entry. She's flanked by a skinny boy with hair as red as hers, and a chubby little girl who looks like a kindergartener.

"Hi, Mandy," she says as she approaches the desk. "I heard you were working here."

"Mom," I reply. It's enough of an explanation. Everyone knows about my mom and the historical society.

"Babysitting," she says with a nod toward the two kids. "Cousins."

"I don't need a babysitter," the boy protests.

She rolls her eyes. "I know, I know," she assures him. "I'm really just babysitting your sister."

"Right," the boy declares emphatically.

Lexi pays for their tickets, and the kids wander to the gift shop area. "How's it going?" she asks.

"Not so bad." Then my eyes open wide. "Lexi! Are you making a boat float this year?"

She frowns. "No. We were away the beginning of the summer so I missed the chance to join a crew."

"Want to join mine?"

She looks surprised. "You're making a float?"

"Yes, and we are so behind, and my . . . friend, well, just yesterday he asked if I knew anyone who could help. You'd be perfect!" Lexi is always part of the group building sets and props for school plays.

Her eyes travel to her cousins, who are now crawling under the display tables. "I think you may have just saved my sanity. Now Lara will have to take over the babysitting." Lara is Lexi's younger sister. She grins at me, dimples showing in her heart-shaped face. "Thanks for the rescue!"

"Believe me, you're the one rescuing me! I need the reinforcements!"

*L*exi slows her bike to a stop as we arrive at the turnoff to the house in the woods. "You didn't tell me you're building a boat with Freaky Framingham!"

It's finally sunny, and although I filled Lexi in on most of the details, I confess I did leave out the location. I told her we should just head there together from my house. I was afraid she would back out.

"Don't worry," I assure her. "It's totally fine. And it's not Freaky . . ."

"Oh. My. God." She straddles her bike and stands staring at me. "The new guy! Framingham's grandkid or something. Everyone's been wondering where he disappeared to! He's been with you!"

I blush. "We started working on the boat only a few weeks ago. I think he spends every waking moment working on it or praying for it to stop raining."

We resume biking. Lexi has always been pretty quiet, rarely speaks up in class, isn't one of the girls who spread gossip—or is the subject of any. Cynthia knows her better than I do, because of their school-plays connection. She once told me Lexi's shy, but speaks her mind when she has ideas for designs or how to do things. Right now I'm grateful she's not the type to pry. She probably has a million questions but is too polite to ask any.

We lean our bikes against the porch, and I lead her inside, calling out, "We're here!"

I sent Oliver a text last night saying I was going to bring a helper, but with his spotty cell service I have no idea if he ever got it.

There's no answer, so I head for the kitchen. Then I realize Lexi's no longer following me. Just like my mom, and me, she is dumbstruck in the living room.

"I know," I say impatiently, "different on the inside. But come on. Times a-wasting!"

"Right . . ."

Oliver is out back, of course. Even though I'm braced for more arguments, I can't help smiling. He's kneeling by a can of paint, stirring. We're finally going to begin painting. I'm not sure if I should just launch into my plan to get him to see reason, or if I should work up to it slowly.

"Cool lighthouse," Lexi says, walking over to the tower sitting near the shed.

"Oliver, this is Lexi," I say. "Lexi, this is Oliver. He's the mastermind."

"Thanks for doing this," Oliver says. "We still have loads to do."

Lexi studies the structure. "So is this going in the stern?" she asks.

"In the center," Oliver responds.

Okay, I guess we're getting into it now. I'm glad it's Lexi raising the subject and not me this time.

She glances at him, puzzled. "Where you row?"

"Yup." Oliver stands and carefully lays the wooden stirrer on the lid of the paint can. "It's going to be cool. I'll get in the boat and then the lighthouse will be lowered over me." He crosses to the tower and points at the bottom windows. "See? At this scale, they're big enough to put the oars through."

"Uh-huh." Lexi walks around the lighthouse structure, studying it.

"Lexi does a lot of building for the school plays," I say. "She's even been in the boat parade before."

Oliver looks a little uncomfortable. I know what he's feeling. This is his baby, and now someone—a stranger—is assessing it. I suddenly want to protect him.

"The lantern house looks great!" I say.

"The light works," Oliver says. "It's one of those battery-operated candles. I think from a distance it will look like a lantern."

"Definitely." I glance at Lexi. "Uh, he wants it to be as exact a replica as possible."

I had already told her about the problems: that he won't cut a door, that he'll be rowing through the windows. But the most ridiculous issue is the one I'm hoping she'll solve. The fact that he won't cut eyeholes.

"There aren't any windows on the side you'll be facing?" she asks.

"No." There's a hard tone in his voice. His "don't argue with me" voice. I've heard it more than a few times. "And I'm not cutting any," he says. I know this is meant for me because I've hounded him about it all week.

"But how will you steer?" I ask for the ten thousandth time.

"You sit backwards to row anyway," he says. "So what difference will it make?" He turns away from us and opens up another paint can.

I throw up my hands and give Lexi a "see what I'm dealing with" look.

"I totally respect your commitment to accuracy," Lexi says. "But, dude, you have to be able to see."

Oliver just keeps stirring.

I walk around to the front of the lighthouse, then into the shed where the boat we'll be using is stored. I climb into it and sit on the middle bench, where Oliver will be sitting.

I really want Oliver to be able to stick to his vision. But I also don't want him to be insane. It's not like he's an expert rower to begin with.

My eyes travel up to a small painting hung above one of the tool cabinets. I don't know why Framingham hung one of his paintings out here, but I don't know why he does anything. A little girl stands at the front of the painting with her back to the viewer. Way in the background, looking tiny, is a barn. An equally tiny man leans against the barn wall, but even as small as he is I can tell he's looking at the little girl. Because she's in the foreground, she's huge in comparison.

An idea forms.

I clamber out of the rowboat in my typically clumsy way and rush out of the shed. "I've got it!"

Oliver and Lexi both look at me. They're on opposite sides of the tower, painting. It looks like a somewhat uneasy truce. I hope Lexi isn't mad at me for pulling her into this. I hope Oliver isn't mad that I dragged someone in who might challenge his plans.

"I'll be your eyes!" I declare. "I'll sit in the bow and guide you!"

"But—"

"Hear me out. I know you're worried about scale. But perspective!"

Oliver looks at me blankly, and Lexi's eyebrows scrunch together. Then it's as if a lightbulb goes on over her head. "Perfect!"

Oliver looks from me to Lexi. "What? What are you talking about?"

"I got the idea from the painting in the shed," I explain in a rush. "It's okay if I'm bigger than I should be, because of perspective. It will be as if I'm in the foreground. I'll be the first thing anyone sees—even if just for a second."

"I don't know . . ." I can tell Oliver wants to find a solution, but his perfectionist side is resisting.

"I know!" Lexi says, putting down her paintbrush. "I can make you a costume that will make it look as if you're much smaller."

"What do you mean?"

"Come on," she says. Oliver and I share a quizzical look and then follow her into the shed.

"Get in the bow," she instructs me. I do. "Lean forward." I do.

She turns to Oliver. "I'll make a kind of bib for Mandy. With feet on the bottom. She can lean forward so that the feet will touch the edge of the boat."

"I love it!" I exclaim. "And the dress for the bib can be old-fashioned. I can be Mrs. Gilhooley, the wife of the first lighthouse keeper."

Oliver still looks dubious. "But the illusion won't work when the boat is seen from the side."

Lexi and I look at each other. Then we look at him. Then we look at each other.

I fling my hands into the air. "You can't row without being able to see!"

"You gotta give in a little," Lexi says more calmly.

Oliver slouches and stares down at his sneakers. "Okay," he mumbles.

"You guys paint," Lexi says. "I'm going to try to find a doll's dress that will work for the bib." She claps her hands together. "Come on, people! We have work to do!" She points at each of us, then rushes away.

"And I've always thought of her as shy," I say once she's gone.

"Shy?" Oliver says. "She's like a general." Then he grins at me. "But in a good way."

I'm relieved that he's not angry. I'm even more relieved that he's listened to reason and won't wind up crashing into the shore.

He steps up to me and wraps both arms around me and squeezes. "I'm sorry I've been such a jerk." Then he takes a step back. "Thank you," he says. "It means a lot to me that you care so much about our project."

I tug at the hem of his T-shirt, my eyes down. "It's important to you. So it's important to me."

He lifts my chin with his finger, and I look into those blue eyes that always make my breath catch. He brings his lips to mine, and I taste salt and a hint of peanut butter. But more, too. I shut my eyes and melt against him and detect the flavors of trust, and happiness, and gratitude, and I imagine I taste the same to him.

We pull apart and I lay my face against his chest, listening to his pounding heart. His chin sits on top of my head as he plays with my braid. "I guess we should get back to work," he murmurs.

I nod, making his chin bounce. I take a step away from him, and his hands clasp behind my back, keeping me close. I peer up at him with a grin. "So what now, boss?"

He glances over his shoulder. "The paint needs to dry. Let's finish painting the keeper's house."

We release each other and go into the shed. "Have you decided what color scheme to use?" I ask. Over the years the keeper's house has been painted different colors.

"Well, now that you're going to play the role of the lighthouse keeper's wife, we should paint it the color it was when Mrs. Gilhooley was there."

"Makes sense." I eye the stack of paint cans in the corner. "Any idea what that would be?"

"Not so much, no," Oliver admits.

"I'm sure the info is at the historical society," I say. "Should we go to the library?"

He taps his chin the way he does when he's thinking. I know he's toting up how long it will take to get there, look around, and get back. Then he holds up a finger in his "eureka!" gesture. "The attic!"

"Yeah . . . ?"

"There's a filing cabinet up there full of historical society newsletters and old photos, and other stuff about Rocky Point," he explains.

"There is?" Every day I seem to discover something new and confusing about ol' Freaky.

"See what you can find while I get set up down here."

I salute him. "Yes, sir!"

The house is quiet when I go through the kitchen. A peek out the living room windows shows an empty front yard. Oliver's mom and Freaky are both out. I'm a little relieved—it only just occurred to me that either of them could have witnessed our mini make-out session a minute ago.

The attic is crowded but fairly organized. The filing cabinets are against the back wall, and I manage to get to them without knocking anything over, tripping on anything, or banging into something. Oliver's waiting, so I force myself to keep from poking around, even though my flea market mentality is itching to see what odds and ends live up here. Unfortunately, my eyes start itching too. Dust allergies.

I riffle through the files, and though I don't find any color photos, I do discover a newsletter all about the keeper's house through the years. A quick glance tells me that there are several paragraphs devoted to its various paint jobs.

Mission accomplished. As I squeeze sideways through a narrow aisle, I notice a stack of framed paintings leaning against the wall, their backs facing out.

Curious, I wiggle over to them. I pull the first frame toward me, stirring up a huge dust cloud. They must not have been moved in a while. I let out three gigantor sneezes, then peer down. Even upside down I can tell it's a beauty. I lean it against my legs and pull the next one forward.

"What are you doing?"

I whirl around, making the paintings clatter.

Framingham stands in the doorway glaring.

"I—I'm sorry. Oliver wanted me to find these." I hold up the historical society newsletters.

He just continues staring.

I turn and straighten the paintings. "These are so good," I say. "I bet a gallery would snap you right up. You should enter them in the Fourth of July art show."

"Little know-nothing girls should mind their own business." He storms out of the attic.

What'd I do? I count to ten to make sure I won't run into Framingham on the way down the stairs, and hurry back out.

The screen door bangs behind me and Oliver turns. "I think I made your grandfather mad," I say.

"You didn't go into his studio, did you?" he asks nervously.

"No, it was up in the attic. All I said was that he should put some of his paintings in the art show. He got super angry."

"He's really touchy about his art," Oliver explains, crossing to me. He tucks a strand of hair behind my ear. "Don't let him upset you."

"But I was complimenting him."

"I'm not really sure what the deal is," Oliver explains. "Mom says he was kind of famous for a while, but then he got really bitter about the art world. Mom doesn't even know much."

Just when I think Freaky isn't so freaky, it turns out that maybe he is.

*E*ven though I'm *so* not a morning person, I wake up at the crack of dawn on the Fourth of July. Actually, I woke up every few hours all night, so around six a.m. I decided I might as well just get up. Spinning-brain syndrome.

Justin came home yesterday, and I immediately coerced him into joining Team Candy Cane Jr. The float is finished except for one crucial part: attaching it to the boat. Thanks to Oliver's nutty scheme, that can only happen once we're down at the river.

Today not only are my two favorite guys going to meet, it could also be the day that I drown. Oh yeah—and reveal to gossipy Rocky Point that I have a boyfriend.

At least I think I do.

I'm sniffing the can of coffee Mom left on the counter when Justin comes into the kitchen. I don't like the taste of coffee, but I do like the smell. I'm hoping that I can inhale some of the caffeine to help me wake up.

"What are you doing up so early?" he asks, taking the coffee away from me. He fills the filter basket, asking, "Aren't you the one who always wants to sleep in?"

"Couldn't sleep." I eye him, already dressed in running gear. "What about you? You usually sleep till the crack of noon when you're home from school."

"I'm running in the Red, White, and Blue Five-K Run," he says, "then I'm going to check out my buddies playing at the noon concert." He pulls a coffee mug from the dish drainer and uses it to fill the coffeemaker, then hits the on button. "Where's Mom?"

"Already gone when I got up." I nod toward a note on the fridge. "There's her to-do list."

Justin scans it just like I did a few minutes ago, checking to be sure we aren't on it. She knows all about the boat parade, of course, but it's possible that because it doesn't start until later in the day she expects us to help with historical society events.

The July Fourth celebration is like the Lupine Festival, only on steroids. It's the *true* summer season kickoff, and all the locals know it. This is the first opportunity to catch the eyes (and dollars) of the Summer Regulars. Everyone—year-rounders, Regulars, day-trippers—is trying to cram as much as possible into these two short months, and the frenzy starts today. People who haven't seen each other all year catch up in the town-wide party atmosphere. We're all happy; we're all celebrating together. Sure, a lot of locals are working their butts off today, but even so it's celebratory.

"Free and clear," Justin announces.

"For now," I say, giving him a warning glare. "Remember, you're driving me and Lexi at four."

He leans against the counter, crosses his arms and grins. "So. You and Freaky Framingham's grandson."

"His name is John Framingham," I say, "not Freaky."

Not that I've ever managed to think of him as anything other than Freaky Framingham myself. Still working on that.

I narrow my eyes at him. "You're not going to embarrass me, are you?"

"No promises, Sneezy."

We don't officially have to check in until five, but with all we still have to do our plan is to meet Framingham and Oliver at the launch site at four thirty. I asked Oliver if he wanted to enjoy the festivities beforehand, but he begged off, saying he still had fine-tuning to do.

Am I a bad girlfriend for not offering to help? I'm afraid if I go over there we'll get into a fight—we're both so tightly wound about this project. I figure it's safer to hold off until the last minute.

Which brings me back to the question: Am I an actual girlfriend?

Is it possible to sprain your brain? All this going around in circles in there has me dizzy. I need to lie down. "I'm going back to bed," I tell Justin. "I need to start this day over at a more reasonable hour." I shuffle out of the kitchen. "Don't be late!" I order over my shoulder.

"Yeah, yeah, yeah," he mutters, scrounging for cereal.

The whole day I'm antsy. No matter how many times I lie down, I only manage to get in a few twenty-minute catnaps. In between those completely unsatisfactory mini snoozes, I changed my outfit and fixed my hair twice, phoned Cynthia three times (voice mail), and arranged with Patti and Joanna where we should all meet to watch the fireworks tonight. By late afternoon I'm crawling the walls.

I nearly jump out of my skin when my phone rings. "Are you heading over?" Oliver asks nervously.

"As soon as Justin gets here, we'll pick up Lexi." I pace in front of my window, scanning the street for Justin's car. "He was going to the concert, but that ended ages ago. I'll text you as soon as we're on our way."

"Maybe you should call him to make sure he's—"

"There he is!" I click off, then realize I just hung up on him without even saying good-bye. Oops.

I grab my bag and race out the door. "Took long enough," I snap at Justin as I scramble into the car.

"Whoa," Justin says. "I'm doing you a favor, remember?"

"Sorry, sorry, sorry." I drum my fingers on my leg, trying to will myself to settle down.

Justin gives me a sideways glance. "You okay?"

"No!" I blurt. "And yes!"

Justin laughs. "All righty, then."

At Lexi's I get out and help her load her supplies into the trunk. I slide into the backseat. My nervous energy needs space. Lexi joins Justin up front.

Justin and Lexi are talking, but I'm not capable of following their conversation. My head is too crammed with all the many things that could go wrong. I just hope I'm not the one to cause them.

The launch site isn't too far from where Oliver and I had lunch down by the river. Up past Framingham's house is the spot where the river branches. One part continues on down the hill to the harbor, the other forms an inlet where the boat parade takes place.

Justin parks next to Framingham's pickup. The boat is already off the trailer and down at the shoreline, the keeper's house replica still intact in the stern. I must say, Candy Cane Jr. looks awfully sweet perched up there in the truck bed. Then I hear cursing and realize that Oliver and his grandfather don't think Candy Cane Jr. is all that sweet. More like a major pain in the patootie.

Justin swings out of the car and into action. "Let me help with that!"

As he trots over to the truck, Lexi and I unload two bolts of fabric and stacks of newspapers. I carry the bib I'll be wearing and the toy lantern I bought as a "pity purchase" at a flea market. From a distance no one will notice that one side is missing a pane and the other side is cracked. The important thing is it looks like Mrs. Gilhooley might have carried it, and with a new battery it actually still turns on.

Once Candy Cane Jr. is off the truck, it's a lot easier for them to manage. The three of them carry it to the shoreline, but only place it on the ground once Lexi and I spread newspapers to keep it from getting muddy.

"Gotta say, it looks pretty darn spiffy," Justin says, taking a step back. Then he frowns. "But how—"

I cut him off. "It's all under control." I don't want to have to get into the whole "how are you going to row, much less see?" argument again. "Oh—Justin, this is Oliver," I add, realizing I hadn't introduced them.

"Didn't I see you on the other side of a lighthouse?" Justin jokes.

"That was me." Oliver smiles. "Unless you mean my grandfather. Mr. Framingham."

Freaky just grunts a hello and continues laying out tools on the newspaper beside Candy Cane Jr.

My sneakers sink a bit in the muddy bank and make little sucking sounds each time I lift my feet. Maine being Maine, we had a brief shower this morning, but thankfully, both the weather girl on TV *and* Framingham have declared that the rest of the day and the evening will be completely clear.

Oliver bounces a little on his feet, looking nervous. "Let me show you Lexi's brilliant idea," I say to distract him.

I glance around and spot a large boulder. "Over there," I say to Lexi. She follows me with a roll of fabric. I duck behind the boulder and attach the bib. I put on Mrs. Gilhooley's hat that Mom generously loaned me (after multiple promises to jump in the river after it if it blows off my head) and pick up the toy lantern. Then I rise up to the point where the scuffed doll shoes tap against the top of the rock.

"I'm Mrs. Gilhooley," I announce. "My husband the light-house keeper asked me to say hello."

Justin bursts out laughing, but in a good way. Oliver grins and applauds. Even ol' Freaky seems amused.

"I know you're worried about what it will look like from the side," Lexi says, "so come around here."

As Justin and Oliver head over, she pins the dark brown fabric to my shoulders and fans it out along the grass. "See?" she says. "We'll cover the inside of the boat with this. That way no one will see Mandy, and it will look as if Mrs. Gilhooley is standing on the ground."

"Brilliant!" Oliver exclaims. "This is what you two have been whispering about!"

I stand all the way up. "We wanted to surprise you."

Oliver brushes my lips with his. "I love it," he says softly. "Thank you."

I'm embarrassed for Justin to see me kissing Oliver, so I duck my head. "It was really Lexi who came up with the idea," I confess.

"But I'd rather kiss you," he whispers. As an enormous grin practically eats my face, he adds in a louder voice, "Thanks, Lexi. You've been awesome! We never could have done it without you."

"Well, you haven't exactly done it yet," Lexi points out. "We can celebrate after you manage to get the boat past the judges' stand."

Gulp. Rowing is Oliver's job. Navigating is mine. And we're both novices. Not to mention self-proclaimed klutzes.

As if reading my mind, Justin says, "This should be interesting."

"Suit up and do a test run," Framingham says. "I know you've been practicing, boy, but the load is going to be different from when it's empty."

I force myself to not stare. That was probably the most I've ever heard from him at one time.

"You're right, Pops." I can feel Oliver tense beside me. He's got a lot riding on this. Neither of us really cares about winning. But we don't want to be humiliated, either. This was all Oliver's design—mostly, anyway—and Lexi and I gave in to his insistence that he can row blind. We're about to put all that bravado to the test. And we all know it.

As Framingham walks back to the truck, he rolls his shoulders a few times and shakes out his hands. I have a feeling lifting and hauling Candy Cane Jr. was his own brand of bravado.

Oliver goes to the rowboat and stands there, assessing. He calls to Framingham, "Do you think I should get into it on land?"

Framingham shrugs. "Safer on ground. But how strong are your friends?"

Oliver glances over at us, worried.

"Come on, help us get Oliver into the lighthouse," I say to Justin.

Oliver sits in his spot in the middle seat. For a moment we all just look back and forth between the rowboat and the lighthouse. "That won't build itself," Freaky says as he ambles over with the clamps we're going to use to attach the lighthouse to the rim of the boat.

"So how are we going to do this?" I say, worrying as the time keeps passing and people start arriving.

To my astonishment, Framingham takes charge. "Ollie, scrunch down. Once we give the okay, slowly straighten up. Mandy, get in the boat and guide the lighthouse down over him. What's yer name, tall girl?" He snaps his fingers at Lexi. "You, me, and the boy there"—indicating Justin—"will hoist the thing. High."

"Got it," Justin says. Under his breath he mutters, "Hope you got your measurements right."

"We tested it," I snap. It's true. When we finished the chicken-wire tower, before we put on the papier-mâché, Freaky, Oliver's mom, and I lowered it down over Oliver. It worked on land. I just hope we can manage it once it's on the boat.

I clamber into the boat, Oliver scrunches, and the three of

them raise the lighthouse. I reach over to help them get it above Oliver and centered. I shove it a bit more to the left, and Oliver disappears inside the tower.

"You okay in there?" I ask.

"Yeah," comes his muffled reply.

"Are you sitting all the way up?" Framingham asks.

The lighthouse shifts and wiggles but it doesn't flip over. "I am now." We all exhale loudly with relief.

Freaky, Justin, and Lexi step away delicately as if any sudden movement might topple the structure.

"Does it look straight?" I ask them.

Lexi walks all the way around it. "Looks good. Time to clamp it on."

Framingham and Justin get to work as I climb out of the boat and help Lexi with the blue-green fabric we also brought. Once they're done, we cover the wooden platform and metal clamps with the fabric, the idea being that it will look like waves.

"Still okay?" I ask.

"Excellent," Oliver replies.

"Let's get this baby in the water!" Justin says.

Framingham has returned to his truck and leans against it, arms crossed. I guess he's done. Justin, Lexi, and I grunt and heave and shove, and finally get the rowboat into the water. I hop into it, making it tip.

"What's going on?" Oliver calls from inside his prison.

"All okay, just getting settled," I assure him.

"Oars?" Oliver asks.

"Coming!" Justin calls. He and Lexi slip oars in through the portholes. I'm relieved when they begin to move rhythmically, which means Oliver not only has a good grip, but actually has been practicing as he promised.

We immediately ground.

"What happened?" Oliver shouts.

"Sorry, sorry, sorry!" I say. "I wasn't navigating. Don't do anything until I get set up."

"Hang on," Justin says. He wades into the water and holds the rowboat still. I am going to owe him big-time. Except no one seems annoyed. In fact everyone seems to be having fun. Even, I realize, as I take a quick look, ol' Freaky Framingham.

"I'm getting into position," I tell Oliver, being his eyes. "Lexi is tying the bib on. Now she's pinning the fabric."

I sit still as Lexi arranges fabric in the bow so it will look as if the doll shoes are standing on a boulder, and then brings it around me to hide my body.

"Done!" Lexi declares. She moves all around the boat in the water, taking photos.

"Is the lantern lit?" Oliver asks.

"I'll get it," Justin calls, rushing forward. "There's going to be a kind of a lurch," he warns. Lexi holds the boat steady.

Justin carefully gets into the boat. It tips side to side, but the lighthouse holds. Yay, clamps! Justin flicks the switch on the battery-operated candle in the lantern room. "All set."

That reminds me to do the same to mine. I click on the toy lantern.

"Adorable," Lexi declares.

By now the boat parade official, Mr. Saunders, has arrived. He quickly wades into the shallows. "You're not supposed to launch until it's your turn," he tells me.

"Do we have to get out of the water?" I ask plaintively. I *really* don't want to have to ask Justin, Lexi, and Framingham to haul us out and then put us back in again.

"What's happening?" Oliver's stifled voice asks.

Mr. Saunders looks startled. "There's someone in there?"

I want to ask him if he thinks Candy Cane Jr. is rowing herself, but I don't since we're asking him to bend the rules for us. I put on a pathetic face and say, "It will just be too hard to pull us out and then bring us back in."

"What number are you?"

"Five."

He glances at the people arriving with their boats. He looks down at his clipboard. "You okay if we make them third?" he calls out to them.

There's a brief stomach-tightening moment as the entrants confer with each other. Then I see shrugs and hear "Sure!" and "Fine," and "No problem," and I relax again.

Well, relax-ish.

"Get over as far as possible to make room for the first two boats," Mr. Saunders instructs.

"Thank you SOOOOOO much!"

Framingham ambles back down to the boat, then slips a hefty pair of wire cutters under the brown fabric by my feet. "Just in case," he says. He jerks his head toward the invisible Oliver. He lowers his voice and adds, "Lad can be stubborn. Can't imagine where he gets it from."

Then he winks, pats the boat, and stands. "Have fun." He gives the boat a little shove so that we move more out of the way, then heads back toward the truck.

I have the astounding impression that I might have just gotten a glimpse of the "real" Freaky. And that this was his way of letting me know he's not really mad at me for the other day in the attic.

The first boat isn't fancy, but has cuteness going for it. A dad wearing typical lobsterman gear rows a boat with lobster traps hanging from bow and stern. Four little kids wearing homemade fish costumes wave. A mom sits in the stern holding a baby dressed as a lobster—a popular infant Halloween costume around here. It takes them a while to launch because all kinds of relatives insist on taking videos and snapping pictures.

Next up is a boat full of scantily clad mermaids, and I'm secretly glad that Oliver can't see anything from his spot inside the tower. My brother Justin happily helps the girls get the boat launched. I have a feeling this boat is going to be a hit with the boys lining the banks.

Then it's our turn.

"Showtime," I tell Oliver.

"Now?" Oliver asks.

"Now!"

My stomach clenches. I've just realized that even though Oliver is the one powering the boat, I'm really the one in charge. It's all up to me to get us through this.

Oliver's oars hit the water with a splash. "Hey!" I yelp.

"Sorry! Sorry!"

He gets the oars under control, and we glide away from shore. First challenge: get around the bend without snagging on any boulders or low-hanging trees, or going aground.

"Straight," I instruct Oliver. "Straight." I keep my voice calm and even. Almost singsong. Our first task is to get far enough away from shore to make the turn without disaster. But not so far that the spectators won't be able to see us.

"Turn!" I call out.

"What?" I hear Oliver ask.

"Turn!" I screech.

"Which way?" Oliver shouts back.

It just now occurs to me that we should have practiced the route. Not to mention tested our ability to hear each other since Oliver is *inside* Candy Cane Jr. sitting backward to row—and facing *away* from me. Too late now.

"RIGHT! RIGHT! RIGHT!" I holler.

Oliver adjusts quickly (points to Oliver!), and we move into the correct position. Up ahead the first boat is getting *awww*s, and the boatload of gyrating mermaids is getting a lot of whoops and catcalls. I'm hoping they don't totally eclipse us and we glide by the shore without anyone even noticing.

I underestimated our fan club.

"Candy Cane!" someone screams onshore. I think it's Lexi.

"Look!" a voice sounding suspiciously like Justin's shouts. "It's Mrs. Gilhooley!"

A rhythmic cheer goes up. "Candy Cane! Candy Cane!" I detect a strong Brooklyn accent in there. Joanna must have stopped texting her boyfriend long enough to join in.

I grin from ear to ear. It's amazing to hear the applause and chanting and know it's for us. I suddenly understand the rush Cynthia says she feels onstage.

"What's happening?" Oliver asks.

"They're cheering for us!"

I think he says "Cool," but it's hard to tell under all that papier-mâché and chicken wire.

Then the sound changes. The clapping falls off, there's a bit of a hush, and then I hear Justin yell, "Mandy! Watch out!"

I snap out of my reverie. Oliver is a righty, and with no visual cues he's rowed us more toward shore than keeping a straight and centered heading. We're closer in than we should be. Here there are rocks and debris—all just waiting to snag our boat and topple Candy Cane Jr.

"Pull left," I yell.

But he doesn't hear me. The next boat must have appeared behind us because a new section of the crowd starts applauding.

"Left, Oliver! Left!"

"What?" Oliver calls through the papier-mâché.

"Left! Left!"

I turn to yell it directly at the tower, ripping up the fabric, Mrs. Gilhooley's dress flapping and feet kicking as I swing around. "LEFT!"

People onshore join in. "Left! Left! Left!" they shout.

The boat finally straightens back out, and there's loud applause again. I swivel in the seat and rearrange my various pieces, though I know it looks totally sloppy compared to Lexi's careful job. *Oh well,* I think. We already passed the judges before this little mishap, when we were still looking good. I silently vow to ignore the shore and pay attention only to navigation.

"We're starting the curve now," I instruct Oliver. We'll have fewer cheerleaders here—this section tends to fill up with families living on the west side of the inlet. That'll make it easier for me to concentrate.

We row around the inlet and land just opposite from where we began without any further incidents. It's only been about a fifteen-minute trip, but I know Oliver must be exhausted. And hot. And if he is anything like me, totally stressed. Maybe even claustrophobic.

We safely make it to where we can get out, and thankfully, a bunch of people come help us the minute we reach shallow water. Someone detaches the fabric from my shoulders, and I undo the costume bib. I drop Mrs. Gilhooley into the boat and leap out. I hold it stable as three dad types unclamp the lighthouse and lift it off Oliver.

He's drenched in sweat, his hair plastered to his face. Someone hands him a bottle of water, which he accepts gratefully. He's too winded to speak or even climb out of the dinghy. I lean over and fling my arms around him anyway, tipping the boat a bit. "We did it!"

He's still breathing in gasps but says shakily, "I'm totally gross."

I stand back up and hold out my hands to help him. "Yeah, you are!" I say with a laugh.

Once Oliver is out of the boat and we've stumbled through the shallow water, the same dad types drag the dinghy out of the way of the arriving boats. I know we should be helping, but given our natural clumsiness and Oliver's exhaustion, I figure we're doing them more of a favor by standing still.

Oliver pours the rest of the bottle of water over his head and rubs his wet face. He takes in a long breath, then blows it back out.

"I wish you could have seen them," I say. "They were clapping and cheering for us."

"I *kind of* heard it," he says with a rueful smile. He shakes his head hard, like a puppy, spraying me with water.

"Hey!" I scream.

"Sorry!" Oliver smiles and lays a wet arm across my shoulder. I don't mind. "As much as I hate to admit this," he says, "I really should have listened to you. And Lexi. Eyeholes would have helped. And rowing from inside was no fun."

"Well, we survived," I say. "That's all that matters."

Oliver twists to look at Candy Cane Jr. "Yeah . . . I guess. . . ."

"I've figured out something about you," I tell him. "It's like you once said to me. You're excellent on the micro scale. But when it comes to macro . . ." I shrug as I trail off.

"What do you mean?" Oliver asks, turning back around. When I don't answer, he bangs his hip into mine. "Come on, you can't leave me hanging."

I hope he doesn't get mad, but I continue. "Your measurements were perfect. Your staples absolutely evenly spaced. The lantern house, the stripes, it's all just right, all the little details."

"But . . . ?"

"But let's just say the big picture kind of gets crowded out."

"Like giving up the ability to see in exchange for a completely accurate model," he says with a sheepish grin.

I give him a little squeeze. "Don't feel bad," I tell him. "I'm good at the big picture, and totally sloppy in the details." I frown. "I guess that makes us opposites." That seems like maybe it's a bad thing.

"I'd say that makes us complementary, not opposites. It's why we make such a good team."

He leans down and kisses me, but I step back. This is a bit too public, with the other parade entrants coming and going. Not to mention any minute now Framingham's blue pickup will appear.

I glance up the slope and spot the truck pulling up. Freaky climbs out and ambles down the hill.

"Good job," Framingham says. Oliver beams. I can see his grandpop's approval means a lot to him.

Together the three of us load Candy Cane Jr. onto the truck and the boat onto the trailer. Oliver climbs into the truck cab, then leans out the open window. "See you at the beach for the fireworks," he says.

"Near the dock," I remind him.

He taps my nose with his finger, then settles into his seat. I step back and watch the truck drive away.

I glance around and realize people are staring. This has to be the biggest Freaky sighting all summer. I wonder if they think I'm a big weirdo because of it.

I have a momentous realization: I don't care. Not only do I like—maybe even more than like—Oliver, I've actually grown fond of Freaky. Hopefully, instead of his freakiness rubbing off on me, my total and complete ordinariness will rub off on him. At least in the eyes of the Rocky Point gossipers.

I text Justin I'm ready for him to pick me up. Then I watch a very elaborately decorated boat coming toward shore. A canopy made of netting hangs over the top, the poles disguised with seaweed. "Under the Sea" from *The Little Mermaid* blasts from hidden speakers. The guy rowing is dressed in a scuba outfit, and three people manipulate larger-than-life-size puppets: a jellyfish, a lobster, and a crab. Glow sticks nestled in the netting and seaweed give it an otherworldly, underwatery look.

"Amazing," I murmur. "I bet I know who'll win first prize!"

I hear a horn honk and see Justin pulling up. I scramble up the muddy little hill. "You did great!" Justin says as I get into the car.

"Yeah," I say, "I'm kind of astonished we survived."

"We all are, believe me," Justin says. "So where to? Back to Freaky's?"

I give him a look.

"I'm sorry, *Mister* Freaky?" Justin jokes. "It sounds more respectful."

I smack his arm, but I'm laughing.

"He's different from what I thought," Justin says. "*Mr. Framingham*, I mean."

"I know, right?" I already told Justin about Framingham being an artist, and also about how touchy he was about his paintings. "Just drop me off at home so I can shower and change, please." I bite my lip as I watch houses decorated with flags and red-white-and-blue bunting go by the window. "And Oliver?"

"What about him?" he asks as he makes the turn onto Dumont.

"Is he . . . different from what you thought?"

A sneaky little smile crawls across his face. "Mandy has a boyfriend," he singsongs. "Mandy has a boyfriend."

"Stop it!" I protest.

But he keeps singing. "Mandy and Ollie sitting in a tree. K-I-S-S-I-N-G!"

"Cut it out," I shriek through my giggles.

Justin switches to making kissing noises.

I poke his side. "You." Poke. "Are." Poke. "Evil."

He laughs his sinister-villain laugh. The he waggles his eyebrows at me. "You better be nice to me, sis. So far I haven't spilled any of your secrets—"

"I don't have any."

"Or interrogated him about his intentions, or questioned him about his weird attachment to Candy Cane or—"

"Okay! Okay! I get it. You are the best brother ever and I am lucky to have you and when are you going back to school already?"

He laughs and stops to let a bunch of parents with little kids with balloons and painted faces cross the street. There were kiddie events all day in the Square, and now these kids are probably on their way to find a spot for the fireworks. Or grab some food on the piers, though there will also be booths set up near the docks, too. Yep, another seafood extravaganza.

As Justin pulls into our driveway, a thought rattles through me. I'm making my debut tonight as Oliver's girlfriend. Or maybe *he's* making *his* debut as my boyfriend.

If that's what we actually are. We haven't discussed our "status"—we've been too busy building the float and, okay, kissing, to talk about what the kissing means. *Don't overthink,* I order myself.

Between Candy Cane duty and building the float I haven't had a chance to see or even talk to anyone. Not Patti, not Joanna, not any of my school friends (well, mostly they're Cynthia's, but whatever). None of them know about Oliver and me. And now we're about to go public.

I think I'm more nervous now than I was before the boat parade.

I run my fingers up and down my seat belt. "So, um . . ."

Justin stops with his hand on the door. "What?"

I flush. This is embarrassing, but I really do want to know. "So do you like him?"

"Freaky? Yeah, he's aces."

I roll my eyes again. Justin brings that out in me.

"Yes, sis, I like Oliver. And what's more important, you like him. And probably even more important to you"—he pokes me—"is that he likes you."

I lean back in my seat and feel the tension fall away, like it's being swept out to sea. "He does?"

Justin scoots out of the car. "Don't go all girl on me, Sneezy. You know he does. Don't pretend you don't."

I'm about to protest, then realize he's right. Oliver likes me. I know it. And he knows I like him. And that's exactly how it should be.

*T*he barge that sets off the fireworks is stationed between Rocky Point and Hubbard Island, so pretty much all sides of the bay provide good views. And all sides get crowded, particularly the U-shaped sandy beach that creates the cove. The band and the officials use the two ferry docks on the bay, so no one gets to sit there, but they make a great meeting point. That's where I head to find Patti and Joanna when Mom drops me off at the wharf.

I pass the same food booths that were at the Lupine Festival, but now that the Summer Regulars have arrived—and a whole lot of day-trippers have invaded— it's *really* crammed. I forgo my bloob pocket just in case Oliver and Lexi beat me here. I don't want him to have to face Joanna and Patti without me.

Music blasts from the loudspeakers, and the whole wharf has a party atmosphere, with lots of people sporting red, white, and blue. It's mega packed even as I make my way down the rocks to the shore. I hope I can find my friends in all this! Light spills from the docks, and the booths illuminate part of the beach, but it's still fairly dark as I get closer to the water.

I had nothing to worry about. I hear Joanna's unmistakable Brooklyn accent and use it as my guide. I try to avoid stepping on any toes or fingers as I pick my way carefully through the people perched on mossy rocks and sprawled on the sand. It's like a human obstacle course.

"I can't hear you!" Joanna's yelling into her cell phone, one hand covering her other ear. "We should text. TEXT!"

Joanna sits on a portable beach chair that holds down one corner of a blanket. Patti lounges on another edge, her legs stretched out in front of her. What's interesting is the guy Patti's leaning against. As I approach, she lifts her face to him. He bends to kiss her, then she gets up and kneels to rummage in a cooler holding down another corner of the blanket.

So Patti found herself her summer romance. Interesting.

"Hey, everybody!" I greet as I drop onto the blanket.

"Mandy!" Joanna cries. "Little Miss MIA!"

"Sorry," I say. "But between working at the lighthouse and building the boat float, I've been super busy."

Patti swings around with her back to the water. "Mandy, do you know Kyle Marcus?"

I look at Kyle, who's now sitting cross-legged next to her. His face is familiar. Curly blond mane. Freckles. "Were you on the soccer team with my brother? Justin?"

"You're Justin Sullivan's sis?" He grins. "Cool. Is he coming?"

"He's around here somewhere," I say, scanning the crowds. "We might run into him. So what have you vacationers been up to while I've been slaving away?"

"Well," Patti says, "Grumpy over there has spent most of the time at the library checking e-mail and gazing at pictures of her beloved Brooklyn. Not to mention her beloved."

Joanna scoops sand at Patti. "I haven't been that bad."

"That's true. We were able to pry you away from Wi-Fi long enough for a trip to Hubbard Island." Patti looks at me a bit apologetically. "We were going to ask you if you wanted to come, but we know you're not all that into the biking and hiking."

"And sneezing and itching eyes," I agree. "My allergies kick in around now, so being in all that nature isn't exactly big fun."

"You looked like you were having a good time in the boat parade today," Joanna says. She holds up her soda can in salute. "Excellent float!"

"Thanks," I say. "It was all Oliver's idea."

Joanna swivels her head. "So where is this mystery man of yours?"

Patti scoots forward. "Is he really Freaky Framingham's grandson?"

"Word really gets around in this town," I say.

"Another reason I miss Brooklyn," Joanna mutters.

"He'll be here," I say. I rise up on my knees and scan the crowd.

"Talking about me?"

Hands appear on my shoulders. Oliver's hands.

"You found us!" I say, glancing up. I'm so relieved that I hadn't said too much. He would have heard every word.

"With Lexi's help," he says, settling next to me. "She's talking to some friends over by the dock. She'll be over in a minute, she said."

"So you're the genius behind the mini Candy Cane," Joanna says.

"I don't know if 'genius' is the right word," Oliver responds. "'Nut job,' maybe. Though I think Lexi and Mandy might refer to me as Pain in the Butt."

"Guys, this is Oliver," I say with a laugh. I nod toward my

friends. "The one clinging to her cell phone is Joanna; that's Patti and her friend Kyle."

"Hey, man," Kyle says. He stands and stretches. "I'm off. Gotta go sell some lobster."

Patti stands and gets up onto her tiptoes to give him a quick kiss. "Later," he tells her.

"You bet."

To us he adds, "If you get hungry, stop by our booth. It's the second one in at Main Street and Water. Don't you dare go to Jake's. And say hi to Sully for me."

"We promise!" I call after him as he heads off.

"Who's Sully?" Oliver asks.

"Justin. One of his many nicknames."

The minute Kyle is out of hearing range, Patti grabs my hands. "So you know him? Tell me everything!" she demands.

"Looks like you already know plenty," I tease.

"But you're here with him all year! And by the way, where have you been hiding him?"

"I guess you just hadn't been paying enough attention," I say.

"Well . . . ?"

I frown. "I actually don't know much. He was a year ahead of Justin."

"Oooh," Joanna says. "A college man!"

"Actually," Patti says, "he's not in college. He told me that his dad needed his help, so he didn't go."

"That's right," I say, remembering. "His dad's one of the lobstermen. I think it's a whole family operation. Uncle. Cousins, too, maybe."

"Rough," Joanna says. "To have to give up college to go into the family business."

"I don't know," Oliver says. "He can always go later. I think it's kind of noble. Pitching in for the family." He grins. "Of course, I'm totally incapable of going into my family's businesses, so it's easy for me to talk."

"Mandy's kind of in the family business this summer," Patti points out. "That lighthouse is practically a family member."

"Yeah," Oliver says, tucking a strand of hair behind my ear. "And I think it's really sweet."

"Okay, now we need to know all about *you*!" Joanna says, setting her sights on Oliver. Gotta give the boy props. He's not running screaming into the night.

"Not much to tell. Here from California. And," he adds, putting his arm around me, "having a much better time than I thought I would."

"So . . . how'd you meet?" Patti asks in a singsongy voice.

I squinch my nose at her. My way of warning her not to get too—well, let's just call it "cute."

"Candy Cane," Oliver tells them.

"That job I didn't want?" I say. "It turned out to have some surprise perks."

"Is that what I am?" Oliver asks, pretending to be offended. "A perk?"

"You're a lot perkier than I am," I quip.

"Definitely perkier than Joanna," Patti grumbles.

"What?" Joanna glances up from her cell. "What are you saying?"

"Quit with the texting already!" Patti complains. "We're getting the dish on the new guy!"

I shake my head, but Oliver seems amused.

"Speaking of dishes," he says. He starts emptying a shopping bag he brought with him. Wrapped sandwiches, cut veggies with some kind of dip in a plastic tub, and more of those giant cookies.

"Oh, my hero!" I squeal. I grab one of the sandwiches. I wave it at the others. "I can guarantee all of this is super delish!"

"Oh good," Lexi says as she joins us. "I didn't miss the food!"

Oliver scoots over to make room for her. "Pops insisted I bring enough to feed an army, so dig in."

"Oliver's grandfather is an insanely good cook," I promise them. "Your taste buds will be in ecstasy."

Lexi picks up a sandwich and unwraps it. "It's true. Ol' Freaky is a freaking brilliant cook."

Everyone freezes. All eyes flick to Oliver. I carefully study the sandwich in my lap.

"Freaky?" he repeats. He looks around, but now everyone's avoiding his eyes. "Mandy?"

I swallow my bite of mozzarella, pesto, and arugula sandwich. "It's, uh, kind of a nickname. It's stupid. Just kid stuff."

"Oh." Oliver looks down and fiddles with the laces of his sneakers. He clears his throat. "Look, I know he's kind of eccentric, but he's actually—"

"He's awesome," Lexi says, cutting him off. "He knows all this stuff about art, and building things."

"If people would get to know him," Oliver says sharply, "they wouldn't be so mean."

"That's not fair," Patti argues. "He doesn't *let* us get to know him. He's like this recluse up in the woods. The only time I ever saw him in town he practically growled at anyone who tried to talk to him."

I stroke Oliver's arm, sorry I brought him here, sorry that he had to hear this, sorry that—well, just sorry. "Patti's right," I say gently. "Until I got to know him, I thought he was kind of scary. You know how kids are."

Oliver gives a little nod and takes a sandwich. I'm encouraged by the fact that he's still sitting here.

"And now that I've been spending all this time up at the house, I see him differently," I say.

Oliver unwraps his sandwich and takes a bite. As he chews I can tell he's thinking. Mulling. I reach for the cooler with sodas and hand him a can. He pops it open and takes a swig. "It's okay," he finally says. "I thought he was pretty odd when I first got here too. And he's definitely got his moods. So I understand. And this town seems pretty big on nicknames."

He smiles weakly to show he's not mad, and I see everyone relax. My own shoulders drop back to where they belong, and my stomach unclenches. The sandwiches get distributed, and after Patti takes a bite, she says, "Oh man. Lexi's right. These are freakishly good!"

"From now on," Lexi says, "that's what we mean if we call him Freaky. That he makes freakishly good food."

Oliver laughs for real, and I know the awkwardness is definitely over.

"You think these are good," I say, "wait until you taste the cookies!"

"Did someone say cookies?"

"Hi, Vicki," Lexi says. She moves over to make room.

"That was the cutest boat," Vicki says to me, but she's eyeing Oliver. I can't tell if it's because he's so good-looking, because she's never seen me with a boyfriend, or because of the Freaky connection.

"This is Oliver," I say. "From California." I lean into Oliver and look up at him. "Vicki's in some of my classes."

"California?" Vicki says. "Cool." She reaches for a cookie, then looks around at us for permission.

"Go ahead," Oliver says with a smile. "I brought plenty."

"How'd the performance go?" I ask, munching my sandwich.

Vicki's in drama club with Cynthia, and for the last few years they've been performing on one of the stages set up in the Square on the Fourth.

"I skipped it this year," she says, then gazes at the cookie. "Wow, this is good."

"Why?" Lexi asks. "You always do it."

Vicki shrugs. "Cynthia's the one who's into it. I'd rather just enjoy the great big party, since most of the summer I'm babysitting."

"Then why do you do it?" I ask.

Vicki shrugs. "You know how Cynthia can be."

I'm about to ask what she means when my hand is crushed under a stranger's foot.

"Yeowch!" I yelp.

"Sorry," I hear someone call.

Normally part of the fun of the Fourth of July is the giant and crowded beach party. But tonight I'd rather not get stepped on and have a bit more private time with Oliver.

"What time is it?" I ask.

Joanna checks her cell phone. "Eight forty-five."

That gives us fifteen minutes before the show begins. "I have an idea," I whisper to Oliver. "A better place to watch the fire-works. But we have to hurry."

"Okay."

I grab a cookie and stand. "We're going to take off."

"But you're going to miss the prize announcements," Vicki says.

The ribbons are given to the boat-float winners just before the fireworks begin, along with the usual announcements, thank-yous, et cetera.

"Somehow I don't think we're going to win," I say.

"Unless there's a prize for the most foolhardy," Lexi comments. She shakes her head and picks up another sandwich. "I still can't believe you pulled it off."

"If we win," Oliver says to Lexi, "you accept for the team."

Lexi gives him a thumbs-up as she chews.

We head toward the wharf, stepping around blankets and skirting kids racing around waving pinwheels and sparklers. "Do we have time for me to grab some sodas from the booth?" Oliver asks.

"If you hurry."

"Don't move." He rushes away into the crowd. The lines at

the booths aren't bad now since the fireworks are about to start, and soon Oliver reappears carrying a take-out box. He hands me a soda. Then he holds out something else.

A lobster roll. For me.

He looks so adorably proud of himself. "I got it at Kyle's booth, as promised."

"I'm not really hungry," I say.

"Aw, come on," he says. "Kyle says theirs are the best. After all, it's a day to show our patriotism. Eating a lobster roll in Maine could be considered a patriotic act."

I smile weakly as I take it from him. My nose wrinkles at the smell. *Wash it down with soda*, I tell myself. Mask the flavor with a bite of cookie. You can do this.

He's still watching. I take a teeny-tiny bite, hoping to get mostly roll. But the reason Kyle's family has so many fans is because of how overstuffed the rolls are.

Dis-*gus*-ting.

My taste buds want to leap off my tongue, and I force myself to swallow without gagging. It's not easy. I immediately take a big swig of soda, swishing it all around my mouth as if it's mouthwash. I take another gulp of soda, trying to wash away the grossness of lobster chunks drenched in mayo. I actually shudder.

Luckily, Oliver is loving his lobster roll so much he actually shuts his eyes and practically swoons. Excellent. I take advantage of his closed eyes and drop the sandwich.

"Oops!" I say as he opens his eyes. "Clumsy me."

"I'll go get you another," Oliver says.

I grab his arm. "No! We, uh, we don't have enough time."

"We can split this one," he says, holding it out to me.

"You have it. I can have them anytime, remember? But we actually do have to hurry."

I take a huge bite of Freaky's cookie—chocolate chip with walnuts—to disguise the lingering fish flavor and grab his arm.

"Where are we going?" Oliver asks as I lead him away from the wharf.

"To the most fitting place to celebrate this day," I say.

Then he gets it. "Candy Cane!"

"Exactly. We spent the day with Candy Cane Jr., so now we should spend the evening with the lady herself."

"I like the way you think." Now that he knows where we're headed, Oliver picks up his pace. We're practically running as we reach it. He follows me around to the entrance. "We're going inside?" he asks.

I give him a smug smile "We're going to the top."

I fish out my keys, and together we shove open the door.

I've never been in the lighthouse at night. It's pitch-black, which I'd expected, and also pretty spooky. "Hang on," I say. "Hold the door open."

Even with door propped the moonlight barely makes a dent in the dark. "Take this," I say, handing Oliver the rest of my cookie. "I need both hands. Actually, finish it," I add. I anticipate some kissing before, during, and after the fireworks, and I can't bear the idea of Oliver having fish breath.

That taken care of, I carefully shuffle to the entryway bench. It's a much easier target than the lamp on the table farther in. I flip up the seat and rummage around inside. "Bingo!" I exclaim, pulling out a flashlight. I flick it on. Oliver lets the door shut and takes the flashlight as I pull out another one.

I train the light on the table with the lamp. "Over there," I instruct Oliver.

He walks to the table, then stops. "Let's not."

"Let's not what?" I ask as I stand.

"Turn on the lights. Let's pretend we're way back in time. We're in the era of Mrs. Gilhooley."

"I don't think they had these." I wave the flashlight.

"They had lanterns. These will stand in for those."

I shake my head and smile. "You're not going to make me put on Mrs. Gilhooley's outfit, are you?"

"Maybe next time."

I cross to the doorway leading to the spiral staircase. "I wouldn't want to climb these in the dark in that dress."

Something about being in the tower with nothing but our flashlight beams to guide us keeps us from speaking. Maybe it's because we're concentrating hard—it would be bad to take a misstep, and we're both self-admitted klutzes. But there's also something mysterious and private and magical about climbing with only our flickering lights that invites silence.

It gets me thinking about the footsteps of all those lighthouse keepers who made this very same climb in the dark. Oliver may be right—there is something compelling about the history of this place, once it starts to seem more personal.

But neither of us can stay quiet when we emerge into the lantern room. "Oh my," I breathe. Oliver gasps behind me.

I know this is the view tourists travel to see, but none has ever seen it like this. I quickly turn off my flashlight, and Oliver does the same with his. We carefully place them by our feet.

The lantern room is made entirely of glass panes fitted into metal frames, giving us a panoramic view of all of Rocky Point. Straight ahead the new(er) lighthouse flashes signals from its rocky outpost where the bay and the harbor join together to become the wide-open sea. Out the windows on my left side, I can see the lights from the ferry docks and the food booths. Tiny fluttering green dots that remind me of fireflies sparkle along the coast. I'm guessing they're glow sticks carried by all of the kids huddled around their parents. Across the bay, lights on the Cranston peninsula dot the shoreline.

On the right-hand side it's pretty dark in the harbor. I can make out the running lights on boats where people are holding their own Independence Day celebrations on board. I turn all the way around and look at the town—the lit homes, the streetlamps, the illuminated shop windows. "It doesn't look real," I murmur.

"Like something out of a storybook," Oliver agrees. "This must be what it looked like to all those keepers who had to make sure the lantern stayed lit."

"Beautiful."

We're both lost in the timelessness of this moment. It's as if history is seeping into me, the way it has seeped into the stones of the tower.

Boom!

We both jump. "Wh-what was that?" I stammer, clutching the guardrail.

Oliver starts laughing. "There seems to be some sort of event going on. . . ."

I look up at him, then smack my head. "D'oh! Fireworks."

"They were the reason we came up here, right?" Oliver kisses the tip of my nose. "Or were they just an excuse . . . ?"

I lay my arms on his chest, with my hands on his shoulders. "A little of both."

He lowers his head to kiss me when we're both startled by another explosion. "Kissing later," I say. I spin him around to face the right direction. "Fireworks now."

"I'm sure there's a bad joke to make but I can't—"

Boom!

We stand mesmerized by the colorful display. There's something about how gorgeous they are—but last only for moments—that gets to me. All this effort and risk just to give us a fleeting vision of something exquisite.

We're too far away to hear the music programmed to go with them, but there's something even more dramatic watching them streak across the sky accompanied by nothing but natural sounds. Just the water splashing against the rocks below and people so far away it's hard to discern what's music and what's chatter, though every now and then shrieks, laughter, and applause drift up to us.

I'm super aware of how close Oliver is, the sharp little intakes of breath when an explosion surprises him, the laughter when he realizes he startled. He keeps glancing at me as if he's enjoying my enjoyment of the fireworks as much as his own.

Best idea ever, I congratulate myself with a smile.

As the rousing finale booms and bursts and explodes, Oliver

moves behind me and encloses me by placing his hands beside mine on the guardrail. I feel his warmth against my back, welcome heat in the chilly tower. I feel protected, and think again about the original lighthouse keepers—the extraordinary risks they took every single day just doing their jobs. What did Mrs. Gilhooley feel like, living here to watch over sailors and ships, before there were real roads and everything was done by ship? How brave they must have been. And how lonely.

The applause on the beach is loud enough to hear in the tower. It's an incredible feeling knowing that we've shared this not just with each other but with all of Rocky Point. All of Cranston. All those boats. All of time, it feels like.

"Spectacular," Oliver says in a long exhale.

"I did good?" I ask, leaning against him.

"You did good."

I turn and smile up at him. It's hard to see his face in the dim light, but I can see he's gazing down at me with something that looks a lot like love. It startles me, how open he is, then I remember I've got my own neon-sign face. He must have seen that same look on me.

Then our lips meet, and his hand tangles in my hair. I stroke the back of his neck, and as the kiss grows deeper, I press against him and move my hands to his back to pull him closer. Our breathing grows more ragged, our kissing more determined, our touches more intense.

We break apart and I take in a deep breath and I hear Oliver do the same. Then he brings his face close to mine and whispers, "Now we have another special place, like the spot by the river."

"Mm," I murmur as his mouth moves along my neck. Then we're kissing again and Rocky Point vanishes.

"We, uh, we should go," I finally say reluctantly. "Mom will be waiting."

"I guess," Oliver says with a sigh.

We turn toward the archway and my foot hits something. It clatters down the stairs. "Oops," I say. "I think that was a flashlight."

"It really was just luck that we didn't drown today, wasn't it?" Oliver comments wryly. "We're quite the pair."

I giggle. "Too bad being clumsy is one of the things we have in common."

Oliver holds up his flashlight. "Should I do the honors? Since you were my eyes in the boat?"

I gesture to the stairway entrance. "After you, fearless leader."

"I'm only suggesting this because you weigh less than I do. If I trip and land on you, I think it'd be a bigger problem."

"How about neither of us trip, okay?"

"Works for me," Oliver says.

"Let's just hope the ghost of Anna Christine doesn't object to our being here. She just might push us down the rest of the way."

"You didn't tell me Candy Cane is haunted," Oliver says, sounding gleeful. "Somehow that makes it even more perfect. So who is she? I mean, who *was* she?"

I tell Oliver the sad tale of the young widow waiting for her husband to return. He'd been blown off the rocks as he made his way in a torrential storm to keep the lantern lit. I get kind of goose-bumpy telling the tale as we s-l-o-w-l-y make our way down the stairs, Oliver in front holding the flashlight, me clutching the back of his T-shirt. Two reasons: One, it's a little hard to see his tiny flashlight beam, and this clues me in to when he's on the next step. And two, if he does start to fall, I can hopefully snatch him back.

A loud clatter nearly topples us in surprise. "What was that?" I squeak.

Oliver laughs. "Anna Christine just tossed your flashlight the rest of the way down the stairs. Using my foot."

We continue down the circular staircase, the rough stone walls giving off a damp smell, the metal railing cold under my hand. I grip it so tight I'm pretty sure my hand is going to be permanently cramped.

"Made it!" Oliver cheers as we arrive at the ground floor.

I stop and soak in the atmosphere for a moment. "I'm starting to get it," I say.

"Get what?"

"The . . . I don't know . . . the connectedness people feel when they come here. Why they want to see the lighthouse." I snort a little laugh. "Ohmigod. Maybe I'm even understanding my mom more!"

"Oh, not possible!" Oliver teases.

"Shut up," I say with a laugh. "But speaking of Mom, I need to get to the Square. Do you want a ride? Or are you hitching with Lexi and her gang?"

"I'm not sure I can find her now," Oliver says. "Your mom won't mind? It's kind of out of the way."

"Are you kidding? How can she not give the boy who loves Candy Cane as much as she does a ride?"

"I think she'll like me even more if I convince her daughter to love Candy Cane too."

I slip my arm around his waist. "I'm getting there."

We walk in companionable silence, soaking in the tangy salt air and ocean breeze. We stay close to the shoreline, figuring we'll head inland after checking to see if any of my friends are still at the beach so we can say good-bye. We help each other up and over the uneven rocks, feeling the spray around our ankles as water splashes the boulders.

The parties are all breaking up. People call to one another, parents corral or carry kids, and the booths are being dismantled. We arrive at the dock and continue along the beach, but it looks as if everyone has already left. We link pinkies as we wander slowly among the departing crowds, sand and seashells crunching underfoot.

Suddenly I stop.

"Do you see them?" Oliver asks.

Moonlit night. Oliver. Holding hands. A tiny soft laugh sneaks out of me. We're actually acting out one of my images from the romantic montage that flipped through my brain the very first time Oliver came to Candy Cane.

Amazing.

Reality is so much better.

*O*ther people may be in Rocky Point on vacation, but I'm not one of them. I'm back at Candy Cane (mama, not junior) way too early.

Today when I shove open the reluctant door, I'm filled with the memory of last night. How romantic it was. How special. How *Oliver*. But I also discover I'm feeling a weird kind of let-down. Cynthia talks about this—how after a show closes she gets blue. All that work and excitement and build-up and then . . . it's over. And real life begins again.

And me being me, I'm also more than a little worried that despite last night, now that there's no project for us to work on together, Oliver and I won't be . . . well, won't *be*.

I try to shake off my anxiety as people straggle in. From the looks of them, they were up as late as I was last night. But they're cheerful enough and seem to get a kick out of the photos of the various keepers lining one of the walls. Once they move off, I get up and study the keepers too. They all have such interesting faces. "Why did you take this job?" I ask each one of them. None of them answers—which is probably a good thing. In my mom's notes I read about Keeper Abe McCarthy, who couldn't take the isolation and went kind of crazy. Don't want to follow in Abe's footsteps!

I cross back to my desk, trying to picture Oliver. What's he doing right now? I swivel my desk chair back and forth, imagining him . . . where? How *will* he spend his time now that he's not here measuring or at home building? I grin. He's probably measuring and building something new.

I step through the Keeper's Café screen door since I overslept and didn't have time to pack a lunch. I'm startled to see Mrs. Gallagher behind the counter. She shoots me a giant smile. "Hello, Mandy. Loved your boat last night!"

"Thanks," I say as I take a seat at the counter. "Is Celeste out sick?"

"No, no," Mrs. Gallagher assures me. She drops a menu in front of me. "It's one of her days off. I volunteered to be her relief."

"Oh," I say. A sudden flash of anxiety rushes through me. Could Oliver be with Celeste? I tell myself to calm down, and order a salad.

After lunch, with all the visitors in town for the Fourth, I'm busy enough that I am forced to give up my obsessing. When I close up Candy Cane, there he is, sitting on the bench, a spanking new bike leaning against the picnic table.

"What are you doing here?" I ask forcing myself to not skip across the grass.

He unfolds in that languorous, relaxed way of his and stands. "Habit. I got so used to meeting you after you were done that my feet just took me here." He gives me a quick peck. "Or maybe it was my lips that lead the way."

"Ha-ha." I nod toward the bike. "That looks new."

"It is. It's a lot faster than walking, and I figured it would be better than asking Mom for rides all the time."

I unlock the shed and retrieve my own trusty steed. Together we start walking them toward Weatherby.

"All day I felt weird," Oliver says. "Like there was something I was supposed to be doing. Then I remembered—we already did it!"

"I know exactly what you mean."

"Do you have to go straight home? I thought we could go hang by the river again." He gives me a sidelong glance and waggles his eyebrows. "Pops made snacks. . . ."

"Well, in that case, how can I say no?"

I give Mom a quick call at the library, and then we ride to Oliver's house. We stash the bikes, he makes a quick trip to the kitchen, then I follow him to "our" spot by the river. Not so long ago I felt so nervous around him, and today I feel at ease in a way that's new to me.

"So what did you do all day?" I ask as we settle onto the flat rock.

"Not much. Got the bike. Ran into Celeste."

I stiffen. So they *were* together. I wasn't just being paranoid. "Oh yeah?" I say, forcing myself to be super casual. "Where?"

"Over at the bookstore. She was looking for used textbooks. Did you know she's getting an engineering degree?"

"Nope." Great. Ethereally beautiful and mathematically inclined. I could just picture them bonding over graph paper.

"Were you busy today?" He hands me an aluminum-foil packet.

"Pretty busy." I keep my eyes on the packet as if it requires great skill to unwrap it. Then my eyes widen, and my head snaps around to look at him. "Is this what I think it is?"

Oliver smiles proudly. "A homemade bloob pocket. I don't know if it will be as good as the ones you get in the booths, but I figured since you didn't get a chance to have one yesterday . . ."

I grin at him, all jealousy evaporating as I take a huge bite. He remembered not only my bloob pocket obsession *and* my nickname for them, but also went out of his way to bring me one.

"Ohmigod," I say, though my mouth is so full it comes out more like "mowfigumph." I swallow and ask, "How is this even possible?"

He shrugs. "Pops is a genius."

I give him a blueberry-pastry-flaked kiss. "*You're* the genius for getting him to make them."

"Okay, I'll take the credit."

After some more blueberry-tinged kissing, we lie on our backs, fingertips touching, listening to the sounds around us. I just hope my allergies don't kick in to ruin the peaceful setting. My sneezes have been known to make cats run for cover.

Oliver lets out a long, contented sigh. "This place is really great."

"How come you never visited before?" This is something I've been wondering.

"Mom and Pops didn't get along. He divorced her mom when she was still pretty young. From what she says, it sounds like that breakup was ugly, and she was really angry at him for a long time. That's probably why she and Dad worked so hard to avoid the usual divorce drama."

I roll over onto my stomach and pluck a strand of grass from the ground. I split it in two, then pull up another one. "So why now? It doesn't seem like she's really taking time off."

Oliver flips over onto his stomach too, his shoulder grazing mine. I lean my head against his shoulder, smelling laundry soap, sunblock, and what I now call *eau de California*. "A bunch of things, I guess. My dad's mom got sick last year, and I think that reminded her that Pops is getting up there in years."

"He looks pretty healthy to me," I say. "A little creaky maybe."

"Yeah, he's fine. But, you know . . . I think the whole mortality thing hit her."

"Is your grandma okay?" I ask.

"Not great, but hanging in." He rolls away from me and rummages in his sack. Pulling out a bottle of water, he takes a swig then offers it to me. As I take it he adds, "She also . . . I think Mom understands him better now."

"Because she's grown-up now?" I wonder if once I'm an adult I'll understand Mom better too.

"No because . . . well, Pops split just as he was getting super successful. Which her mother resented like crazy."

I hand him back the water bottle. "Understandable. She was with him when he was nobody, and once he got famous . . ."

"Exactly. But the same thing kind of happened with us. Mom hit it big and things just soured."

I sit up. "So you're saying being successful ruins marriages? That would just suck."

He sits up too. "No, it's not that. It's . . . it's more that it was a huge change. Change makes things . . . complicated. A couple will either work it out or they won't. If there were already serious cracks in that foundation . . ." He shrugs.

"I get it."

"With Mom it wasn't like 'Oh, now I'm rich, and I'm going to trade you in for a shiny new model.' It was more that her priorities changed. Pressures changed. Daily life changed. I think she stopped being so angry when she started to look at things from Pops's point of view."

"Makes sense, I guess. . . ."

"Also Pops wanted to see more of the world, paint different kinds of pictures. Nana was a total homebody. Shy. Never wanted to leave her hometown. Liked it that way. They never compared goals. Until it was too late. I think a bit of that happened with my folks too."

I swivel around to face him. "You and your mom talk a lot, don't you?"

He shrugs. "I guess. Don't you? With your mom, I mean."

I tug at the grass. "Mostly she just tells me what I'm doing wrong."

"Oh, that can't be true."

"Believe it."

Oliver stands and holds out a hand to help me up. He pulls me into a hug. "It's easy to talk to you. I've never talked so much to a girl in my whole life."

"Must be this place," I say, looking up at the canopy created by the trees and the happy blue sky, and listening to the sound of the water and the drone of unseen insects. Like a tiny little bubble of peace. "Because I've never talked so much to a boy in my whole life either."

He tightens his hold. "*Our* place," he whispers as he moves aside my hair and brushes my neck with his lips. I shut my eyes and allow the tingles to spread through me.

After a few more kisses, he says, "Want to go see *Far Far Away*? It's supposed to be really good. It's playing—" He stops when he sees my frown. "Sorry, do you have plans? Am I taking up too much of your time? I always do this—just assume—"

"No! No, that's not it." I don't want to tell him I already saw that movie and kind of hated it. "You're definitely not taking up too much of my time."

That's when it hits me. Time. Our time together has an expiration date. I grab him in a fierce hug. "I—I want to spend as much time as possible with you," I say, my voice suddenly cracking.

"Wh-what's wrong?" he asks. I can't answer; I can only shake my head. His body tenses. "Oh. Right."

He peels me off him and takes a step back. "You're thinking about . . ." He rakes his hand through his hair. "I've been trying *not* to think about that myself."

I can't look at him. "But don't we have to think about it?" My voice squeaks like a mouse's.

"Why?"

He catches me off guard with that one, and my head snaps up. "What?"

His face mirrors the misery and confusion I'm feeling. "Do we have to focus on the end? Can't we just . . . I don't know . . ." His shoulders rise, then drop again as he searches for words.

I blink back the threatening tears as I try to come up with an answer. "Stay with the micro?" I say softly. "Avoid the macro?"

A smile begins in his eyes and spreads to his lips. "Something like that, yeah."

I have told myself time and again not to overthink. *Today*, the *micro*, is fantastic. I'd only ruin it if my brain kept going for the macro, the big picture, the future. Stick with what's in front of me. No matter how much it might hurt later. Do I really want to give up what's so fantastic now?

"It's a deal," I say, and seal it with a kiss. I lean away from him, our arms around each other's waists, our hips pressed together. "I'd love to see *Far Far Away* with you." Why spoil things by telling him the movie he's looking forward to seeing is a tedious bore? I'll just sit in the dark next to him and be happy to have both him and air-conditioning.

We fall into a kind of routine, if something that makes me feel different than I've ever felt before can be called "routine." Each day he meets me at Candy Cane. Sometimes we go to the movies; sometimes we grab a bite to eat; sometimes we go to "our" place by the river. I confess, I make him pick the movies and the places to eat. Since he loved *Far Far Away* (gag) I know we have different taste. I don't want him to not like what I pick. I've sat through some clunkers, but it's a sacrifice I'm willing to make.

On my days off he shows up at my house and says, "So which Rocky Point should it be today?" remembering that first day at the river when I told him about there being multiple Rocky Points, all in biking distance. "You choose; you're the guest" is always my answer. After a week or so he stops asking. We just go.

Today he arrives at my door on his bike with a huge grin on his face and wearing an enormous battered backpack. A castoff of Freaky's, I assume.

"What are we up to today?" I ask.

"Hubbard Island! A full day of hiking, biking, bird-watching—the whole nature experience. I read about it in my guidebook, and I figured what better way to see it than with a native, right?"

My insides fall to my feet. A whole day trapped on an island doing the outdoorsy. So not a good look for me. "Uh, I'm not a native of Hubbard Island. . . ."

"You know what I mean," he says with a laugh. "Grab whatever you think you'll need and let's go. I checked the ferry schedule, and the next one leaves in about twenty minutes."

Tell him, my brain screams. *Tell him this is not something you want to do.* But somehow what comes out of my mouth when I look at his face all lit up with excitement and expectation is just "Sure."

Oliver waits on the porch while I go and try to figure out what I should bring as a survival kit. I check the bathroom medicine cabinet and find some allergy pills. Should I take one now in a preemptive strike? But this is the kind that makes me drowsy. I tuck them into a pocket in my backpack just in case. A pack of tissues—an absolute necessity. Bug spray. Sunblock. I sigh. This is why I'm not a big fan of the great outdoors. I have to pack an arsenal to fight off whatever Mother Nature has in store for me.

I leave a note for Mom telling her where I am. She's going to be pretty surprised; like the lighthouse, Hubbard Island is another of those Rocky Point attractions I've never been particularly attracted to.

Of course, Oliver changed my mind about Candy Cane, so

maybe he can change my mind about Hubbard Island, too.

I push through the screen door and Oliver jumps up. "Ready?"

"Ready."

I hope.

*T*here are two ferries from Rocky Point, one that goes to Cranston, the peninsula just next door, and the other to Hubbard Island. The one to the island is a lot more touristy, and we're not the only ones walking our bikes onto the deck. I can tell today is going to be one of Maine's rare scorchers.

I have to admit the ferry ride over is nice, with the breeze from the water cooling us, and the boats bobbing on the bright blue water with the evergreens of Hubbard Island in the background. It's not exactly romantic to be packed in with dozens of other cyclists with our bikes between us, though. *Keep an open mind*, I tell myself.

We disembark with everyone else and push the bikes up to the rustic cabin serving as a visitors' center. "I'll be right back," I tell Oliver, standing my bike near an information kiosk filled with brochures, maps, and scenic postcards. There's even the one of Candy Cane that I'm selling at the lighthouse. Before Oliver can ask me where I'm going, I scurry around the building to find the restroom. I don't know when the next chance to do this will be.

When I come back around, Oliver is sitting beside our bikes, studying a map.

"So where should we go?" Oliver asks.

"You're the one with the map; you tell me," I say.

"Yeah, but you're the one from here."

"The last time I was on Hubbard was probably in the fifth grade," I say.

"Oh. Like people who live in New York never go to the Statue of Liberty. You don't do the tourist things."

"I guess. . . ."

"Okay, so . . ." He squints at the map, then shrugs. "Let's just follow a trail."

Thank goodness I've been biking to Candy Cane every day. I'm in much better shape than I was at the start of the summer. Even so, I'm sweating pretty quickly since the path Oliver picked is mostly uphill. I know somewhere on the island there are supposed to be spectacular views, a waterfall, and good spots to swim where the water is warmer than in the bay, but I have no idea where they are. Besides, views are views. I can see them most anytime.

Oliver can't, I remind myself. It's why he's so big on all this.

The path is too narrow for us to ride side by side. This is not good. It means nothing distracts me from the driplets of sweat snaking down between my boobs, the stickiness of my hair on my neck, and how uncomfortable this dumb bike seat is. I totally wore the wrong clothes. I'm overdressed but underprotected. If he had let me know beforehand, and I didn't have to race for the ferry, I'd have been better prepared.

I try to take my mind off my discomfort by watching Oliver ahead of me. Only instead of getting my focus off the stupid gnats flying in my face, seeing his ease on his bike annoys me. I really really really want to take a break, but I don't want him to think I'm a total wimp. Besides, he's so far ahead of me that he'd never hear me if I asked him to stop. He's not even checking to be sure I'm keeping up with him.

Is that good boyfriend etiquette? I don't *think* so!

Oliver finally slows to a stop when we reach a fork in the path. And for the first time since we started riding he turns around. His big grin irritates me. Is he not even sweating? Do boys from California not sweat? In Maine we're not very used to the heat, since we only have it a few weeks a year. I'd like to see him try to get through a Rocky Point winter. I'd definitely win that contest.

"Which way should we go?" he asks cheerfully.

I'm about to say "Whichever," because seriously, I don't care, but instead what comes out is a giant sneeze. Then another. And another.

Uh-oh.

I sling around my backpack and fumble for my tissues. Just in time. "AAAAA-choo!"

Birds take flight, squirrels scurry, and Oliver still has that giant smile on his stupid face. "You okay?" he asks.

"Fine." Only now that my allergies have kicked in, they're *all* attacking at once. My eyes itch and water. I swipe at a tear trailing down my cheek. Before I turn into a dripping mess, I tell Oliver, "Just pick a direction. Let's go."

Oliver looks a little startled by my tone but starts riding again. I feel around in my backpack for the allergy pills. It may be too late, since they take a while to work, but I'm desperate. I realize that Oliver has the water bottles, so I pick up my speed.

Bad move. My streaming eyes make my vision fuzzy, and I miss seeing the root Oliver has just swerved around. I hit it hard and go flying.

I let out a shriek. The world blurs as I tumble up, down, and sideways. I land hard, scraping various parts, slamming others. I can hear the bike's chain whirring, and feel something poking my ankles. I lay stunned, staring up at the patch of blue between the thick pine trees.

Have I mentioned that I'm really not the outdoorsy type. *And* a klutz?

At least this got Oliver's attention. As I sit up checking for broken bones, he turns and rides back. "Are you all right?" he calls.

No. I'm embarrassed and bruised, and I have gravel burn on my hands. Along with pine needles and leaves in my hair. "Yes. I'm fine."

Why do my brain and my mouth come up with different answers to questions?

He drops his bike and rushes over. "You sure?"

He reaches for my bike, but I yank out my foot and kick the bike away from me. "Yes, I'm sure," I snap.

His head pulls back like a turtle's. "Ooo-kay."

I sigh. "I'm fine. Just . . . feeling stupid." I start to stand, and he instantly tries to help me. But I'm so sweaty and gross the last thing I want is for him to touch me. I step out of reach and again his head does the turtle thing. To cover, I bend over and brush the dirt off my knees and twist around to do the same to my backside.

"Can you check my bike?" I ask. "Make sure it's okay?" He's the micro guy, right? That should be a good task for him and give me time to pull myself together.

He picks up my bike and straddles it, checking the alignment, the handlebars, and the seat position. When he steps off and kneels down to examine the chain, I go through his back-pack. Water. Excellent. I take the allergy pill and wash it down, then use the water to clean off my scrapes. Nothing too serious, just some stinging.

By the time I'm done, he's given my bike the thumbs-up. "Ready to get back up on the horse?"

"Huh?"

"The old saying? If you fall off a horse, you're supposed to get right . . . Forget it."

"Right." I yank the handlebars away from him. "Lead on. To wherever it is we're going."

He gives me another one of those quizzical looks, so I fake-smile at him, wondering about the condition of my face. Red and puffy eyes? Equally red and puffy nose? My allergies are making me itch from the inside out, and it's not a fun feeling. Come on, modern medicine. Work fast, please!

I follow Oliver, and now what had been minor discomfort has transformed into actual aches and pains from the fall. I just hope we come to a place to picnic soon. Is he planning to bike the entire island?

The path widens, and he slows down so I can pedal up beside him. We pass a clearing, surrounded by tall pine trees. "How about we stop here?" I suggest.

"No view," he says. "We can do better."

We bike a ways more and come out of the woods to actual picnic grounds. Although a family has claimed one table, and a foursome sit at another, there are still a few empties. "Here?" I slow down.

"Not special enough," he says, and continues pedaling.

I push hard to catch up. My muscles are burning—that ride to Candy Cane hasn't gotten me in as good a shape as I thought. Realizing I'm going to have to do this ride all over again to go back just adds to the cranky. "Who are you? Goldilocks?" I ask.

"Huh?

"When are you going to find the one that's *just right*?"

"I just wanted . . . Fine. Let's stop here." He abruptly stops by a large tree and leans his bike against it.

"Great," I say.

Only not so great. He's right. There's nothing special or scenic about it. We could be in the woods near his house.

"Where's the other water bottle?" he asks, rummaging through his backpack.

"I took it when I fell," I say as I pull it out and take another gulp.

"Don't swig it. That's all the water I packed."

"Are you kidding?"

"Aren't there, like, concession stands?"

I gape at him as he spreads a picnic blanket. "At the dock, yeah. But this is a nature preserve. You know, where they preserve nature? Didn't the guidebook explain that there aren't any food booths here?" I shake my head. "Not exactly a completist now," I mutter.

"You don't have to be so snotty about it."

"Snotty?" I start laughing. "Yep, that's me. Snotty. And drippy. And sweaty. And scraped up and bruised."

"Have a sandwich," he grumbles.

I take it from him, but only because Freaky made it and anything Freaky makes is delicious. As soon as I'm holding it, the smell tells me it's fish. "I'm not hungry." I drop the sandwich onto the blanket.

"Fine. More for me."

Bad move. Claiming I'm not hungry means I can't exactly ask if there's anything else to eat. I pull my knees up to my chest and hug them. We sit silently as Oliver scarfs down his sandwich. I hope he doesn't hear my stomach rumbling.

"So what should we do?" he asks, wadding up his napkin and sandwich baggie. He stashes them into a plastic bag. He clearly thought ahead about garbage, why not water?

I shrug and rub at the bicycle grease around my ankle.

I hear him sigh, then say, "How about swimming? I read that there are—"

I cut him off. "I didn't bring a suit."

"Why not?" He sounds annoyed.

I'm annoyed right back. "You didn't exactly give me much time to get ready."

"So what did you pack?"

I get up and go to my bike. I pull my backpack off the handlebars and stomp to the picnic blanket. I flip it upside down, dumping out my stash: Sunblock. Which I just now realized I forgot to apply. Isn't that awesome? Bug spray. Which we will definitely need as it gets closer to dusk. I'm betting that's when he'll want to take the return ferry. Tissues. Eyedrops.

Oliver studies my supplies. "You have allergies."

"Yup."

"This is all you brought with you? For a picnic on Hubbard Island?"

I kneel down and repack my backpack. "I'm not an idiot, you know. I brought what I needed. And you know what? This picnic is over."

I stand and sling a strap over one shoulder. I stomp back to my bike, slip on the other strap, and walk the bike around to face the right direction. The one leading back the way we came. "I'm taking the ferry back. Now," I announce, hopping on. "And don't you follow me."

"Wow. Overreact much?" Oliver calls behind me.

My body stiffens and I clutch the handlebars. *Don't respond*, I tell myself. *Just walk away*. Well, *bike* away.

Which I do. Muttering the whole time.

The ferry ride back to Rocky Point is dismal. I waited until the very last minute to board, hoping that Oliver would show up and apologize. Then I fumed over the fact that he didn't follow me, even though I told him not to. I waited just a moment longer, debating if I should wait until he *did* arrive, whenever that might be. Finally I just scurried aboard, practically as they were pulling away. I was lucky I didn't wind up in the water. That would have been the perfect ending to a completely rotten day.

By the time we approach the dock, it's sprinkling. I bounce back and forth between worrying about Oliver and thinking it serves him right. You have to prepare for a trip to Hubbard. He pores over those guidebooks—didn't that part stick? Had he checked the weather, brought rain slickers, or enough water, for goodness' sake?

I bike home in the light rain. With each street I get more and more depressed. Sleepy too. The allergy pill has finally kicked in. Another reason I'm glad I'm not on that stupid island. But a creeping feeling starts to take over that *I* should be the one to apologize. All Oliver wanted was to spend the day with me. To have fun. To see the sights.

I push harder on the pedals. Of course, he could have asked me first!

I slow as I make the turn onto my street. Even if he had asked, I would have said yes anyway. That's what I've been doing all summer. Seeing the movies he wants to see. Having him decide on our outings. No wonder he didn't ask me.

"I'm such a jerk!" I mutter as I carry my bike up the porch steps. I let the screen door bang shut behind me. I hope Mom's not home; she hates when I do that.

I've never been in a fight with a boy before. Other than Justin, but brothers don't count. A boy who means so much to me. I go into the bathroom and peel off my wet and dirty clothes. I sit on the edge of the tub, dabbing at my scratches and scrapes with toilet paper. Then my head drops and I cover it with my hands. Misery washes over me, and the tears finally come for real.

I avoid looking in the mirror in the entryway when I arrive for Candy Cane duty. I know what I'll see. Red eyes from crying, a stuffy nose from allergies, and the face of a girl who for no good reason left her boyfriend on an island, and probably lost him forever.

That's a girl I seriously don't want to see.

I didn't try texting Oliver last night. If he didn't respond, I didn't want to wonder if it was because the text didn't go through or because he hated me. Besides, I didn't know what to say.

I didn't even try Cynthia. There would just be too much to explain, and with her all caught up with camp—I've only been getting super-short texts—she barely has time to talk.

"What is wrong with me?" I moan to the empty room. Thankfully, it doesn't answer back.

It's busy enough that it's only when my stomach rumbles so loudly it turns the head of a little boy sitting on the bottom step of the lighthouse tower (I know, I know; I'm supposed to tell him not to sit there) that I realize it's past lunchtime. I consider skipping it since it means I have to face the celestial Celeste. I'm sure she's never been mean to someone who was just trying to be nice to her. But my stomach refuses to be ignored, so I force myself to deal with her perfection.

"Hey, Mandy," she greets me. "Lemonade?"

I nod and take a seat at the counter.

"You going to wait for Oliver to order?"

My head jerks up at this. "Is he coming?"

She looks confused. "How would I know? Aren't you meeting him? It seems like he's always here on the days you work. Though not always for lunch, I guess. . . ."

I fiddle with the salt and pepper shakers. "Just me." I can feel her eyes on me. I wish she'd stop looking. "Salad please. Chicken."

"You got it."

She disappears, and I notice some of the tourists from this

morning sitting at booths. A big group with a baby in a high chair is probably having lunch before checking out Candy Cane. Still, it's pretty sparsely populated. From what I've seen, the boys mooning over Celeste tend to show up just before she's getting ready to close. I wonder what they order.

Celeste returns with my salad, then leans against the back counter, arms crossed. "So you want to tell me what happened between you two?"

I plunge my fork into a tomato. For some reason I can't lift it to my mouth. "I was a total jerk and now he hates me," I blurt.

"He said that?"

"Well, no. But I know he does."

"Do you?"

I let out a shaky sigh. "*I'd* hate me. I treated him really badly, when all he wanted was to explore Hubbard Island."

"So what was the problem?"

"Where do I begin?" Then it all comes out: my allergies and general lack of interest in the so-called great outdoors, his not asking me about going, my not bringing the right things, his better biking skills. Celeste listens patiently. I'm too embarrassed to look up, so I'm well acquainted with every leaf of lettuce and slice of cucumber in my salad by the time I'm done.

"Yeah, you were a jerk all right," Celeste says. "But not because you were so snippy."

"Great." Just what I need. To feel worse.

"The real problem is that you haven't been yourself. You've been whoever you imagine he wants you to be." Her eyes flick over my shoulder. She taps the counter in front of me. "Hang on."

She picks up the coffeepot and goes to refill a customer's cup. I stare at the sickeningly sweet pastries in the case on the counter. That doesn't make any sense.

"I *have* been myself," I tell Celeste as she comes back around the counter. "And myself is annoying and whiny."

"Why didn't you just tell him you didn't want to go to Hubbard? You could have found something else to do. Something you'd *both* think was fun."

I open my mouth to say something, but since I don't know what to say I close it again.

She replaces the coffeepot, then starts rolling silverware into paper napkins. "I bet this isn't the first time either. I bet you've been seeing the movies he wants to see. Going to the parties he wants to go to."

"We haven't gone to any parties," I mumble.

Celeste grins, making her look like a wry fairy. "My bad. That woulda been me."

"You?"

"I know the syndrome all too well. I thought I had to pretend to like the stuff my boyfriend liked—my *ex*-boyfriend that is."

This is fascinating. Not only is Celeste telling me personal things, as if we're, I don't know, equals, but she's admitting she screwed up with a boy. "Why?"

"So he'd like me, of course! Why are *you* doing it?"

"But you—you're—you're perfect!"

This cracks her up. "You're kidding, right?"

I stare at her blankly. She shakes her head and continues. "*Any*way, if it's the right guy for you it's because he likes the real you. Not the you who pretends to be into professional wrestling and Xbox."

"He feels like the right guy. . . ."

"Jeffrey—that's my boyfriend now—he's not into engineering. He's an English major, and he loves those scary movies that I avoid like the plague."

"But you get along anyway?"

She smiles a soft, almost private smile, obviously thinking about him. "Yeah . . . ," she says a little dreamily. "Yeah, we do." She comes back to earth and points at me with a fork. "You don't have to be someone's clone to be close to him. Same thing with friends, too. Sometimes it's your differences that help keep you together."

"Complementary, not opposites," I say, remembering Oliver's words.

She comes around the counter and sits on the stool next to me, leaning on an elbow. "Here's a really tough question. Have you *ever* been yourself around him? Be super honest."

Panic tightens my chest. Has the whole thing been a sham, and the girl Oliver likes—or *liked*, past tense—never even existed?

But as I think more, I know the answer. "Yes. Plenty." Building Candy Cane Jr. At "our" place by the river. Up in the lighthouse tower watching the fireworks. I've been *me* when it has really counted.

"Good. Because from what I've seen, Oliver's really into you. Glad to know it's actually Mandy he likes. Not some imaginary girl, not some Cynthia clone."

This startles me. "What do you mean?"

She shrugs as she slides off the stool. "Hey, I went to Rocky Point High too. This is a small town. Sometimes it seems as if . . . well, look, never mind. Maybe I'm wrong."

"You are," I insist. "Cynthia's my best friend since we were little kids. If we're alike . . ."

"That's the thing. I don't actually think you are. But I could be totally off."

"You are."

I don't want to end in a fight. She's being so nice. Not to mention that hearing she has a boyfriend is super reassuring— and that I never had any reason to be worried that she might be into Oliver. And she says Oliver likes me. These are all things that make me want to hug her, not get into an argument.

I take a long last sip of lemonade. Sweet and tart. Kind of like relationships, I guess.

"Do you think he'll talk to me?" I ask.

"Only one way to find out."

"That's what I was afraid you'd say."

*T*his would be so much easier in an e-mail. But I can't count on Oliver finding Wi-Fi somewhere any time soon. So here I am, pacing in the raggedy front yard, my bike leaning against a crooked tree, trying to work up the courage to knock.

What's the worst that can happen? I ask myself. Bad question. The list is enormous, and all of it makes me want to grab my bike and get out of here quick. *Try again*, I tell myself. What's the *best* that can happen?

"You can do this," I mutter for about the millionth time. The problem is each time I tell myself this, another self counters, "No you can't." Once again I wish that Cynthia were here, not just to give me advice but also so we could come up with a script together that I could follow. We would have even practiced.

I take in a deep breath to fortify myself, stride to the front door, and knock before I can talk myself out of it. Maybe he won't be home. I can't tell if this possibility is a relief or a problem.

I decide I'll try one more time, and if no one answers, I'll chalk it up to "not meant to be." It will suck, and tears spring to my eyes just imagining never being with him again, but what else can I do?

I knock more forcefully this time. I start hyperventilating as footsteps approach, then my breath catches in my throat when Freaky Framingham flings open the door. He looks as startled to see me as I am to see him. "Oliver didn't say you were coming over. He's not here. He and his ma went to the farmers' market."

"Oh. Okay."

"Nah, it's rude of the boy to not be here. . . ."

"He didn't know I was coming." I fiddle with the end of my braid, not sure what to do now.

"Oh. Well, they shouldn't be too long. Got muffins in the oven," he says, turning and heading toward the kitchen.

I could back out now, but that would be bad, right? Even though I'm not exactly sure if that was an invitation, I follow him inside.

I cross the living room, wondering if this is going to be the last time I'm ever here. My throat feels thick, and no matter how much I swallow, the lump won't go away.

I hover in the archway that leads to the kitchen, watching Freaky remove two muffin tins and place them on top of the oven. The smell is tantalizing.

"You just cool a bit," he tells the muffins. He gives me a quick glance over his shoulder. "They're for tomorrow's breakfast."

I nod. The warning is clear. Hands off.

He studies the muffins a bit longer, then sets up some racks on the counter. He taps the tops of a few. "Gotta be patient," he says, I think to me, and not the muffins this time. "Don't want to leave half of them behind in the tins."

He crosses to the fridge. "Kids drink soda, right?" He pulls out a can and holds it out to me.

I take it from him, hoping it will clear the lump in my throat. Freaky dumps the muffins out of the tins and onto the racks, then carefully turns them right-side up. He has a surprisingly delicate touch. He gives me another one of those sideways glances.

"Should probably test them," he says with a twinkle a lot like Oliver's—at least when he's not mad at me. "Wouldn't want to serve subpar muffins to the family."

I manage my first smile since Hubbard Island. Freaky chooses two muffins (he dubs them Lumpy and Lopsided) and puts them on plates for us. I've had dinner here a gazillion times, but I still feel a little nervous being here by myself. Not because I think Freaky is a freak anymore; I just don't really know what to say to him. Or if he knows what a superjerk I was to Oliver.

If Oliver did tell him, Freaky doesn't seem to be holding it against me. His twinkly blue eyes watch me as I take a big bite.

My eyes widen as the flavors collide in my mouth.

"New recipe," Framingham says. "Threw in some shredded coconut and added a little almond flour."

I swallow and lick crumbs from my lips. "Amazing."

"Oliver and his ma seem to go for my baking," he says. "So I want to keep up a steady stream."

"Who wouldn't go for your baking?" I say. "Or anything else you make," I add before taking another bite.

Framingham holds up his lumpy muffin and studies it. He breaks it into two, then pops one half into his mouth. "Hurt feelings come out in all kinds of ways," he mutters as he chews.

My stomach lurches. "Wh-what did Oliver say?" I ask. And what could it have to do with muffins?

Framingham looks at me, startled. "Oh, sorry. So used to talking to myself, I forgot I had a listener. Even with the kids staying here."

If I'm going to get Oliver to forgive me, I should try to find out what he might have told his grandfather. "So Oliver . . . ?" I prompt.

He frowns, as if he's trying to remember his train of thought. He waves a hand when he figures it out. "It's not Ollie. His ma, well, even though she certainly appreciates what's put on the table, she resents it too."

"Why?" I hope that's not impolite, but I figure since he opened up the door by telling me something this personal he won't mind. Between Alice asking me to call her by her first name, and Framingham telling me his problems with her, I feel awfully grown up.

"I didn't do any of this"—he gestures around the kitchen—"when she was small. So something about my doing it now irks her." He pops the second half of the muffin into his mouth. "She eats it all, mind you, second helpings too, but it bothers her."

I have no idea what to say. But this is definitely a conversation I never expected to have with freaking Freaky Framingham. "So if someone's mad at you, what's the best way to make them stop?"

His face twists up, and he slaps the table with a loud "Ha!" I startle and bounce a little in my chair. "I've been trying to figure out the answer to that one for most of your young life. Longer."

I trace an invisible line on the table in front of me, keeping my eyes glued to my finger. "I—I was really mean to Oliver."

Framingham gets up and pours himself coffee from a stainless thermos. The mug he's using is chipped; I wonder if he makes pity purchases too. He leans against the counter and squints into the mug, like a fortune-teller reading tea leaves. "Sorry's a hard thing to say. Sometimes, though, you can tell how important a thing is by how hard it is to do." He crosses to the table and sits down again. "But it's not just saying the sorry. Any fool can say words. It's how you back up those words that counts."

"Yeah . . . ," I murmur. "So you keep trying new recipes? To find the one that will make everything okay?"

He reaches over and pats my hand. I'm so surprised I don't even react. "I knew there was something about you I liked," he says. "That's it exactly."

I grin. "That would be such a cool story. A baker searching for the one perfect recipe to solve all the problems of the world."

He looks impressed. "I like that." He gets back up and starts to move the muffins from the cooling rack to a platter. "Sometimes it doesn't even matter if you get the recipe right. Sometimes what matters is that you just keep trying."

It's so weird that I'm having this conversation with Freaky Framingham. "How come the people you're supposed to be able to talk to are the ones who are the hardest?" I ask, thinking of my mom.

"Depends," he says, his back still to me. "Afraid to disappoint them, maybe? Fear that what we're going to say will make them think differently of us. Or prove something we were afraid they already thought."

Since Mom already thinks Justin is perfect and I'm the problem child, Framingham's theory makes a lot of sense. If she knew I'd behaved like such a brat, the worst thing would be if she chalked it up as typical Mandy. Sometimes I wonder if Dad hadn't died when I was eight and Justin was eleven if he and Justin would have fought like me and Mom, and Dad would have beamed at *me* the way Mom does at Justin. We've been getting along better lately, and I guess our current truce still feels fragile.

"Oliver and his mom talk a lot," I comment.

Framingham comes back to the table for his coffee mug. "Yeah, they're good that way."

I hear the sound of tires on gravel, and my heart speeds up.

"Sounds like they're home," he says. He gets up and heads out to the living room. I hear the door open, then he says, "Ollie, Mandy's here."

I grip the edge of the table to keep from fleeing out the back door. The pounding in my ears blocks out any response Oliver has, so I have no way of knowing how he reacts to this info.

Then he's in the doorway. And then I'm standing up. And then we're staring at each other.

"Hey," I say softly. Probably too softly for him to hear. I clear my throat. "Uh, so hi."

He doesn't say anything. Not a good sign.

I force myself to jump right in. "Okay, so I'm sorry. Super sorry. Colossally sorry."

Freaky was wrong. The hard thing isn't saying sorry—the hard thing is the gap between when you say it and when the other person answers.

Oliver crosses to the fridge and pulls out a soda. Even his back looks angry.

"Um . . . I'm trying to apologize here," I say, shifting my weight and then shifting it back.

I hear him pop the can, then he takes a swig. "Yeah, I got that." He turns around. "I'm trying to figure out what you're sorry for."

"For—for all of it. I mean, you're obviously mad at me, so clearly I have reasons to apologize, right?" I'm so confused. Doesn't he think I owe him an apology?

"Yeah," Oliver says. "But what I'm trying to figure out is what happened. You were acting like I was the one who did something wrong, but I can't for the life of me figure out what."

"That's part of what I'm saying sorry for." I sit back down and rest my forehead on my hands. "I messed up, didn't I?"

"I don't know! Did you?"

I raise my eyes to meet his. Now he doesn't look angry; he looks genuinely confused. And upset.

"You did everything right," I explain. "Well, except for maybe where you didn't ask me if I wanted to go, you just . . . well, that part doesn't matter," I add quickly when a flicker of temper crosses his face. I plow on. "I should have told you. I'm not really big on the communing-with-nature kind of scenario. Allergies. Falling down. Well, you saw. It wasn't a pretty picture."

"Why didn't you just tell me?"

I throw up my hands. "You didn't give me a chance. You were all excited, with a big picnic and guidebooks."

"Big whoop."

He still sounds mad. He comes closer to the table. "Why do you think I'd want to do something that wouldn't be fun for you?"

He's got me there. I pick up tiny muffin crumbs with my fingertip.

He slides onto the chair across from me, where Framingham had just been sitting. "Have you been doing that all along? Only pretending to like stuff? Humoring me?"

I can't respond, knowing he's not going to like my answer.

"So this whole thing? It's all been fake?" He stands up with such force the chair wobbles. He grabs it and rights it with a thud.

"No!" I'm on my feet too. "None of this is fake. None of the real parts."

He glares at me like I just said something really dumb, which come to think of it, I just did. "I mean, the important parts, the parts that make things real." Ugh! Why is this so hard?

"So what *were* you pretending? The things that you don't consider"—here he uses air quotes—"important?"

"Movies," I blurt. "I hated *Far Far Away* when I saw it the first time and even more when we saw it together."

His eyebrows rise. "Really? I thought it was—" He stops himself and shakes his head. "But why would you do that? And why do you keep making me pick what we do? That's why I didn't ask you about Hubbard. I thought you liked being surprised. I figured that's why you always have me choose."

Huh. That would have been a better reason than the actual one. "I—I was afraid you wouldn't like what I picked," I admit. I finally look directly at him despite the tears welling in my eyes. "And then you wouldn't like *me*."

We hold like that for a moment, and I'm stunned as I watch all the angry drain out of him. Stunned and relieved. He does that sideways thing with his mouth. "Sardonic," I think, is the SAT word for it.

"Are we done fighting now? Apology accepted?" I ask.

"On one condition," he says, making his way around the table.

"Ooo-kay," I say cautiously.

"From now on, you have to be more honest with me. If you don't like something, tell me. If you want to do something different, tell me. It's been a lot of pressure to keep coming up with things for us to do."

I cross my heart with my index finger. "Absolutely. Scout's honor." Exactly like Framingham said, I have to back up the words with actions.

"I have an idea of something to do," I add. Then I hurl myself into his arms.

When Oliver comes to pick me up the next day at Candy Cane, I actually have an activity in mind. "Can we go through the exhibits?" I ask.

He gives me a skeptical look. "That's more my thing, right? Our deal was—"

I cut him off. "I really want to. That night in here, it got me thinking about what it must have been like to have been the keeper in the old days. I want to learn more about it."

Oliver grins. "Cool. Where should we start?"

I glance around the lobby. "How about right here?"

"I have an idea," Oliver says as I shut the door and lock it. I don't want anyone thinking the lighthouse is still open. "How about you make up a story about whatever we're looking at, then I'll tell you the actual history. I'll bet my true stories are just as interesting as your made-up ones."

I smirk. "Too bad there's no one here to act as judge," I tell him, "because I will so win this bet."

He points to a series of framed pictures hanging above the case. There's a diagram of Candy Cane, identifying the different parts. Beside it is a poster with the headings "Daymarks," "Flash Patterns," and "Foghorns," explaining what each one is.

"Is this a test?" I ask. I put on my best schoolteacher voice. "Daymarks refer to the distinct shape and color scheme of each lighthouse so that a sailor knows where he is during the day when the light's not visible. Flash patterns"—I stop, trying to remember—"are the distinct way the light flashes for a particular lighthouse. Kinda like Morse code, but not. Foghorns—self-explanatory, right?"

"So the question is," Oliver asks with a grin, "who decided Candy Cane should have the red spiral around the tower?"

I grin. Over the years I've entertained Cynthia with variations of this story. I think back until I find the one she liked the best. "Okay, a long time ago, a nearsighted elf was on a mission for Santa in Rocky Point. He accidentally crashed into the original all-white tower. After he came to, the evil lighthouse keeper had him tied up in the tower. He recognized the elf for a magical being, though not quite clear on what kind. Using magic, the elf made the red swirl around the tower. When Santa and his reindeer search party flew over Rocky Point, Santa instantly recognized the giant candy cane as a distress signal, since candy canes are often used as markers up at Santa's workshop. You know, where there may be a message, or something to investigate.

"Using elfin magic, they turned the evil keeper into a buoy and put him out to sea. But it turned out that the elf had fallen in love with his candy-cane tower—and the lighthouse keeper's *non*evil daughter—and so he became the new lighthouse keeper of Rocky Point."

Oliver is smiling broadly. "Okay, that's a much better story than the lighthouse board making the decision, even if they did get into a whopping argument over this particular design. Practically Hatfield and McCoy about it."

"Well, I have to confess, I didn't make it up on the spot. It's from the archives."

"What archives? The historical society?"

"Why would they have a story about Santa Claus in . . . never mind. No. When we come up with a good story, Cynthia and I always say 'put that one in the archives' so that we'll remember it."

"I like it."

"Next?" This is fun. Today his idea of fun and mine are completely in synch.

There are a number of small items in the display case, but Oliver brings me over to a woman's battered shoe. It's obviously from the 1800s from the style, and judging from the large hole in the toe, the dirt, and the fraying fabric, had seen some tough times. "Don't read the label," Oliver says, suddenly clamping his hands over my eyes.

"I wasn't!" I protest, laughing.

"Well . . . ?"

I pull his hands off my eyes. "Got one," I say. "But I think it's going to have a tragic ending."

Oliver holds up his hands in surrender. "So be it. Gotta go where the muse takes you."

I'm tickled by the idea that he thinks I have a muse. "There was a young lighthouse keeper who saved a boatload of passengers after a wreck in a storm. Unfortunately, he lost his glasses during the rescue, but there was a girl he just knew was beautiful no matter how blurry her face. Her graciousness, her charm, her humor, her halo of hair, it all added up to perfection to him. All too soon, a party arrived on land to bring them the rest of the way to their destination.

"Only as they were leaving did he finally muster up the courage to try to speak to her. He ran after the group, realizing he couldn't call out her name because he didn't know it.

"But he was too late. As the driver of the carriage helped her up into her seat, her shoe fell off. Before she could try to retrieve it, the horses took off. He was left holding her shoe. After that, he made inquiries and carried the shoe around, hoping to find the lovely young lady who fit into it."

"Did he ever find her?"

I shake my head. "If he had, there'd be a pair here."

Oliver nods approvingly. "Nice twist on Cinderella. Though a lot sadder . . ."

"So what's the real story?" I ask. "Some lighthouse keeper's wife had it in her sewing basket?"

"Nope. According to the label, it was found in the wall of the keeper's house."

"Wow. If I had known that I would have come up with a murder mystery! That's so creepy!" I edge him out of the way to read the label.

My eyes widen as I read. I had no idea that there was a custom in the 1800s to place an old shoe worn by a loved one who had died into the walls of a house to protect the family from evil spirits. This shoe had been found during the renovations of the keeper's house. The hole in the toe was put there on purpose—it's supposed to allow the spirit of the original owner to flow out and keep the house and family safe.

I turn to smile at Oliver. "That's so cool. I didn't know that there were superstitions on display."

"All part of history," Oliver says. "So the point for this story goes to . . . ?"

"I think this point may go to you."

"Then we need a tiebreaker." Oliver's eyes narrow while he thinks. He snaps his fingers. "Got it!" He takes my hand and leads me to the next room.

I stand in the center, hands on hips. "Well?"

His palms are together in front of his face, the tips of his index fingers tapping his smiling lips. "Right behind you," he says.

I turn, and I know exactly which display he wants me to make up a story about. "The dog collar."

"Yup."

This is a true story that I know, because the dog collar is one of the favorite displays among the kiddies. I try to empty my mind of the facts and focus on the collar, trying to let it tell me a story. "Fog," I say, as images begin to come.

"Fog?" Oliver repeats.

I wave my hand at him to get him to be quiet so I can formulate the story. "This once belonged to the dreaded ghost dog of Rocky Point."

"Good start," Oliver says. He leans on the display case in that way he does, weight on an elbow, ankles crossed.

My voice goes low and creaky, my scary-story voice. "They say in these parts that fog can be a living thing. Ask any sailor and lobsterman and they'll agree—it can be a malevolent force with a mind of its own."

"Spooky." Oliver shudders appreciatively.

"When the moon and tides are right, a howling goes up. All then know the cursed fog is forming into the giant hound, a creature fearsome to behold!"

I let out a howl. Oliver covers his mouth trying not to laugh.

"The creature is impossible to fight, since it's made entirely of fog, yet it can devour men and ships whole." I point at the dog collar. "This is the only hope for mankind. As long as the dog collar is in the hands of good and not evil, the fog dog can be contained. The collar owner says the magic words . . ." I pause, trying to think of where to take this.

"Woof," Oliver moans. "Wooooooo-oooof!"

"Exactly. Those magic words! Then the fog shrinks down to fit into the collar, and then vanishes."

"Excellent story!" Oliver holds his bare arms up for me to see. "Look. Goose bumps."

"Yeah, it was pretty good."

"Archive worthy, I'd say."

I turn and look at the dog collar. "The real story is good too," I say. "That brave dog, ringing the fog bell when his master had slipped and broken his ankle trying to get to it." I shake my head in amazement. "That dog even got the right ring pattern."

"See?" Oliver says. "There are good stories all around you."

I look around the lobby at all the carefully preserved objects, the photos that capture a specific time, place, and face. "Okay, you convinced me," I tell him. "History isn't just the boring dates and wars that we learn about in school."

Oliver's face lights up. "In that case, how about we poke around the historical society?"

I laugh. "You really know how to get on my mom's good side."

"I'd rather be on *your* good side."

"Would that be this side?" I turn one way. "Or this side?" I turn the other way.

He laughs and gives me a kiss first on one cheek and then the other. "Both."

We head out of the lighthouse and bike to the Square. We

lock the bikes in the rack, then enter the hushed library. Mom is at the check-out desk, talking to a family with several kids and a large stack of books. She smiles when she notices Oliver and me, but she looks tired. Once the group moves away, Oliver and I step up to the desk.

"Hi, Mom," I say. "Can Oliver and I check out the files up in the society office?"

Mom tries to hide her surprise but isn't very successful. "This must be your influence," she tells Oliver. "Because she's never wanted to go up there before."

"It didn't take too much convincing," Oliver says.

I squirm a little. It's a little weird to realize my mom may have more in common with my boyfriend than I do.

"This way," I say to Oliver. We tromp up the stairs to the office in the attic. It reminds me of Freaky's, minus the paintings, though there are framed documents and photos leaning against the walls in similar stacks. There's an old card table with some boxes and a phone on it and the cluttered desk that Mom and Mr. Garrity share, and that's about it.

"What do you want to look at?" I ask him.

He shrugs with a grin. "I'm a completist, remember? I want to look at *everything*."

"Oh, right!" I gaze around the room. "Well, there's probably something you'll like in every nook and cranny. Just start some-where."

"Do you know where they keep the info about the keeper's house? I'd love to see the changes over the years."

"Not a clue," I admit. "Why don't you try over there." I point at the filing cabinets along one wall. "I'll start with Mom's desk."

"Sounds like a plan."

Oliver studies the file-drawer labels as I pull open a bottom desk drawer and find a thick folder labeled KEEPER'S HOUSE.

I pull it out. "Found something."

Oliver joins me at the desk and flips open the folder. "This is all about the renovations when they turned it into the café." He carries it over to the table so he can lay it flat.

While he looks through the folder, I riffle through the papers on top of the desk. "These are all current bills for the lighthouse. Insurance. Estimates for repairs. An electric bill." I look up at him. "Some are marked past due. That's bad, right?"

He pulls a paper out of his file. "This explains why the second floor of the Keeper's Café is closed. They couldn't afford to make the repairs to make it safe for the public. Floorboards and staircase problems."

"They're probably waiting for more of the summer visitors and their cash to kick in so they can reopen it," I say, realization dawning. "No wonder Mom seems stressed."

"I guess this is why she's having you volunteer." He holds up another piece of paper. "Last year they paid someone to be the greeter. They save money this way."

"And why Mrs. Gallagher volunteers in the café on Celeste's days off."

I pile the papers back into what I hope had been their original order. In my usual clumsy way, I manage to knock a standing file off the desk. I slide onto the floor to put it back together. It seems to all be memos between the historical society board and various committee members. My eyes widen when I get to the most recent one. My head snaps up. "This says they're closing Candy Cane!"

"What?" Oliver puts down the folder and rushes over. He drops beside me and scans the memo. He turns to look at me, his forehead scrunched with concern. "They can't afford to keep it open anymore."

The disappointment that rushes through me is as surprising as it is overwhelming. Tears spring into my eyes. "But—but they can't!" I grab the paper back from Oliver, and he starts looking through the other memos.

"They are really behind with some pretty big bills," he says. "And there are all kinds of regulations they won't be able to meet if they can't make certain repairs and get additional insurance."

I keep shaking my head. "This can't be happening."

"It looks pretty definite," Oliver says. "Only a major influx of cash—and I mean *major*—will make a difference."

Oliver and I sit on the floor in silence. His hand snakes over to mine and he squeezes it. I'm just dumbfounded. I haven't always loved Candy Cane, but she's been part of my life forever. Literally. I may not have gone to the Candy Cane celebrations very much over the last few years, but it makes me so sad to think no little kids will be going for their first school visit, or that Mom won't be putting on Mrs. Gilhooley's dress for the Lupine Festival and the Fourth of July.

I lean against Oliver. Candy Cane brought us together. Just like Martha Kingston and Abner Rose. When she saved the sailor from drowning and he recuperated in the upstairs room at the keeper's house, they fell in love there. Like my parents. There's just something about the sweet little lighthouse that seems to shine a light on romance.

"She never said a word," I say. I turn to face him. "Why wouldn't she tell me?"

Oliver shrugs. "Doesn't want to worry you? Hoping for a last-minute save?"

"I guess. . . ." It does explain why she looks so worried all the time.

We gather together the last of the papers and return them to the desk. Just as we're shutting the drawer, I hear footsteps.

Mom pokes her head over the top of the stairs. "Closing time," she announces. "Find anything?"

Oliver looks at me, and I give my head a tiny little shake. This isn't the time to ask her about the closing. She might not like that we snooped.

Oliver grabs a book about lighthouses from one of the bookshelves. "Is it okay if I borrow this?" he asks Mom.

"Of course," she says. "Would you like to join us for dinner? You can let me know your secret for getting Mandy interested in our history here."

I roll my eyes.

"And maybe help me figure out how to get her to stop doing that," she adds with a laugh, lifting her chin toward me.

"Whatever," I grumble, and push past them to clomp down the stairs. Behind me I hear them laughing. How can she make jokes with all that's going on? The more I find out about her, the less I feel like I know her!

*M*om shakes her head with a smile. "That imagination of yours, Mandy." Over dinner Oliver told her about the game we played at the lighthouse.

I always thought she said this in disapproval. Now I recognize she's saying it with some parent combo of admiration and amusement. This is another gift Oliver gave me.

"I've always loved that elf story," Mom says as she scoops ice cream. "And that's why you came into the library? To get more material?"

"Kind of," I say.

Mom returns the ice cream container to the freezer. "To me history *is* a collection of stories. It's not always taught that way, I know," she says in my direction, "but once you scratch the surface, it all becomes alive, and rich, and fascinating." She sits back down and dips her spoon into her bowl.

"I was wondering, Mrs. Sullivan," Oliver says, "would you like to keep Candy Cane Jr.? I mean, that is . . ." He flushes a little as his voice trails off.

I squeeze his knee under the table. I know this is his way to try to make up for the fact that it looks like she may be losing the real Candy Cane.

All through dinner I tried to figure out a way to bring up the awful subject. But it never seemed quite right to bring up something so upsetting. Maybe she didn't tell me because she's too devastated to even talk about it.

"That's so sweet of you, Oliver," Mom says. "But don't you want it?"

"Well, it's not like I can take it home with me on the plane," Oliver says.

"That'd be quite a sight," I say with a laugh, focusing back in on the conversation. "You could wear her, like you did in the boat."

"I'd like to see him try going through airport security," Mom jokes.

"Can you see me fitting into Mom's car like that?" Oliver says. "We'd have to cut a hole in the roof for the lantern house!"

"The car rental company would have a lot of questions," I say.

We're all laughing now. "Perhaps if Mrs. Gilhooley explained things . . . ," Mom says.

I haven't seen Mom laugh like this in a long time. I give Oliver's knee another squeeze. He puts his hand on top of mine and pats it.

"Are you sure your grandfather doesn't want it?" Mom asks.

Oliver shakes his head. "I kind of think he'd love for me to get it out of the garage, actually. But it would feel weird to just toss her."

"Well, I'd love it. It would make a nice addition to the historical society office. Thank you."

"Maybe if you can get the second floor of the Keeper's Café open, it could go up there," I say, hoping this will open the imminent closing as a topic of conversation.

Mom's face shadows a moment. "That would be a lovely idea, yes." She reaches for our empty bowls.

As we pass them to her, I ask, "Do you think you'll be able to reopen it?" I know I'm kind of pushing it, but I go there anyway.

Mom takes the stacked bowls and carries them to the sink. "Did Mandy ever tell you that her father proposed to me at the lighthouse?" she says with her back to us.

Okay. The subject is obviously off-limits. For now.

"No," Oliver says.

She turns and leans against the counter. "That lighthouse has been very special to me for so many reasons, but I think that's the biggest."

"Even bigger than your wedding there?" I ask.

Mom has a wistful smile on her face. "In a way . . . I guess because it was so private. The wedding was fantastic," she adds, coming back to the table, "but the proposal was . . . magical."

She smooths out her napkin, then gives us a mischievous look. "I probably shouldn't tell you this, but we snuck in late at night. I was already a volunteer for the historical society so I had a key. Anyway, it was incredibly romantic up there in the tower, with the stars up above and all of Rocky Point below."

I look down so she can't see my blush.

"Sounds perfect," Oliver says, and I know he's remembering the Fourth of July too.

She stands and gathers our napkins. "I do wish we could still host weddings," she says.

"Why can't you?"

"The costs are just too high. We wouldn't turn a profit. Catering, insurance, the extra people required. Marketing to get clients. We're having enough trouble." She waves a hand. "Never mind.

Let's get back to convincing Mandy that the real stories about the lighthouse are nearly as interesting as the fabulous ones she invents."

"You should tell Oliver some of the local legends and ghost stories," I say.

She grins. "How easily do you scare?" she asks Oliver.

I lean back in my chair, trying to grapple with the mom sitting in front of me. She still has those worry lines between her eyebrows, but I've never heard her call my stories "fabulous." Mostly she tells me to stop daydreaming and get to my homework. I'm discovering all sorts of new things this summer—and not just about boys!

*H*ey, Mom, is it okay if I go with Oliver and his mother over to Cranston?"

Mom looks up from the front-porch swing. "Sure, honey." She closes her battered paperback and peers at me over her reading glasses. "Something happening over there?"

I perch on the arm of the swing. "Just some shopping, I think. But Oliver's mom is going to show Oliver the house where she grew up. And where his grandfather keeps his boat."

"He goes all the way over to the Cranston wharf?" Mom looks puzzled. "Why doesn't he dock over here somewhere?"

"According to Oliver, Framingham only fishes alone and doesn't want anyone asking to tag along."

"Funny," Mom says. "Your dad was like that."

I slide off the arm to sit on the seat beside her properly. "Really?"

"Some people like to fish with friends. Your dad thought it was the perfect time to think. Alone."

"Did that bug you?" I don't think I'd like it if Oliver wanted to spend time doing something that he wouldn't want to share with me. Though, come to think of it, there are probably plenty of things Oliver enjoys that would drive me around the bend. Okay, never mind.

"At first," Mom admits. "But frankly, sitting still for such a long time? Definitely not my cup of tea."

"Oliver also said that Freaky doesn't like attracting attention or—as he put it—'feeling the prying eyes upon him' every time he wants to go out on the water."

"Sounds like Freaky."

"Mom!"

"You started it," Mom says.

I push the floor with my feet to set the swing in motion. "I really have to come up with something else to call him! But Framingham always feels strange and *Mr.* Framingham doesn't seem right."

"Ask Oliver. Or his mother."

"She told me to call her Alice. Do you think he'd be okay with me calling him by his first name?" I try to remember what it is. John, I think.

She shrugs. "Only way to know is by asking one of them." She tilts her head and looks at me sideways. "You're spending a lot of time over there. You sure they don't mind?"

"I—I don't think so. . . ." I turn to face her. "Do you think they don't like it? Alice always invites me to stay, and Freaky always makes enough food to feed the whole town. . . ." It hadn't occurred to me before that maybe I was wearing out my welcome.

"I'm sure it's fine. I just miss you, is all."

"Really?" It's out of my mouth before I can stop it.

She tugs on the ends of my braids. "Of course, silly." She leans back again and adds, "Don't worry. I understand. I know there are more fascinating ways to spend time than with your boring old mom."

I'm not sure what to say. I mean, she's not wrong. It's not that she's boring. Well, she kind of is, but only in that way that moms are. Though these last few weeks I've been seeing her kind of differently.

But compared with Oliver? Sorry. No contest!

A horn honks, and we both look out at the street. Oliver's mom pulls up.

"Will you be home for dinner?" Mom asks.

"Probably not." I shift my weight to one foot and fiddle with the strap on my bag. "You don't think they mind, do you?"

"Of course not. How could they mind having you around?"

I lean over to give her a quick kiss. I realize when I straighten back up that it's been some time since I've done that. The surprise on her face shows me just how long.

"See you," I call as I race to the street. I climb into the backseat and we take off.

Cranston is a bigger town than Rocky Point and a lot more twenty-first century. As we approach the outskirts, where several big-box stores claim space, Oliver's mom suggests we check out her old house first. "Then," she says, turning off the highway to take a smaller, wooded road, "we can get to the stores and the farmers' market."

But as we drive around for a bit, she grows perplexed. "The roads look right," she says, "but the houses are different."

"Uh, Mom, it's been a while," Oliver says. "It looks like there's been all kinds of building around here."

She drives up one street and then circles back around and drives up it again. Finally, she stops the car in front of a cleared piece of property with houses on either side. "Oliver, go check the numbers on the mailboxes," she says.

"I think it's gone," she murmurs as we watch Oliver jog first to one side of the grassy plot then to the other.

He climbs back into the car. "Seven forty-one Moosehead and 745."

"That's it," she says, nodding. "That's what's left of the place. We were 743."

"Oh man . . . ," Oliver breathes.

"It's fine," she says, patting his knee. "In a way it's heartening to know that things actually do change. Even in Cranston."

"Do you want to look around anyway?" Oliver asks.

"Nah," Alice says. "There's a pretty view of Candy Cane, but it's not like you never see the lighthouse." She gives me a wink over the seat. "And I don't think I'd even recognize your grand-father's boat in the marina down there." She turns the ignition key. "Let's just head into town."

We drive to Main Street (do all towns have a Main Street?), and as Oliver pokes around in a hardware store, Alice and I wander through the bustling farmers' market. I spot a brightly colored poster stapled to a telephone post. The state fair! I had forgotten all about it.

I see Oliver crossing the street carrying a huge shopping bag. I wave wildly to attract his attention in the crowd. He grins and crosses over.

"Looks like you found what you were looking for," I say, eyeing his haul.

"Yep," he says.

I wait for him to elaborate but he doesn't. "That's all you're going to say? Wow, you really are becoming a closemouthed Mainer."

He laughs. "I'll tell you later. Maybe. I'm still trying to decide if it should be a surprise."

"Okay, now you *have* to tell me. Because if you don't, I'll make up a wild story, and then the truth will just be boring."

His mother joins us, carrying a large bag of her own. "I think your grandfather will approve of my selections," she says. "At least I hope so. He's awfully finicky about his veggies."

"Hey, Mom, do you mind if Mandy and I take the ferry back?" Oliver asks.

"Of course not. It's a beautiful day for it."

As we stroll back to the car, I point out the state fair poster. "We should definitely go," I say. "My friend Cynthia will be back by then. We can get a whole group together."

"Sounds fun," Oliver says.

Alice drops us off at the ferry dock. Oliver does a quick check of the schedule. "Oh good. We'll be back in time."

"For what?"

"Pops asked me to drop off some film to be developed. I forgot to do it on the way here."

"He's a photographer, too?" Will I ever stop being surprised by ol' Freaky?

"Not in the way you're thinking. He takes photos to use as references for his painting, and he refuses to use a digital camera."

"Ah."

We buy our ferry tickets, then board, claiming spots at the rail on the top deck. As is typical in Maine, the once bright and sunny day turns darker. "Is it going to rain?" Oliver asks. "Should we go below?"

"I think it's just fog," I say. "Let's stay up here."

I like fog. Other people think it's gloomy. I think it's romantic. Mysterious. So much of Maine is pointy and sharp. Fog softens the edges.

I gaze at Candy Cane as the pink-hued fog starts to roll in. "I can't believe it's going to be closed down," I say.

Oliver pulls me into his side. "I know."

"She didn't even tell Justin." I called my brother to find out if maybe she had confided in him, but he was as shocked as I was.

I bang the railing with my palms. "I wish there were something we could do about it."

"Maybe there is," Oliver says. I turn to face him. "I don't know what, exactly, but if we put our heads together . . ."

I nod slowly, hoping some idea comes to mind, but right now my brain is full of the stacks of bills raining down on an empty lighthouse-shaped bank.

"If it closes, it really will become haunted, " I say. "All that will be left of it will be the past. No new memories will get made there."

Oliver weaves his fingers through mine. "If it had been closed, we probably would never have met," he says softly. "I hate to even think about that."

I slump against him and gaze forlornly at Candy Cane. "She just looks so lonely out there," I say, then straighten up sharply. "The postcard!" I've never paid attention to the lighthouse from the Cranston side. But the person who painted the image used on the postcard sure had.

"I'm going below," I tell Oliver. "I have to check something."

I scurry down the metal staircase, gripping the handrails. The fog makes things wet, and I don't want to slip—as it would be oh so me to do. I hurry to the bow on the lower level. "I don't believe it," I murmur.

Oliver comes up behind me. "What are you looking at?"

"The view!" I say excitedly. "Look at the angle. Whoever painted the Candy Cane postcard painted it from a *boat*. From this side of the bay."

"You're right," Oliver says, leaning on the railing.

"I always wondered why it looked different from all the other pictures I've seen."

"The artist could have been a Cranston local. Or a visitor."

"We'll never know," I say. "The postcard lists the artist as anonymous. I just may have to make up a story about it."

"Do you want to stay here below?" Oliver asks.

"Nah, let's go back up on deck. But how about a lemonade first?"

Oliver digs into his pockets and comes up empty.

"I've got money," I tell him. "My treat."

I buy us a lemonade from the snack bar and pick up two straws. "So are you going to tell me what was in that huge bag?" I ask as we climb the stairs back up.

"Maybe . . . If you ask really nicely."

The weather has driven most of the passengers below so we have the deck pretty much to ourselves. With the thick fog it's as if we're in our own world. A world made up of just Oliver and me, with a soundtrack of lapping water, gull cries, and the mournful foghorn.

"How about a lemonade bribe?" I ask, peeling first one straw and dropping it into the oversize plastic cup, and then the other.

He smirks. "Depends on how good the lemonade is."

We lean against the rail and sip on our straws. I release mine as a small giggle escapes my lips.

"What?"

I wipe my mouth with the back of my hand. "Nothing." I don't want to tell him that we're acting out the second fantasy image from my romantic montage. Sharing a lemonade with two straws. I lean into him and kiss the side of his neck, where he tastes salty, then the side of his face, then his lips.

"My next project," he whispers.

I pull my head back so I can look at his face. "What?"

He clears his throat. "The stuff in the bag. It's for my next project. This bribe is working better than the lemonade."

I laugh. "I see. So what is your next project?"

"I'm going to make another scale replica. But no rowing is involved this time."

"Small enough to take home?"

"Maybe. Or give to the historical society. Your mom seemed so happy to get Candy Cane Jr. The keeper's house I made for the boat, it wasn't all that detailed. So I'm going to pick a specific keeper, and make an accurate replica of the keeper's house when he or she lived there. I thought I'd show it at the craft fair."

"Which craft fair?" I ask. There are agricultural contests at the state fair, but I can't remember if they have an arts-and-crafts thing too.

Oliver looks surprised. "The Good-bye to Summer Festival."

The lemonade cup slips right out of my hand and splashes into the water. "Ohmigosh! I'm so sorry!"

"That's okay," Oliver says, peering down at the waves. "I was done anyway."

Good-bye to Summer is the town event held just before Labor Day weekend. I must have blocked it out this year. Because this year I won't only be saying good-bye to summer.

I'll be saying good-bye to Oliver, too.

August

$\mathcal{D}$on't dwell," I tell myself.

The realization that Oliver's departure is a fact, and not some tragic twist in one of my more dramatic stories, sits like a lump in my stomach.

"But how can I stop?" I ask my reflection in the mirror. I know we made a deal and that I was the one who insisted we stay focused on the micro. On the todays we have. Not the tomorrows we won't.

But my brain keeps flipping to the next page on the calendar, where it says September. When Oliver and his mom will be back in sunny California, and I'll still be here in Rocky Point, getting ready for another deep freeze.

"Today," I murmur. "Stay focused on today. And only today. No looking ahead."

I cross to my desk and glare at the *actual* calendar. My eyes widen. "Yes!" I cheer. I've been so busy with Oliver that I completely lost track of the days. The big purple circle filled with exclamation points—Cynthia's coming home!

$\mathcal{C}$ynthia phoned when she got in last night. We couldn't stay on long; I could hear chaos in the background and Mrs. Crowley calling for Cynthia to come help unpack. We made plans for a sleepover and then hung up. We'll catch up tonight—I'm already planning on zero sleep!

To add to my good mood, a Lighthouses of Maine tour group arrives just after I open. That's twenty tickets sold, and I'm willing to bet they'll buy souvenirs and maybe even eat in the café. They swarm through the lighthouse, upstairs and down.

After an hour or so, I'm writing in the ledger the number of magnets (four) and postcards (fifteen) sold. With most of the tour group in the café, it's quiet enough that I hear the conversation wafting in from the exhibit room behind me.

"Not much to look at in this one," a man says.

"Sure, it's pretty with those stripes and all, but . . ."

"Why is it even on this tour?" a woman complains as the trio enters the lobby. "It's not exactly significant."

I slam down my pen. "Not significant?" I stand and cross to the portraits of Martha Kingston and Abner Rose. "It was significant to *them*. She was the keeper's seventeen-year-old daughter. Her widowed father had gone inland for supplies when a terrible squall kicked up. Martha kept the lantern lit and nearly froze to death because she wouldn't leave the tower. She slept fitfully beside the lantern to make sure she didn't fail in her duty.

"Despite her efforts, a small fishing boat crashed on the rocks below, the sea churning so fiercely that despite seeing the light, the few men on board lost control. She left her post to help them out of the freezing waters. One man—Abner—caught sick and stayed behind at the tower to be nursed back to health after the others traveled by land to parts unknown. You may have guessed their ending—they married and became the next generation of keepers—but you may not know that Martha was one of the first suffragettes in Maine. Abner supported her in this, convinced by his experience that women are just as capable as men."

I'm on a roll now, reading aloud the framed letter thanking the then-keeper for the aid and assistance provided back in 1894 and another from the 1920s from a little kid who lived in Cranston who said that after his daddy died, he could go to sleep at night because the light from the giant candy cane made him still feel safe. I finish up and turn to face the stunned trio. "That all seems pretty significant to me."

I hear applause form the entryway. I spin around. "Cynthia!" I shriek.

"Mandy!" she squeals, and we fling ourselves at each other.

Out of the corner of my eye I notice my captive audience dispersing. I see that they have been suitably chastened as they shuffle out the door. "More souvenirs to choose from in the Keeper's Café," I call after them.

"Those were cool stories," Cynthia says.

"They weren't stories," I say. "They're facts. History."

"Really? I guess your mom made you memorize stuff for the tourists."

"Actually, no. Not Mom. Oliver and I—"

"That's right! The boy!"

She hops up onto my desk, scattering the research I'm doing for Oliver's new project. I bend down to gather the papers, avoiding Cynthia's swinging feet. Weirdly, I don't really feel like talking about Oliver. Not yet.

"Is he as freaky as Freaky?"

I stand and look around for a safe place to stash the clippings. I give up and shove them into my backpack. I straighten up again. "Freaky's not all that freaky."

Cynthia feigns a look of horror. "Uh-oh. Did he convert you to his cult?"

That had been one of my better Freaky stories, one I'm a little ashamed of now.

She hops off the desk and grabs my arms and waggles them. "Oh no! The aliens have replaced Mandy with a pod person! What have you done with my best friend?"

I giggle and shake her off. I hold my arms straight out in front of me and stomp around the lobby. "Not pod person," I intone in a gravelly voice. "Zombie. Must. Eat. Brains." I stalk Cynthia, moaning, "Brains. Braaaaains!"

We collapse in a heap on the steps to the tower. She slings an arm across my shoulder. "Missed you!"

"Missed you back!"

"Did you really?" She knocks her shoulder into me a few times with a big smile on her face. "Or were you so busy flirting that you forgot all about li'l ol' me?"

I realize she doesn't know how serious Oliver and I are—she still thinks we've just been playing some kind of flirting game. "Actually . . . ," I begin.

She stands and wanders the lobby, picking things up, putting things down, riffling brochures. "Any of the Regulars turn out to be interesting? Or was Oliver the only crush-worthy boy this summer?"

I stand and straighten the things she's mussed. "Patti's been seeing Kyle."

"Who?"

"He was ahead of Justin at school. Blond curls. Works for his dad. Lobster dudes."

"Oh, right! Him. So she found her summer fling after all."

"I guess. . . ."

"Is she going to break his heart when she goes? Leaving him behind and all."

"Hard to say."

"Or maybe he'll break hers. . . ." She turns to look at me, smirking. "Hope she's still in that fling-only/nothing-serious zone the way she was when I left."

"Why?"

She looks at me as if I asked a dumb question, and speaks to me as if I'm a child—and a not very bright one. "Because in three weeks it's over."

I swallow and turn away, fiddling with the pages of the ledger. Luckily, a kid comes in to ask if we have a bathroom. I send him to the café, and the interruption lets me change the subject.

"How was camp?" I ask. "Were you the lead in, like, *everything*?"

An odd expression crosses her face, a mix of embarrassment and something I can't quite identify.

The door to the café opens, and one of the trio I had regaled with Candy Cane lore comes in with two tour members in tow. "Tell them the stories you told us." She turns to her friends. "She has a real knack. Makes the experience so much richer. The history comes alive."

"Uh, I . . . okay." I glance at Cynthia, and she tips her head toward the door, indicating she's going into the café. I nod, then launch back into my impromptu lecture.

Finally, the tour group leaves and Cynthia returns. "Man, the food's as bad as ever there." She wanders the lobby. "You must have been so bored."

I shrug. "Sometimes."

"Seriously? What do you do when no one's here. Play games on your phone? Does it even work here?"

"I manage. . . ."

She glances at me with a questioning look, then smiles. "I'm going to lay out and catch some rays till you're done."

"I thought we weren't meeting till after dinner?"

"How could I pass up spending quality time with my girl before Mom gets into her back-to-school frenzy?"

Before I can tell her that Oliver's going to pick me up, she's out the door. Well, I wanted them to meet. No time like the present.

I love Cynthia to pieces. She's the sister I always wish I had. I've been envious of her in the past, but today I'm outright jealous. Does she have to be so effortlessly gorgeous and allergy free?

I glance at the clock, ticktocking till my worlds collide. Cynthia disappeared somewhere, but she knows I finish up at four, which is exactly the same time Oliver will arrive.

"Please like each other," I murmur as a mantra. "Only not too much," I add just as the big hand reaches twelve and the little sticks to four.

Cynthia sails into the lobby. She must have gone home, because now she's wearing a bright blue sundress that perfectly complements her skin, hair, and eyes, not to mention her show-stopping figure. "Freedom, Free-ee-dom!" she belts out. (It's from the musical *1776*, which she performed at a previous July Fourth festival.) "Ready to go?"

"Uh, not quite."

I peek out the window. Yup, there he is. I grab my bag. "Okay. Listen, since we were going to meet after dinner . . ."

"I know, I know. You can't even be in the house while Mom makes her fish stew."

"Well, because of that," I explain as we leave the lighthouse, "Oliver's here." I pull the door shut and lock it.

"You have plans?"

"Not exactly. He just comes to meet me after work. Some-times we go to—"

"Every day?" Cynthia asks.

"Pretty much." We turn and start walking.

"Which Rocky Point today?" Oliver calls. Then he realizes Cynthia isn't a Candy Cane visitor and that she and I are together. "Oh, hi," he says.

"Well, if it isn't the flea market find," Cynthia teases.

"What?"

She laughs. "That's where we first saw you. At the Lupine Festival flea market."

"That's right." He smiles. "I hope I'm not one of Mandy's for-lorn unbuyables." I told him about my "pity purchases." He kisses the side of my head.

I squirm. Cynthia squirms. Oliver looks back and forth between us and takes a step away from me. I can tell he's wondering what's wrong. I'm wondering the same thing.

"Mandy said you're just back from camp," Oliver says.

"It wasn't *camp*," Cynthia corrects him. "Not like canoeing and making lanyards. It was professional performing-arts training."

"Right, Mandy said."

We stand there awkwardly. "Want to . . . ," I start.

"Should we . . . ?" Oliver says at the same time

"How about . . . ," Cynthia also says.

We all give nervous laughs. "Someone go first," Oliver says. He takes my hand.

"What did you mean before?" Cynthia asks. "Asking 'which Rocky Point'?"

"Oh, it's an idea of Mandy's. That there are multiple Rocky Points."

"Are they each equally dull?"

"We don't think so," Oliver says, and squeezes my hand.

Cynthia raises an eyebrow at me. "My my my. I guess someone's been doing a good PR campaign for sad little Rock Bottom."

"Aw, that's just mean," Oliver says with a grin. "This place is cool."

Cynthia's still looking at me. "Yeah?"

"Well, it's not so bad. But you have to admit," I say to Oliver, "there's not a whole lot to do."

"Are we going to just stand here looking at the oh-so-not-exciting view, or are we going someplace?" Cynthia says.

"I thought we could do some more research at the historical

society," Oliver tells me. His eyes flick to Cynthia. "Unless there's something else . . ."

"What kind of research?" Cynthia asks.

"Info about the keeper's house," Oliver says.

"He's building a replica," I say.

"Didn't you already make one?" Cynthia asks. "I saw those photos you posted."

"This one will be more detailed," Oliver explains. "I'm double-checking the floor plans so that the scale works and that it's completely accurate."

I wish that didn't sound so nerdy. I know Oliver's more fun and interesting than he's sounding.

Cynthia pokes me. "I can't believe you did the boat parade. So dorky!"

"Yeah, well . . . it turned out to be fun," I say, glancing at Oliver. "Lexi worked on it; did I tell you?"

"And that girl . . ." Oliver snaps his fingers a few times, trying to remember the name. "Vicki Jensen. She said she wished Mandy had asked her to be part of the crew."

"She did?" Cynthia says, crossing her arms.

This is getting tense. "Hey, you probably don't want to hang at the historical society—"

"You *do*?" Cynthia is looking at me more and more like I'm someone she doesn't know. I don't like how it feels.

"It makes Mom super happy. She hasn't been on my back since I started poking around up there." I don't want to get into the whole Candy Cane closing problem right now. The situation is already awkward.

Cynthia nods slowly. "Ahhh. Smart girl."

Now Oliver is looking at me quizzically. What is with me? I'm making it sound as if the only reason I'm going through the files is to suck up to my mom.

"I'm helping Oliver with the research." Now I sound like I only do it to make him happy.

Cynthia smirks at him. "He really did indoctrinate you."

"What does that mean?" Oliver says, just short of snapping at her.

"Hey, don't be offended," Cynthia says. "Be flattered."

I need to end this before it turns into an actual fight. "You want me to bring anything over for tonight?" I ask Cynthia.

"Nope," Cynthia says. "I've got plenty of movies to catch up on. And maybe we can do a little makeover." She flips the end of my braid up and down. "Someone hasn't been using conditioner."

I brush her hand away.

"I think Mandy is exactly the way she should be," Oliver says, putting his arm around me. "Why do girls think putting on more makeup makes them somehow more appealing?"

"Well, builder boy, we like to achieve our full potential."

This is so not going the way I had hoped. Here are my two favorite people in the world (well, Justin goes in that category too), and they're not getting along. At all.

I get that he's a fox, but seriously, Mandy. He's so . . . I never thought of you as going for the dweeb."

"He's not a dweeb," I protest.

We're up in Cynthia's bedroom, where the primary topic of conversation has been how *not* for me Oliver is. It's not like I didn't expect something like this tonight. It was obvious that she thought he wasn't exactly cool from their brief interaction. And I fielded similar comments from Oliver at the historical society, though it was the fact that she was "pushy and shallow" that bothered him. It made it hard to concentrate on our attempts to brainstorm solutions to the Candy Cane problem.

"What do you really know about him?" Cynthia asks.

"What are you talking about? I've spent nearly every day with him; I've hung out with his mom, his grandfather . . ."

"Right. *Freaky*."

"He's really not a bad guy." I pick at an imaginary spot on one of her bedposts. "You just have to get to know him."

"Yeah, like that'll ever happen." She finishes brushing her hair and hops onto the bed. "What I mean is, do you have any idea about Oliver's life at home? Where he actually lives. Where he'll be going in just a few weeks."

I stare down at a pillow and stroke the fringe.

"Remember Arabella Swenson?" she says.

The name chills me. Bella Swenson is the cautionary tale for all of us thinking of having a summer romance with someone from away. The guy she was gaga for turned out to have a steady girlfriend back at home. Though I wonder how serious it really was if he was fooling around with someone else all summer.

"And Billy Winston," she adds.

The boy version of Arabella. But even worse, since that girl's boyfriend came up to spend Labor Day weekend, and poor Billy had to see them all over town together.

"Why are you ruining this for me?" I ask.

"I'm looking out for you," Cynthia says.

"Well, don't." I stand and flop down onto the air mattress. "Since when are you the boss of me? I'm a big girl."

Somehow I don't think I'm helping my own argument.

*T*he next morning Cynthia goes into the bathroom, and I pretend to still be asleep. I hear her sighing heavily—it wouldn't be the first time she used this tactic to try to wake me. I just roll over, bringing the sheet up and over my head.

I lie there wondering what I should do. We had planned to spend the day together, since I don't have Candy Cane duty, but now I'm not so sure. Does Cynthia even want to? Do I?

"I know you're awake, Mandy," she says. "Your feet are doing that thing they do when you're anxious."

Busted. When I worry, my feet seem to have a mind of their own. Banging together or toes wiggling or bouncing up and down. I yank my feet back under the sheet.

"I'm sorry we had a fight," Cynthia says.

"Me too," I say. I push the covers back down and sit up. "You'd like him if you got to know him."

Cynthia winds a strand of hair around her index finger. That's what she does when *she's* anxious. "Maybe. But there's still the fact that he lives—"

I cover my ears. "La-la-la-la-la-la," I babble.

She throws a pillow at me, but at least she's laughing. "Okay. No reality speech. At least not this morning."

I climb off the air mattress and onto her bed. "Yeah, we should at least have breakfast first." I squinch my nose. "Oh, wait, is your mom still on her health-food-only diet?"

Cynthia flops back down onto her bed. "Ugh. Yes."

I flop beside her. "Then I guess we'll be going out."

I want to say, "Too bad we can't drop by at Freaky's—we'd get an awesome meal." But this isn't the time to push it.

Now I just have to work on Oliver's attitude toward *her*.

A few times during the summer there are gallery nights in a bunch of neighboring towns, including ours. Everyone gets dressed up, and it's like a town date night. When we were kids, we felt very sophisticated wearing nice clothes, sipping lemonade from little plastic cups, and nibbling on squares of cheese stuck on frilly toothpicks. We were allowed up past our bedtimes, which made it even more special.

A few nights after the dreadful first meeting between Cynthia and Oliver is the last gallery night of the summer. We decided to make it a girl's night. So no Oliver, no Kyle, and Joanna even promised to leave her cell phone at home. I felt a little bad, since Oliver hadn't been to any of the earlier gallery nights. Something always had come up with his mom or his grandfather. But I could use some quality girl time. I also don't want to be one of *those* girls. The ones who ditch their friends because of some boy.

We only have two actual galleries, but displays are also set up in the Square for local artists, and many shops stay open late. And because this is Maine, there's a lobster roll booth at one end of the Square and a booth selling all things blueberry at the other. Guess which side I'm planning to hang around.

"Cynthia!" Lexi cheers as we climb out of Mrs. Crowley's car in front of Scoops. Patti, Joanna, and Vicki all snap their heads in our direction.

Cynthia is quickly surrounded and peppered with so many questions she can't answer any. She holds up her hands to get everyone to quiet down and announces, "First things first!"

I think she's going to ask them about me and Oliver or maybe Patti and Kyle, but instead she asks, "What are the Scoops front-runners?"

We all laugh. "None of us agree," Joanna says.

"You'll have to catch up on the tastings," Patti says. "The vote is coming up soon."

Scoops is packed, but we cram inside with everyone else. As we push toward the counter, Cynthia says hi to a few more people. Harried "taste ambassadors" (a worse job title than "greeter," though their paychecks probably make up for it) bustle around carrying tiny pink tasting spoons.

Cynthia and I make it to the front, where Patti is holding a cone and a tasting spoon. She lifts the spoon. "Peach coconut," she explains. She finishes it and licks her lips. "Mm." Then she gazes adoringly at the cone. "But I'll always be true to mocha chocolate chip."

I drum my fingers on the counter. "Should I risk it and get a pecan graham cracker cone, or just a taster?"

"You've had the other four new flavors?" Joanna asks.

"Oliver and I have been known to detour past Scoops," I admit with a grin.

"I'm surprised you bother," Vicki says. "With all the deliciousness that Freaky makes. That Fourth of July picnic was wicked good."

Cynthia turns with a triple chocolate cone in her hand and a surprised look on her face.

"He doesn't make ice cream," I explain, then order a pecan graham cracker in a cup. Live recklessly, right?

"Ooh," Lexi says, stepping to take my place at the ice cream counter. "You should buy him an ice cream maker. See what he comes up with."

"What are you guys talking about?" Cynthia asks.

"Freaky is amazing in the kitchen," Vicki explains.

"Seriously?"

"Seriously," Lexi confirms. "We decided we could still call him Freaky because he's a freaking good cook!"

"Uh, and not because he's, you know, kind of a freak?" Cynthia asks.

"We should make space," I say, noticing the line growing huger outside. We file out.

"But he's not," Lexi says behind me. "I mean, yeah, he's a character, but he was super helpful whenever we had questions about making the boat."

"Oh, Cynthia!" Vicki squeals as we reassemble our clump on the sidewalk. "It's so sad you missed the boat parade. Their entry was adorable!"

Patti starts laughing. "I can't believe Oliver was so stubborn."

"Believe it," I say as we traipse down Main Street toward the Square. The night is clear, perfect late-summer weather. Warm enough to wear dresses—which we all are, along with bug spray—without the mugginess that sometimes creates an ick factor.

"What do you mean?" Cynthia asks.

"Didn't you tell her?" Lexi asks me. My mouth is too frozen from pecan graham cracker to respond, so I just shake my head. "It was hilarious. He refused to cut holes in the tower in order to see. It wasn't accurate, he said."

Cynthia smirks. "Not too bright."

My eyes flick to her, but she's focused on licking the drips on the sides of her cone.

"Have you met Oliver yet?" Joanna asks, tossing her napkin into the garbage can.

"They're such a cute couple," Vicki agrees.

My mouth thaws enough to allow me to smile.

"We should totally think about doing a boat together next summer!" Patti says.

"One that doesn't involve rowing blind!" Lexi says with a laugh.

"I hear you've been going out with Kyle," Cynthia says to Patti. "So how's that going?"

Patti smiles with a slightly wicked grin. "It's been an excellent . . . diversion."

"Ah, keeping it light," Cynthia says.

"Exactly."

Cynthia sends a smug look my way, which I ignore.

"It's going to be hard, won't it, having Oliver leave soon," Lexi says sympathetically.

I smile softly at her. I know she truly likes Oliver, so she feels bad for me. I shrug and leave it at that. I swallow and say brightly, "So, Cynthia, tell us all about camp!"

"Yeah, superstar, how many hearts did *you* break?" Patti teases.

"Did any big Broadway directors snap you up?" Joanna asks.

"What shows did you do?" Lexi asks.

Cynthia takes a swig of her bottled water. "We didn't do full shows," she explains. "We did scenes from *Les Miz*, *Wicked*, and *Rent*."

"And I bet you were the star in each one," Vicki says.

Cynthia tucks her chin as if she's being modest, but I can tell something's wrong.

I'm probably the only one who notices, but Cynthia's eyes aren't matching her smile. When she looks up again, her eyes are locked onto mine. She's sending me a message: Change the subject.

"We should all go to the state fair over in Franklin," I suggest.

"That would be so fun!" Vicki says.

"But we can bring our guys, right?" Patti asks. "It'll be fun to smooch at the top of the Ferris wheel."

"Will Oliver still be here?" Lexi asks.

I take a last lick of my spoon and nod. I glance around for a garbage can to toss it in.

"Great, so he can come too," Patti says. "Kyle would feel weird being the only guy in a group of girls." She bangs her hip into Joanna's. "Bringing a virtual Sam doesn't count. At least, not to Kyle."

"Ha-ha," Joanna says. They make silly faces at each other.

Vicki slides her arm through Cynthia's. "Looks like we're the only single ones here. We should find us some boys to flirt with. There's lots of visitors tonight!"

"I have better things to do than moon over boys," Cynthia says. She slings her arm across Patti's shoulder, so that they make a linked threesome. "Not when I've got my girls."

"Well, it's gallery night," Joanna declares. "Think maybe we should go look at some art?"

"If we must, we must," Cynthia says.

"Yeah, I could use some fizzy water," Vicki says. "We can get freebies."

We arrive at the Square and head inside Paterson's Gallery. Joanna and Patti make a beeline for the beverage table, while Vicki drags Cynthia around in search of flirting partners.

I spot a table with snacks. I wiggle through the art lovers (or, at least, art *observers*) to get myself some crackers—that pecan graham cracker ice cream was a tad too sweet. I need to balance it out with something salty.

"Yes, that's an Oliver," a voice says, stopping me.

Hearing Oliver's name, I glance over. An overdressed man and a woman in a long flowing summer dress stand in front of a large painting of what looks like the Cranston marina.

"A John Oliver," the man says with admiration. "Those are rare."

"Some say he destroyed many of them after some terrible reviews in San Francisco and New York."

"That's too bad."

The woman cocks her head, studying the painting. "Yes and no. It would be wonderful if there were more of them in the world, of course. But being so rare makes them incredibly valuable. I managed to snag this at an estate sale down east. It's already sold. And for a pretty penny, I tell you."

Too bad this John Oliver wasn't also a lighthouse keeper. Now, *that* would make a great story to tell tourists. I could combine the Artists and Artisans tourists with the Lighthouses of Maine tourists.

"No one to flirt with here," Vicki whispers as she and Cynthia join me. "Let's go."

We gather Patti and Joanna and find Lexi outside. "They've lined the Square with Brad Ainsley sculptures," she says, pointing.

"Cool!" I turn to Patti and Joanna. "Have you seen his stuff?"

"I don't think so," Patti says as Joanna shakes her head.

"They're hilarious," Cynthia says.

We wander down the row of sculptures. We're near the side of the Square by the lobster booth when I see one I remember from the Lupine Festival exhibit.

"Oh, look!" I point toward it. "It's Ship-nado!"

The girls laugh as we approach it. "Good title," Lexi comments as we surround the ships-trapped-in-a-vortex structure.

"Mandy!" a familiar voice calls.

I turn and see Oliver waiting on line at the lobster roll booth. I wave and turn back to the girls. "Do you mind if he just comes over to say hi?"

Cynthia looks peeved, but everyone else is fine with it. I gesture him to come over.

He holds up a finger to say "one minute," then turns back to order his lobster roll. "Just for a sec, I swear," I promise the girls.

Oliver lets a group of kids wearing college T-shirts pass, then crosses over to us. "Hi, everybody! Don't worry, I wouldn't dream of horning in on your girls' night. Just wanted to say hi."

"Are you with your mom?" I ask.

"She's over at the bookstore."

"Anyone else?" Cynthia asks.

"If you mean Pops, no." He looks around at the bustling, cheerful scene. "Not exactly his kind of thing."

"I bet," Cynthia says.

"Those look wicked good," Vicki says, nodding toward the lobster rolls. "I'm going to go get one."

Lexi and Patti join her, while Joanna goes in search of something to drink.

"Don't you want to get that to your mom?" Cynthia asks, nodding toward Oliver's hands, each clutching a fully loaded lobster roll.

"Actually, it's for Mandy." He holds one out to me. My stomach heaves.

"You eat seafood now?" Cynthia stares at me.

"Why wouldn't she?" Oliver asks.

"Because she hates it, that's why."

Now Oliver stares at me. "Is that true?"

"Uh . . ."

Cynthia throws up her hands. "This is ridiculous. You actually pretend to like fish just because of some boy?" She stomps away.

Oliver gapes at me. I dig my toe into the dirt and stare down at it. "So, uh, I guess I never got around to telling you . . ."

"Our deal was that you stop doing this!" He tosses the extra roll into a trash can, totally exasperated.

"You keep buying them without asking—"

He whirls around and points at me. "This is why you're always dropping them! You're not *that* clumsy. No one is. It's because you hate them."

"Well, kinda, yeah."

"You would have saved me some bucks if you had told me the truth."

"And been a lot less hungry." I smile weakly, hoping my little joke will help.

"Do you pretend with Cynthia, too?"

Okay, joke's not helping. "Pretend what?"

"Pretend to like what she likes. Pretend to be like her. Are you ever yourself with *anyone*?" Now *he* stomps away.

I can't believe it. We have just two weeks left and we're fighting? This is . . . this is . . . I have no words for what this is because instead I have tears.

I blink hard. I refuse to cry in the Square. Refuse. Refuse. Refuse.

"Oliver take off?" Vicki asks, taking a bite of her lobster roll.

"'S cool that he didn't try to crash girl's night," Joanna says.

"Hey, just because Kyle's working the lobster booth doesn't mean he was trying to muscle in," Patti protests. "One kiss and that was it!"

I swallow a few times, trying to get myself under control.

"Mandy, what's wrong?" Lexi asks.

I clear my throat. "Allergies," I claim.

"Yeah, as in allergic to jerks." Cynthia appears behind the other girls. They turn to look at her. "You had a fight over that stupid sandwich, didn't you?"

Now all their heads swivel toward me. I shrug.

"Seriously?" Joanna asks. "A sandwich?" She shakes her head. "And I thought Sam and I got into weird arguments."

"Maybe he *is* a jerk," Patti says.

"He's not," I say. "I mean, he did overreact. And didn't give me a chance to explain . . ." I frown.

"I don't get it," Vicki complains. "Why would anyone be mad about a lobster roll?

I sigh. "It's complicated. It's not really about the sandwich." I push my hair away from my face. "I don't want to get into it. I just want to have fun and forget it. Okay?"

Cynthia slings her arm across my shoulder. "You'll feel a lot better after we get you a blueberry pocket."

Somehow I doubt it. But it's worth a shot.

So what *was* the deal with the lobster roll?" Cynthia asks.

We're up in her room getting ready for bed. I turn on the pump for the air mattress. The noise makes it impossible for me to answer. I need a minute to decide what—and if—I want to tell Cynthia.

She lies on her bed on her stomach, arms dangling over the

edge as she fiddles with her collection of flip-flops. I turn off the pump and sit, back still to her, and hug my knees.

"It was a whole thing, earlier this summer." I sigh. "Something he was actually right about."

I stand and stash the pump under her window and sit at her desk.

She sits up and crosses her legs, waiting.

"I know you don't like him, so it's weird to talk to you about it," I blurt.

She frowns. "But I like *you*," she says finally.

I drop my head. How can this be happening? That I can't tell Cynthia my every single secret, every feeling and thought, no matter how strange or silly or outrageous.

She slides off her bed, then plops onto the air mattress and puts her feet on top of my fidgety ones. "Stop that," she orders.

"Okay, so the seafood thing was part of a big fight about my not being honest with him about what I like and don't like. The same thing you got on my back about."

"Wow." She makes a shocked face. "The boy and I agree about something!"

"Celeste too."

"Celeste Ingram?"

"Yeah, she's working at the Keeper's Café."

"She knows about your fight?"

I nod. "Not this sandwich one. The earlier one." My eyes flick to her and away. I rub a nail-polish stain on the desk. "Celeste thinks I do it with you, too. That I go along with you even if I don't really want to."

"Is that true?" Her eyebrows knit together, confusion on her face. "Why would that be true?"

"I—I didn't really think I did it until she pointed it out," I say in a small voice.

She stands and throws up her hands. "Why would you copy me? I don't want you to do that! If anything, I want to be more like *you*!"

Shock gets me to my feet. "No way!"

"You've got this great, wild imagination! Everybody likes you without you even trying! You—"

"What are you talking about? You're the interesting, cool one. I'm just the sidekick."

We stare at each other, eyes getting wider and wider. At the exact same moment we burst out laughing and fling our arms around each other. "How's this?" I suggest. "We alternate who's Batman and who's Robin."

"Who's Aladdin and who's the genie."

"Who's the Doctor and who's a companion."

Cynthia takes a step back. "We need to come up with all-girl examples."

I smirk. "Maybe girls don't need sidekicks. They can be *equal* besties!"

We hug each other again, then flop down onto the air mattress.

"Look, I like to imagine a summer romance, but really? Not into it," Cynthia says. "Why would anyone want to get involved knowing it will end?"

Before I can protest she adds, "But maybe I'd change my mind if I met someone who affected me the way Oliver affects you."

I settle down and she continues. "I do think he's in the nerdy category, but to each her own. It would be a lot worse if we went for the same type, wouldn't it?"

"You've got a point," I say. "By the way, since I'm now in that all-honest-all-the-time zone, I have a confession."

Cynthia sits up and looks down at me, frowning. "Yeah?"

"I'm not crazy about musicals."

Cynthia pretends she's been struck in the heart, flopping back down and shuddering. "Noooooooooooo," she moans. She stops flailing and says, "Okay. I forgive you."

We lie on our backs, each drifting in our own thoughts. "You're right, you know," I say softly. "Freaky *is* kind of freaky. One minute he's weirdly nice, and then the next he can practically growl. And thinking about Oliver leaving . . ." My voice cracks as tears well in my eyes. "And now we're in a fight. Do you think that was our good-bye?"

Cynthia weaves her fingers through mine. "We just won't let it be."

"Thanks," I whisper.

We're quiet again, then Cynthia says, "I have a confession to make too."

I roll over onto my side so I can look at her. "Ooo-kay."

Tears suddenly stream down her face without warning.

I sit up, alarmed. "Cynthia, what's wrong?"

She covers her face with her hands. "It was terrible."

"What was?"

"Camp. It was awful. Nobody liked me, and I got the worst parts in each of the shows."

"But you're the best!" I protest. "You're better than anyone else here!"

"That's the thing," she says, using her hands to wipe her face. "Everyone at the camp is the best in our hometowns. And there were also people from places like New York and Boston and LA and who were getting professional lessons. How could I compete? What I'm doing here in Rock Bottom is strictly amateur hour." She gives a shaky sigh. "And they let me know."

"Just some meanies," I insist. I get up and grab a box of tissues from her dresser and hold it out to her. "Did you make *any* friends?"

She sits up and yanks tissue after tissue out of the box. "The other losers." She swipes at her face.

I sit back beside her and sling an arm across her shoulder. I lean my head against hers. "I'm so sorry. But look, you'll keep training. And now you've set the bar for yourself super high. You know what you're aiming for. Then no one can knock you down. And if anyone tries"—I make a fist and shake it at her—"they'll have to answer to me!"

She laughs. I laugh. And everything's just fine.

The next morning Mom picks me up at Cynthia's, and when we arrive back at the house, Oliver is sitting on the steps, his bike parked nearby.

"Morning, Oliver," Mom says cheerfully as we head up the walk to the door.

Oliver stands. "Hi, Mrs. Sullivan. Mandy," he adds a bit tentatively.

I don't say anything. Is he here to yell at me some more? Make it an official breakup?

Mom goes inside and we're alone. Well, alone-ish, considering we're standing in my front yard. Next door Mrs. Jackson picks up her newspaper from the bush where the delivery boy tossed it. Thunder the dog walks Mr. Martin past us.

"Your pals adore you, just so you know," Oliver says.

Interesting start. "Yeah?"

"Yeah. They ambushed me at Scoops."

"They went back?" He looks confused. "Never mind. What do you mean?"

"Basically they told me off," he says. "That I was a jerk. That you're the best thing that could ever possibly happen to me. The one with the New York accent—"

"Joanna."

"She suggested I choke on a lobster roll."

I cover my smile. That's so Joanna. "I never told them what the fight was about. Not really."

"Cynthia had filled them in, I suppose."

"Look," I say. "I know you're not crazy about Cynthia, but she's my best friend, whether you like her or not. And you haven't exactly been very nice to her."

"She hasn't exactly been nice to me," he protests hotly.

I run my hands through my hair, exasperated. "You told me to be honest, right? Well, this is me. Sticking up for my friend. The way she sticks up for me."

We both cross our arms and glare at each other as if we're in a staring contest. Oliver folds first. His body sort of collapses, as if he were a balloon losing air. "Point taken."

"I can like you both, right?" I ask softly. "Even if you don't like each other."

"Of course." He winks. "Theoretically anyway."

"Well, that's my theory and I'm sticking to it." I tip my head toward the screen door. "Want to come in?"

He smiles. "Sure."

As we settle onto the front-porch swing I say, "Just so you know, that fish thing. It really was the last thing I didn't mention. I didn't know how to after all those sandwiches."

"You've been lucky. Every time you've stayed for dinner, Freaky made something *other* than fish."

"I've wondered about that." I tilt my head, considering. "Do you think he knows about my fish aversion?"

"You always complain about this being such a small town," Oliver says. "Maybe everyone knows. Everyone except me, that is."

"You're from away," I tease. "We Mainers don't open up the gossip pipeline all that easily."

"Not to outsiders anyway." He touches his ears gingerly. "All last night my ears were burning."

I smack his arm, laughing. "Ego much?" Then I bring my legs up and curl into his side. "Okay, since it's all about the truth now, yeah, you were definitely a primary topic of conversation."

He rests his hand on my leg and stretches the other along the top of the sofa swing. He uses a foot to gently make the seat sway. We both let out long, contented sighs.

Even though Cynthia scared me, mentioning the possibility of Oliver having an at-home girlfriend, not one single molecule of me believes it. For one thing, I don't think he'd get all on my case about not being honest if he was keeping that kind of secret. Besides, I know this boy. *Really* know him. Maybe even better than I know myself, since I seem to still be figuring out how to actually be Mandy, plain and simple.

I know another thing too.

I love him. Truly and really. I love him. Simply and with no reservations.

And shockingly, given my usual state of insecurity, I know he loves me, too.

Not wish. Not hope.

Know.

I also know he's leaving. Every time I think of it my heart squeezes. But I keep focused on the micro. Today. This minute.

Which is just about perfect.

I haven't been to a state fair since I was . . . I guess about your age," Oliver's mom says.

Alice is driving Oliver, Cynthia, and me to Franklin to meet up with Patti and Kyle, Lexi, Joanna, and Vicki. I sit in the back-seat with Cynthia, all too aware of the tension she and Oliver are both pretending doesn't exist.

It makes for a weird drive.

"How about you girls?" Alice looks at us in the rearview mirror. "Do you come every year?"

"When we were younger," Cynthia says. The state fair is one of those things that's super fun when you're a little kid, and great to do when you're older and can go to the nighttime events. But when you're not dating, and can't drive, it's less of a "thing." Cynthia hadn't been all that pumped for this outing, but she wants to hang with Joanna and Patti before they head for home.

"It'll be fun," I say, hoping I'm right.

The fair is set up in the same spot every year since the 1890s. It features a midway with games and delectably junky food, a track where there are tractor pulls, a Native American dance performance, a crazy-cars parade (I'm relieved Oliver didn't know about that—he would have come up with some outrageous float for us to build in forty-eight hours!), vendors, a petting zoo, 4-H exhibitions, and lots of rides.

"It's really nice of you to drive us," I tell Alice as she navigates the crowded parking lot. Trailers and trucks surround the wire fence draped with banners announcing the fair and various attractions. Oliver, Cynthia, and I slide out of the car. Oliver leans back into the window. "Thanks, Mom," he says.

She takes a look at her watch. "How about I pick you up at seven? We can meet at"—she scans the lot—"that light at the far corner." She glances at her cell phone on the dashboard. "It looks like there's a really good signal here, so if there's any problem . . ."

"I know the drill," Oliver says. He pats the car and then she drives off.

Leaving me standing between my boyfriend and my best friend. Who aren't exactly fans of each other.

"We should look for the others," I say. I figure there's safety in numbers.

As planned, the girls (and Kyle) are just inside the entrance. We buy our tickets (Oliver buys mine—so cute!), and Oliver immediately starts poring over the map and schedule of events. No surprise there. His complete (or is that "completist"?) absorption gives me a chance to chat with the girls as we decide what we want to do in a far less scientific and organized way than Oliver's.

By the time Oliver looks up from his papers, everyone has scattered. "Where'd they all go?" he asks.

"Don't worry. Plans and backup plans have been made," I tell him.

Everyone has a different strategy for a day at the state fair. Patti seems to always be hungry, so she dragged Kyle to the food booths on the midway before doing anything else. Cynthia never eats until after she rides the most gravity-defying, stomach-churning thrill rides, so that's where she and Vicki immediately raced to. Lexi and Joanna are into the carnival games, no matter how rigged they seem to be.

Me? I have something else in mind entirely.

Oliver pretends to pout. "And why wasn't I consulted?"

I grin and slip my arms around his waist. "You complained that it was a lot of work having to come up with things to do all summer. Today, I'm in charge!"

He wads the map and the schedule into a ball, tosses it into the air, and catches it. "I put myself entirely in your hands."

"Oh, really?" I run my hands up and down his back. "Sure you won't mind?"

"Oh, I'm sure," he says. He leans down and lets his lips ever so lightly brush mine. "In fact," he says, his voice husky, "I wish you'd never let go."

I quickly duck my chin, staring at my vivid blue high tops. My eyes fill with tears, and I clutch the back of his T-shirt, willing them to disappear. He pulls me closer and his arms come up around my shoulders and his head tucks into mine. I'm completely enveloped, and it makes it worse and better and worse.

"I know," he says shakily. "But we can't . . . dwell."

I laugh and wipe my face, breaking the circle he made around me. "Don't dwell. That's exactly what I'm always telling myself." I push him lightly in the chest, making him stumble back.

He looks at me in surprise. "What?" he asks, hurt all over his face.

"I was doing so good!" I wail. "Not dwelling. Not thinking! Just . . . being. And then you have to be so sweet and . . ."

He grabs one of my flailing hands and brings it to his chest. "You've been great. Probably a lot better than me."

"Really?" I squint up at him. We're having this intense and personal conversation at the entrance to the state fair at high noon. Well, it is what it is. At least we're surrounded by strangers, not neighbors.

He nods solemnly. "Really."

"Is it bad of me to be happy that you're having as much trouble with this as me?"

He smiles. "Very bad." He gives me a ridiculous, lip-smacking kiss, complete with a loud *mwah!* I giggle and push him away.

"Come on," I say, tugging his hands and walking backward so I can pull him in the right direction. "There's something I want to do first."

"Hey, you're in charge. I'll follow you anywhere."

I bang into a garbage can.

"Except for maybe there," he jokes.

"Very funny." I turn around and we walk side by side, hands in each other's back pockets.

We stroll through the crowds, taking in whiffs of fried goodies, and somewhere under there the scent of animals and hay. We pass the thrill rides as I lead Oliver to the area where the calmer, gentler rides are set up.

"This is where we're going?" Oliver asks as I buy tickets for the carousel.

"If we don't do anything else all day," I say, "I want us to do this."

He shakes his head and smiles that twisty smile that he uses when he's humoring me, but I don't mind.

The merry-go-round's tinkling music slows down as it comes to a stop. I gesture toward the horses. "Pick one," I say as we step up onto the platform.

He walks among the horses and poles and chariots and finally settles on a light brown horse with a dark brown mane and tail.

He pats its backside. "Hello there, Trigger," he says. He swings up onto the saddle.

"Scoot back a little," I tell him. I grip the pole and in a completely awkward way manage to seat myself in front of him. We don't really fit, but that's okay. Oliver wraps his arms around me and rests his pointy chin on my shoulder. This is the third fantasy scene from my romantic montage from all the way back in June. And now it's real. Like everything else has been. Maybe more real than anything else in my life till now.

W hy did I eat that last funnel cake?" Patti moans. She sits on the curb, holding her stomach. People stream throughout the parking lot—families with kids leaving, older teens and adults arriving—as we wait for Oliver's mom.

"You're not going to hurl in my car, are you?" Kyle asks anxiously.

"Aren't you glad you're riding with us?" I whisper to Cynthia.

"No lie," she agrees.

"Are you sure you don't want this?" Oliver asks me, holding out a stuffed lobster he'd won at ringtoss. "Or does your aversion to seafood extend to toys, too?"

"Uh, every kid in Maine has one of those," I tell him. "You keep it."

Lexi and Joanna each chomp down on their grilled corn on the cob, while Cynthia fiddles with her ridiculous oversize sparkly sunglasses. She pushes them up onto her head. "I think they work much better as a tiara, don't you?"

"Definitely," Vicki says. She's wearing her own absurd pair.

"You guys don't have to wait for my mom to get here," Oliver says.

"Yeah, they do," Kyle says. "No food in the car. Dad will kill me." He waggles a finger at Patti. "And no puking."

"I'll do my best," Patti says, standing.

"There she is," Oliver says, pointing at the silver car coming into view.

He waves her down, and we say good-bye to the group. I hear Kyle anxiously asking Patti if she was really ready to get into a moving vehicle as I slip into the backseat after Cynthia.

"Have fun?" Alice asks as she winds her way around the lot.

"Yeah," Cynthia says, sounding a little surprised.

"We never made it to the 4-H exhibits," I say to Oliver. "Hope that doesn't offend your completist sensibility."

"His what?" Alice asks.

As we head away from Franklin, I explain the completist concept, which has Alice nodding and laughing. Cynthia just watches the streets go by.

Once we're on the highway, Oliver asks, "What did *you* do all day, Mom?"

"Actually, I finally went to the lighthouse," she says. "It really is charming."

"Oliver did a good job with Candy Cane Jr., didn't he?" I say.

"He certainly did." Alice smiles at him. If she weren't driving, she'd probably ruffle his hair.

Alice takes an exit, and we're back in more familiar wooded terrain. "What do you think your mother will do now that the lighthouse is closing?" she asks.

Oliver looks over the seat at me and then at his mom. "How do you know about it, Mom?" he asks.

"She and I have discussed it quite a bit. She knows I'm a financials person, so we strategized possibilities."

"Mom hasn't actually mentioned it," I admit. "Oliver and I found out about it by accident."

"Candy Cane is closing?" Cynthia asks. "It's not much, but it's the only reason tourists come to Rock Bottom. Why would they close it?"

Her tone tells me she's surprised, but it's not that big a deal to her.

"There's just not enough money for upkeep," Alice explains. "The thing is, a business like that can't survive on just a summer economy. There's too much competition." Her eyes catch mine in the rearview mirror. "I know Candy Cane is special to you, but you have to find a way to make it special to outsiders.

"The only way it will work is if it's generating income year-round," Alice continues. "Which means locals have to support it, and not only with fund-raisers. Not to mention needing a large influx of cash, pretty much immediately."

"There's the auction at the Good-bye to Summer Festival," I say hopefully.

"Every penny of this year's auction will have to go to existing bills. There won't be anything left over for next season. In fact, it may not be enough to cover what's already owed."

I shut my eyes. "We can't just let it close," I murmur.

I feel Cynthia pat my hand. "We'll think of something," she says to my surprise. "We always do."

I call this meeting of Operation Save Candy Cane to order," I say.

We're not in the library, because I don't want Mom overhearing us. She still hasn't told us about closing, and also if we don't come up with a plan, I don't want her to be disappointed. But we need the Internet so we're on one of the benches nearby. Oliver and I sit on the grass with Lexi. Cynthia, Celeste, and Vicki share a bench with Justin on Skype.

I lay out the problem. Everyone's shocked, of course, but no one has any ideas. "I don't know if anyone would want it," Oliver says, "but I'll donate the keeper's house replica I'm working on to the auction instead of the art fair."

I beam at him. "Thanks."

"What would bring more tourists?" Vicki asks.

"Not just tourists," Justin says from my laptop. "Oliver's mom said we need more year-round attendance."

I look around the Square, watching people go in and out of the stores. "They stay open all year, so why can't Candy Cane?" I ask, gesturing at Main Street.

"Too bad the food at the café is so bad," Celeste says.

"It might actually make more sense to close the café to save money," Justin says. "It probably costs more to run it than it earns."

I write that in my notebook as something to suggest.

"People go for those replicas and restorations," Lexi says. "Maybe the Keeper's Café can be turned back into what it looked like in the 1880s or something."

"That would probably take a lot of money," I say, but write that idea down too.

I tap my chin with my pen, trying to think of what made the most impact on the visitors. "Stories," I say.

"Stories?" Celeste repeats.

"That's what can make Candy Cane more special," I say. "The stories."

"Brilliant!" Oliver says, already getting where I'm going with this.

"Like the ones you told those tourists the other day?" Cynthia asks.

"But more!" I'm getting excited. "We . . . we act them out! We tie them in to holidays! We do stories based on history and made-up ones too!"

"From the archives!" Cynthia says.

Oliver laughs. "Yeah, *your* archives *and* the ones at the historical society."

"This could work," Justin says. "Something that people in town can do all year long."

"Everyone's always trying to find things to do with their kids," Vicki says. "I should know. I babysit a lot, and there's not much to choose from."

"School groups too," Celeste adds. "I remember going on trips for stuff like this in Cranston. Why not here in Rocky Point?"

My head keeps nodding with each idea.

"Then maybe we'd want to keep the café open," Celeste continues. "So they have somewhere for lunch."

"I'll get everyone from drama club to act in them," Cynthia says.

"But you'll always be the star," I promise.

"I can build anything we might need," Lexi says.

Oliver frowns.

"What?" I ask. Everyone's so excited. Why is he looking so down? "You don't think it's a good idea?"

"I want to help too," he says. "But this will all happen after . . ." He stops himself and shakes his head. Then he puts his hand on top of mine and smiles. "This is good."

He feels left out. Candy Cane means a lot to him, too. "You can help us put together a proposal. Your mom's input would be great! Then we'll give it to Mom to bring to the next meeting."

"We still have to figure out a way to bring in money *now*, though," Lexi says.

"At least enough to keep it open to put these ideas into place," Justin says.

"Yeah . . ." I stare down at my list. It is definitely not long enough.

"At my school they do auctions where people donate not just stuff but also services," Oliver says. "Massages, dance lessons, whatever. Maybe you can do something like that?"

"Freaky should donate catering services," Lexi says. "I'm still thinking about those sandwiches from the Fourth of July."

"And cookies," I add. "Mmmm."

"Somehow I don't think that's going to happen," Oliver says with a laugh. "But I suppose I could try."

"Listen, this is a great start," Justin says from the screen. "But I have to get to class." He signs off, and I reach up and shut the laptop.

"So I guess we're done for now," I say. "Keep thinking, though."

"Will do!"

"For sure!"

Lexi, Vicki, and Celeste take off, leaving me with Cynthia and Oliver.

"You know, I'm kinda surprised you're all in on this," Oliver says to Cynthia. "Knowing how you feel . . ."

"Just because the lighthouse doesn't matter to me," Cynthia replies huffily, "doesn't mean I don't care what happens to it. Not when it means so much to the people I love best."

Oliver's eyes widen a little, then he says, "Sorry. That was wrong of me." He looks down at his clasped hands. "And that makes it extra great of you to be involved."

Cynthia looks from me to Oliver to me to Oliver. She grins. "Truce?" she says.

He looks up with a grin and shoves his bangs out of the way. "Truce."

We're all systems go on Operation Save Candy Cane. Celeste and Cynthia have been working on getting auction donations. The two of them together pack a powerfully persuasive wallop—both beautiful, and with Cynthia's outgoing energy, how could they miss? Oliver has nearly finished his little keeper's house replica to donate to the auction, and he and Justin are putting together the proposal for Oliver to give to his mom. Vicki's asking the parents of the kids she babysits what might work to bring them to the lighthouse. I'm doing some of everything.

And for now, in case our plans don't work, we're keeping it all from Mom. Who still hasn't mentioned this little bit of HUGE NEWS about closing Candy Cane.

Today I'm up in the attic again, rummaging through Freaky's files for Oliver. He decided to make his model from the year when the lighthouse keeper's daughter, Martha Kingston, saved Abner Rose. He picked it because, just like me, they remind him of us: brought together by Candy Cane. We're going to write up the story too, in a fancy font, and print it on thick paper to include with the model. I'm poking around for anything that might be useful. We've already been through everything at the historical society about it.

I pull out a thick folder that seems to be full of articles and pictures that could be potentially helpful. I cross to the window for better light and—unsurprisingly—trip over something. The folder flies out of my hands, scattering pages everywhere.

"Oh, great," I mutter. I get on my hands and knees on the dusty floor and start collecting the papers. I crawl under a table that has paintings leaning against it, hoping I don't knock them over.

I reach for an article titled "Women Lighting the Way," which could have information about Martha Kingston in it. Then I stop, hand in air.

I'm looking at a painting—well, part of it—leaning with the image facing the table. The image and the signature. A signature that rings a bell.

John Oliver.

I crawl back out from under the table and squeeze past the sofa with sprung springs and the chair missing its upholstery. I come around to the paintings. All of them are stacked picture side in.

Carefully, soooo carefully, I pull the paintings out and slide them into what are hopefully safe places to rest them. I don't look at the others; I'm after that John Oliver.

I take a deep breath before turning it around. Could Freaky Framingham actually own a valuable John Oliver painting? Why would he just stash it up in the attic?

I turn it around and gasp. I actually stumble backward a little, thankfully not into anything that could fall over.

"It can't be . . . ," I murmur.

I'm looking at a very familiar image. Candy Cane. In the fog.

The picture on the postcard sold all over Maine. The one I've been selling all summer.

"I was right!" I exclaim.

This painting—the original that the postcard had been made from—includes the bow of a boat. The boat the artist had been on to capture the image. It had been cropped out, along with the signature, when it was made into the postcard.

I shake my head several times, unable to believe what I'm seeing. I turn and look at the paintings that had been resting in front of this one. My mouth drops. They're *all* signed John Oliver.

Something clicks in my brain, and I feel so wobbly I actually sink to the floor to process.

"You looking for something particular?" Framingham stands in the attic doorway.

How does he sneak up on me so easily? My head snaps up. "It's you! You're John Oliver. Why doesn't anyone know?"

He frowns and steps into the attic. He frowns more deeply when he sees that I'm sitting among his paintings. "I don't want them to. And you're not going to tell."

I stand carefully and gape at him. "But someone *must* know—this postcard is sold all over Maine!"

"Direct deposit. An account in Boston."

"Is Framingham your real name?" Has he been living under an alias all this time?

A small smile plays on his lips. "John Oliver Framingham is the full handle."

I look down at the painting. "Why would you keep it hidden up here? It's so beautiful."

He stops as if he doesn't want to get closer. He leans against an old dresser. "It's the one that was my breakthrough," he says. "Oliver's ma was too young to remember it. I never let her in the studio because of the chemicals. I suppose I've got what they call a love-hate relationship with it. Brought me into the limelight, but then trapped me in endless requests for lighthouses. I had to get out of Maine, find new vistas, new subjects. Some took. Most didn't."

I study the painting. "You painted it from a photo you took from your boat from the Cranston side."

He nods.

I frown, thinking. "This is why none of the recent paintings are signed. You don't want anyone to know."

He nods again.

"But it's so sad," I tell him. "They're just . . . wasted up here." I turn back to the paintings. "If I could paint this beautifully, I'd want everyone to know. I'd hang them all over the house just so I could see them."

"You ain't me."

I glance at him again and see pain etched on his face.

He takes a step closer, as if maybe he's a little less afraid of the paintings now. "They're from a time when . . . Well, let's just say I'm not very proud of the me that painted them. It was a very selfish time. I didn't know that then. I know that now."

He must be talking about leaving his family, about the things Oliver's mom was angry about. "I wish they didn't make you feel bad," I say softly. "Because I bet they made a lot of people really happy. Just looking at them."

"Maybe." He doesn't sound very convinced. He rubs his face with one hand, then sighs. "Well, let's put them back."

Together we drag the paintings back to their position. I pick up the file I found for Oliver and follow Freaky out. When I get to the door to the attic, I turn to gaze at the backs of the paintings.

"I'm trusting you, girlie," Freaky says with a sharp edge to his voice.

"I won't tell anyone," I promise. "Even if I think you're wrong. Totally and completely."

"Won't be the first time," Freaky says, a touch of humor returning to his eyes.

Then he does something absolutely unexpected. He ruffles the top of my head, just like Alice does to Oliver.

Before I can react, he lopes down the stairs, leaving me gaping behind him.

*T*he thing about having a lot at stake at this year's Good-bye to Summer event is that it doesn't give me time to dwell on the Good-bye to Oliver aspect. Each time I start to get morose, someone calls about Operation Save Candy Cane, and I have something new to do.

This is where Oliver's micro nature comes in super handy. He's amazing at list making, and has even drawn up charts of what has to be done by when and by who.

The project also gives us something to focus on when we're together other than his imminent departure. Still, every now and then I catch him looking at me sadly, or nervously. I know my own face reflects the exact same miseries.

We made a pact to not talk about it until after we get through Operation Save Candy Cane. Which doesn't leave much time for good-byes. He's leaving before Labor Day weekend, like a lot of the Regulars who need to get ready for school, get back to work, and otherwise return to their "real" lives. The lives that we in Rocky Point aren't actually part of.

And here come those tears again.

I wipe them away as I reach for my chiming phone. Five new texts. "Whose brilliant idea was this again?" I mutter. Oh yeah. Mine.

"What idea is that?" Mom asks, coming into the kitchen.

"Just some more ideas for the auction," I say. I told her about finding contributions for the auction since she has to register them all, but not that it's part of a larger plan to save Candy Cane.

I hold up my phone. "Cynthia and Celeste got Kyle's dad, Mr. Marcus, to donate a bucket of bait, and Ms. Hughes three hours of after-school algebra tutoring. And we're all donating baby-sitting hours."

Mom's eyes crinkle, and I think she might be about to cry along with that smile. She comes over and kisses the top of my head. "Have I told you how amazing it is that all of you kids are helping this year? It means so much. I just hope . . ."

I glance up when she stops speaking. She's blinking rapidly. Uh-oh. "Hope what?" I ask.

She shakes her head and crosses to the sink. "I hope you're not running yourself ragged with this on top of everything else you're doing."

"'S cool," I say. Funnily enough, it actually is. I think I may have the micro gene too. I'm really loving pulling all this together. Cynthia says it's like that with shows, too—it's a huge amount of organizing, but everyone works as a team, so it's fun and culminates in something to be proud of. I hope that's how I'll feel after tomorrow. Only then will we know if we actually managed to save Candy Cane.

Problem is, even with the additional auction items, Alice thinks we still won't raise enough money to make a dent in the amount that's actually needed.

Mom starts washing the breakfast dishes. Oops. That was supposed to be my job this morning, since she had to race out to a meeting. I jump up from the table. "Sorry, Mom," I say, stepping beside her at the sink.

"Nah, it's fine," she says. "You've been working hard. You deserve a break."

"You sure?" I ask. "You've been working hard too." Like, around-the-clock hard.

"I actually find it soothing," she admits. "Nicely mindless." She glances sideways at me. "Do you have plans with Oliver today?"

"I might go hang over there later. He's finishing up his keeper's house model."

My phone buzzes, and I cross back to the table. Another text from Justin. *Proposal finished.*

The water turns off, and I feel Mom looking at me. "Mandy . . . ," she begins very gently.

I can tell by her tone that I don't want this conversation to happen. Certainly not now. It's either her confession about Candy Cane closing, or it's something about Oliver leaving. I don't want to get into the first one because maybe it will all be fine. I don't want to get into the second because, well, just because.

I hold up my phone. "I need to answer this in an e-mail," I tell her, and quickly leave the kitchen.

Up in my room I pop Justin an e-mail, telling him to send the proposal to Oliver *and* to me, since Oliver's Internet connection is so wonky.

I read through the proposal. It's really great, but there's a big problem. These are all ideas to sustain Candy Cane once repairs are made and bills taken care of. Nothing we suggest can happen without a major flow of cash first.

I lean against the back of my desk chair and twirl my pen in thinking mode. Slowly an idea begins to take shape. An idea so perfect—and perfectly outrageous—that I throw down my pen and race out of the house before I can chicken out.

I bike to Freaky's in record time. I leap off the bike and hear it crash to the ground, but I don't care. In moments I'm banging on the front door.

Oliver opens it. "Hey!" he says with a big smile. "Do you want to—"

I cut him off. "I need to talk to your grandfather." If I wait another second, I just won't have the nerve to do what I'm here to do. "In private," I add.

He takes a step back, probably pushed by the force of my determination. He's so surprised he doesn't ask a single question; he just points toward the kitchen and says, "Shed."

I rush outside and find Framingham doing something with the big collection of tools in his shed. I know he doesn't like being interrupted, and if I make him mad, he's more likely to say no, but we're down to the wire here.

There's so much at stake for me, for Mom, for Rocky Point, the words force themselves out all on their own. "The painting of Candy Cane," I say. "Please. Would you be willing to sell it?"

"What?" Framingham stares at me as if I just sprouted a second head.

"At the auction. To save the lighthouse. "

He nods. "Yeah, Alice and Ollie mentioned the lighthouse is closing. It's a sorry thing, to be sure."

"But we can stop it from happening! Oliver, and my friends, and my brother, we're all trying to come up with ideas. But none of them will work without something drastic."

"And my painting somehow figures into this?"

"A John Oliver painting would probably raise enough money to keep the lighthouse going for at least another year, maybe more, while we try to find other ways to bring in funds." I launch into the whole scheme, but he quickly holds up a hand to stop me.

"That's all very well and good, but I'm not interested in selling." He turns back to his work table.

Tears spring into my eyes. "But you don't even like the paintings. They make you sad just to see them. You could do so much good if you'd just . . ." My voice chokes up and I have to stop.

How can I get him to understand how special Candy Cane is? Not just because of all the time Oliver and I have spent together there, but because of *everything* that's happened there—the people, the stories, the history. I'd hate to see that all disappear.

And then there's Mom. I think about losing Oliver in a couple of weeks. I've only known him for two and a half months, and already the pain burns in my chest. Mom lost my dad, the man she loved and lived with for years. That pain must have been unbearable. "My mom," I choke out. "I don't want to think . . . It's so much more than a lighthouse to her. It's like a symbol of her relationship with my dad. It would break her heart."

Tears are now running down my face, but I ignore them. They're not just from pain, they're anger, too. "You don't like those paintings because they remind you of when you were selfish. You have a chance to do something the opposite of selfish with them. Won't you do that? Please?"

"Can't you see I'm busy here?" he snaps without even turning around. "Why don't you go along and let Ollie show you his model or something."

My mouth opens and then closes again. I whirl around and stomp out. I drop onto the bench at the picnic table. I have to get myself together before heading back into the house. Even though I'm furious, I'm not going to spill Freaky's secret identity. I keep my promises. If I go inside now, I don't know what will come out of my mouth when Oliver asks me what's wrong.

I wipe my face with the bottom of my T-shirt, trying to get myself to calm down. I hear muttering from the shed. Probably Freaky complaining to himself about me.

A shadow makes me realize Framingham is now standing behind me. Just like him, I don't bother turning around.

"I hear you, girlie. I hear how important this all is, but so is my privacy."

I don't think that's a very good excuse, but I figure it's not a good idea to keep yelling at Oliver's grandfather, so I keep my mouth shut.

He sits beside me on the bench, his back against the table. "Do you know what would happen if folks hear that John Oliver is none other than ol' Freaky Framingham?"

My mouth drops and I turn to face him.

His eyes twinkle. "You thought I didn't know about that lovely moniker, huh?"

"I—I—I . . ." I shake my head.

"Those danged artist tours, they'd be crawling all over my property. I've been famous; I know what it can be like."

My brain clicks frantically, searching for a solution. I get the strongest feeling that he's trying to find a way to say yes. "What if we say it's an anonymous donation? That someone who knew about the postcard decided to give it to the historical society?"

"You think there's anything done anonymously in this little town?"

"The postcard is."

A smile slowly spreads across his face. "I think I know a way to make this work. But no one can know. Not even your mother."

"Not even Oliver?"

"How about you hold off until after they leave town. That's a big secret for anyone to keep. Think you can?"

"To save Candy Cane, you betcha!"

Then I do something as startling as Freaky ruffling my hair. I throw my arms around him.

And he even hugs me back.

*T*he next day my phone rings, and I see that at least for now, Oliver has cell service.

"Hey, you," I say. "How goes the building?"

"Just waiting for the paint to dry," Oliver says. "Then it is officially done!"

"Congratulations." I lean back in my desk chair and slowly spin in it, taking in the souvenirs of this summer that I've accrued. The plushy lobster toy Oliver convinced me to take after the state fair. The spreadsheet he devised to determine which new flavor should win the ice cream contest at Scoops. (Neither of

our choices won. Pecan graham cracker? Are they kidding?).
Mrs. Gilhooley's "bib." An evergreen branch tacked to my bulle-
tin board that Oliver pretended was mistletoe (since it's Christ-
masy). A sparkly rock from the river near "our" place.

"Uh, so I wanted to ask you something," Oliver says.

I stop the chair with my feet, wary. "Yeah?"

"This antiseafood thing of yours. Is it just eating it, or do you
hate being around it, uh, generally?"

I turn the chair so I'm facing my desk again. "You want to go
to the lobsterbake tomorrow."

A highlight of the Good-bye to Summer Festival for many
(not me) is the lobsterbake held on the cove's sandy beach where
everyone watched the fireworks. For those not from Maine, a
lobsterbake is a super-traditional party meal, though there are
big arguments about the best recipe and technique. The way we
do it in Rocky Point is like this: Giant steel washtubs are placed
on rocks over coal fires. Salt water goes into the tubs, then the
lobsters, which get covered with a layer of seaweed. Next there's
a layer of clams and mussels and more seaweed. The last to go in
is corn on the cob, which is also covered with seaweed.

As you can tell, I've been to them, but only when I was forced
to as a small child. It's mostly for visitors to Rocky Point, since
it's pretty pricey and most of the locals are working at it in some
capacity or other.

"Would you . . . would you want to go?" Oliver asks tentatively. "Mom's kind of into it."

"Of course she is," I tell him. "Everyone who comes to Maine
has to experience a lobsterbake on the beach."

"Will you come too?" Oliver asks.

"To be honest, it's not my thing. I'd have to bring my own food, I'd be trapped among the creepy crawlies, I'd—"

"I get it," Oliver says, cutting me off. "So we won't go."

"No, no!" I say. "You definitely should go."

"But I'll be leaving . . . I mean, we only have a few days left. Don't you want . . . " He clears his throat. "Don't you want to spend that time with me?"

"Of course I do!" I exclaim. "It's just—I don't want to keep you from doing something I think you'd really enjoy."

"I get it. I do," Oliver says. He sighs.

I take a deep breath then say, "You know what? Let's go. Together."

"Really? But you—"

"Really." Relationships are about compromise, right? "You just have to promise not to try to make me eat anything."

"Promise."

"Or do classic boy moves like chasing me around with a squirming lobster."

He chuckles. "Do I have to promise that? Cuz that sounds like fun."

"It's a deal breaker, buddy. Promise or else!"

There's a knock on my door, and Mom barges in. She's wired, pacing back and forth, radiating a crackling energy. I've never seen her like this. It's freaking me out.

"Call you back," I tell Oliver. I put down the phone. "Mom?"

"I don't believe it," she's muttering over and over.

"Mom! What's going on?"

She stops her pacing and stands by my bed, one hand holding the headboard as if to keep herself steady. "I just got the most amazing call." She spots my phone. "Was that Oliver?" Now her face grows a bit crafty. "Is this something the two of you cooked up?"

"I have no idea what you're talking about!" Then it hits me. Freaky must have come through. He waited till we were down to the wire, but he came through.

Mom settles onto my bed and gathers herself. "I just got off the phone with Oliver's mother. It seems she has a client who owns a John Oliver that he'd like to donate to our auction!" She pops up off the bed again.

"And not just any John Oliver!" she continues. She bends down to look me straight on and puts her hands on my shoulders. "The *Candy Cane* John Oliver!"

I'm confused how to react. I'm not supposed to know anything about this. Luckily, Mom is so jazzed I don't have to come up with anything. She straightens up and shakes her head. "I'm so sorry. You probably have no idea what I'm talking about."

She perches on my bed again. "John Oliver had been a pretty famous artist from Maine, though no one is sure where he actually lived. His paintings are quite valuable. So as soon as Alice mentioned it, of course I was thrilled." She pops up again. "And then I saw it! She sent me a picture she snapped with her phone."

She takes in a deep breath. "It's of Candy Cane! The most amazing thing of all? The postcard we've been selling all these years—it's a reproduction of this very painting! I had no idea it was a John Oliver!"

She plops back onto the bed as if she needs to catch her breath. Which I'm guessing she does. Just watching her is making me hyperventilate.

"That's awesome, Mom!" I say. I get up and sit beside her. "So now you'll be able to keep Candy Cane open, right?"

Her head snaps to look at me. "How do you . . . ?" She waves a hand. "Never mind. Everyone knows everything in Rocky Point."

Not *exactly* everything.

My laptop pings with an incoming e-mail. The proposal from Justin. No time like the present, I guess.

I hit print and then turn to face Mom. "So . . . we found out that Candy Cane was in danger of closing. And we don't want that to happen. So we did this." I collect the pages from the printer, then hand them to her.

"What's this?" she asks. She looks up at me quizzically. "Operation Save Candy Cane?"

I settle beside her on the bed. "It's a proposal for you to take to whoever makes those decisions. It's all ideas about how to get the lighthouse to bring in money year-round. Oliver's mom is going to look it over too."

Mom's eyes turn shiny. "You—you did this?"

I shrug.

She flips through the pages. "You *did*. This has you all over it. The stories . . . the . . ." She holds the proposal against her chest. "I—I don't know what to say."'

"Say it will work!"

*B*ecause of the amazing addition of the John Oliver painting to the auction at the very last minute there was some scrambling to do. It was too late to get the info into the newspaper, so we printed up flyers that the Operation Save Candy Cane crew handed out all morning. The auction will take place at four, so everyone with tickets to the lobsterbake earlier in the day can attend too. Because the painting is so valuable, special precautions had to be taken to be sure it would travel and display safely. People took turns sitting beside it in the auction tent in the Square to be sure no grubby little fingers touched it.

Tables with clipboards that listed the donated services that people could bid on lined the tent, and there were a podium with a mike and a long table where the objects up for sale would be displayed. And thanks to Justin, who understands these things, there was even an online version so that anyone around the world could bid—but this was only going to be used for the painting. It was a lot easier for Justin to get the word out in London about the surprise addition to the auction than in Rocky Point because our Wi-Fi connection is so unpredictable.

The Candy Cane painting (which is actually called *The Friend*—I'm not sure if Framingham is referring to Candy Cane or the fog with that title) was in the place of honor. Anyone walking into the tent would see it immediately on its easel in the very center at the front of the tent. I helped Alice write the crafty label description: *An anonymous art collector with a love of lighthouses and a connection to this area has generously donated the iconic John Oliver painting* The Friend *to the Rocky Point Historical Preservation Society. The collector has expressly stated that any funds raised will go to renovations, maintenance, and programming of the Rocky Point Lighthouse.*

Mr. Garrity from the historical society has a background in fine arts, so he helped to make sure it was moved safely. Then Oliver, Alice, Mom, and I ambushed him with the proposal. He promised to read it over carefully and get back to us.

Even though there are lots of activities all day long—concerts at the pier, where Cynthia is singing; windjammer cruises, where Oliver is with his Mom; balloon animals; face painting; and various food-eating contests—I stay in the auction tent. I just can't bring myself to leave the Candy Cane painting. So much work went into getting this to happen; so much is still at stake.

Mom comes up to me and lays her arm across my shoulder. We gaze at the painting together.

"It's so beautiful," Mom says.

"Do you think it will raise enough money to save Candy Cane?"

"I do. I really really do." She glances around. "Where's Oliver?"

"He and his mom are on a windjammer tour."

"Ah, the full Maine experience." She grins as people start filing into the tent, picking up paddles for bidding, and reading the descriptions of the donated items.

"They're going all out," I say. "They bought tickets for the lobsterbake. I'm going to meet them over there after the auction."

"They're not coming?" she asks, surprised.

"They bought their tickets so late that they were only able

to get the five p.m. seating." The company that handles the lobsterbake keeps it all under control by doing timed "seatings," if sprawling on beach blankets and in lounge chairs can be called seating. But it's how they can serve the hundreds of people who want their share of the experience.

"Wait a second." Mom turns to look at me. "You? At the lobsterbake?"

I throw up my hands. "I know!"

She laughs and pulls me into her. "Love makes us do crazy things. Even if it's just the love of a lighthouse."

*M*andy! Over here!" I whip my head around to find Oliver waving frantically from a prime spot on the packed beach. He, Alice, and Framingham have staked out a sandy break between rocks, so that they're using flat stones as end tables. Amazingly, Framingham occasionally nods at passersby. Alice concentrates on cracking apart her lobster.

I told Oliver that I had no idea when I'd really be finished at the auction, so they should just go ahead and start without me. Secretly I was hoping they'd have finished eating before I arrived so I could avoid close contact with the quintessential Maine seafood. I snacked all day, so it's not like I'm hungry—or that there would be anything here for me to eat.

I wind my way through the throngs, stopping for a moment to admire the caterers manning the fire pits. I may not like the food, but the action is really impressive. They're prepping for the next seating, so they're poking the coals to make sure they're still hot. Although the company does lobsterbakes up and down the coast, they use Kyle's family to provide the lobsters here. I spot Kyle dropping a mound of the seaweed that's stacked near the pits onto Patti, who lets out a squeal.

I make hand signals to Oliver, indicating I'm going to stop by the beverage table, and he heads in the same direction.

"Hey, you," he says, giving me a quick kiss. Thankfully, he doesn't taste like lobster.

"Hey, you." I glance around as I wait for the kids around the soda cooler to get out of the way.

"How'd it go?" He takes a step back and looks at me. "It went great, didn't it? I can tell by that grin."

I grip his arms and bounce a little. "It was amazing! Everything sold! I didn't have to bid on a single pity purchase!"

Oliver laughs. "Lucky for your wallet there weren't any broken mugs or toys donated."

We step up to the cooler, and I rummage in the ice. I pull out a soda and hand it to Oliver, then grab one for myself.

We scoot out of the way to make room for other thirsty people. "Mr. Garrity bought your keeper's house," I tell him as we head to where his mom and grandpop are sitting.

"And," I add, "they're so sure that they'll be able to raise enough money to stay open that he's going to add it to the displays in the lighthouse."

"Really?" Oliver beams.

"He said it really does show what it had been like in a particular moment in time," I say. "The write-up we gave it is going to be turned into a label card!"

Oliver clinks my soda can with his. "Congratulations to us!"

We stop to let some kids race by using their corn on the cob as swords. I glance at Freaky and Alice. "I'm kind of stunned that he's here."

"It's nice to see them getting along so well," Oliver says as we start walking again, carefully, to avoid stepping on anyone. "It was kind of tense when we first arrived."

Workers are starting to move through the crowd, collecting dirty dinner plates and handing out bowls with blueberry crumble and ice cream. Now, those I wouldn't mind having.

"They've been acting funny for the last couple of days," he continues. "Almost like they have some kind of plot brewing."

I have to look down at my feet because I'm afraid my face will reveal that I know exactly what plot they've been brewing. As much as I want to, Freaky Framingham's secret isn't mine to tell. Oliver will know soon enough.

"So . . . ?" Alice asks expectantly when we reach them.

Her half-eaten lobster creeps me out, so I stay focused on her face. "The bidding for the John Oliver is going to be extended until midnight because of so much interest from places in other time zones. The last time I checked, the bids were already through the roof."

"You done good, kid," Framingham says. "You done a good thing."

"We all did," I say.

It was hard work but worth every aching muscle and sprained brain cell.

As I settle onto the sand with Oliver on one side of me and

Freaky on the other, my elation over our success suddenly gets put on hold as a thought sneaks in. As hard as putting all this together was, tomorrow will be so much harder. Saying good-bye to Oliver.

But a surprising realization surrounds that painful thought, creating a sort of cushion. The heartache that will come . . . well, it's been worth it too. To have had this summer.

I lean against Oliver and shut my eyes. All worth it.

The next morning Oliver arrives at my house. We had each prepared lists (so us, right?) of what we wanted to do on our final day together.

We're sitting on the sofa swing on the screened-in porch. I look at the paper with his list Oliver just handed me. I start laughing.

"What?" he asks, a little defensively.

I place the paper beside me on the sofa and hand him my list. My list is *identical* to his. "Great minds, huh?" I say.

"'Our Place,'" he reads aloud. "'Candy Cane.'" He smiles at me over the paper. "We even wrote them in the same order."

I swivel on the seat so that I'm sitting cross-legged facing him. I waggle a finger at him. "I don't want to spend the day crying."

Oliver nods. "I don't want that either."

"So, got any ideas how to do that?"

Oliver pushes my hair back over my shoulder. "None." Then he leans away and smiles teasingly. "We could always go back to Hubbard Island. I'll annoy you so much you'll be glad to see me go."

I laugh, despite the raw feeling that's suddenly claimed my throat.

The day we spend by the river is terrible and wonderful, full of intense debates (he's still trying to convince me that *Far Far Away* is a decent movie), stories, laughter, kisses, and long stretches of comfortable silences.

When it grows dark, without even discussing it, we head for Candy Cane. I pull out my key, and together we shove open the (still) reluctant door.

"It took every ounce of restraint to not kiss you that day," Oliver admits.

I smile. He doesn't have to tell me which day he means. I know it was when we fell onto each other trying to get the door open.

"I thought that's what was going on," I say as we stand in the doorway letting our eyes adjust to the pitch-dark entryway. I stand on my toes and kiss his cheek. "I was fighting the same fight."

We only have one flashlight since the other one broke in its tumble down the stairs. I remind myself again to put it on the list of things that need to be replaced. Unbelievable as it is, I'll still have Candy Cane duty after Oliver leaves. Labor Day weekend is busy in Rocky Point. The good thing is, it's official. Candy Cane will be staying open. We made more than enough money on Freaky's painting, even before the final bid. Not only can it stay open, there might even be funds left over for some improvements.

Up in the lantern house it's a lot darker than it was on the Fourth of July. No fireworks, no bright clip lights on booths on the piers. Just the regular harbor lights and streetlamps.

"Someone built a fire on the beach," Oliver comments.

I'm looking at the sky. Tomorrow he'll be on the other side of the country. We'll share the same stars, but have a continent between us. I take in a shaky breath.

Oliver clicks off the flashlight, and I'm grateful. I don't want him to see me cry. Not when we promised. His lips find mine.

"Mandy," he says when we gently pull apart. "I know you don't want to talk about this, but don't we kind of need to?"

"Why?" I murmur, staring down at my feet, which I actually can't see in the dark.

He rakes a hand through his hair. "What's the plan? Are we going to stay in touch? Try long-distance? I might be back next summer."

"Might . . . ," I repeat.

He looks down at his feet too, our heads lightly touching.

"I—I don't want to make a promise I can't keep." His voice thick and creaky.

"I—I know." We're doing it again. That matching stammer.

He inhales and straightens up, resting his chin on top of my head. "Stick with the micro, right?"

"Micro. Right." I blink away my tears and shift my head so that we're looking at each other in the moonlight. "And right now the micro is perfect."

"So we figure it out day-to-day?" he asks.

"It's too hard to see the big macro picture."

"But we stick to our deal," Oliver says, bending a little to bring his face directly in front of mine. He grips my arms. "Honesty only."

I swallow and say, "Honesty only."

He wraps his arms around me and I melt into him. "So, being honest, this has been the most amazing summer of my life. Most amazing *ever* of my life."

I squeeze him hard and let the tears come. After all, they're honest too.

*O*liver left today. That's the lovely thought that greets me the moment I open my eyes. I feel like I'm made out of rocks. I force myself up, trying to relieve myself of the sensation of being crushed. I trudge downstairs, each step weighing a million pounds.

When I galumph into the kitchen, Mom's sitting at the table. "Hey, sweetie," she says sympathetically.

I nod, not trusting my ability to speak, and just lean against the doorjamb. I feel her eyes on me, and I'm grateful she's taking her cues from me and not asking any questions. She doesn't need to. My misery must be radiating.

"Justin will be home in time for dinner," she says.

Justin. Right. I brighten a little.

I'm trying to decide if there's anything I can possibly eat on a morning like this, when there's a knock at the door.

"So early?" Mom says, glancing at the wall clock. It's just past eight o'clock. She pushes up from the table and goes to answer the door, but calls for me a moment later.

Puzzled, I pad out of the kitchen. I'm even more puzzled when I see Freaky standing on our front porch. He's holding a large cooler. Perched on top is a teeny tiny model of Candy Cane.

"The lighthouse is from the boy," he says. "The rest from me. A . . . care package. Thought you might need it today."

Speechless, I pick up the insanely adorable baby lighthouse. Mom takes the cooler.

Freaky turns and heads for his truck so quickly our thank-yous are drowned out by his engine roaring to life. We stare after him as he drives away.

Mom plunks the cooler in front of the sofa swing and sits. "That man continually surprises me."

I drop beside her and flip off the top of the cooler. It's filled with sandwiches, dips, cookies, breads, and muffins. I place Baby Candy Cane on the sofa and pull up a jar.

"'Mandy's Tikka Masala,'" I read from the label. My eyes widen. "This is the sauce he made that first dinner I had over there."

"What is all this?" Mom asks, staring at the goodies.

I lay a hand on her arm. "It's amazing is what it is. Wait until you try it."

Mom raises an eyebrow and unwraps a blueberry scone. Her eyes grow practically as big as the treat she holds. She takes a bite, swallows and says, "You're not kidding he's a good cook."

She pats my knee. "You made quite an impression on him." She takes another bite and gazes at the scone thoughtfully. "I wonder if he'd be willing to sell these at the café." She frowns. "Not likely, I suppose. I know he's not all that interested in getting involved in community events. But still—"

I start laughing.

"What?" she asks. "The idea's absurd, I know, but he is unpredictable. Maybe he could be persuaded."

"You have no idea how unpredictable he is." I launch into the whole story. How I discovered the painting and Freaky's secret identity. I know I wasn't supposed to tell, but I can't keep something this huge from Mom.

By the time I'm finished, she's staring at me so hard I think her eyes are going to fall into my lap.

"You did all that? The proposal. The auction items. *And* convinced Freaky Framingham to go out on such a limb and be so generous?" She shakes her head. "I don't know what I'm most surprised by."

"Me either, frankly."

She pulls me into her. "Have I told you lately how proud I am of you?" She kisses the top of my head as she stands. "I think I need another cup of coffee to process all this." She opens the door to the house. "Coming?"

"In a bit."

I lean back and give the swing a tiny push. Back and forth. Back and forth. I pick up Baby Candy Cane and realize there's a small envelope taped to the bottom. Inside is a little card with a picture of a starry night on it.

No matter what happens, know that this summer was real. Not a story.

Keep it forever in the archives.

I love you.

Oliver.

I shut my eyes and feel the swing's gentle motion. He loves me back. It's real and it's been right.

My brow furrows as a new thought enters. It's good that he's gone. It hurts, yeah, but I learned so much from him. And one of the things I learned is that I need more practice at being "just Mandy." Not a Cynthia clone, not the girl I think a boy wants me to be.

Then I'll really be ready for a forever kind of love, not just a summer one. And who knows? Maybe that will happen by next summer—and Oliver really will return.

A smile grows across my face, a smile bigger than I thought possible on the day Oliver left.

I sit and swing a little while longer, then rummage in the cooler and find a cookie. I unwrap it as I head into the house. "Mom?" I call. "If I do it right, maybe Framingham will agree to sell his cookies at Candy Cane by next summer."

After all, I have a whole year to work on him.

And on myself.

RIVETED

BY *simon* teen ♥

BELIEVE IN YOUR SHELF

Visit RivetedLit.com & connect with us on social to:

DISCOVER NEW YA READS

READ BOOKS FOR FREE

DISCUSS YOUR FAVORITES

SHARE YOUR IDEAS

ENTER SWEEPSTAKES FOR THE CHANCE TO WIN BOOKS

Follow @SimonTeen on

to stay up to date with all things Riveted!